The
BRIGHTEST
OF DREAMS

Books by Susan Anne Mason

CANADIAN CROSSINGS

BOOK THREE

BRIGHTEST OF DREAMS

Susan Anne Mason

BETHANYHOUSE

a division of Baker Publishing Group

Minneapolis, Minnesota

Published by Bethany House Publishers
11400 Hampshire Avenue South
Bloomington, Minnesota 55438
www.bethanyhouse.com

Bethany House Publishers is a division of
Baker Publishing Group, Grand Rapids, Michigan

Printed in the United States of America

Library of Congress Control Number: 2019949894

ISBN 978-0-7642-1985-6 (paper)
ISBN 978-0-7642-3548-1 (cloth)

Cover design by Koechel Peterson & Associates, Inc., Minneapolis, Minnesota/Jon Godfredson

Author is represented by Natasha Kern Literary Agency.

20 21 22 23 24 25 26 7 6 5 4 3 2 1

For all the British Home Children
and their descendants
who have made their home in Canada.
May this story shine a light
on the hardships they endured
and demonstrate the strength and courage
it took to forge a new life here.
Thank you for making Canada
an even stronger country!

Trust in the Lord with all your heart and lean not on your own understanding; in all your ways submit to him, and he will make your paths straight.

Proverbs 3:5–6 NIV

PROLOGUE

Derbyshire, England
Spring 1919

Quinten Aspinall stood in the Earl of Brentwood's study, awaiting his employer's imminent return. With any luck, after his daily ride over the estate, his lordship would be in good spirits and more receptive to Quinn's petition.

Even so, Quinn couldn't banish the nerves that dampened his palms as he struggled for a calm that had escaped him of late. Would Lord Brentwood understand Quinn's reasoning and agree to his request, or would his employer deem it necessary to terminate Quinn's position at Brentwood Manor?

Quinn took in a breath, attempting to focus on his blessings rather than his trials. The war was over. He'd survived. A major accomplishment to say the least. Yet that blessing paled when he thought about the fate that had befallen his family.

Becky, Cecil, and little Harry. *Lord, keep them safe—wherever they are.*

That simple prayer cemented his commitment to his present course of action. He would do whatever was necessary to find his family and bring them home.

After recovering from his injuries, Quinn never imagined he'd be asking for a leave of absence to travel overseas. But then again, he'd never imagined his mother would place his three younger siblings in an orphanage or that the orphanage would ship them off to another country.

The door creaked open, and Lord Brentwood strode into the room.

Quinn straightened his shoulders and clasped his hands behind his back in the proper servant stance.

"Mr. Aspinall! Davis told me you were here. Home from that blasted war, I see." The exuberance on Lord Brentwood's ruddy face matched his tone. He tossed his riding gloves on the desk. "Good to see you again, lad. How are you feeling?"

Quinn reached out to shake his employer's hand, the old rush of affection rising in his chest. In truth, he'd missed this place and his position as the earl's personal valet. "I'm happy to report I've been given a clean bill of health."

"Excellent." His lordship moved to the credenza that housed his favorite spirits. "Does this mean you're here to reclaim your old job?"

Quinn hesitated, mindful that his answer might alter the man's jovial mood. "Yes and no, my lord."

The earl's hand stilled on the crystal decanter. "That sounds rather cryptic. Care to elaborate?" He poured a hefty splash of brandy into a snifter and carried it over to the massive cherrywood desk, the place where he usually spent each afternoon taking care of business pertaining to the estate.

"I do wish to resume my duties, sir, but . . . perhaps not right away." Quinn swallowed. "I require a short leave of absence first."

The earl frowned. "Does this have something to do with your family?"

"It does." Of course his lordship would figure that much out, since Quinn had always made it clear how much his family meant to him. "I need to make a trip to Canada."

The earl's glass halted halfway to his mouth, a curious gleam brightening his eyes. "Canada? Whatever for?"

Memories of Quinn's visit to the Dr. Barnardo's Homes for children crowded his mind, threatening to unravel his carefully held control. "Upon my return to London, I went to see my mother." He swallowed. "I found her living in a workhouse, my younger siblings now in an orphanage."

"I'm sorry to hear that." The earl's brow furrowed.

"I then paid a visit to the children's home, only to learn that my brothers and sister have been shipped off to Canada as indentured workers without my mum's knowledge." Growing restless, Quinn wished he had leave to warm himself by the flames in the fireplace. Since his time in the trenches, he couldn't get used to the constant dampness that seemed to perpetually seep through his bones. "Unfortunately, my mother is in ill health. I fear she'll not last the summer."

Visions of his emaciated mother had haunted Quinn for the four years he was away at war. He never imagined her looking even frailer than when he left. But when he'd found her bedridden in a workhouse infirmary upon his return, he knew he had to do something. Quinn suspected guilt played a large part in her listlessness, as though she deserved to die for abandoning her children. If he could find Becky, Cecil, and Harry and bring them home, it might give his mother a reason to get well. She didn't deserve this life of hardship solely because her husband had died prematurely.

Heaven only knew Quinn had tried his best to help her over the years, sending almost every shilling he earned back home to care for the family. To find out now that it had all been in vain was beyond excruciating.

"So, you're asking for a leave to find your siblings?" The earl studied him from behind the enormous desk.

"Yes, my lord."

"And if I refuse your request?"

Quinn resisted the urge to look away from the man's direct gaze. "Then I will respectfully have to resign my position. Though it would pain me to do so."

"It would pain me also." Lord Brentwood shifted on his chair and leaned forward. "Whereabouts in Canada will you be going?"

"I'm not sure of the exact location. The ship lands in Halifax, Nova Scotia. From there, it will depend on where my brothers and sister were sent. I haven't been able to discern that information as of yet." Quinn clenched his hands into fists against his rising agitation. He still couldn't believe the director of the Dr. Barnardo's Homes wouldn't give him any information other than the name of the ship and the landing point in Halifax.

Quinn shoved one hand into his pocket until his fingers met the familiar iron key he carried with him everywhere—the last thing his father had given him before he died. It had been the key to their family home in London, and by giving it to Quinn, his father had effectively bestowed upon him the title of head of household. The cool metal reminded Quinn of the promise he'd made and gave him the boost of courage he needed to continue. "If it's too much to ask that you hold my position, I'll certainly respect your decision, sir. But this is something I have to do. I won't rest until my family is back together again."

The earl nodded. "A sentiment I understand all too well." A shadow crossed the man's features and, for a moment, real anguish flashed in his eyes.

To Quinn's chagrin, he realized he'd not even inquired about the earl's family and how they had fared since Quinn left for the war. "I trust Lady Brentwood and Lady Amelia are both well?"

"They are. Thank you for asking." He paused. "My niece, on the other hand, is a different story."

"Miss Julia?" Quinn sucked in a breath at the memory of the vivacious girl. She'd come to live with the earl and his family at the age of thirteen, following the sudden death of her parents. After an appropriate time to grieve and become accustomed to her new home, Julia had eventually found solace in the company of her cousin, Amelia, and the squeals of girlish laughter often rang throughout the halls of Brentwood Manor. "I hope nothing dire has happened to her."

"Not in the way you're thinking. But bad enough." The earl pushed up from the desk. "Julia insisted on helping with the war efforts—against my wishes, I might add. She went off to aid the medics with the wounded soldiers, a task no proper young lady should undertake."

"Having been a wounded soldier myself, I think it a noble undertaking. I know I appreciated any help I received."

The earl shot him an annoyed glance.

Quinn almost bit his tongue. He would have to get used to keeping his opinions to himself when they were not asked for.

"I had a feeling nothing good would come of it." His lordship lifted his chin in a manner that meant only one thing. Disapproval. "Right before the war ended, she ran off with one of the Canadian soldiers."

"Oh. How . . . unfortunate." Why did the weight of disappointment hit Quinn so hard? It wasn't as if he could ever have hoped to win the girl's affections. She would never have looked twice at a servant, except maybe to request a task be done.

"I believe your trip to Canada could prove most fortuitous." The earl leaned an arm on the back of the chair, a pensive look on his face. "While you're there, I'd like you to find Julia and bring her home."

Quinn snapped to attention. "I beg your pardon?"

"Julia's departure has devastated my wife and daughter. I'll admit I came down rather hard on the girl, and unfortunately, we parted on bad terms. A circumstance I greatly regret." He let out a sigh. "I'd go in search of her myself, but I can't afford time away from the earldom right now. In the aftermath of the war, I've lost three of my tenant farmers—two in battle and the other from illness. I simply must rectify the situation, or the future of Brentwood could be in jeopardy." His lordship came to stand by the fire, his strong profile highlighted by the flames. "Since you're already headed overseas, I must take advantage of our association and ask for your help." The earl moved back to his desk and pulled a velvet pouch from one of the drawers. "I'm prepared to give you whatever funds you might require to cover any expenses incurred on my behalf."

Quinn's mind reeled. He couldn't afford to be distracted from his main goal, yet he didn't wish to refuse his employer, not without a very good reason. "Do you know where she's living in Canada?"

"The man she left with, Private Samuel McIntyre, hailed from Toronto. That much I was able to discern. It would be the most logical place to start."

Even with Quinn's limited knowledge of Canadian geography, he knew enough to realize that Toronto was a far cry from Halifax. But then, it was feasible that his siblings might have been sent somewhere near there. The Barnardo organization had a receiving home in Toronto, and many of the orphans ended up on farms in the province of Ontario. Still, it would take time away from Quinn's own search to have to look for the earl's wayward niece.

An uncomfortable idea twisted Quinn's gut. "Is it possible that Miss Julia might be married to the man by now? I can hardly wrestle her away from her husband."

"I don't believe that's the case." The earl's shoulders drooped suddenly. "Amelia admitted several days ago that she recently received a letter from Julia, postmarked from Toronto. She said her cousin sounded rather desperate. That she needed to find a new place to live, but money was an issue, and she didn't know what to do. Though Amelia was not happy about it, I insisted on seeing the letter." His brows swooped down. "I hate to think of my niece being in trouble. I want her to know she can come home, though I fear she may not have that impression right now." He straightened, adjusting the sleeve of his riding jacket. "Finding Julia will no doubt be a challenge, one I'm willing to reward handsomely should you succeed."

Quinn stared at his employer, the man's impressive carriage and intelligent gaze confirming that he was every inch a person of title. The earl had given Quinn a position in his household at a time when he'd been quite desperate, and over the years his lordship had promoted him from footman to his personal valet.

In truth, Quinn owed the man a great deal. How could he refuse to help him? Besides, if Julia was indeed in dire straits and Quinn could offer her some assistance, then he had to try. "Very well, your lordship. I'll do my best. But even if I do find Miss Julia, she may not wish to return to England. I won't force her to board a ship against her will."

"I understand." The earl pursed his lips. "Perhaps an added incentive might ensure you do your utmost to persuade her." He walked toward Quinn, a gleam in his eye. "If you succeed in your endeavor, I will reward you with one of the tenant farms for your own. Free and clear."

Hot tingles shot straight up Quinn's spine. His own property? A place where he could reunite his family and fulfill the promise he'd made to his father nine years ago? How could he turn down the chance—no matter how slim—to provide a real home for his mother and siblings?

He squared his shoulders and nodded. "You have my word, sir. I'll do everything in my power to bring your niece back to you."

CHAPTER 1

Nova Scotia, Canada
May 28, 1919

Quinten strode along the Halifax sidewalk with determined intent. Today he would obtain the information he needed—even if he had to throttle the stubborn clerk to get it.

He'd just bid farewell to Emmaline and Jonathan, friends he'd made on the long voyage over. During their time at sea, Quinn had spent many hours talking with the pair, though poor Jonathan had been indisposed for a good deal of the trip due to extreme seasickness. Another young woman named Grace had also joined their entourage, and they'd discovered the three of them shared a similar quest. Emmaline had come to Canada in search of her father, and Grace was looking for her sister, a young war widow, in the hopes of bringing her back to England. Grace had left for Toronto the same day the ship docked, while Emma and Jonathan opted to stay in Halifax until he had sufficiently recovered to travel again. This morning, the pair had boarded a train bound for Toronto, and Quinn heartily wished he could have joined them.

If he'd been able to ascertain the whereabouts of even one of his siblings by now, it might have been a possibility. However, an overly zealous clerk in the inspection office stood between Quinn and his next destination. Today, he would not leave without that information.

With a grunt, he opened the heavy door and stepped inside. The Inspection Office, he'd learned, was the first stop for all immigrants. Anyone who failed the medical inspection would be quarantined or, at worst, sent back home.

Inside the room, an acrid smell of smoke and rotting wood lingered. More than a year after a devastating explosion had laid waste to a good part of the harbor, as well as the city itself, the horrific effects remained, and with the windows still boarded up, little fresh air could enter to dissipate the unpleasant odors. The city must have suffered serious financial consequences due to the scope of destruction. Why else would so many buildings still not be repaired?

Quinn glanced at the counter and held back a groan of frustration. The same difficult man sat there, writing in his ledger. Would today be any different from the last four times he had talked to Mr. Churly?

An apt name to be sure.

Despite their previous run-ins, Quinn pasted on a smile, determined to win the man over to his way of thinking. Sooner or later, he was bound to give in.

"Good morning, Mr. Churly." Quinn removed his hat with a slight bow. "How are you this fine day?"

The man glanced over his pince-nez glasses and gave Quinn a stony stare. "Your cheerfulness will get you nowhere, Mr. Aspinall. My answer will be the same today as it has been the last three times you've been here."

"Four," Quinn said quietly.

"I beg your pardon?"

"I've been here four times. This makes my fifth."

Mr. Churly snorted. "Then you're five times a fool, for my answer has not changed. I am unable to divulge the whereabouts of your siblings. That information is confidential."

From the corner of his eye, Quinn became aware of movement. He glanced over to see a young woman emerge through a curtain from a back room. She came forward carrying an armful of books and set them on the counter, sparing Quinn a sympathetic glance. He recognized her from his previous trips to the office.

"Never mind gawking, Miss Holmes. Get back to your station." The clerk's harsh tone made the girl wince.

"Yes, sir." She gave a slight lift of her shoulders, as though apologizing to Quinn, before ducking back into the recesses of the building.

Quinn held back a sigh. Unlike the boorish Mr. Churly, Miss Holmes exuded sympathy. Quinn sensed an underlying desire to help him. If only he could speak with her alone, he was certain he could persuade her to give him the information he so desperately needed. Unfortunately, it appeared Mr. Churly never took a break from his duties.

"Please, sir." Quinn took out the worn photograph he carried with him, one depicting all his siblings together, and laid it on the counter. Perhaps the sweet faces of Becky, Cecil, and Harry would sway the man. "I've traveled a very long way to find my family. It would mean the world to me—and to my very ill mother back home—to learn where my siblings are and how they're faring. Won't you help me?" Quinn was not above begging at this point.

As the clerk begrudgingly glanced at the photo, his hand stilled on the ledger. Then he cleared his throat, placed the pen in the inkpot, and released a loud breath. "It's not that I don't empathize with your plight, Mr. Aspinall. But from what I understand, the children who are sent here through Dr. Barnardo's organization—the ones who aren't orphans, that is—have been relinquished by their parents. The families no longer have any rights to them. You certainly cannot interfere with your siblings' placements. They will be subject to binding contracts, and as such, their employers won't take kindly to anyone trying to contact them or perhaps attempting to lure them back home."

"I understand, sir." Emboldened by this divulging of at least some bare facts about the children's plight, Quinn leaned forward to look the man in the eye. "I only want to ensure they are healthy and happy so I can report back to my mother."

May God forgive me for this fib.

When Quinn had learned his siblings had been shipped off to Canada without his mother's consent, he'd vowed to do everything in his power to get Cecil, Becky, and Harry back where they belonged.

Maybe then his mum would have a reason to live.

The man gave him a long look, this time not in anger or annoyance but in sympathy. Hope fluttered to life in Quinn's chest. His lips curved upward in anticipation of the man's capitulation at last.

But then the clerk shook his head again. "I'm sorry. I could lose my job if I gave out that type of information." He lowered his voice. "Your best bet would be to try the Fairview receiving home on the outskirts of the city. Some of the orphans are processed through there. Otherwise, I'd suggest traveling to Toronto. I understand Dr. Barnardo's has several receiving homes in that area. Perhaps you'll have more luck there. Now, if you'll excuse me . . ." He rose from his stool, gave a stiff nod, and disappeared through the curtain behind him.

The same stab of disappointment pierced Quinn's chest. He still had no concrete idea where his younger siblings had been sent. Yet maybe he'd received one tidbit of information he could use. All he had to do was figure out the location of the Fairview home.

He pocketed the photo, shoved his cap back on his head, and turned for the door. A brisk wind blasted his cheeks the moment he stepped outside. Though it was almost June, the proximity to the ocean kept the temperature at springlike levels. Quinn huddled inside his overcoat and pulled the collar up around his ears, scanning the buildings across the street. Perhaps he could find a taxicab. Surely the driver would know the whereabouts of the residence.

"Excuse me, Mr. Aspinall?" A tentative voice came from the alley between the Inspection Office and the next building.

Quinn turned to see the young woman from inside. She moved into the light, not fully coming onto the walkway. Wordlessly, she held out a piece of paper, her eyes imploring him.

He walked closer, effectively blocking her from sight, and accepted the paper.

"I have to get back before I'm missed," she said. "But this might help with your search." She turned to go, but Quinn reached out a gentle hand to stop her.

"Wait. How . . . ?"

"There were only three children with the name Aspinall. It wasn't hard to find." She pulled her shawl closer around her.

"Thank you, miss. You have no idea how much this means to me."

"I think I do." Her eyes filled with moisture. "My younger sister went missing during the explosion a year and a half ago. I searched for two days, fearing she'd been killed, until a kind woman helped me find her in one of the emergency medical centers. I can only imagine what you're going through, being so far from home." She gave a wobbly smile. "Godspeed on the rest of your journey. I hope you find them safe and in good health."

"Thank you again." He squeezed her hand before she disappeared down the alley.

As he watched her retreating back, Quinn prayed the girl wouldn't get in any trouble for helping him. With unsteady fingers, he opened the folded paper. The scrawled handwriting read: *Rebecca Aspinall, Hazelbrae, Peterborough. Cecil and Harrison Aspinall, Dr. Barnardo's Homes, Toronto.*

He lifted his head to stare blindly down the street. Where on earth was Peterborough? Toronto, he knew, was a large city. He'd learned as much from his friends on the ship who were headed there. Quinn refolded the paper. He would find out where Peterborough was in relation to Toronto, and if it made sense to go there first, he would. If not, Toronto would be his next destination. Too bad he hadn't learned this yesterday. He could have joined Emmaline and Jonathan on the train this morning.

But no matter. God's timing was always perfect. Quinn had to believe that. He shoved the slip of paper into his pocket and headed toward the train station.

"Yer rent's two weeks overdue. If you want to stay, I need payment in full today."

Julia Holloway's foot stalled on the first stair that led up to her room on the third floor. She'd hoped to sneak by without her landlord hearing her, but he must have been waiting for her to arrive home.

She turned to find the man, clad in a filthy undershirt that didn't quite cover his belly, staring at her from the open doorway to his apartment. The sharp smell of sauerkraut and onions, mixed with ripe body odor, was enough to make Julia gag.

"Are you going to give it to me now, or do I have to follow you up to your room?" Mr. Ketchum adjusted one brown suspender over his shoulder.

"That won't be necessary." Julia swallowed back her fear as she rummaged in her bag for the last few dollars she had left. Funds she'd set aside to buy groceries. But eating would have to wait. She clutched the bills in a ball and held it out to the landlord.

"Count it out proper-like," he instructed, making no move to take the offering.

Slowly she smoothed out the wad and counted it for him, bill by bill. "Four dollars." She held her breath as she waited for him to take the money.

His eyes narrowed. "That's not the full amount."

"I . . . I know, but I get paid tomorrow. I'll get the rest to you then. I promise." She hated the quaver in her voice but was powerless to stop it. Her part-time janitorial job didn't pay much, and if she got evicted from this hovel, she didn't know where she'd go. There wasn't anywhere better she could afford, not on her limited income.

Leering, Mr. Ketchum scanned her figure from the kerchief tied around her hair, past her plain dress, to the unflattering boots on her feet. "I can think of another way to pay me." He took a step toward her.

Julia used every ounce of willpower not to flee. "As I've told you repeatedly, sir, I'm not that type of girl." She held out the money, willing her hand not to shake.

Finally, he grunted and snatched the bills from her. She pushed her fingers into the pocket of her apron, discreetly wiping away the grime of his touch.

"I want the rest by tomorrow, or you'll find your things out in the alley." He spat a brown stream of tobacco onto the floor by her boot, then turned and lumbered back into his flat.

Julia did not waste a second. She flew up the three flights of stairs and down the hall to the room at the farthest end. With shaking fingers, she unlocked the door, let herself inside, and shut it, sliding the lock into place. She leaned her forehead against the wood, waiting until her heart rate slowed. Only then did she take a full breath and turn around.

A gasp strangled in her throat. The blankets from her bed lay in a twisted heap on the floor. Her pillow had been ripped open, feathers spewing everywhere. The drawers in her small dresser had all been pulled open, her clothing rumpled and tossed.

How dare he! Heat flooded her cheeks at the thought of Mr. Ketchum rifling through her undergarments. If he'd been searching for cash, he hadn't found a thing. She kept her money on her person at all times for this very reason.

She crossed the tiny space to retrieve the blankets and straighten the bedding, doing what she could to sweep up the feathers. Despite the horrid living conditions, she did her best to keep the room clean and tidy. It helped that she didn't have many possessions. Her one satchel with a few changes of clothing was all she'd brought when she left England. Her fingers sought the gold chain around her neck, the one memento she'd kept from her former life. Inside the filigree locket was her only photo of her departed parents. Nothing in her life had been the same since their untimely deaths.

Had she known that fleeing to Canada would only result in more tragedy, she never would have left Brentwood Manor and the protection of her uncle. How had her shiny dreams for the future turned into such a nightmare?

She ran the chain through her fingers, then resolutely tucked it back beneath the bodice of her plain cotton dress. In this neighborhood, it wasn't wise to display anything worth stealing.

Julia walked over to the window, rubbed more of the dirt away so she could see the street below, then wiped her palm on her apron. Would she ever feel clean again? She yearned to soak in a hot tub filled with scented water, a luxury from home she often dreamt about. The best she could manage here was a quick wash with cold water from the ewer on her nightstand. Even if she managed to find the shared lavatory free, she could never relax in the tub, not with the many unscrupulous types in the building.

Oh, Sam, why did you leave me? Why couldn't you accept the help that was offered you?

She bit her lip, fighting the sting of tears. This kind of thinking would get her nowhere. It wouldn't help her toward her goal of saving enough money to escape this ghastly existence. And it wouldn't help her find her purpose in life. After what had happened to Sam, Julia was more determined than ever to do something worthwhile. To be of service to those who suffered. Her thoughts turned to the injured soldiers she'd assisted during the war, a ministry that had brought her such fulfillment. Too bad her uncle could never understand that.

Julia pressed a hand to her mouth, fighting a roll of nausea and homesickness. If only she could go back to Brentwood and see her aunt and her dear cousin Amelia again. But that simply wasn't possible. Uncle Howard had made it clear that if she chose to leave with Sam, he would cut her off from his money and his protection. His ultimatum had only fueled her stubborn pride and made her more determined to go.

Now, in the aftermath of the bridges she'd burned, Julia had never felt more alone. Whatever her future held in store for her, she would have to discover it on her own.

CHAPTER 2

Quinn stood outside the iron gate that guarded the walkway to a rather quaint-looking house. Tall and narrow, with a turret on one side and wraparound porch in front, the character of the building was eminently suited to a boardinghouse. Another of his shipmates, Grace Abernathy, had recommended this establishment, saying that her sister had found it charming and the proprietress who ran it very kind. Now if only Mrs. Chamberlain had a vacancy, he might finally have a place to settle for a while.

How long that might be, Quinn had no idea. Uncertainty was the constant of this voyage; he never knew what to expect around the next corner. The train trip to Toronto had been uneventful in itself, giving him a long time to reflect on the next steps required to find his siblings, as well as how best to go about tracking down the elusive Julia Holloway.

Lord, you've helped me get this far. I have to trust you to guide me from here.

A man came around the corner of the house, wielding a bushel basket and a rake. With his cap slung low over his forehead, the man's face wasn't visible, yet something about him seemed familiar. When he lifted his head and spotted Quinn, the man dropped the basket and grinned.

"Quinn, old chap. You're here." Jonathan Rowe rushed over

to open the gate, then came out to clap him on the shoulder. "I thought you were staying in Halifax awhile longer."

"So did I. But I finally got some information on the children's possible whereabouts."

Children. Perhaps that wasn't the correct term to use anymore. Becky had to be nearing eighteen, Cecil sixteen, and Harry twelve, but they would always be children to Quinn. He swallowed, recalling the last time he'd seen them on the day he left to move into the earl's household. The sight of their precious faces pressed against his side. The sound of their cries. He couldn't even begin to imagine how scared they had been years later, shoved aboard a steamship on their way to a foreign land. Alone. Surrounded by strangers.

Quinn forced away the anger that seethed just below the surface every time he thought about it. Jonathan didn't deserve his irritability, nor his unpleasant mood. He summoned a wide smile. "It's good to see you again, Jon. I trust you and Emmaline have found accommodations here. I only hope there's room for one more." Quinn managed what he hoped to be a lighthearted tone to his voice.

But Jonathan didn't smile in return. Instead, a look of regret crept over his features. "I hate to be the bearer of bad news, but Mrs. Chamberlain doesn't take male lodgers." He nodded his head toward the side yard where he'd first appeared. "I'm staying in a cot over the garage, but only because she needed a temporary groundskeeper."

"Oh." Quinn's optimism faded faster than the rays of the sun behind a cloud. "I don't suppose she could recommend another place to stay?"

"There's a YMCA on College Street. That would've been my next destination if Mrs. C. hadn't offered me this position."

"How far is College Street?" A bone-deep weariness settled over Quinn. He felt like he'd been traveling forever. He couldn't remember the last time he'd had a proper night's sleep or a hot meal.

"I'm not sure. Come up to the porch, and I'll see if Mrs. C. is around. You look like you could use a glass of lemonade." Jonathan opened the gate wider to allow Quinn onto the property.

"That would be appreciated. Thank you." He followed his friend to the homey wraparound porch.

Jonathan gestured to the wicker chairs. "Have a seat. I'll be right back."

Quinn had only been sitting for a couple of minutes when the front door opened and a plump woman bustled out, followed by Jonathan, who carried a tray of drinks.

"Hello there. I'm Harriet Chamberlain, and you must be Mr. Aspinall. Jonathan and Emmaline have spoken most highly about you."

Quinn jumped to his feet. "Yes, ma'am. But please call me Quinten."

Her pale eyes sparkled. "That's a fine English name. I had a cousin with the same name back home."

"You're from England?" He should have known by her faint accent.

"Yes. I came to Canada as a young girl many moons ago." A shadow passed over her features, but then she smiled again. "Emmaline's not here right now. She'll be sorry she missed you."

Jonathan handed Quinn a glass, and the three took a seat.

"I understand you don't accept male tenants," Quinn said after a long drink that drained half the glass.

"I'm afraid not. But the YMCA has reasonable rates. It's a very respectable establishment. You should do fine there."

"Thank you. I'll just need directions to find it. This is indeed a large city."

"And growing by the day." Mrs. Chamberlain chuckled. "How long will you be staying in Toronto?"

"It all depends on what I find out about my siblings." Quinn frowned, his gaze scanning the tree-lined street in front of them. "I need to locate one of Dr. Barnardo's Homes. The one on Peter Street." He'd long since memorized the information on that scrap of paper.

Mrs. Chamberlain went white, and lines popped up on her forehead. "That's a name I haven't heard in some time."

"You know the place?"

"Oh, indeed." Her mouth was a grim line, which quelled Quinn's faint stirring of hope. "It's where most of the young lads are sent when they get off the ship."

A shiver of foreboding traveled down Quinn's spine. "Why does it sound like that's a bad thing?"

She glanced over at him. "The house itself isn't bad. The boys are treated well there. It's where they go afterward that's the problem."

"How so?" Quinn set his empty glass on the wicker table at his side.

"The majority of boys are sent to work on farms in the area. It's not an easy life. I'll tell you that straight out. And many aren't treated half as well as the cattle in the barns."

"How do you know this?"

She stared ahead, and for a second Quinn thought she hadn't heard his question. But then she turned to look at him. "Years ago, my sister and I were brought over on just such a ship, along with a large group of other children. We were taken to the girls' receiving home in Peterborough."

Quinn stiffened on his chair. "That's where my sister was sent."

Mrs. Chamberlain reached over and laid her hand on Quinn's arm. "I only pray your sister had a better experience than Annie and I did." Moisture rimmed her eyes. "I made it out alive. Sadly, my sister didn't." She pressed her lips together and turned to fumble in her pocket for a handkerchief.

"I'm so sorry." Quinn's throat thickened. "How old were you, if I might ask?"

"I was nine. Annie twelve. We fought to stay together, but no one wanted two girls. So they sent us to different farms, hundreds of miles apart." She crumpled the handkerchief between her callused fingers. "It was dreadfully hard work. Up before dawn each day to do all the morning chores—milking cows, collecting eggs, getting the firewood chopped to start the stove. But at least the people who took me in were fairly decent. Unlike Annie's situation."

"She wasn't treated well?" He hated to ask, dreading the answer.

She shook her head. "Annie ran away twice, but each time the authorities brought her back. They didn't seem to care about the bruises covering her body. The farmer said she'd been disobedient and deserved the punishment. Apparently, his word was good enough for them." Mrs. Chamberlain dabbed her eyes. "If only that was the worst of it."

Quinn glanced over at Jonathan, who had remained silent throughout the conversation. But the look of disgust on his face reflected Quinn's own feelings. "Did she die by the farmer's hand?" he asked quietly.

"Not directly, but he's still to blame. Not only did he mistreat her, he got her pregnant." She paused. "Annie hanged herself. She was only fifteen, and it was all too much for her to bear." A tear slid down the woman's cheek. "I know there's not much I could have done, but I wish she hadn't felt so alone. With no other choice."

Quinn shook his head, the lemonade souring in his stomach. "I'm very sorry for your loss. I only pray my sister was more fortunate."

"I do too." Mrs. Chamberlain seemed to gather herself. "Perhaps conditions have changed for the better over the years. However, it doesn't hurt to be prepared for whatever you might find."

He nodded and rose. "Well, I've taken enough of your time. I'd best find the YMCA before it gets too late. Thank you for the lemonade—and the advice."

"You're most welcome. Oh, you'll be needing the address." Mrs. Chamberlain stood and took a slip of paper from her apron. "I wrote it down for you. There's also the Red Triangle Club, a branch of the Y that caters to soldiers. It's farther away though, and lately they've been full. I think the College Street facility would be a better option." She handed him the paper. "If you can't get a room, let me know. I'll have my friend Reverend Burke see if one of his parishioners can put you up temporarily. And you must join us on

Sunday at Holy Trinity Church. The majority of parishioners who attend are originally from Britain, so you'll feel right at home."

"Thank you, ma'am. I'll keep that in mind." Quinn smiled as he pocketed the address, the tightness in his chest easing for the first time since leaving English soil. Maybe he wasn't completely alone in this journey after all.

For the rest of the evening, Harriet couldn't get Quinten and his siblings out of her mind. All during dinner with her boarders, she could barely keep track of the conversation going on around her. Now, after the day's chores had been completed, she sat in her favorite armchair in the parlor, trying to gain control of her emotions by reading her Bible.

Yet her thoughts kept returning to Quinten and his search for his family. She gripped the leather book tighter. The lad's story had dredged up all the sorrow and despair of her own childhood, feelings she'd thought she'd left firmly in the past—the fear and loneliness of losing her parents and being sent away, the grief at being separated from her dear sister, and the eventual tragedy of losing Annie.

Clearly, she'd been fooling herself that she'd gotten over these memories. It had taken her a long time to come to terms with Annie's suicide. Talks with different ministers over the years had helped Harriet come to a place of understanding and peace about it. Yet even though a scab had formed over her wounds, it hadn't taken much prodding for the bleeding to begin again.

"Is everything all right, Harriet?" Rev. Burke's deep baritone shook Harriet from her thoughts.

She blinked and looked up from the book in her lap. "Geoffrey. I didn't hear you knock."

He smiled as he entered the room. "Clearly not. Which is why I let myself in. I hope you don't mind."

"Not at all. You know you're always welcome." She set her Bible aside and rose. "Let me make us a pot of tea."

He came forward to lay a hand on her shoulder. "Tea can wait. Why don't you tell me what's troubling you?" Genuine concern radiated from his eyes.

"It's nothing, really. Just a foolish old woman reliving events that should remain in the past."

He studied her. "What's happened to bring on this bout of melancholy?"

She let out a sigh. "A friend of Jonathan and Emma's came by today. Right off the boat from home." Harriet twisted the string of beads at her throat. "The young man is looking for his siblings, who were sent here through Dr. Barnardo's organization, like Annie and I were years ago."

"Ah, I see." Gently, he steered her to the sofa. "It's brought up all those difficult memories."

"It has."

"What can I do to help?"

She sighed. "There's nothing anyone can do. It will pass. It always does."

Geoffrey took a seat beside her and placed his hand over hers. "Is there anything you can think of that might help put the tragedy behind you once and for all? Give you the closure you need?"

Harriet pulled her hand away. "Put it behind me? Geoffrey, I will never forget what happened to my sister. And I will never stop grieving her loss, no matter how much *closure* I get." She stood and walked to the fireplace, where the only photo she had of her sister graced the mantel. The gentle girl with fair hair and wide eyes. Eyes that once sparkled with joy but later knew only despair.

Geoffrey came up behind her. "I'm sorry. It wasn't my intention to make you feel worse."

She brushed at the unexpected dampness on her cheek and turned to look at her friend. He didn't deserve her sharp tongue. "You're only trying to help. As always." She managed a smile. "Besides, what you said isn't anything new. I've thought about it a lot over the years, trying to determine why losing Annie that way continues to haunt me." She shook her head, the guilt and shame rising up once more. "I don't even know where she's buried, or if she has a gravestone. Shouldn't I at least know that much?" She shivered involuntarily, for that would mean returning to Hazelbrae, something she swore she would never do.

"You could start by trying to find out." He studied her as though determining if he should say anything further. "One thing I sometimes advise my grieving parishioners is to find a way to pay tribute to their loved one. Something meaningful to both the deceased and the bereaved." He paused to stroke his chin. "What if you did something to honor Annie, like plant a tree or start a scholarship in her name? Something that would have meaning for you as well."

Harriet's throat tightened and she nodded. "I've often thought about a memorial of some kind but could never decide what might be fitting." She reached over to pat his arm. "Thank you, Geoffrey. This is just what I need. To stop dwelling on the negative and focus on something positive. I will give the whole matter a good deal of consideration."

He smiled, crinkles forming around his eyes. "All in a day's work, my dear."

CHAPTER 3

The Dr. Barnardo receiving home was a very ordinary-looking building. Nothing except the sign above the door indicated its purpose. Quinn forced his feet forward to cross the street, nerves jumbling in the pit of his stomach. What would he learn today about the fate of his brothers? Silently, he offered up a prayer for good news as he entered.

A large coatrack and umbrella stand graced the musty entranceway. Quinn walked down the hall to what appeared to be a reception desk. A rather severe-looking woman sat entering information in a large book. She looked up when she noticed him and scanned him from the top of his hat to the shoes he'd recently shined in his room at the YMCA.

"Can I help you, sir?"

"I certainly hope so." He mustered his most charming smile. "My name is Quinten Aspinall. I'm looking for information on my two brothers. I believe they came here about four or five years ago from the Dr. Barnardo's Homes in London, and I'd like to find out where they are now."

Immediately her features hardened. "I'm sorry, sir, but I am not at liberty to give out that type of information." She shut the leather journal in front of her with a decisive slap.

Quinn stepped closer to the desk. "I understand there are rules of propriety that must be followed. But surely you can tell immediate family members about their status." He reached inside his jacket. "I have identification if that helps."

The woman rose, her harried gaze darting to the staircase leading to the upper level. "I'm afraid I don't have the authority—"

"Then might I speak with the person in charge of this establishment?"

Her hand fluttered to the high collar of her blouse. She let out a breath and nodded. "One moment, please, and I'll see if Mr. Hobday has time to speak with you." She gestured to a bench against the far wall.

"Thank you." Quinn bowed slightly and took a seat.

The woman started up the staircase. Once she was out of sight, Quinn went straight over to the journal on the desk. His heart pumping, he quickly opened the first page. There he found a neatly scripted list of names and dates.

He flipped the pages, scanning for any entries in 1914 while listening for the sound of approaching footsteps. After hearing Mrs. Chamberlain's accounts of the dire conditions some children lived in, Quinn wasn't taking the chance of being denied information on his brothers. Perspiration slicked his palms as he attempted to move quickly through the journal. Finally, a name jumped out at him. *Aspinall, Harrison, age 7. Mr. T. Wolfe, Caledon, Ontario.*

Quinn quickly memorized it while continuing to scan. On the next page, he found *Aspinall, Cecil, age 11. Mr. A. Simpson, Collingwood, Ontario.*

Mentally repeating the information, he closed the book and made sure it looked the same as the woman had left it, then returned to the bench. He wiped his damp palms on his pant legs and made an effort to slow his breathing, wanting to appear calm and in control when the director appeared.

At last, footsteps sounded on the staircase, and the woman came into view, followed by a slim gentleman who looked to be about forty. Quinn got to his feet as they approached.

"This is Mr. Aspinall," she said to the man before returning to her desk.

"Thank you, Mrs. Allen." He came forward, hand extended. "I'm Mr. Hobday, the superintendent of this establishment. Won't you come into my office where we can speak in private?"

Quinn followed him down a hall to a large room with long rectangular windows that faced the front street.

"Please have a seat." Mr. Hobday gestured to the chairs in front of his desk.

"Thank you." He sat and waited until the man took his place, praying for the right words to convince the fellow to give him the information he wanted.

"I understand you're looking for your brothers, Mr. Aspinall." The superintendent folded his hands on the desktop.

"That's right. Harrison and Cecil Aspinall. They came over in 1914. My mother became ill and was unable to provide for them. I was away at war and had no idea she'd placed them in Dr. Barnardo's Homes." Quinn swallowed the bitterness that arose every time he thought of his mother's actions. Why hadn't she told him how dire her circumstances had become? If he'd known, maybe he could have done more to help or even postponed joining the war.

"Most unfortunate." Mr. Hobday shook his head. "However, you need to understand that by placing the children in the care of Dr. Barnardo's organization, your mother relinquished her parental rights. They are now bound by their individual indentures to their employers until the age of eighteen." He shuffled a stack of papers. "I'll tell you plainly that the farmers don't take kindly to any interference with their workers. You'd likely be run off the property with a shotgun if you attempted to see them."

Quinn's hands tightened into fists. Mr. Hobday made it sound like his brothers were prisoners working out their punishment. He could almost picture them in iron shackles, tethered to the barn wall. Quinn fought to regulate his breathing. He could not afford to lose his temper and alienate this man. Despite the information he'd memorized about his brothers' whereabouts, Quinn might need Mr. Hobday's help at some point in the future. He'd prefer to have the superintendent as an ally rather than an enemy. "I understand the delicate nature of your business, sir. It must take extraordinary skill to balance the orphans with all the people who wish to obtain their services."

The lines on the man's forehead eased. "Indeed, it is a thankless job at times."

"Tell me, Mr. Hobday, is there any sort of follow-up once the children have been placed? To ensure everyone is . . . happy with the arrangement?"

"Yes, there is." The man's shoulders relaxed, and he looked Quinn in the eye for the first time. "We send inspectors out to interview the children and the employers. The inspectors take their job very seriously."

"I see. And how often does this occur?"

"Once a year."

"That infrequently? A child could be suffering for a full year before anyone comes to check on them."

The man's frown reappeared. "If a farmer is unhappy with the child, believe me, we hear about it forthwith."

"No doubt." Quinn leaned forward. "But what happens if the *child* is unhappy, or worse yet, maltreated? What recourse does he have then?" He couldn't help but think of Mrs. Chamberlain's sister. What options did Annie have when she found herself in an unbearable situation?

Mr. Hobday's mouth pursed with displeasure. "I'm sure you understand we cannot cater to the whims of ungrateful and often unruly children, Mr. Aspinall. Every child is out of sorts at first. But gradually most of them settle in and become good workers."

"Most? What about the others?"

"Some run away or create such havoc that the employer is forced to return them. In those instances, we keep the boy here for an attitude adjustment, a retraining of sorts, and then attempt to place them on a more suitable farm."

"Do you keep records of these individuals?"

"We do." He shifted his weight on the chair, causing it to creak.

"Would you mind checking to see if either of my brothers experienced this type of 'retraining'? It might ease my mind to some degree, without jeopardizing the terms of your confidentiality."

He held the man's annoyed gaze for several seconds before Mr. Hobday inclined his head. "Very well." He pulled open a bottom desk drawer and withdrew a leather book. Then he put on a set of spectacles and opened it. "You said 1914 was the year of arrival?"

"I believe so, yes."

He scanned the pages, running a finger down the inked paper, until he stopped. Carefully he removed his glasses and looked up at Quinn. "It appears Cecil ran away from his first placement. Several times, in fact."

Quinn straightened on the chair, his heart racing. This was the first tangible account of one of his siblings. "Does it say why?"

"Apparently he didn't like the family he was living with." The man set his jaw.

Quinn held back a barrage of questions, knowing Mr. Hobday would not answer them. The situation must have been dire for his brother to run away. "What happened to Cecil then? Did he come back here?" It struck Quinn then that the information he'd memorized earlier might no longer apply since Cecil had been moved.

Mr. Hobday looked back at the book. "Yes. He stayed here for a month and was then placed on a new farm. The inspector's report several months later indicated that Cecil was adjusting well to the new location."

A measure of tension trickled from Quinn's tense muscles. That was at least a relief. "But you won't tell me *where* he was placed."

"Not the exact farm, no." A long pause ensued. Finally, the superintendent let out a heavy sigh. "All I can say is that he was sent north to a town called Elmvale. But be advised, Mr. Aspinall, any interference with these children will not be tolerated. Do I make myself clear?"

Quinn rose. "Perfectly." He pointed to the ledger. "Are there any more entries for either of my brothers?"

Mr. Hobday replaced his glasses and continued to peruse the listings. "Nothing further for either boy."

"Thank you. I appreciate your time. And your candor." Quinn paused. "I'll keep your advice in mind." He headed for the door.

"Mr. Aspinall."

"Yes?"

"Please don't do anything to jeopardize your brothers' contracts. I cannot stress how important this is. If your brothers leave before the terms are complete, not only will they forfeit any money owing to them, they could be subject to legal ramifications."

Quinn swallowed. "Surely you don't mean jail?"

"In some cases, that could be the penalty. More often it involves a hefty fine."

"I understand, sir. Thank you." Quinn put on his hat and continued out the door. It appeared these indenture contracts held far more weight than he had imagined. But he'd come too far to let anything sway his mission, legal implications or not.

If his brothers decided to leave their employment and return to England, they would have to take their chances.

CHAPTER 4

"Your brothers are in Elmvale and Caledon?" Mrs. Chamberlain's brow furrowed as she and Quinn walked out of church on Sunday morning. "How did you come by this information? Surely the director didn't tell you this."

"Not at first." Quinn stood to the side to let the other congregants pass. He was surprised how much he'd enjoyed the service. Somehow the atmosphere in the charming brick building reminded him of home. "The man came around after we'd talked for a while." Quinn didn't reveal that he'd also stolen a glance at the main ledger, fearing he might have broken some law. Best if no one knew that part.

"Impressive," Mrs. Chamberlain said. "You must have won his trust. But then, I understand there's a new superintendent since Mr. Owen retired. Perhaps he is more forthcoming than his predecessor."

"It appears so." Quinn breathed in the scent of budding roses that lined the church walkway and attempted to rein in his impatience. He needed to bring the conversation back to the point at hand. "I was hoping you might know where these towns are located."

Mrs. C. nodded. "Caledon is north of here. Over an hour by train. Elmvale is about double that distance, I believe."

"Oh." His stomach knotted. He would have to inquire at the train station if it would require two separate trips. Not to mention there'd still be a voyage to Peterborough to find Becky. It was beginning to look like Quinn would be in Canada a lot longer than he'd anticipated. But before he left Toronto, he needed to look into Julia Holloway's whereabouts.

Jonathan and Emmaline joined him on the walkway, while Mrs. Chamberlain excused herself to speak with Rev. Burke. Emmaline looked as fetching as she had on the ship with her colorful outfits. Today she wore a bright blue suit with a matching feathered hat.

She grinned and came forward to give him a hug. "Quinn. I'm so happy to see you. Jonathan told me you'd been by while I was out."

"It's good to see you too." He smiled. "How is the search for your father going?"

"Very well." She took him by the arm. "It turns out my father is a prominent member of society and is running for mayor."

"You've met him, then?"

"Just once." Her expression fell. "It didn't go as well as I'd hoped."

Jonathan fell in step beside them. "Her father was more than shocked by her arrival and is taking some time to process Emma's presence here. But I'm sure he'll come around."

"I hope things go more smoothly next time you meet." Quinn patted her arm.

"How is your search going?" Emma lifted a hand to hold her hat in place as the breeze picked up.

"I'm making a bit of headway, but it looks like I have three separate towns to visit now. However, before I leave Toronto, there's something else I must do." He paused as they neared the street and turned to Jonathan. "You mentioned a soldier friend you intended to look up while you're here. Have you made contact with him?"

"Not yet, but I plan to soon. Why?"

Even though much of the church crowd had dispersed, Quinn lowered his voice. "I'm looking for a Canadian soldier who spent some time in a military hospital in England before being sent home to Toronto. Do you have any idea of the best way to find him?"

Jonathan frowned. "You didn't mention this chap on the ship."

Quinn shifted on the walkway. "I'm doing a favor for my employer back home. He's trying to find his niece, who came with this fellow. His lordship asked me to be discreet as he's unsure of the nature of their relationship."

"A wartime romance?" Emmaline's brows rose.

"Perhaps," Quinn replied. "But I believe she initially came over as a caregiver. The man was in a wheelchair."

"Oh, I'm sorry." Emmaline's features softened. "Sounds similar to Jon's friend."

Jonathan nodded grimly. "Reggie lost a leg in battle. In his last letter, he said he's been seeing a doctor at the military hospital here who's helping him adjust."

Quinn brightened. "That might be the perfect place to start. Where is this hospital?"

"I don't know. But Mrs. C. might."

"Did I hear my name?" The woman walked over, the cheery-looking minister right on her heels.

"You did." Jonathan smiled. "First of all, Reverend Burke, this is Quinten Aspinall, a friend we met on the ship."

"Pleased to meet you, my boy." He shook Quinn's hand. "Always happy to talk to someone from back home."

"Thank you, sir. And may I say I enjoyed your sermon this morning."

"You may indeed." The man gave a hearty laugh.

"Mrs. C.," Jonathan said, "do you know where the military hospital is? Quinn is looking for a soldier who may be there."

"I'm so sorry. Is he a friend?" Mrs. Chamberlain's curls lifted in the warm breeze.

"No. I'm actually checking on him for my employer back home. When Lord Brentwood found out I was coming here, he asked me to look up Private McIntyre if I landed anywhere near Toronto." Quinn held his features in check while a bead of perspiration slid from under his cap.

Mrs. Chamberlain turned to the minister. "Geoffrey, what's the name of the doctor who's working with the injured soldiers?"

"Dr. Clayborne. He works at the military hospital on Christie Street. I've heard he's doing wonders for the wounded. That would probably be the best place to start."

Quinn looked from Mrs. Chamberlain to the minister. "Thank you," he said. "Until recently, I felt so alone on this journey. You have no idea how much I appreciate your support."

Rev. Burke clapped a meaty hand on Quinn's shoulder. "We're right here whenever you need us, lad."

Swallowing a lump in his throat, Quinn nodded. "I'll let you know how I make out."

On her hands and knees, Julia moved the bucket of water across the floor of the hospital corridor. She wasn't supposed to be working today, Monday being her usual day off, but the man who normally did the afternoon shift had called in sick, and they'd asked her to fill in. An extra shift meant a few more dollars toward the back rent she owed Mr. Ketchum. She only prayed another payment would be enough to keep the landlord from evicting her.

She rinsed the scrub brush in the bucket, then began scouring the tiled floors. After an hour, her back groaned in protest. She had no recourse but to ignore it. There were many more hours to go before she'd finish all the floors on the lower level.

A low murmur of voices caught her attention. Perhaps Dr. Clayborne was working today. The thought brought a smile to her lips. In her opinion, the man was a guardian angel. During the time Julia spent as Sam's caregiver, Dr. Clayborne had been extremely solicitous, allowing her to observe their physical therapy sessions and giving her advice as to what she could do to benefit Sam's recovery. But more importantly, the kind physician had helped her deal with the fallout from Sam's tragic death, and it was because of Dr. Clayborne that she had this job at all.

She moved around a corner and paused to sit back and catch her breath before starting the next corridor.

The voices drifting out into the quiet hallway became more distinct.

"Thank you for seeing me, doctor. I'm hoping you can help me locate someone."

Julia perked up, the lilt of the stranger's distinct British accent beckoning to her like a beacon from home. She knew she shouldn't eavesdrop, but she couldn't help glancing at the open door to Dr. Clayborne's therapy room.

As much as she wanted to hear the conversation, Julia knew she could be fired if anyone caught her. She returned to scouring the floors with added vigor, hoping the physical exertion would help her forget her problems—and her homesickness—for a while.

"The man's name is Private Samuel McIntyre. He spent some time in hospital in England before returning home. I thought he might have come here for further treatment."

Julia's hand slid on the soapy surface, and she all but fell face first onto the linoleum. Why would someone from England come all the way here to ask about Sam? Other than ending up in a British hospital during the war, Sam had no real ties to England. Yet the stranger's voice sounded vaguely familiar, like a memory she couldn't fully grasp.

"Is he a relative?" Dr. Clayborne asked.

"No. Just a fellow soldier. I'd like to learn what's become of him since he's returned."

A long pause ensued. Julia could picture Dr. Clayborne's serious features studying the man before him, attempting to determine if he should divulge any information.

"I'm afraid I'm not at liberty to discuss my patients."

"I realize that, and I hate to impose. Could you at least tell me how I might contact him?"

Julia's heart seized as a spasm of pain ripped through her. She wanted to jump up and run away before she overheard anything else. But her knees remained glued to the hard floor. Her wet hands clenched the folds of her dress, dark stains of moisture spreading across her skirt.

"I'm afraid that's impossible," Dr. Clayborne answered tersely.

"I can assure you I have no ill intent. I simply wish to speak to him."

"As I said, that's not possible." A heavy sigh. "I'm sorry to inform you that Private McIntyre is dead."

Julia crumpled over her knees. Visions of blood and death, ones she'd tried so hard to erase, rose up to swamp her.

"I'm terribly sorry," the stranger said. "I . . . I thought he was doing well, despite being confined to a wheelchair."

"Yes, well, it wasn't his physical health that did him in."

Julia clapped a wet hand over her mouth to keep from gasping. She'd never heard such bitterness from the physician before.

"Forgive me," Dr. Clayborne said. "That was uncalled for, as well as unprofessional. However, it galls me when a man has so much to live for and, despite all the resources offered him, chooses to end his life."

"He killed himself?"

"I'm afraid so." Another pause ensued, then, "Are you all right, sir?"

"Yes, fine. This has come as a shock is all."

"I apologize for blurting out such tragic news. Let me get you some water."

Julia pushed to her feet and tossed the brush into the water with a soapy splash. Who was this person looking for Sam? Was he really a fellow soldier who'd served in the war? There was something recognizable about his voice. Or was it only his accent?

She had to find out.

Moving closer to the doorway, she gingerly peered around the frame. A tall man leaned against the wall, running his fingers through his dark hair.

Dr. Clayborne handed him a cup of water and then, upon spying Julia, stopped cold. "Miss Holloway? Is there something I can help you with?"

"N-no, thank you, doctor. I was checking to see if the room was empty so I could clean in here." Her heart pounded against her ribs. Surely, he would know she was fibbing by her flaming cheeks if nothing else.

The stranger jerked away from the wall. His eyebrows rose as he looked her over from head to toe. A flicker of recognition passed over his features before he schooled them into a neutral expression.

Julia stared back, curiosity overcoming her discomfort at his perusal. She took in his wide shoulders, the shock of dark hair across his brow, the piercing gray eyes heavily fringed with thick lashes. While no one characteristic stood out, he did seem familiar. Was he one of the soldiers she'd treated at the medical center back home?

"Miss Holloway?" the man croaked out. "Julia Holloway?"

"Th-that's right. And who are you?"

"You probably don't remember me. I'm Quinten Aspinall."

She frowned. Where did she know that name from?

"We met at Brentwood Manor." He moved closer, the pallor of his skin making his gray eyes seem to glow.

Her uncle's estate. Had she been introduced to him at one of the balls her uncle had thrown in her honor? "I'm afraid I can't place you, Mr. Aspinall. Are you a friend of my uncle?"

The man's chin dipped downward. "I'm your uncle's valet."

The quiet dignity in his voice jarred her memory at last.

The unobtrusive young man who tended to Uncle Howard's every need. Julia had always thought of him as steadfast and unceasingly loyal. Not to mention very handsome—for a servant.

"Of course. Mr. Aspinall." Her manners kicked in and she gave a slight curtsy, as though greeting him in Brentwood's grand entranceway. "How nice to see you again."

And how very odd to be addressing a servant so familiarly.

As she straightened, she smoothed a hand down her skirt, and the wet fabric brought reality rushing back. The last time she'd seen this man she'd been a frivolous young girl, concerned only with what gown to wear to the next soirée, sought after by a flock of eligible bachelors in London. Now she was a penniless worker, scrubbing floors for a living, wearing rags for clothing. Mortification burned her neck and ears.

Oh, how the mighty had fallen.

Quinn did his best to keep the shock from his face. The scrubwoman before him bore almost no discernible resemblance to the vivacious girl he remembered. Gone were the extravagant gowns, flashy jewels, and elaborate hairstyles.

As his gaze skimmed over the large water stains that marred her simple skirt and the bedraggled kerchief that contained her blond tresses, he wanted to weep at the image before him. But it was her hands that grieved him the most. Red and raw, her knuckles looked like a prizefighter just finishing twelve rounds in the ring.

She must have caught his stare for she stuffed her hands into her pockets.

A throat cleared, drawing Quinn's attention back to the doctor. He'd nearly forgotten the man was there.

"It appears you two have some catching up to do," Dr. Clayborne said. "I'll be in my office down the hall if you need anything, Miss Holloway." He threw Quinn a rather pointed look that seemed to dare him to do anything to upset the girl.

"Thank you, doctor." Once the man had left, Julia lifted her chin in a manner reminiscent of her cultured upbringing. "Why are you looking for Sam?"

Quinn drew himself up to his full height and focused on her eyes. Brown and luminous, they were the one thing about her that hadn't changed. "The truth is, I was looking for him in order to find you."

Her chin trembled. "Why on earth would you . . . Oh." Her features hardened, and her eyes went flat. "My uncle sent you, didn't he?"

"He did." There was no point in denying it. She'd find out sooner or later anyway. He only hoped she would let him explain.

"I can't believe he made you come all this way. For what purpose?" Julia clutched the tattered neck of her blouse and took a step back, as though she expected him to snatch her away.

This was not how Quinn had planned to approach her. He needed time to determine the right words to convince her to come back to England with him. "Would you allow me to buy you a cup of tea and attempt to explain the reason for my journey?"

She bit her lip nervously, and her gaze darted toward the door. "I'm working right now. I don't get off until ten o'clock."

"I could come back then and walk you home."

"No." She clamped her mouth shut, then sucked in a breath. "I must ask you to please leave. You may tell my uncle that you've seen me and I'm fine. That's all he needs to know. Good day, sir." She rushed out of the room.

Frowning, Quinn followed her. "There's much I need to speak to you about, Miss Holloway. Where are you staying?"

"That is none of your concern." She grabbed a scrub brush from a metal pail of grayish water. "Uncle Howard made it very clear that if I left with Sam, he no longer wanted anything to do with me."

"But—"

"If you'll excuse me, Mr. Aspinall, I have a lot to accomplish before the end of my shift."

How could a scrubwoman manage to make him feel like he'd just insulted a member of the royal family? She stared at him, arms crossed, until he had no other choice but to leave.

"Very well. I hope to see you again before I return to England." He tipped his hat and reluctantly headed down the corridor.

As Quinn climbed the stairs to the main floor, he set his jaw, his mind grappling to make sense of what he'd just learned. Private McIntyre, the man Julia had come abroad with, had taken his own life. How had this affected her? Had she been in love with the man? Even if she was merely his caregiver, she must have been devastated by his death. And why was she now scrubbing floors in the military hospital?

Nothing about Miss Holloway's situation sat right with him, and he wouldn't rest until he determined what was really going on.

Since she'd made it clear his interest was not welcome, the only way he could see to accomplish his goal was to follow her when she left tonight. If he knew where she was staying, he might feel better. And at least he'd know where to find her once he devised a plan to woo her back to England.

Because one way or another, he *would* come up with a means to persuade her. He couldn't risk losing the once-in-a-lifetime opportunity of getting his own farm and being able to provide a home for his family at last.

No matter what he had to do to accomplish it.

CHAPTER 5

By the end of her shift, Julia's back ached and her knees throbbed. Thankfully Dr. Clayborne had left in a hurry for some medical emergency soon after Mr. Aspinall's departure, so he hadn't had the chance to question her about their relationship. Perhaps, if she were fortunate, the doctor would forget all about Quinten Aspinall.

As she planned to do.

She stepped out onto the sidewalk and let out a long breath, the walk home suddenly seeming more than she could endure. For some reason, she was more tired than usual after her shift, so much so that her very bones ached. But she had no choice since the streetcars had stopped for the evening.

The shadows appeared extra dark as she forced her feet to move faster. She'd never felt unsafe walking home in the evening, but tonight her nerves were getting the best of her. The visit from Mr. Aspinall must have unsettled her more than she'd realized.

For a moment, she allowed her mind to wander back to Brentwood Manor, where she'd spent her teenage years with her cousin, Amelia. Though their fathers were brothers, the two girls had been raised in entirely different circumstances. Julia's father, the younger of the Holloway brothers and therefore not the heir, had become a minister, and their family had lived very modestly in several vicarages over the years.

Until the day her parents had died in a tragic carriage accident and Julia was sent to Brentwood.

Amelia had done her best to school Julia in the ways of the nobility, but Julia had found the rules so confining and was always worried about a misstep of one sort or another.

Like the time she had noticed the attractive young man in uniform standing in the great hall and had whispered to Amelia, "Oh my. Your father's valet is rather handsome, don't you think?"

Amelia had looked at her in horror. "For pity's sake, Julia, he's a *servant*! You have plenty of handsome, rich men to choose from. You needn't pay the staff any mind at all, unless it's to ask them to fetch your bags." Amelia's voice had been loud enough that Julia was certain the valet had heard her.

Mortification had burned her face, and from then on she'd remembered never to talk about a servant again.

How incredibly odd—and rather troubling—that all these years later, her uncle's valet was here in Canada looking for her.

An auto's horn blared, startling Julia from her thoughts. The streetlamps in this part of town were sparse indeed, and her unease continued to mount as she walked. At last, she reached her building, grateful to see some of the tenants sitting on the curb, smoking cigarettes, more than likely trying to escape the confines of their stuffy rooms.

"Evening, Miss Holloway," one man called. "You're working late tonight, I see."

"I am indeed, Mr. Wood." She paused at the foot of the stairs to smile at the older gentleman. "How is Mrs. Wood? Is she over her cold yet?" The man's wife had suffered with bronchitis most of the winter, the cough lingering well into spring.

"She's much improved at last. She said to thank you for the last batch of soup you brought her." He winked at her, his eyes crinkling.

"It was no trouble at all." Last week, Julia had asked the soup kitchen for an extra ration, which she'd taken up to share with the Woods. "I'd love to stay and chat, but I've an early shift tomorrow."

"You have a good night, then," Mr. Blackmore said. "But watch out for Ketchum. He's been asking for you."

Her stomach twisted. She still owed the landlord the remainder of the rent—not to mention two months of arrears. "Thanks for the warning. I'll tiptoe past his flat."

Suddenly a man appeared out of the shadows. "Miss Holloway? Might I have a quick word before you go in?"

Julia froze. Her spine snapped into place as a slow curl of anger rose through her chest. "Did you follow me here, Mr. Aspinall? After I told you I didn't need an escort?" Though her nerves were jumping, she sent him an icy glare.

He shot a glance at Mr. Wood and Mr. Blackmore, who'd risen to their feet. "Forgive me, but I sensed I might not get the chance to speak to you again if I didn't."

"It's very late, Mr. Aspinall. I'm in no mood right now—"

"I didn't mean tonight." He held up his hands in mock surrender. "Only that we make arrangements to meet at your convenience."

"Is this fellow bothering you?" Mr. Wood came up beside her. "Because we can make sure he leaves."

"Thank you, Mr. Wood, but it's all right." Anxiety twisted her stomach into knots. How could she get rid of this man without causing any undue commotion? The last thing Julia needed was to give her landlord any further reason to evict her. She let out a sigh. "Very well, Mr. Aspinall. My shift is over at three thirty tomorrow afternoon. Meet me at the hospital, and I'll allow you to buy me that cup of tea."

The man's face flooded with relief. "Thank you, Miss Holloway. Until tomorrow, then."

He gave a bow and stepped back from the building.

Julia gathered her skirt and started up the cement stairs, resisting the urge to wait for him to leave. Somehow, she knew he would see her safely inside before he departed. A heaviness weighed in her stomach at the thought of having to meet him tomorrow. Now the man would surely report back to her uncle all the unpleasant details of her menial job and decrepit living conditions.

Oh, why had she broken down in a moment of weakness and written to Amelia? Even though she'd asked her cousin not to reveal anything about Julia's dire circumstances, Amelia must have divulged the contents of the letter to her father. Why else would Uncle Howard have sent his employee to find her?

She pressed her lips together, warding off unpleasant memories of her last altercation with her guardian and his shouted ultimatum. *"If you leave my home to run off with that soldier, you'll be on your own, cut off from any further financial assistance. And you won't be welcome here again."*

If only she hadn't openly defied him, she might still have a home to return to. But now her pride simply wouldn't allow her to go crawling back, even if she'd had the money to do so.

No, she would have to figure a way out of this mess on her own.

No matter what Quinten Aspinall had to tell her tomorrow.

As Julia made her way to her room, her initial relief at having made it by Mr. Ketchum's flat gave way to an increasing sense of dread that thickened her throat and slowed her steps.

It had been too easy. If her landlord had indeed been asking about her, as Mr. Blackmore claimed, he would have been listening for her footfall as he had the other day. There was no way he'd give up so quickly.

Her instincts proved correct when she rounded the corner of the third floor and found the hulking figure standing in the corridor outside her door, arms crossed over his barrel chest.

"Good evening, Mr. Ketchum." She forced a smile to her lips, offering a prayer that the man would be reasonable. For once.

"It will be—after I get my money." His thick brows crashed together. "I was expecting you home sooner. Not avoiding me, I hope."

"Of course not." Julia fumbled in her bag for the key. "I was asked to cover someone's shift today." She pushed the door open an inch. "Unfortunately, I didn't have time to see about an advance on my pay."

"Advance? You told me it was payday."

She swallowed. Was that what she'd told him? She couldn't actually remember what she'd said in the panic of the moment. "I meant that I was going to ask for an advance. Payday is next week. But I promise I'll—"

"I'm sick of your promises, missy." He took a menacing step forward. "If you can't pay me right now, you have two choices. Pack your things and leave immediately. Or . . ."

Her throat constricted. "Or what?"

"We can negotiate a different type of payment." He lowered his head toward her, his mouth hovering near her ear. "Services in lieu of cash."

His sour breath made Julia's stomach lurch. From the leer on his face, she knew exactly what type of services he expected. Unwelcome images of another man flew to mind. A man who had used her naiveté against her in a most vile manner. Her breath became shallow and her hands shook. She stepped back from the landlord, edging one foot inside her door. "The answer is still no."

His eyes became black coals of fury. "You'd rather sleep in the gutter with the rats?"

Courage stiffened her spine. "That's right."

Steely fingers wrapped around her upper arm, biting into the flesh.

A strangled cry escaped her before she bit down on her lip.

"You're forgetting about the outstanding amount you still owe me." He squeezed tighter. "I could send for the constable right now. I'm sure he'd have a nice jail cell ready and waiting for you."

A frantic pulse beat in her throat. Where were Mr. Wood and Mr. Blackmore? Had they come in yet? She tried to wrench her arm free, but the bully twisted it cruelly. The only thing she could do was pray that one of the other tenants would come to her aid.

She took in a breath and screamed as loud as she could.

Quinn stared at the two men who'd been sitting on the front stoop when he arrived. They now moved closer, assessing Quinn with unfriendly eyes.

"Don't bother coming back here," the thinner man said. "It's clear Miss Holloway doesn't want to talk to you."

"And I'd forget about meeting her tomorrow as well." The second man, at least twenty years junior to the first, crossed his arms. "She only agreed to meet you in order to get you to leave."

Quinn pushed his shoulders back and kept his gaze even. "I have no undesirable intentions, I assure you. Miss Holloway's uncle, the Earl of Brentwood, sent me to find out how she's faring so far from home."

The thin man snickered. "Well, la-di-dah. If Julia has such fancy relatives, why would she be living here?" He waved a dirt-encrusted hand toward the building behind him.

Why indeed? "That's what I intend to find out."

A faint cry sounded from somewhere inside the building.

Quinn stiffened. He scanned the bricks, spying an open window several floors above.

When a second, much louder scream pierced the night, Quinn immediately raced up the steps to the building. If Julia was in trouble, he had to help.

"Third floor," one man shouted after him.

Without hesitating, Quinn took the stairs two at a time until he reached the third story, where he paused to determine which direction to take next.

A muffled grunt drew him to the right. At the end of the hallway, two figures stood very close together. As he got nearer, he saw a beefy man had Julia by the upper arm. She was struggling against him, but her slight frame was no match for his brawn.

Quinn marched forward. "Take your hands off her immediately."

The man froze, then whirled to face Quinn. "Who the devil are you?"

"That is of no consequence. Let her go. Now."

Julia's eyes went wide, and her bottom lip quivered.

"This is a private matter between me and my tenant."

"Being a landlord does not give you the right to assault your tenants."

"This tenant is in arrears, and I'm within my rights to get my money by whatever means I deem necessary."

For such a creepy character, he certainly had command of the English language. Almost as though he'd memorized the law book pertaining to landlords' rights.

"And this is how you collect your rent? By bullying defenseless women?"

"None of your business," the burly man snarled. "You're trespassing on private property. If you don't leave immediately, I'll have you arrested."

"By all means, telephone the authorities. I don't mind explaining why I felt the need to enter this hovel."

And a hovel was indeed the best description. Paint curled off the walls, while the stench of urine and rotting meat was enough to turn his stomach.

The landlord released his grip on Julia's arm and moved toward him. Although Quinn stood a good head taller, the other man outweighed him by a fair bit, judging by his bulging belly.

Quinn stood his ground. "How much does the lady owe you?"

That brought the man up short. A greedy new light sparked in his eyes. "Twenty-one dollars."

Still not totally familiar with Canadian currency, Quinn sensed this was a rather high sum, especially for someone who cleaned floors for a living. He withdrew his money pouch from his jacket, loosened the drawstring, and shook out some of the gold coins the earl had given him to cover expenses. It seemed only fitting to use the earl's money to help Julia. He chose one and handed it to the man. "I think this should more than cover any outstanding debt."

The man's eyes widened. "Is that real gold?"

"It is." While the man fingered the coin, Quinn walked toward Julia, who hovered by an open door. "Now, if you'll excuse me, I'll help the lady pack her belongings."

Julia's mouth fell open.

"There's no need to be hasty." The landlord shoved his loot into a pocket. "If this payment turns out to be legitimate, she can stay. At least until next month's rent is due."

"How gracious of you. However, I believe Miss Holloway will be looking for more suitable lodging. Good evening."

With a hand under her elbow, Quinn ushered Julia into her room and shut the door behind them.

"I . . . I . . ." Julia rounded on him. "What do you think you're doing?" Color returned to her ashen cheeks.

Quinn remained by the door. "You can't stay here. Not with a lecherous oaf like that on the prowl."

She crossed her arms, her nostrils pinched. "You have no right to interfere in my life."

"Miss Julia." He stared directly into her brown eyes. "Please allow me to ensure your safety and find you somewhere decent to live."

"Do you think I *want* to live in a place like this?" She practically hissed at him. "It's all I can afford on the wages I earn."

Quinn paused to carefully consider his next words. "I'm acquainted with a woman who runs a very respectable boardinghouse. She also has many connections in the city. Let me take you there, for tonight at least, and I'm sure she will help you find alternate accommodations. Something within your budget."

He waited while she considered her options. A host of emotions flickered over her lovely face. She possessed a beauty that no amount of hardship could mar.

At last her shoulders slumped. "Very well. Anywhere would have to be better than here."

"Don't worry. If Mrs. Chamberlain can't come up with a solution, I'm sure there must be another equally horrid place with a room to let," Quinn teased, hoping to coax a smile.

Julia's lips twitched, then grew into a reluctant smile. "Fine. I'll pack my belongings."

Julia came to a halt on the walkway. Before her, the boarding-house loomed tall in the darkness, yet the welcoming glow of light from the front window shone like a beacon of hope. Could she really stay in this lovely residence?

"Maybe the landlady is in bed for the night," Julia whispered. "I don't want to disturb her."

Quinn—as he insisted she call him—mounted the steps to the long porch and rapped loudly on the front door. After several seconds with no response, he repeated the action. "She won't mind. Especially when she hears about your circumstances."

Julia bit her lip. As much as she appreciated Quinn's intervention with Mr. Ketchum, the fact remained that she was now homeless, dependent on the kindness of strangers for a place to sleep tonight.

The door opened, and a plump woman in a bathrobe appeared. She squinted through the screen. "Quinten? Is that you?"

"Yes, ma'am. I'm sorry to disturb you so late, but I have a bit of an emergency." He gestured to Julia. "This is Miss Julia Holloway, an acquaintance from home. She's in dire need of a place to stay tonight."

Heat bloomed in Julia's cheeks. How she hated being the object of people's pity. "Nice to meet you, ma'am. And I'm terribly sorry to bother you."

"No bother at all, dear. And both of you please stop with all the 'ma'ams'. You can call me Mrs. C., or Harriet if you prefer." She swung open the screen door. "Please, come in."

Julia entered the house and found herself in a cozy foyer. Quinn followed and set her bag in the corner.

"I've just finished my nightly tea," the woman said, "but I'm sure there's some left in the pot if you'd like a cup."

"We'd love one," Quinn said before Julia could answer.

Mrs. C. pointed to a room on the right. "Make yourself comfortable, then. I'll be right back."

Clutching her handbag, Julia entered the parlor and looked around. A large floral sofa and overstuffed armchairs surrounded the fireplace. Above the mantel, a painted landscape of an English cottage made Julia's throat tighten with another attack of homesickness.

"What a lovely room," she said as she took a seat on the sofa.

"It is indeed." Quinn smiled. "Reminds me of my childhood home. Before my father died." A flash of sorrow passed over his features.

Julia peered at him, suddenly aware of how little she knew about him. What kind of life had he lived before he came to Brentwood? All she remembered was a young man in servant's livery. Now she found herself wanting to know what had led him to become employed in her uncle's household.

He came to sit across from her. "Please don't worry, Miss Holloway. Everything will be fine. I promise." His earnest gray eyes radiated sincerity. Could she accept his gesture of kindness? The last time she'd accepted a stranger's charity she'd lived to regret her misjudgment.

Yet something about Quinn felt safe and dependable. Still, it wouldn't hurt to be cautious. "What makes you so certain everything will turn out fine?" she said in a soft voice. "I doubt I'll be able to afford the rent here."

He studied her. "I don't know Mrs. Chamberlain well, but I do know she has a big heart and is especially sympathetic to immigrants. In fact, she helps the minister at her church run a support group for newcomers." He chuckled. "Be warned. She'll do her best to get you to join them."

"That might not be so bad." Julia attempted to smile. "I don't have many friends here. And now that Sam is . . ." She pressed her lips together to fight back a rush of tears. When would she ever be able to say his name without breaking down?

"I'm very sorry about your friend." Quinn's voice was gentle. "It must have been a terrible blow."

"It was. I . . . I was the one who found him." She closed her eyes, fighting visions of Sam's lifeless body on the bed, surrounded by blood-soaked sheets, his face as pale as the walls behind him.

"Why?" Quinn's one-word question tugged at her very soul.

How many times had she asked herself that same question? "Why would he take his life?" he asked.

"I don't know for certain." She frowned. "It happened after he'd received some bad medical news. News I wish I'd known about. Maybe then I could have done something to prevent his death." She drew in a sharp breath, pressing a hand to her abdomen, then slowly released it, willing the persistent nausea to leave her.

Quinn stared at her with open sympathy.

"I knew he had an appointment with Dr. Clayborne that afternoon, but he insisted on going alone. And later he wouldn't tell me what the doctor said. He locked himself in his room, saying he wanted to be alone. The next morning, when I went to wake him, I found . . ." Her throat seized.

"You don't need to explain. I can imagine the rest."

Julia shook her head. "I can't help feeling responsible. As his caregiver, I should have checked on him. I should have known." She pinched her eyes shut, trying to block out the pain.

Warmth surrounded her chilled fingers as Quinn took one of her hands in his. "Don't do that to yourself, Julia. You can't blame yourself for Sam's actions."

She opened her eyes to find Quinn's face close to hers, empathy swimming in his gaze. She clung to his hand, drinking in the comfort he offered, until the unbidden memory of Dr. Hawkins and his brand of comfort made her pull her hand away.

The sound of rattling cups preceded Mrs. Chamberlain into the room. "Sorry I took so long. I decided to brew a fresh pot after all." She set a tray on the table in front of the sofa and looked at Julia, taking in her distraught appearance. "Oh, my dear. Please don't fret any longer. I have a small room available on the third floor. One of my boarders is making it up for you now."

Julia dabbed her cheeks with her handkerchief. "That's very kind of you. But I . . . I don't think I can afford the rent."

"Now, now. I'll hear no talk of money tonight. There'll be plenty of time to discuss the future tomorrow, when you're rested."

Rested? Julia's gaze flew to the ornate clock on the mantel. It was already after midnight. How would she be at the hospital by seven o'clock and clean all day on so little sleep?

"I have to work very early tomorrow. And I don't know how to get to the military hospital from here." A bone-deep weariness made thinking a chore. At this rate, she'd get no sleep at all.

"No need to worry. We're all early risers around here. One of our girls, Nora, works at a bank right across the street from that hospital. She'll help you get there on time."

All the muscles in Julia's back sagged, and she sank back against the cushions.

Mrs. C. pressed a cup into her hands. "Drink your tea, dear. By the time you're done, the room will be ready."

Quinn drained his cup in one long gulp and set it back on the tray. "Thank you so much, Mrs. C. Now that I know Julia's in good hands, I'd best be going." He rose from his chair.

"You're welcome, Quinten. Come by and see us whenever you like."

Quinn gave Julia a long look. "I plan to do just that. Sleep well, Julia. Until tomorrow."

CHAPTER 6

Quinn paced the sidewalk outside the military hospital the next afternoon, waiting for the end of Julia's shift. He hoped she wouldn't try to avoid him by exiting through a back door or an employee entrance. He imagined she might be feeling embarrassed and perhaps a tad put out with him for the way he had dealt with her landlord.

Still, Quinn didn't regret his actions. He could no more walk away and leave Julia to that man's mercy than he could leave his little sister in such a situation. Honor dictated he take action to aid the earl's niece, who had obviously fallen on hard times.

Since she'd come to Toronto as Private McIntyre's personal caregiver, Quinn guessed her employment had died with Sam. And since Julia had no formal training as a nurse, only her experience in the war, he doubted it would be enough to earn her employment in the field.

Yet scrubbing floors? Surely there was some type of work more in keeping with her skills. Something less demeaning. He'd have to be careful how he approached that topic of conversation and somehow bring up the suggestion that returning to England might be her best option.

A door opened, and Julia exited onto the sidewalk. Upon seeing Quinn, she hesitated, then gave a tentative smile. "Good afternoon, Mr. Aspinall."

"Good afternoon. And remember, it's Quinn." He held out his arm to her. "I found a charming eatery on the next street. I doubt they have true English tea, but I'm willing to brave it if you are."

She gave a light laugh that went straight to his chest, loosening the tension there as they started toward the corner. "I've yet to find a truly good cup of tea," she said, "though Mrs. Chamberlain's came very close."

"I thought so too. How did you sleep?"

"Quite well. And Mrs. C. was kind enough to provide me with a bagged lunch. I don't know how I'll ever repay her. Or you, for that matter." She looked at him with solemn eyes.

"No need to repay me. The money came from funds your uncle provided for any expenses I might incur during my search for you. I thought it only fitting to use a portion of it to pay your landlord, since I couldn't bear the thought of you being indebted to that man."

They turned onto the next street, and Quinn pointed to the restaurant he had in mind. When she nodded, he escorted her inside. The place bustled with noise and activity. Most of the booths, as well as a long row of stools at the counter, were filled with boisterous patrons. The hostess led them to a small table by the window where they could watch the traffic passing by.

Once the waitress took their order for tea and biscuits, Julia folded her hands on the tabletop. "So, my uncle paid you to find me." The quiet words held a trace of hurt. "That's why you came to Canada?"

"Not exactly." Quinn kept his tone even. "I'm here to find my three siblings. When I told the earl of my intended trip, he leapt at the chance to have me look for you as well." He leaned forward, needing to make her understand. "Your uncle loves you very much, Julia. He regrets the ultimatum he gave you and wants you to return home. The money he gave me was simply to allay any additional expenses I might incur on his behalf." There was no reason to tell her about the generous advance the earl had given Quinn on his pay, nor the promised tenant farm, since it had no bearing on the truth of his words.

"I see." Her cheeks grew rosy as she toyed with her napkin, her lashes sweeping down.

What was going through her mind? Would she forgive her uncle for his harsh treatment and agree to come back? Perhaps Quinn should have asked his lordship to write a letter asking her to return. Maybe then she might be more inclined to trust the validity of his claim.

In the ensuing silence, Quinn took a moment to assess her. At least she appeared more rested today. The dark circles under her eyes were less prominent. She'd removed the kerchief from her hair, and the long blond locks he remembered were pulled back into a rather severe roll at the nape of her neck.

She raised her head, a frown marring her brow. "Have you had any luck finding your siblings?"

"Not yet." He gripped the water glass in front of him. "It's turned out to be a complicated process."

"How did they end up so far from home?"

"That's a rather long, sad tale. One I won't bore you with." He attempted a smile.

But she didn't return it. Her gaze remained solemn.

The waitress reappeared with two small metal teapots and a plate of biscuits. Julia poured some milk into her cup, then added the steaming brew.

Quinn stirred a spoon of sugar into his and tried to come up with a way to return the conversation to coming back to England. But how?

Julia took a sip, studying him over the rim. "I'd like to hear about your siblings, if you don't mind sharing the story."

Quinn hesitated. He was far more interested in learning about the events that had led to her dire circumstances. Yet maybe if he told her about his own situation, she might be more inclined to trust him.

"I was fifteen when my father died," he began. "Being the oldest, I gave up any notion of going to university and found work to support my family. I did a variety of odd jobs until I was fortunate enough to get hired on at your uncle's townhome as a footman."

"That was before I came to live with him, I imagine." She began to nibble at one of the biscuits.

"Yes. By the time you arrived, I'd been in his employ over a year, and we'd moved more permanently to his estate in Derbyshire. At that time, the earl promoted me to his personal valet, which was indeed an honor and a privilege. I admire Lord Brentwood a great deal. He's been very good to me."

Her gaze fell to the table as she fiddled with her spoon. "For all his high-handed ways, Uncle Howard is a good man," she admitted, a tad begrudgingly. "I only wish he . . . I wish we hadn't parted under such difficult circumstances." She looked up again. "But back to your story. Where were your mother and siblings during the time you worked for my uncle?"

"Living in a small flat in London. Mum earned a meager amount cleaning and sewing. But it was my salary that provided the majority of income." He took a breath. "I used to see them on my days off, until the move to Brentwood Manor. Then it became too far to travel for one afternoon a month."

She set her cup down with a loud clank. "Is that all the time off you were allowed?"

He shrugged. "I didn't mind, except that I couldn't see my family. Then the war started and everything changed."

Her face darkened. "Did you enlist right away?"

"Pretty much, as all the young men did. The earl was kind enough to send a stipend to my mother every month as a supplement to my soldier's pay."

"That was kind of him." She nodded gravely. "I guess you were already gone by the time I left Brentwood to help with the war effort, much to my uncle's chagrin. He didn't approve of my involvement with the wounded men. It never occurred to him that helping in some small way would allow me to feel useful for once."

"As I recall, his lordship expressed his opinion about it on the few occasions I visited Brentwood while on leave." Quinn's lips twitched as he bit into a biscuit.

"Ah, I suppose being his valet, you were privy to many such complaints about my behavior." Her brows rose in a haughty manner, which immediately reminded Quinn of the high-spirited girl he remembered.

"A good valet never reveals his master's private conversations."

She raised her cup to her lips as though to hide her smile. "I'm sure you would never have known I was gone, save for my uncle's rants."

"On the contrary. I was very much aware of your absence." The minute the words left his mouth, his neck heated. Why had he admitted such a thing?

Julia's brown eyes widened. "You were?"

"Well, yes. The manor was far less cheerful with you gone."

"What a lovely thing to say." Her face softened as she patted a napkin to her lips. "When I first saw you at the hospital, I couldn't place you, but I knew I recognized your voice," she said. "I remember you at Brentwood. I often thought how lucky my uncle was to have such a devoted employee. You were so steadfast and . . . unflappable."

A laugh escaped him. "Unflappable. Well, I suppose there are worse qualities to be remembered for."

She giggled, and a blush spread over her cheeks.

Quinn stared into her warm brown eyes until she lowered them. He gave himself a mental shake. Had he taken leave of his senses, flirting with Julia that way? He had absolutely no business behaving in such a manner with Lord Brentwood's niece.

A waitress appeared with more hot water for their tea. Julia busied herself pouring another cup, while Quinn struggled to strap down his emotions. He needed to remain aloof, in control. And he definitely needed to turn the conversation around to focus on her.

"What happened to your family while you were away at war?" Julia asked before he could begin.

Quinn pushed his plate away, his appetite gone. Just thinking about that time was enough to make his stomach twist. "When I returned from duty, I discovered the flat where they'd been living had been rented to someone else. I found my mum in a workhouse in London." He paused and took a drink to wash away the bitterness from his tongue.

"How dreadful. Were the children with her?"

"No. It turns out she'd placed them in an orphanage to spare them that fate. She intended it to be a temporary measure until she was able to find work and a decent place to live, but that never happened." He blew out a frustrated breath. "If only she'd told me how dire her circumstances were, I would have tried harder to make sure they had enough money."

Julia placed a hand on his arm. "You did the best you could, Quinn. There was nothing else you could have done."

Looking into her earnest face, he longed to believe her. The tea, along with the constant ache of guilt, churned in his gut.

"How did they end up in Canada?"

"The Dr. Barnardo's Homes where Mum left them are known for sending large numbers of orphans to Canada. Supposedly to give them a better life, living with a family and working on a farm. The idea sounds noble enough in theory, but I'm certain my mother had no idea of their intention."

"That's terrible. No wonder you're desperate to find them."

"Indeed." Quinn attempted to push aside the stress brought on by reliving such unpleasant memories. "What about you? I assume that after Private McIntyre's death you were left without employment."

Her features grew pinched, and she nodded. "Also without accommodations." She set her cup down. "Before the war, Sam inherited his parents' home. But upon his death, the house passed to a male cousin who kept only some of the staff." Her gaze flickered. "Unfortunately, he made it clear he had no need for my services and demanded I leave immediately."

Quinn did his best to hide his outrage. How unfeeling could a man be to evict a single woman with no ready means of securing another place to live?

"I'll admit I was rather desperate. Dr. Clayborne was kind enough to get me the position at the hospital. Still, it's only part-time, and most landlords aren't willing to lease a flat without the guarantee of a more secure source of income." She bowed her head over her plate. "Which is how I ended up in that horrid building."

Quinn made a sympathetic murmur while carefully choosing his next words. "Did you ever consider going back to England?"

When she raised her head, tears shimmered in her lovely eyes. "Even if I'd had the money for my passage, I wouldn't have been welcome at my uncle's home."

"I know you didn't part on good terms, but if you were in trouble, I'm certain he would have helped you, no matter how angry he was."

"Perhaps. However, my pride wouldn't allow me to admit he'd been right." She sighed. "I hated the thought of returning a failure and wasn't about to beg. I decided to work until I could save enough for better accommodations or for a ticket home."

Quinn raised a brow. "And how is your plan going?"

"Not very well." Her lips twitched. "Turns out I'm a rather poor money manager. Though it's hard to manage what you don't have."

All the more reason she should jump at the earl's offer.

Quinn's heart beat hard in his chest. He leaned forward. "Julia, your uncle gave me enough funds to cover your passage home. Would you consider coming back to England with me when I return? You can stay at Mrs. Chamberlain's until I find my siblings. Then we could all go back together." He could picture it so clearly in his mind. The lot of them on the deck of the ship, laughing and sharing stories. He'd come back a hero, bringing the prodigal daughter back to her loving family. Julia would be safe, and Quinn would reap his reward.

She wiped her mouth with a napkin and set it down. "I know you mean well, but I really must do this on my own. Uncle Howard hurt me deeply when he disowned me, and I don't know if I can forgive him quite so easily." She lifted her chin. "When and if I return, I'll do it on my own terms. It's a matter of pride and self-reliance. You understand."

The wind left his sails in a whoosh as his beautiful dream faded. He blinked, not sure what else he could say to change her mind.

"However, if I've managed to save enough by the time you're ready to leave, I'd be happy to join you on the trip back." She gave him such a blinding smile that Quinn forgot to breathe.

Heat blasted through his chest, and he knew with startling clarity that he would slay any dragon or overcome any obstacle to make sure Julia was all right before he ever left Canada. Despite everything, he couldn't help but admire her courage and determination to make her own way in the world. He could certainly understand those sentiments, since he'd been struggling for years to do the same.

He nodded. "It's a deal, then. And I intend to hold you to it."

Color stained her cheeks once more, but she laughed. "Very well. It's a deal."

Quinn pulled out some money to pay the bill. "May I walk you back to the boardinghouse?"

Julia's lighthearted mood instantly turned sour. She'd been so engrossed in her conversation with Quinn that she'd forgotten her main problem: the necessity to look for new accommodations. "I really must find somewhere else to stay. I know I can't afford to pay Mrs. Chamberlain's rates." She picked up her purse and rose from her seat.

"What if I told you," Quinn said slowly, a hint of trepidation in his voice, "that your rent has been paid for the next month?"

She stopped to stare at him. "What do you mean it's been paid?"

Looking sheepish, Quinn shrugged.

A burst of anger shot through her system as understanding dawned. She opened her mouth, ready to give him a piece of her mind, but he touched her elbow and leaned close. "Let's discuss this as we walk, shall we?" He opened the restaurant door and waited for her to exit.

Not wishing to make a scene, she marched along the sidewalk, certain that steam must be whistling from her ears. "You had no right to do that, Quinten Aspinall. I will pay my own way or sleep in the streets."

When she glanced over at him, the faint twitch of his lips only increased her annoyance. "Are you laughing at me?"

"Never." But then his grin stretched across his face, belying his claim. "I'm sorry. It's just that you look so . . . adorable all riled up that way."

"Hmph." She lifted her chin and kept walking, willing her lips not to curve.

He came up beside her again. "Please tell me you're not seriously thinking of living in the streets. Anything would have to be better than that."

"Not anything. Trust me." Visions of the leering Mr. Ketchum rose in her mind, and she shuddered. She'd take rats running over her rather than submit to that type of payment.

"Right, then, let's look at this from a different angle. What type of work would you ideally like to do?"

She stopped at the next corner. "Nursing. Or some other position that ministers to the suffering."

A streetcar sailed by, its bells clanging, warning the other traffic to steer clear. When the road emptied, they made their way across. Quinn kept a hand under her elbow, a gallant gesture Julia found reassuring and more than a little appealing.

"After watching Sam struggle," she continued, "I wanted to find a way to help other men like him. Dr. Clayborne says the rate of suicide among returning soldiers is very high. Their physical wounds can be treated, but there's no real relief for their emotional turmoil."

"A noble yet daunting goal. I imagine it would involve specialized training?"

"Yes. Either nursing or social work would require college courses. Which is another problem, since I have no money for those either." The frustration of her situation continued to eat at her. No matter which way she turned, she reached an impasse.

"Let's speak with Mrs. Chamberlain when we return. Perhaps

this newcomers group of hers might offer you a solution. Or at least the possibility of finding a better-paying job."

She glanced at his profile as they stopped again to wait for the traffic to clear. Such a noble chin and jaw, as well as a high, almost aristocratic forehead. Quinn looked more like someone from the upper class than she did. "May I ask why you're worrying about me when you have your own problems to contend with?"

When he turned to look at her, the intensity of his gaze made her pulse flutter.

"What kind of man would I be if I left you to the mercy of that landlord? Once you're safely settled at Mrs. Chamberlain's and I know Reverend Burke has agreed to help you, then I'll be able to focus on my own affairs."

Julia swallowed the lump forming in her throat. *What kind of man indeed?*

"I think," she said softly, "that you are a most honorable man. And I'm very grateful for your help."

Quinn's cheeks turned ruddy. "Glad I could be of service."

"I won't forget your kindness, and I promise to one day return the favor." Her voice quavered. Other than Dr. Clayborne, no one had shown any concern for her since Sam's death. Her thoughts turned to Richard Hawkins, Sam's family physician. She shuddered and quickly pushed the memories away. It would serve no purpose to relive her shame over how easily he'd manipulated her into believing he was a caring person.

Every instinct told Julia that Quinn was nothing like the deceitful Dr. Hawkins. Instead, this humble man, a servant in her uncle's employ, treated her with more respect and consideration than she'd received in a long time.

He smiled and winked. "Be warned. I intend to hold you to that promise too, Miss Holloway."

CHAPTER 7

"I'm so glad you agreed to come to the meeting tonight." Mrs. Chamberlain gave Julia a warm hug as they entered the hall in the basement of Holy Trinity Church. "I'm sure you'll find it's like a wee taste of home."

A damp, somewhat musty odor met Julia's nose as they entered the large room. Several people stood talking beside a table along the far wall.

"These meetings are always fun." Barbara, one of Mrs. C.'s long-term tenants, looped her arm through Julia's. "Especially now with the men back from war. They really appreciate our home-baked pies."

Now Julia understood why the girls had insisted on baking all afternoon.

Armed with two baskets of pies and muffins, Barbara and Mabel marched over to the table and began to unload their wares.

"Never mind them, dear." Mrs. C. chuckled. "Those two are more interested in finding husbands than helping Reverend Burke with the newcomers. Not that there hasn't been a romance or two started here. But our main concern is seeing that people like you have the opportunity to find stable jobs, decent housing, and, of course, a place to worship on Sundays."

Julia smiled. "Any help at all will be greatly appreciated, though you've already done more than enough."

"Nonsense." Mrs. C. shook her head. "I could never let a fine young girl like you stay in one of those hovels. I've written numerous letters to the mayor over the years to do something about that area of town. Unfortunately, they've had little effect so far."

Julia laughed. "Is there any cause you don't champion, Mrs. C.?"

"I only support the causes I feel strongly about. I love this city, and I intend to see it live up to its full potential. Just like the girls who live at my house."

Warmth spread through Julia's chest. With someone like Mrs. C. on her side, her circumstances would surely have to improve.

"Here comes Reverend Burke now. Looks like Quinten's already bending his ear."

Julia's heart sped at the sight of Quinn crossing the room. He was so tall and handsome next to the shorter minister. And when his intense gaze found hers, she had to resist the urge to pat her hair and make sure no pins were slipping.

What was wrong with her? He was her uncle's valet. Back home, she wouldn't even be allowed to speak to him unless discussing a household matter. But here in this foreign land, where the social class structure was much more relaxed, Julia found herself wanting to be around the man who made her feel so safe and valued.

"Mrs. Chamberlain. Miss Holloway." Quinn gave a polite bow. "It's good to see you again."

"And you, Mr. Aspinall." Was it only yesterday since Julia had spent so much time talking with him?

"Now listen here, you two. We're not that formal around here." Mrs. C. laughed. "Are we, Geoffrey?"

The reverend raised a bushy brow. "Indeed we are not, Harriet."

A hint of pink infused Mrs. C.'s cheeks. "Forgive my manners. Julia, this is Reverend Burke, the minister here at Holy Trinity."

"A pleasure to meet you, my dear." Grinning, he took Julia's hand in his. "I hope you don't mind, but Quinten has been filling me in on your situation. I'm sorry you've had such a hard time of it, but I'm certain we'll be able to help you improve your circumstances." He waved a hand around the room. "We have a far-reaching network among our members. And everyone here has been in your shoes at one time or another. I'll put out some feelers to see if anyone knows of any possible job opportunities."

"Thank you, Reverend. You have no idea how comforting that is." Julia swallowed hard. "I've been feeling so alone since . . . my friend died."

Rev. Burke nodded gravely. "And I remember how overwhelming the city feels at first when you're far from home. Which is why Harriet and I make it our mission to help immigrants any way we can. Now, if you'll excuse me, I need to get this meeting under way. We'll talk again soon."

Quinn escorted Julia to the metal folding chairs positioned in a semi-circle facing the dais and sat down beside her. The hour-long meeting flew by with Rev. Burke, as well as several other people, speaking on various issues, mostly concerning the poorer citizens of the city. Somewhat self-consciously, Julia introduced herself to the assembly, along with two other ladies and a man also new to the group.

Later, during refreshment time, Julia was amazed at how many people came to speak with her and offer their assistance. She was chatting with Barbara when a touch at her elbow made her turn.

"Excuse me, Julia. Might I have a quick word?" Though Quinn smiled, the unease in his eyes made her pulse quicken.

"Of course." She excused herself and followed him to a quieter spot.

"I wanted to make sure you felt comfortable with Mrs. C. and Reverend Burke before I leave." He stood with his hands clasped behind his back, as he used to do when performing his duties. However, something about his demeanor radiated anxiety.

"I feel right at home. They've both been most kind." She smiled. "Don't worry. I'll walk home with Mrs. C. and the other girls. You don't have to wait." The fact that he was so concerned about her safety made her appreciate how much of a gentleman he was. Most of her peers back in England were nowhere near as solicitous.

"That's good to know, but I didn't just mean tonight." He exhaled slowly. "I'm planning on leaving tomorrow to travel north and look for my brothers. Once I've found them, I'll start searching for my sister."

"Oh, I see." Why did it feel like a hole had opened in her stomach? "How long will you be gone?"

"Several days. Maybe longer if I run into difficulties." He reached for her hand. "But I won't leave if you're not comfortable with your present . . . arrangement." His gray eyes searched hers.

Between the intensity of his gaze and the warmth of his hand, Julia found it hard to formulate an intelligent response. She swallowed. "You don't have to worry about me, Quinn. You've paid my way for now at the boardinghouse. And Reverend Burke seems to think he'll be able to find me a better position." She forced a smile so he wouldn't detect the anxiety creeping into her system.

"Promise me you'll stay with Mrs. C. until I return."

"Why is this so important to you?" She peered at him, a sudden suspicion growing. "Did my uncle make you agree to watch out for me?"

He stiffened. "This has nothing to do with your uncle."

"But you barely know me. I don't understand why you feel so responsible for my well-being." She lifted her chin. It still chafed somewhat being in his debt when she wasn't clear on his motives. And after the fiasco with Sam's physician, Julia still wasn't sure she could trust her own judgment.

Quinn let out a breath. "You may find this difficult to believe, but I consider you one of the family. Perhaps it's because I was accountable for your uncle's welfare, as well as those living within Brentwood's walls. I couldn't bear thinking about you living in the type of horrid conditions you were before."

The sincerity in his gaze was almost too much to take. "I'll be fine, Quinn. Thank you for your concern."

"Very well, then." The lines of tension around his eyes eased. "I look forward to seeing you again upon my return." He lifted her hand to his lips.

Warmth spread up her arm and soon enveloped her cheeks. "Godspeed, Quinn. I pray you have good news to bring back."

"And I as well. Good-bye for now, Julia."

He held her gaze for several seconds before releasing her hand and striding away.

"Keep him safe, Lord," she murmured. "And may he find his siblings in good health."

The hours on the train to Elmvale the next day gave Quinn too much time to think. Never had he been so torn by a decision. First, he feared he was making a mistake going in search of his brothers before trying to find Becky. But Peterborough was two hours in the opposite direction, and by choosing to go north first, Quinn could check on both boys at once. Even though he worried about Becky's welfare, she was almost eighteen, whereas Harry was still only a boy of twelve. All Quinn could do was to pray that the Lord would keep everyone safe until he could get to them.

Second, he hated leaving Julia behind. In some manner, he felt he was shirking his duty, which was silly. She was in excellent hands with Mrs. Chamberlain. Quinn had already spoken to the woman and enlisted her help in ensuring Julia's well-being. He'd also taken Jonathan and Emmaline into his confidence and requested them to befriend Julia in his absence. Everyone had assured him they would treat her as one of their own.

That notion alone gave Quinn a small measure of comfort as the train approached the Elmvale station. For the present time, he must put Julia out of his mind and concentrate on his brothers.

Quinn had decided to travel to Elmvale first, the town farthest away. If he was able to locate Cecil, the two of them could then make their way back to Caledon, where Harry was staying. Quinn would be grateful to have Cecil's company on the second leg of his trip, and if all went according to plan, the three of them would travel back to Toronto together.

After that, Quinn needed to go to the placement home where

Becky had been sent. But he hoped to put his brothers in Rev. Burke's care before he set off on the next phase of his quest.

And he also wanted to see Julia again. Depending on her circumstances at the time, he was toying with the idea of asking her to accompany him to find Becky. His instincts told him he would be more favorably received with a woman along. After all, a man claiming to be Becky's brother might be viewed with suspicion.

He shook his head as the train came to a grinding halt. There was no point in getting too far ahead of himself. *"One step at a time, lad,"* as his father always said.

Minutes later, Quinn settled his hat on his head, stepped down onto the platform, and simply stared. Other than the train station in front of him, the landscape spread out around him in a sea of green. Nothing but miles of rolling hills and trees. How would he ever find Cecil's farm?

He headed over to the depot, hoping someone would be inside. Thankfully, a man was stationed at the desk.

"Good afternoon," Quinn said. "I wondered if you could help me."

"I'll do my best," the man said with a smile. "Are you looking for a place to stay?"

Quinn's accent likely made him think he was a visitor.

"Actually, I'm looking for my younger brother who works on one of the farms in this area. Unfortunately, I don't know the name of the owner."

The thin man frowned. "That could be like looking for a needle in a haystack. There are hundreds of farms in this neck of the woods."

Quinn's spirits sank. No wonder Mr. Hobday had revealed the name of the town. He knew it would be near impossible to find anyone with such limited information.

"What's your brother's name? Maybe I've met him."

"Cecil Aspinall." Quinn leaned an arm on the counter. "He's about sixteen, and he's been working here for several years now."

The man's brows shot up. "Cecil? I know the boy. He often

comes to meet the train and pick up shipments for Mr. Sherman. A very polite young man."

"That's fantastic." Quinn could scarcely believe his luck at finding someone who knew Cecil so quickly. "Can you give me directions to Mr. Sherman's property?"

A shadow crossed the clerk's face. He straightened some brochures on the counter before meeting Quinn's gaze. "I'd be very careful if I were you. Mr. Sherman isn't exactly the friendly type. He won't appreciate you nosing around his farm."

Quinn straightened slowly. "Thank you for the advice. I'll be sure to knock on the front door and introduce myself in a most proper manner before I start 'nosing around.'"

The clerk studied Quinn for a moment, then shrugged. "Suit yourself, mister. The Sherman farm is on Rural Road Three. About eight miles due north of here."

"Eight miles?" Quinn's stomach dropped. "I don't suppose there's anywhere nearby to rent a horse?"

"Now, there I can help you. Hank's Livery is two blocks that way." He pointed to the right.

"Thank you, sir. You've been most helpful."

"Good luck with your brother."

From the serious look on the man's face, Quinn wondered exactly what he would find on the Sherman farm.

CHAPTER 8

Julia knocked on the door of Dr. Clayborne's office, then took a step back. Her heart beat hard against her ribs, and her breath felt too heavy to escape her lungs. The gnawing fear that had kept her up at nights now demanded she take some sort of action. To deny or confirm her suspicions once and for all.

"Come in."

Julia inhaled deeply, then stepped through the door.

Dr. Clayborne sat at his desk, surrounded by stacks of books and papers. "Miss Holloway. What can I do for you?"

Her mouth went dry, and no words would come out. This was a bad idea. Dr. Clayborne had already been so good to her. She couldn't ask him for any more favors. "Never mind. I . . . It's not important."

"Is there a problem with your job?" He pushed his glasses up his nose. "If they're not treating you well, I can speak to your supervisor."

"No. That's not . . ." She wrung her hands together. "As I said, it's not important." She started to turn toward the door.

"It was important enough to bring you here after your shift." The doctor's kind gaze held hers. "Why not tell me what's on your mind?"

How did she begin to confess her shame? What if he had her fired once he learned her secret? "It will keep for another time."

She reached for the doorknob, but the whole room seemed to tilt. She grasped the handle, her head buzzing.

"Miss Holloway?" The doctor's voice sounded like it was coming from inside a tunnel.

She pressed one hand to her forehead, the other gripping the doorframe to keep her upright. She would not faint. She would *not*.

"You've gone completely white." Dr. Clayborne took her arm and guided her over to a chair. "Put your head down, take deep breaths, and I'll get you some water."

She did as he asked, and by the time he returned, her vision had cleared, though her stomach now threatened to rebel.

Dr. Clayborne held the glass to her lips. "Take a few small sips. It should help settle your system."

The cool liquid soothed her parched throat. She inhaled deeply again and at last met the physician's gaze.

"Are you unwell, Miss Holloway?"

Her hand shook, sloshing the water in the glass. "I don't know. That's why I came." Her eyes stung with sudden tears. "I need to know . . ." She gulped. Did she have the courage to continue?

"It's all right. I'm a doctor and I don't shock easily. You can tell me anything."

The gentleness in his voice made the tears shake loose and spill down her cheeks.

"I need to know if I might be . . . pregnant."

Under the blazing sun, Quinn pulled the energetic brown gelding to a halt and removed his cap. With his sleeve, he wiped the perspiration from his brow. He hadn't realized the summers in Canada were this hot. At the end of a long country lane, a battered mailbox with the name *Sherman* painted in faded black letters stood sentinel.

Quinn squinted down the dirt road and could just make out the roof of a barn in the distance. Should he risk riding up on horseback? Perhaps it would be safer to walk. He'd have a better chance to avoid buckshot that way. And the horse wouldn't be in danger.

Quinn tied the reins to the post, took a moment to bow his head and pray for a good outcome, then started down the road. As he walked, all his senses went on high alert, watching for any sign of workers on the property. Specifically, someone who might resemble his brother. Yet he encountered nothing but acres of rolling green fields.

When the barn came into view, Quinn's pulse sprinted, and a bubble of hope rose in his chest. Was it possible he was about to see his brother again? If so, would he even recognize Cecil after so long?

Repressing the urge to head straight to the barn, Quinn recalled the station master's warning and instead made his way to the farmhouse. It was a plain white clapboard home with a screen door and a sagging porch. Quinn climbed the stairs and knocked on the doorframe. Immediately, a vicious barking erupted from within. Quinn backed away in case the creature launched itself through the screen.

"Quiet, Hercules." A woman's sharp command made the noise cease.

Seconds later, a tall, austere woman appeared, a mangy-looking mutt at her side. She frowned at Quinn through the screen. "Can I help you, mister?"

Quinn swallowed, suddenly uncertain how to proceed. "I hope so, ma'am. I'm looking for my brother, who I believe works for you and your husband. His name is Cecil Aspinall."

A flicker of recognition flashed through her eyes, but then her features hardened. "I think you have the wrong farm."

He stepped forward, already prepared for the obstacles to come. "Could you at least tell me if you know Cecil? He works on a farm in this area. I was certain it was for a Mr. Sherman."

"Can't expect me to know the names of all the help around here." The brackets around her mouth deepened as her lips pulled down even lower. "Now, I'd thank you to get off the property before my husband gets back. Believe me, he won't be as accommodating as I am." She scowled at him again for good measure and slammed the wooden door, making the screen rattle.

Quinn expelled a long breath. The woman knew more about Cecil than she'd said. Yet harassing her further would not help Quinn's cause. He had no choice but to leave.

Certain she would be watching him through a window, Quinn retraced his steps down the lane. When he passed the barn, he slowed his stride, reining in the desire to charge inside and see if Cecil was in there. However, since the entrance would be visible to anyone looking from the house, Quinn kept going until he rounded a bend and was out of sight behind a crop of trees. Then, ducking low, he pushed through the foliage and painstakingly made his way back to the far side of the barn, counting on there being another entrance into the structure.

Sure enough, a small rear door stood open, allowing him a partial view of the dimly lit interior. Quinn brushed the grass and leaves off his clothes, and with his heart in his throat, stepped inside. The immediate stench of manure hit him as he waited a few seconds to get his bearings. Rows of cattle stalls lined the far wall, and a layer of straw covered the dirt floor of the main aisle.

Movement farther down the barn brought Quinn's attention to two people who came into view. He ducked out of sight into an empty stall and held his breath.

"Fill the wagon from the hay shed and get those cattle fed," one man said. "And while you're at it, bring back a couple of bales for the barn."

"Yes, sir."

Quinn's pulse sprinted at the younger man's British accent. Could it be Cecil? Or just some other immigrant worker brought over from England?

Heavy footsteps stomped off, and judging by the sounds being made, it seemed the second person was fiddling with a harness. Quinn dared to peek over the stall door. A very thin boy bent over a leather-and-chain contraption. He wore a large floppy hat that hid his face, making it impossible to tell if it might be his brother.

The lad straightened and moved to open one of the stall doors. Seconds later, he led a sway-backed horse out of the enclosure, the hooves kicking up a cloud of dust in its wake.

"Come on, Rigby. Time to take the wagon out."

Before he could change his mind, Quinn stepped into the open. "Excuse me."

The boy whirled around, still clutching the horse's reins. His eyes widened, the freckles standing out on his pale skin. The strap of his denim overalls slipped down, revealing a stained white shirt beneath. The knees of the boy's pants were so worn, Quinn could see skin showing through. But it was the thinness of his limbs—the bony elbows and shoulder blades—that struck Quinn hard. The lad bore some resemblance to the brother he remembered, but Quinn couldn't be sure.

He swallowed. "Cecil? Is that you?"

"Quinn?"

For a second, Quinn's throat closed up, and he could only nod. His eyes stung with sudden tears as the boy launched himself at Quinn. He caught Cecil and pulled him into a fierce embrace.

Cecil hugged him hard and then pulled back, smiling widely. "What are you doing here? How did you find me?"

"It's a long story. But I'm here now. That's all that matters." Quinn gripped the boy's shoulder. "I've come to bring you, Harry, and Becky home."

A flicker of alarm crossed Cecil's face. "Did Mum send you? How's she doing?"

Quinn held back a sigh. "Not well. She's in the workhouse infirmary and quite weak. Which is why we all need to go back. Once we're together again, I know she'll pick up."

"I . . ." Cecil frowned and glanced down the aisle. "I wish I could leave, but I can't."

"What do you mean? You're not a prisoner here, are you?"

"Close enough." He scowled and moved away, picking up the horse's reins once again.

Quinn followed him. "All the more reason to come with me. We can be on the next train back to the city."

"I told you, I can't. I'm bound by my contract." Cecil glanced nervously around the barn. "You'd better leave now before Old Man Sherman comes back. He won't be happy to find you here."

Quinn threw out his hands, barely suppressing the urge to shake his brother. "Cecil, I've crossed a blasted ocean to find you. You can't just dismiss me after less than five minutes."

Cecil shot Quinn an agonized stare. "You don't understand. If he finds me talking to you, he'll take it out on me. I've worked hard to earn his trust. I won't ruin that now."

Quinn squeezed his fingers into fists at his side. How could he simply walk away from his brother now that he'd found him? "I don't believe this," he said. "I never once considered you wouldn't want to come with me."

"Please, Quinn. I have chores to finish." A fly buzzed around Cecil's neck, and he swatted it away. Beads of sweat dripped from under his hat. It was obvious from the way he kept looking behind him that the boy was nervous. But he let out a sigh. "Look, I don't mean to be rude. Maybe on my next afternoon off we can get together and catch up. I'd love to hear how things are going back home."

Quinn held back the retort that leapt to mind. He never imagined that his brother would barely speak to him. Would refuse to go back with him. Perhaps he needed to give Cecil time to get used to the idea of going home. "Very well. I'll go for now, but I'm not giving up. You can count on that."

Cecil gave a quick nod before heading down the center aisle, the horse in tow.

Quinn struggled with an immense feeling of disappointment. He only hoped he'd have better luck with Harry. "Wait." Quinn charged after Cecil. "Have you heard from Harry at all?"

For an instant, Cecil's feet faltered, then he stiffened his spine. "Haven't seen him since I left Toronto."

Quinn frowned. "Well, I intend to find him, and when I do, we'll both be back." He jabbed a finger at him. "Be warned. I'm not leaving for England without you."

Cecil went still, then came to stand toe to toe with Quinn. "I only have eighteen months left before my contract is up, and then I'll be free to do whatever I wish. Do not ruin this for me, Quinn." He snapped a leather switch against his palm, his eyes burning with a host of emotions.

"I wish I could leave it at that, but I can't. I didn't want to tell you this way. . . ." Quinn paused, searching for the words. "Mum may not last the summer."

Cecil stood breathing hard for a moment, his thin chest puffing in and out. Surely he would realize the gravity of the situation and come home for Mum's sake. But the boy shook his head again. "Harry and Becky will have to be enough. Now, if you don't mind, I have a herd of cattle to feed."

CHAPTER 9

Julia finished buttoning her blouse with shaking fingers. Dr. Clayborne was waiting for her in the outer office, one that belonged to a colleague, since his own office was not equipped for this type of examination. Filled with books and papers, it was only used for verbal consultations with his patients, while the bulk of his work was conducted in the physical therapy room.

Dr. Clayborne had assured her that no one would mind him using this room, and he'd found a nurse willing to assist him in the examination. Would they have been able to come to any conclusions about her condition this soon or would she have to wait for the bloodwork?

Either way, Julia dreaded walking through that door. *Lord, help me to be strong and to bear whatever the doctor has to say.*

She brushed a strand of hair off her forehead, picked up her handbag, and went to face her destiny.

Seated behind a large desk, Dr. Clayborne's features betrayed little, but as he watched her take a seat, his eyes filled with sympathy.

Julia's stomach dropped. Bile coated the back of her throat, her body already aware of what was to come. "It's not good news, I take it."

"That depends on how you look at it, I suppose." He gave her a slight smile. "Your suspicions were correct, Miss Holloway. I believe you are indeed expecting. From the information you've given me, I suspect you're about three months along."

Julia covered her mouth with a trembling hand. "Dear Lord," she whispered. "What am I going to do now?" Her eyes burned with the threat of tears, her mind spinning. How long would she be able to work? She'd have to hide her condition as long as possible, for without an income, how would she live?

"If you don't mind my asking," Dr. Clayborne said, "what about the baby's father? Surely he should take some responsibility for the situation."

Julia focused her gaze on her lap, where she twisted a rather worn handkerchief between her fingers. The thought of facing that man again—the one she'd thought so kind but who had taken advantage of her in the worst possible way—brought another wave of nausea. "I'm afraid that's out of the question."

"I see." The physician leaned over his desk, his forehead creased. "Forgive me if I'm getting too personal, but I couldn't help noticing the time of conception coincides roughly with the date of Private McIntyre's death."

She clamped her lips together to stop their trembling.

"Is Sam the father of your child?"

The gentle question ripped at Julia's heart. If only this baby were Sam's. At least then she could look forward to seeing a resemblance to someone she truly cared about. Instead, the child was the product of a man who'd used his position of trust to prey on Julia at her most vulnerable moment.

"I'm afraid not. While I was very fond of Sam, our relationship was not a romantic one."

An awkward silence descended. Julia tried to breathe normally under Dr. Clayborne's scrutiny, but her lungs felt incapable of fully inflating.

"Did the father make promises to you? If so, where is he now?"

"No, it wasn't like that."

His brows shot up. "You weren't forced—?"

"Please, I don't wish to talk about it." She swallowed the acid rising in her throat. Even if she could speak of it, just picturing Dr. Clayborne's reaction would keep her silent, not willing to risk losing the one ally she had. She forced herself to meet his gaze.

"Very well. I respect your right to privacy." He hesitated. "Will you at least tell the man? Give him the opportunity to do the right thing?"

She shook her head. Facing Dr. Hawkins, admitting her condition—no, she could never do that. No matter how dire her circumstances. "I don't think so. It's a rather complicated situation."

"I see. Well, then, what can I do to help?"

The tears she'd kept at bay now welled anew. They brimmed over her lower lashes and dripped down her cheeks. "I don't know," she whispered. "I need to keep this confidential for as long as possible. I can't afford to lose my job."

The doctor remained quiet for several seconds. "Perhaps I could look into possible maternity homes for when you can no longer work."

The sympathy on his face was more than she could bear. But she needed his support since he would be the only other person privy to her condition. "That would be helpful. Thank you."

Dr. Clayborne rose and came around the desk. "Try not to despair, Julia. I'll be praying for you, that God will provide you with the people and the resources you need to see you through this trying time."

"I appreciate that." She got to her feet, still somewhat shaky.

He steadied her with a light touch to her elbow. "Come and I'll call you a cab. Once you're home, I prescribe a cup of tea, followed by a good night's sleep. Matters are bound to look better in the morning."

She secretly doubted that would be true. If anything, the world would appear even bleaker once the enormity of her situation sank in. "Thank you, but I'll take the bus. The fresh air will do me good." In reality, she didn't want to waste her limited funds on a taxi.

"If you're sure you're all right."

"I'm fine. Thank you again for everything." With as much dignity as she could muster, Julia left the office and made her way outside.

For some reason, as she walked down the street, her thoughts flew to Quinn, and she thanked her good fortune that he was not around to witness her utter demoralization. Despite his chivalrous attempts to help her, she now found herself in a worse situation than ever.

By the time Quinn returned, she would need to have her composure in place so he wouldn't detect anything amiss. And then she would have to sever all ties with the man before he could learn of her disgrace. For she couldn't bear it if he or her uncle ever knew the truth.

After almost an hour's journey, Quinn came to a stop in front of the dirt road leading to the Wolfe farm. He'd walked all the way from the Caledon train depot, following the station master's very specific directions, and during the entire trip, he'd been trying to come up with a different way to approach Harry. Talking to the farmer or his family, as Quinn had tried to do with Cecil's employer, probably wouldn't help him. Mr. Hobday's words came back to Quinn. *"But be advised, Mr. Aspinall, any interference with these children will not be tolerated."* It appeared the man wasn't exaggerating.

So, what could he do differently this time to ensure a better outcome?

The most logical course of action seemed to be trying to find Harry without involving the farmer. He only prayed his youngest brother would be happier to see him than Cecil had.

The sun heated Quinn's shoulders as he started down the road, making him wish he could remove his jacket, but he wanted to make a good impression should he run into anyone in charge, so he kept it on. As he came closer to the main barn, Quinn stepped off the path and crossed a grassy area to a slatted wooden fence. Bending low, Quinn followed the line of fencing toward the barn, hoping he wouldn't be too noticeable. When he reached the wooden structure, which, from the peeling paint and missing boards, looked like it had seen better days, Quinn crouched behind a wide tree trunk.

Several men went in and out of the double barn doors, one leading a cow by a rope. A second man drove a flock of sheep in from the pasture. All the workers looked too old to be indentured British boys. So where was Harry?

When the coast was clear, Quinn sprinted across to the barn and around the back. He stopped in the shade of a tree and took a minute to survey the area.

A second later, Quinn's heart rate shot up. In a nearby pigsty, a thin boy shoveled muck into a bucket while the pigs ate from a trough at the opposite end, snorting their pleasure. Could this lad be Harry?

Staying behind some shrubs, Quinn moved closer. The boy's back remained to Quinn, and he almost groaned in frustration. Since no one was in the vicinity, Quinn took a chance and approached the pen.

"Excuse me. Can you help me with something?"

The boy turned. Dark circles hugged eyes that appeared sunken. Cheekbones stood out against the rest of his gaunt face. He glanced up, then looked down at the ground. "You'd best talk to Mr. Murdoch, the farm foreman." He went right back to shoveling the slop.

Though Quinn could make out some familiar traits, he couldn't be sure the boy was his brother. "I'm looking for Harrison Aspinall," he said. "I understand he works here."

The boy's hands stopped moving. Slowly he turned around again. A mixture of fear and suspicion flashed over his face. "I'm Harrison. Who are you?"

Quinn winced. Had it been so long that Harry no longer remembered him? He stared for a moment, taking in his brother's features. In the hazel eyes and swath of freckles across his cheeks, he found traces of the youngster he remembered. Yet Harry's thinness and rather stooped posture belied his age of twelve. By the looks of him, Quinn would have thought him no more than nine. He swallowed the lump in his throat and moved closer to the fence, where he took off his cap and attempted a smile. "Don't you recognize your own brother?"

Harry went white. His mouth fell open, and the shovel slipped from his fingers into the mud. "Quinn? Is it you?"

"Yes, Harry. It's me. I've come to take you home."

The boy gave a strangled cry. In a flash, he scrambled over the fence and threw his arms around him, pressing his face into Quinn's chest. Harry's frail body shook so hard that Quinn automatically tightened his grip on the boy. When he did, the protrusion of every sharp ridge in the boy's spine bit into Quinn's palm. Despite the stench of unwashed body and pig manure that wafted upward, Quinn pulled Harry closer, hardly able to believe he'd found him. Though he longed to savor the moment, urgency made him end the embrace.

"Get your things, Harry. We need to make it to the station before the next train is due to leave." *And before the farmer has time to miss you.*

Harry's face, blotchy with tears, crumpled even more. "I can't leave, Quinn. I have chores to do." His eyes widened as he scanned the area around them.

Quinn frowned. Maybe Harry didn't understand his meaning. "Not anymore. I'm taking you away from here for good. Home to Mum, where you belong. Come on. No time to waste." He propelled Harry toward the barn. "Change your clothes and wash off some of that . . . dirt."

Harry came to a stop. "I don't have any other clothes. This is it."

Quinn fought to keep his dismay and his distaste from showing. He'd have to take Harry as is, manure and all, and hope to sit at the back of the train so as not to offend the other passengers. "It's all right. I'll buy you some new ones tomorrow. Now let's get a move on."

Deftly, he steered Harry toward the cover of foliage in the hopes of avoiding detection. But they'd only gone a few feet when loud footsteps sounded behind them.

Harry gasped and stopped dead. "It's Mr. Murdoch. We can't let him see us." The boy clutched his stomach like he might be sick.

In a protective gesture, Quinn shoved Harry behind a bush and ducked down beside him. A burly man strode over to the pigsty, scanned the area, then strode into the barn, frowning.

"He's looking for me. I have to go." Harry looked panicked.

Quinn rested his hands on the boy's shoulders. "Harry, what do you want to do? Come with me or stay here?"

Harry's eyes widened, darting from Quinn to the barn and back. "I . . . I don't know." His body began to shake beneath Quinn's fingers.

Was it fair to expect the lad to make such a quick decision when he was obviously terrified?

"Listen, I know you have work to do. Why don't you take some time to think it over? I'll come back in the morning and we can make a decision then."

Harry bit his lip. "You promise you'll come back?"

"First thing tomorrow. I promise. Have your belongings ready to go, just in case, and don't tell anyone I was here." Then Quinn pulled the boy in for a quick hug. "Now, off you go and try not to worry."

"All right. Bye, Quinn." Harry scurried off toward the barn.

Quinn waited until the boy was out of sight before pulling his cap lower on his forehead and settling into a more comfortable position amid the bushes. He wanted to wait a bit longer to make sure this Murdoch character wasn't giving Harry a hard time, and after several minutes when nothing seemed amiss, Quinn started back through the foliage toward the main road.

As he walked, Quinn's gut churned. He hated leaving Harry here when he was so clearly anxious, but what could he do? Drag the boy off the property? That wouldn't be fair to him and would feel too close to kidnapping.

Quinn would find a room for the night and return at dawn the next morning. Hopefully by then, Harry would have come to terms with leaving the farm, and Quinn would be able to get him away without any trouble.

CHAPTER 10

"I believe I've found the perfect position for you." Seated in Mrs. Chamberlain's parlor, Rev. Burke beamed at Julia.

"My goodness, that was fast." She forced a light laugh that she hoped sounded convincing. Yet she doubted her false smiles were fooling anyone.

Mrs. Chamberlain had informed her at dinner that Rev. Burke was coming over to discuss a possible employment opportunity. Two days ago, such news would have been cause for great excitement. But how could she start a new job now, when she'd only have to leave once her condition became apparent?

Julia's whole future now stretched before her as a vast unknown. The tentative idea of going back to England with Quinn and his siblings was no longer a possibility. For a brief moment, learning that Uncle Howard had forgiven her had allowed Julia to believe she could return to Brentwood. But her pregnancy changed everything. She could never subject her uncle's family, especially her dear cousin, Amelia, to such disgrace. It would tarnish her uncle's name, not to mention ruin Amelia's prospects for a good marriage.

In addition, Julia grieved the loss of her dream to have a career. Any type of schooling would now be impossible. She wouldn't be able to support herself, let alone afford tuition. Dr. Clayborne might have to find her a maternity home sooner than expected.

"That's wonderful news, Geoffrey." Mrs. Chamberlain passed

him a plate of ladyfingers. "I knew you'd find something suitable for Julia."

"What sort of position is it?" Julia tried to appear as interested as they both expected her to be.

"One of my parishioners, an elderly widow by the name of Mrs. Middleton, has been in the hospital for several weeks now. When I went to visit her again yesterday, she told me she might be released soon. But there's a slight problem." He rested his cup on his lap. "The doctor feels she needs more care and asked if she had a son or daughter she could live with."

"Oh, that's unfortunate." Mrs. C. shook her head as she poured more tea into her cup. "Mrs. Middleton's only son died a couple of years ago in the war. Such a tragedy."

"Indeed. But that gave me a brilliant idea." Rev. Burke's face brightened. "I suggested she hire a live-in companion. Naturally I had you in mind, Julia."

She bit her lip. What a perfect job this would have been.

"Oh my word." Mrs. C. clapped her hands together. "That's ideal. Though I will certainly miss your company, dear."

Julia managed a weak smile. What could she say? If she refused to consider the position, they would think her extremely ungrateful—and possibly be a little suspicious. And she was not ready to tell anyone about her pregnancy, not until she'd had time to sort through her options and determine whether she could keep the baby or not. She would go along with the idea for now.

"It does sound wonderful." She paused, shifting position on the sofa. "Do you think we'd get on well together?"

"I'm sure you would," Mrs. C. said. "Violet is a kind and . . . spirited woman. Although she's been more despondent since her son died. You might be just the tonic she needs." She patted Julia's leg, her expression eager. "And you'll love her house. It's a beautiful Victorian manor, which she always keeps in impeccable condition."

Julia forced an expression of interest. "Well then, how do we proceed from here?"

Rev. Burke took a pipe from his pocket and tapped it on his

palm. "I'll tell Violet you're interested. Then perhaps you could go up to the hospital tomorrow and visit her. See if you think you two would make a good fit." He glanced at Julia as he lit the pipe.

"I can do that. Thank you, Reverend Burke." Maybe once she met Mrs. Middleton, she'd find a viable excuse not to take the job.

"My pleasure. I have a feeling you two will get on famously." He leaned back in his chair, seeming quite pleased with himself.

Julia kept her smile in place, wishing she could show more enthusiasm. If circumstances were different, she would have jumped at the chance to work for this lady. No more rodents, no horrid stenches in the hallway, no boorish landlords to plague her. No more depending on the kindness of others to support her.

If only one major error in judgment hadn't ruined all that.

The next day, Julia entered the main lobby of the Toronto General Hospital and headed for the information desk, where she inquired about Mrs. Middleton.

The clerk directed her to the third floor. After taking the stairs, Julia hesitated outside the doorway to the room, nerves swirling through her system. Rev. Burke had been kind enough to set up this meeting, but now that she was here, Julia suddenly felt deceptive. Maybe she should come right out with the truth before Mrs. Middleton began counting on having someone to stay with her when she went home. Taking a deep breath, Julia knocked on the partially opened door.

When a firm voice bade her enter, she walked inside, bracing for whatever she might see. Since the minister hadn't been clear about the woman's medical condition, Julia prepared herself for the worst. Instead, she was pleasantly surprised.

Mrs. Middleton sat up in bed, looking alert and well-groomed. Silver spectacles highlighted intelligent blue eyes. Her graying hair was fixed in a thick plait that lay over one shoulder.

"Mrs. Middleton?" The woman must have clout or money, because somehow she was in a private room. Fresh flowers adorned the nightstand and the windowsill, their fragrance overpowering the pervasive medicinal hospital smell. "I'm Julia Holloway."

"A pleasure to meet you, Miss Holloway. My eyesight's not as good as it used to be, so you'll need to pull a chair up close."

Julia did as she requested and perched on the edge of the seat.

"Thank you for coming. I realize this is a somewhat unorthodox location for a job interview." The woman smiled.

"Reverend Burke says you've been here for some time. I hope you're feeling better." Julia didn't want to pry into the woman's business, but she had to at least address the issue of her health.

"I'm much improved after a nasty fall, the result of a weakened heart. Thank you for asking. Unfortunately, these pesky doctors don't want to release me unless I have someone at home to help me."

"I see." But Julia didn't really, as Mrs. Middleton looked perfectly healthy. She waited for the woman to explain further.

"The plain fact is, I'm getting old. My heart isn't behaving as it should, and I'm losing my vision. Reverend Burke suggested a live-in companion to help take care of my personal needs. I don't require a cook or housekeeper, since I have those already." She squinted at Julia. "It would be a trial-and-error situation, since I've never done anything like this before."

"I've had a little experience in this area," Julia said slowly. "I came to Canada with a wounded soldier who'd lost the use of his legs. He needed someone to help him adjust to his new circumstances. I took care of him until he . . ." Her voice faltered, and she took a moment to collect herself. "He passed away a few months ago."

"I'm so sorry." The woman peered at her. "It sounds as though you were fond of him."

"I was." Was Mrs. Middleton fishing for information as to the nature of their relationship? Julia supposed it could be misconstrued. "Private McIntyre and I developed a friendship at the infirmary in

England where we met. It was a relationship based on trust and mutual respect, otherwise I would not have come with him to Canada."

"Thank you for sharing that. I appreciate honesty in a person."

Julia did her best not to flinch. What would the woman say when she learned Julia's secret?

"Reverend Burke said you're working at a hospital now. Are you a nurse?"

"Not exactly." Julia didn't want to admit what she actually did there. Instead, she focused on her other experiences. "However, during the war, I did assist the medical staff with the injured soldiers."

"You know some first aid?"

"Quite a lot, actually. Working with the doctors, I learned to treat all types of wounds, as well as various other illnesses."

"Well, that could come in handy. What other skills do you have, Miss Holloway?"

Julia squeezed her hands together. Should she just tell the woman now before this interview went any further? She moistened her dry lips. "I'm a decent cook and a better baker. Before my mother died, she taught me to make bread, as well as the flakiest pastry you could imagine." She allowed herself the pleasure of remembering those happy times with her mother for a moment. "But then, you said you already had a cook."

"I do, but it never hurts to have someone able to fill in when necessary. What else?"

Julia swallowed, suddenly aware of how lacking she was in job skills. "I'm an organized person, one who pays attention to details. I'm well-educated and well-read. I can play chess and the piano. . . ." She trailed off, attempting to come up with something more substantial.

Mrs. Middleton studied her. "You seem like an intelligent young woman, tidy and clean—" she glanced at Julia's attire—"though not very stylish."

Julia ran a hand over her best navy skirt, thinking of all the beautiful clothes she'd left behind in England. Perhaps she should have worn her one good dress, but she wanted to come across as sensible, not frivolous. "I left home rather quickly and wasn't able to bring my gowns with me."

Mrs. Middleton arched a brow. "I'm sure there's more to that tale. Perhaps you'll tell me one day. I do love a good story."

With no ready answer, Julia blinked but remained silent.

"What I'm trying to say is that I think you'll do nicely for the job. If you can put up with an old bird like me." Mrs. Middleton chortled out a hoarse laugh.

Julia chuckled too. It was hard not to like this feisty woman. But she couldn't in good conscience accept the post without being completely honest. "I imagine we'd get along just fine," she said. "However, there's something you need to know, which might change your mind."

"Oh?" The woman's eyes sharpened on Julia's face.

The hard spokes of the chair bit into Julia's back. Her breathing grew labored, imagining the woman's reaction. "Before I tell you, I must ask for your discretion."

Her fair brows rose. "Discretion is my middle name, child. Now, what is it?"

Julia's heart pounded in her chest. Once she spoke the words, her condition would become a reality. Her world might never be the same again. She inhaled and released a long breath. "I've just learned that I'm expecting a baby. Sometime before Christmas, if the doctor is correct." Heat climbed into her cheeks. She stared at the woolen blanket on the bed, not daring to look up.

Several seconds of silence ensued until Mrs. Middleton cleared her throat. "That does change matters, doesn't it?"

Julia pressed her lips together and nodded. "I'm sorry to have wasted your time, ma'am. I couldn't bring myself to tell Reverend Burke why I couldn't accept the position." She stood up, clutching her handbag.

"Hold on a minute." Mrs. Middleton waved a blue-veined hand. "Let me catch my breath here."

Julia froze by the chair. "It's all right. You don't owe me any more of your time."

"I realize that, girl. But it occurs to me we're both in a pickle of a situation and maybe we can help each other out. At least for a time, anyway."

"Y-you'd still consider hiring me?" Julia couldn't believe the woman hadn't tossed her out on her ear.

"First, I'd like to know if the father of the child is still in the picture."

Julia straightened and lifted her chin. "No, ma'am. I hope to never see him again."

"Another story I look forward to hearing." The woman studied her. "That being the case, I'm willing to take a chance if you are."

Julia's throat tightened. Never in her wildest imagination did she think Mrs. Middleton would accept an unwed pregnant woman as her companion. "If you're sure, I . . . I'd like that very much."

"Good. It's settled, then. All I need now is for my doctor to tell me when I can go home." She sank back against the pillows. "He has another couple of tests he wants to run, so it may be a week or more. I'll let the minister know when they give me a release date, and he can pass it on to you."

"Thank you so much, Mrs. Middleton. And if there's anything I can do in the meantime, please let me know. I'm staying at Mrs. Chamberlain's boardinghouse if you need to reach me."

"I will do that. Good day, Miss Holloway."

"Good day." Julia left the room with a new lightness to her step, almost giddy with relief.

Maybe her life wasn't over yet. And maybe, despite how it appeared, God hadn't forgotten her after all.

CHAPTER 11

The sun wasn't even visible over the horizon when Quinn arrived at the Wolfe farm the next morning. He'd spent the night at a rooming house in the center of town, although he'd barely slept a wink, anticipating seeing Harry again this morning. Since Quinn didn't want Harry to have to walk such a great distance to the train station, especially carrying all his belongings, he rented a small cart and pony at the livery. It would also make for a hastier escape if things went badly with the farmer or the foreman.

The idea that Quinn might be breaking some sort of law by taking Harry away ate at his conscience. Yet the fact that his brother was a child, one who might be suffering abuse at the hands of his employer, overrode any legal issues as far as Quinn was concerned. The lad had only been seven years old when he was sent to Canada, without any say in the matter. From what Quinn could see, the last five years had not been kind to Harry, and Quinn could not sit idly by and let the boy endure six more years of suffering. If it meant Quinn got thrown in jail, it was a chance he was willing to take.

The early morning warblers were out in full force, serenading Quinn along the way. He could have enjoyed the tranquil ride through the countryside if only he could be certain what would happen with Harry.

Please, Lord, let him be ready and willing to leave, and help us get away without any trouble.

After tying the pony to a tree on the edge of the Wolfe property, Quinn made his way to the barn, a host of nerves swarming in his belly. How would Harry be feeling about the situation today? Would he be brave enough to come with Quinn? Something told him he'd have to deal with Murdoch before he would find out.

Sure enough, before Quinn even reached the rear entrance, the beefy foreman appeared on the path, a rifle in hand. "You're trespassing on private property, mister. I'd advise you to turn around." He raised the weapon and aimed it at Quinn.

"I'm Quinten Aspinall, Harry's older brother. I've come to take him home."

"I don't care if you're the king of England." The big man moved toward him. "The boy belongs to Mr. Wolfe. He has a contract that says so."

Heat blazed in Quinn's chest. The arrogant sod acted as though Harry were his personal property. As though he owned him outright.

"The only place Harry belongs is home with his mother, and that's where I'm taking him." Quinn reached into his jacket. "I'm even willing to offer Mr. Wolfe some compensation. I don't have much, but . . ." He opened his money pouch and took out some coins.

"You think that paltry sum will make up for years of lost labor?" The man spat on the ground.

Anger moved through Quinn's system. "Harry is not a prisoner. You can't forcibly confine him."

"You're wrong. The law is on Mr. Wolfe's side." Murdoch smirked. "Don't make me call the authorities."

Quinn hesitated. For all his bravado, he really didn't know if Murdoch was conning him. Would they arrest Quinn for trying to take Harry? Every instinct told Quinn to get his brother away from this place. That Harry was being abused. But would it be tantamount to kidnapping? He decided to call the man's bluff.

"Go ahead. Call the authorities if you must. As soon as I talk to Harry, we'll be on our way."

"You seem pretty sure of yourself, English."

Quinn clenched his back teeth at the derision in Murdoch's voice. He glared at Quinn, who held his ground and refused to back down.

At last the man moved to one side of the door. "You have five minutes to say your good-byes to the kid. If you're not back by then, I start firing this rifle."

Quinn gave a tight nod and strode into the barn. One of the cows inside let out a low moo. Tiny dust motes floated in the air. "Harry? Are you in here?" He continued down the corridor. "Harry?"

No answer. Was his brother in the barn at all, or had Murdoch let Quinn make an erroneous assumption? Noise drew his attention farther down the aisle. A moaning sound echoed from what Quinn guessed was a tack room or storage area, but when he opened the door, he was unprepared for the sight that met him.

Harry lay on a pile of straw in the corner, his knees pulled up toward his chest, writhing in pain.

Quinn rushed to kneel beside him. "Harry, what's wrong? Are you ill?"

The boy didn't answer, just continued to thrash about.

Quinn looked around the tiny space, not much bigger than the size of a closet. Harry's boots sat in one corner. His denim overalls hung from a peg on the wall. A metal bucket filled with something putrid stood by the door. Was this where Harry slept each night? Did they not have a room for him somewhere in the house? Surely anything would be more comfortable than this squalor. Even the animals had a nicer area.

He laid a hand on Harry's back. Immediately the boy winced and pulled away from him. Quinn looked closer and his gut clenched. Markings he'd thought to be shadows were actually purple bruises encircling Harry's upper arm.

He lifted the boy's threadbare shirt. Large red welts crisscrossed Harry's back. Reining in his reaction, Quinn gently turned him to take a look at his stomach. More welts and bruising marred the boy's thin chest and abdomen.

Harry groaned and finally looked at Quinn. Raw pain and fear darkened his hazel eyes. Quinn pressed his lips together to keep from roaring at the universe. How could someone treat another human being in such a vile manner?

"Who did this to you? Was it Murdoch?"

Harry shook his head.

"Who, then? Wolfe?"

A flicker of terror flashed over Harry's face.

"Your employer did this? What sort of monster is he?" Quinn closed his eyes for a brief moment in an attempt to collect himself. Then he held out a hand to his brother. "Come on. I'm getting you out of here."

With Quinn's help, the boy slowly got to his feet but remained hunched over, unable to stand straight.

"Where are your belongings?"

Harry pointed to the straw.

Frowning, Quinn rummaged under some of the hay and found a small trunk. Harry's initials were carved in the front. He dragged it over, resisting the urge to open it. "Anything else?"

"My boots and overalls."

Quinn fetched them both and helped his brother into the foul-smelling clothing.

Layers of newspaper lined the soles of Harry's boots. Quinn forced a neutral expression as Harry stuffed his bare feet inside. At least he wasn't insisting on staying.

Quinn hoisted the small trunk, finding it remarkably light, and wrapped his other arm around Harry's waist to support him. Thank goodness Quinn had thought to bring a cart. The boy would never have made it to the station on foot.

But first they had to get past Murdoch. And Wolfe had better not show his face, or Quinn couldn't guarantee what he might do. His fists burned with the need to give the man a taste of his own medicine.

Murdoch whirled around, rifle in hand, as they exited the barn. "What the—"

Quinn shot a glare at the man. "Do not start with me, Murdoch. Not after what you've done to my brother. I should call the constable and report the lot of you."

"Hey, I had nothing to do with it." A nerve pulsed in Murdoch's jaw. Was the bully actually nervous? "Whatever punishment the old man sees fit to dish out is his business."

"But you did nothing to stop it, did you?"

The big fellow shifted on his feet, his expression grim.

"Tell Mr. Wolfe that as of today my brother no longer works for him. I pray to God he's never allowed to hire anyone other than an adult again. Someone who can fight back." He paused. "And tell him I will be reporting this to Mr. Hobday at the Toronto office."

Murdoch pressed his lips into a hard line but offered no further resistance.

Without another word, Quinn led Harry away from the Wolfe farm for good. As they hobbled down the dirt road to where he had left the pony, Quinn's thoughts turned to the promise he'd made to return for Cecil. But as much as Quinn yearned to go back for him, he needed to get Harry to a doctor. Not only to assess his injuries but to determine how malnourished the lad was as well. And since Quinn didn't know if there was a hospital in the immediate area, that meant traveling back to Toronto right away.

Cecil would have to wait.

Julia had just finished her light breakfast when Mrs. Chamberlain bustled into the dining room the next day.

"Good morning, Mrs. C." Despite her unsettled stomach, Julia managed a cheery smile.

"Good morning." Mrs. C. chose a cup from the sideboard and filled it from the large teapot stationed there. "How are you this fine day?"

Bright sun streamed in through the window, infusing the room with light.

"I'm well, thank you."

Mrs. C. pulled out a chair and sat down. "I'm so happy about your new position. Working for Violet Middleton is a perfect solution for both of you."

"Indeed, I believe it is." Julia smiled, her mind at ease for the first time in ages. It was wonderful to have new hope for the future when mere days ago everything had seemed so bleak. "I'm looking forward to it."

Mrs. C. reached for a scone from the basket on the table. "Luckily Violet doesn't live too far away, so I'm sure we'll still see a lot of each other."

"I'd like that." Julia swallowed hard. Would Mrs. C. still hold her in the same regard once she learned of her pregnancy? Or would the woman politely distance herself from Julia? "But I won't be moving out for a week or more yet."

"You're right. No use getting ahead of myself." Mrs. C. looked up from buttering her scone. "I almost forgot. I have news about Quinten. He telephoned earlier."

The air stalled in Julia's lungs. Despite her erratic heartbeat, she tried to appear unconcerned. "Oh? Has he returned from his trip?"

"Yes. He arrived yesterday with one of his brothers. Sadly, the lad is in rather rough shape. Quinten had to take him for medical attention."

"How terrible. I hope he'll be all right." Julia frowned. Quinn must be so disappointed to have his reunion marred that way. "What about his other brother?"

"There was no mention of him. But I'm sure we'll find out soon enough. Quinten plans to come by later."

Julia almost dropped her teacup but quickly recovered her composure. "It will be good to see him again." She avoided Mrs. C.'s gaze and focused on her saucer.

"Do you have to work at the hospital today?"

"No, I've finished there." She laid her napkin over her plate. "I wanted to be available whenever Mrs. Middleton was ready to come home."

"How thoughtful. Though I don't imagine you'll miss the manual labor."

Julia chuckled. "I won't, believe me." She drained her cup and rose. "I think I'll go and finish a letter I was writing. If . . . that is, when Quinn arrives, will you let me know?" Heat scorched her cheeks.

"Certainly."

Julia rushed up to her room and checked her appearance in the mirror. Why was she so nervous to see Quinn again? It had only been a few days since he left, but it felt much longer. Her resolution to distance herself from Quinn drifted through her mind, but she pushed it aside.

Instead, she opened her closet and reached for her favorite blue dress. In a matter of minutes, she had it on and had brushed out her hair until it curled softly over her shoulders. She stilled at her reflection in the mirror. Outwardly, her appearance was more than presentable, but it concealed a terrible secret that would destroy any respect Quinn could possibly have for her. And that secret wouldn't remain hidden for much longer.

She set her brush down with a sigh. If she were smart, she would tell him straight out that she couldn't go back to England with him. Sever ties once and for all.

Yet her heart wasn't ready to say good-bye.

For now, couldn't she simply enjoy his friendship? After all, she owed him a great debt for everything he'd done for her, and if she could help him in any way with reuniting his family, she intended to do her best.

A knock sounded on her door. "Julia, there's a telephone call for you," one of the girls said.

Julia rose, her pulse fluttering. Was it Quinn calling to say he wasn't coming after all? She took in a breath, battling a tide of disappointment, and headed downstairs to the parlor, where the phone was located.

"Hello?"

"Julia. Thank goodness I found you."

She froze at the clipped tone, one that definitively did not belong to Quinn. "Who is this?"

"It's Richard Hawkins. Don't you recognize my voice?"

She sank onto a nearby chair. "What do you want?" she whispered.

"I've been trying to find you for weeks. I finally went to see Dr. Clayborne, who told me you'd come here."

Oh, why hadn't she thought to warn Dr. Clayborne? As a fellow physician with a former patient in common, of course he would trust Dr. Hawkins.

"What do you want?" Julia repeated, thankful most of the boarders were out at work.

"I want to know why you disappeared on me." His exasperation bled through the receiver. "I realize you were terribly upset over Sam's death, as we all were, but you acted so strange at his memorial service, and then you simply vanished."

A bubble of disbelief rose in her chest, overriding her nerves. "What did you expect after what you did?" She bit her lip and looked around to make sure no one had heard her.

"If you're feeling guilty about our . . . encounter, please let me allay your concerns. I'm working to rectify the situation, and I think I'll have a solution soon. But I don't wish to discuss it over the telephone. I'd like to come by and see you—"

"No!" she practically shouted, then grappled for control. The last thing she wanted was for him to show up here and create an unpleasant scene. "We have nothing to discuss, and I have no desire to see you. Kindly leave me alone." Before he could respond, she hung up the receiver.

Her heart hammered in her chest as she struggled to even out her breathing. Why would he think she'd want to see him after what he'd done? Surely he didn't believe he could explain away his actions?

Mabel entered the parlor and stopped short. "Julia, you're white as a sheet. Not bad news, I hope."

"No. Just someone I didn't expect to hear from." She forced her lips into a smile. "If you'll excuse me, I need to finish something in my room."

CHAPTER 12

After the upsetting telephone call, the morning hours seemed to pass with excruciating slowness. Julia eventually came downstairs and positioned herself in the front parlor, reading from Mrs. C.'s Bible to pass the time. Perhaps Quinn wouldn't arrive until later in the day. If so, she should really find some chores to help with.

A loud knock on the front door startled her. What if Dr. Hawkins had ignored her wishes and had come to see her after all? Her first instinct was to hide in her room, but since Mrs. C. was upstairs, Julia shored up her courage and went to answer it.

Quinn stood on the porch, cap in hand. His features brightened the moment he saw her. "Julia. This is a nice surprise. I didn't expect you to answer the door."

She returned his smile, ignoring the swarm of dragonflies invading her stomach. "Mrs. C. said you might drop by. Please, come in. Shall I run upstairs and tell her you're here?"

Quinn followed her into the parlor. "Actually, I wouldn't mind a few minutes to talk to you, if that's all right."

Pleasant warmth spread through her chest. "I'd like that." She took a seat on the sofa, while Quinn chose the armchair closest to her. "So, tell me how your trip went." She didn't let on that she knew about his brother. She'd let Quinn relay the details in his own time.

A shadow crossed his features. "Not as well as I'd hoped. Even though I found my brothers, Cecil barely gave me the time of day and refused to leave the farm. And Harry . . ." He paused, the muscles in his throat working. "Harry is in the hospital."

"I'm so sorry. Is he ill?" It must be far worse than she imagined if they kept the boy.

"It's not an illness." Quinn raised his anguished gaze to her. "The man Harry worked for beat him after learning I'd been there. I didn't think anyone saw us, but someone must have told the farmer Harry was talking to me." He shook his head. "I came back the next day and found him barely able to stand from the blows he'd received. He has fractured ribs and a dislocated shoulder, among other injuries. The doctors want to run some tests to make sure there's no internal damage."

"Oh, Quinn. That's truly awful."

"Mrs. C. warned me their situations might not be pleasant, but it's far worse than I could have imagined." He dragged a hand across his jaw. "Harry's so thin, I can count every rib and vertebra. They practically starved him. And he was living in one of the barn stalls with nothing more than a bit of straw for his bed." He paused again, seeming to collect himself. "What I don't understand is how the authorities could allow this sort of treatment. The superintendent at the Dr. Barnardo office said they sent inspectors only once a year, but even then, shouldn't someone have noticed the condition he was in?"

Tears stung Julia's eyes. Her heart ached for Quinn and his brother. She leaned forward to lay a hand on his arm. "Is there anything I can do to help?"

"Not as far as Harry is concerned. Other than pray for him." He hesitated. "But I could use your help looking for Becky."

Julia's composure faltered. She gripped her hands together. "What can I do?"

"I was hoping you might accompany me to the receiving home where Becky was sent. I had a difficult time at the boys' home. I can only imagine what type of reaction a man arriving at Hazelbrae looking for a young woman might receive." His eyes softened, taking on a pleading look. "I figured if you were with me, I'd have a much better chance at gaining any sort of cooperation."

Julia hesitated. "Is it far away?"

"Not very. We could be there and back by train the same day."

She pondered the idea for a moment. If the trip took only one day, she'd be back in plenty of time for Mrs. Middleton. And how could she refuse Quinn's request after everything he had done for her? She smiled at him. "I'd be happy to go with you."

"Really?" Relief spread over his handsome face, easing the lines of tension on his brow.

"Of course. I owe you at least that much after all the help you've given me."

"Thank you. That means a lot."

"You're welcome." She leaned back against the cushions. "While you were gone, Reverend Burke found me a position as a live-in companion to one of his elderly parishioners. But I won't be needed for about a week."

"That's good news." He reached out for her hand and squeezed it. The warmth of his fingers contrasted sharply with her chilly ones.

Under his approving look, she found she couldn't hold his gaze and gently pulled her hand free. She didn't deserve such admiration. If he ever learned the truth of how far she'd fallen, he wouldn't want anything to do with her.

"You're pleased, aren't you? Because if not, I'm sure Reverend Burke could find you something different."

"I'm very pleased. Mrs. Middleton seems like a lovely person."

"I'm glad." Quinn leaned forward, his gray eyes radiating sincerity. "All I want is for you to be safe and happy."

Julia's throat tightened. Why couldn't she have met such an honorable man before this? If she had, perhaps her life wouldn't be in shambles now.

"Besides," he continued, "I have a selfish reason for being pleased about this job. With your room and board paid for, you'll be able to save enough for your passage home." He winked at her.

Her pulse fluttered. She attempted a smile but failed miserably.

Her secret sat like a lump of hard coal in her belly. He deserved to know she wouldn't be going with them. At the very least, she owed him honesty.

"Quinn, there's something you should know—"

"I thought I heard a male voice down here." Mrs. Chamberlain came bustling into the parlor. "Quinten, how nice to see you again."

Quinn shot to his feet, biting back his disappointment at the interruption. What had Julia been about to say? "And you, Mrs. Chamberlain. I hope you don't mind me dropping by like this."

"Not at all. Julia dear, did you offer our guest some refreshments?"

"N-no, I'm sorry. I didn't think to." Julia bit her lip, looking overly distressed for so simple a transgression.

"Please, don't worry about that," Quinn said. "I can't stay long. I have to get back to the hospital to check on Harry."

In truth, he'd worried about leaving the boy alone in the first place, but the urgent desire to see Julia again had won out. Besides, the doctor had told Quinn that with the amount of pain medication Harry had received, he'd likely sleep for a few hours.

"Is your brother ill?" Mrs. C. asked, concern shining in her pale eyes.

"No, ma'am." Quinn relayed the story. But as he did, the color drained from the older woman's face. "The doctor assures me Harry will recover. It will just take some time, especially in his weakened condition."

Mrs. C. reached out to grasp the arm of the chair and lowered herself to the seat, as if her legs wouldn't hold her.

Mentally Quinn berated himself for being so insensitive. Of course this would bring back memories of all the suffering she and her sister had endured. "Forgive me, Mrs. C. I shouldn't be telling you all this. I don't want to bring up unpleasant memories for you."

She shook her head. "No, no. We must speak of such matters. They've been kept hidden for too long as it is."

"I don't understand." Julia frowned. "What does Harry's situation have to do with Mrs. C.?"

Quinn looked at the landlady for permission and when she nodded, he briefly explained her history.

Tears filled Julia's brown eyes. "How could anyone be so cruel? Especially to orphaned children?"

"It's beyond comprehension, really." Mrs. C. straightened on her chair, a bit of color returning to her cheeks. "I've been fooling myself that our Newcomers Program at the church is doing enough to help immigrants, but in reality, we should be addressing this issue head on. It seems the abuse of children has been going on for decades."

"What can we do about it?" Julia dabbed a handkerchief to the corners of her eyes.

"I'm not sure. But I intend to raise the issue at our next meeting. Perhaps if we all put our heads together, we can come up with a plan."

Quinn nodded. "That would be a good start. Unfortunately, it doesn't solve my immediate problem." Reluctantly he rose, his gaze straying to Julia. "I'd best get back to the hospital."

It astounded him how much he hated to leave. Everything about Julia—her beauty both inside and out—drew him to her like a bee to nectar.

Mrs. C. got to her feet as well. "We'll all be praying for Harry and for you, dear."

"Thank you, Mrs. C." He picked up his hat and turned to leave.

At the front door, he realized Julia had followed him.

She lifted her handbag from the hall table. "If you don't mind," she said, "I'd like to go with you."

Quinn hesitated. He'd love nothing more than to spend additional time with Julia, but he had no idea what he was in for. "It's kind of you to offer, but it could be a very long wait."

"I'll stay as long as I can. You shouldn't be facing this alone." She gave him a long look as she pinned on her hat. "You helped me at one of my worst times. I'd like to return the favor."

His throat tightened, making speech impossible. He sent her a grateful look and then held the door open for her.

As they headed outside together, Quinn's shoulders lifted, and for the first time in days, his burdens felt considerably lighter.

From the parlor window, Harriet watched Quinten and Julia make their way down the sidewalk, her unease only growing.

Lord, why have you brought this man and his problems to my doorstep? After all these years, I thought I'd paid my dues, done my best to help the newcomers to this country. But why is all the pain from the past coming back to haunt me now?

She sniffed and dabbed her cheeks with her handkerchief, the answer welling inside her. The atrocities against orphans coming here from their homeland had been going unchecked for far too long. Someone needed to speak out on behalf of the children and shine a light on this injustice. If she'd been braver, she would have done something before now. If only to right the wrong that had caused Annie's death.

The uncomfortable truth made her wince. She'd eased her conscience over the years by letting her husband take the lead. They'd started the boardinghouse to provide affordable housing for immigrants, a noble venture in itself, but clearly not enough. And she'd also helped Geoffrey with the Newcomers Program. But it didn't address the true problem and did nothing to solve the fact that children still suffered at the hands of unscrupulous people.

Lord, show me what to do. Show me where to begin. And please grant young Harry your healing grace.

With a last blow of her nose, she marched into the hall to get her purse. She needed to see Geoffrey right away. If anyone could help her determine her next course of action, he could.

CHAPTER 13

Seated on the hard chairs at the children's hospital, Julia began to feel stiff all over. She glanced at the large clock on the wall. They'd been here for three hours. Three hours with no change in Harry's status.

Upon their arrival, Quinn had been met with unfortunate news. Harry had experienced a setback and was unconscious, a fact that clearly worried the doctor. Quinn had rushed to his brother's side, and since the hospital only allowed one visitor per patient, Julia opted to stay in a nearby waiting area. Every so often, Quinn came to update her, and she could tell he was torn, hating for her to be alone, but not wanting to leave Harry.

It had become clear to Julia that Quinn suffered great guilt over the beating his brother had endured, and no matter what she said to ease his burden, he remained stubbornly entrenched in his culpability. Julia prayed for a way to make him see that it wasn't his fault.

She rose from the chair and stretched her lower back. Her stomach growled, reminding her it had been some time since she'd had anything to eat or drink. Over the last week, she'd learned it was better for the nausea not to let her stomach get too empty. She should really find something to eat. But she didn't want to leave without seeing Quinn again.

She gathered her purse and set off down the hall. Perhaps she could peek into Harry's room and get Quinn to step out.

Two inquiries later, Julia found where Quinn was holding vigil. Harry shared a ward with five other patients, his bed partially curtained to maintain some degree of privacy. The boy lay very still, his face as pale as the sheet that covered him. Quinn sat on a stool by Harry's side, his head bent over his folded hands. Eyes closed, his lips moving soundlessly, Quinn appeared to be praying.

Julia hesitated, her confidence wavering. The scene was too intimate, too personal. What right did she have to intrude? She was about to back out when Quinn lifted his head and spied her.

Immediately, he shot to his feet. "Julia. I'm sorry. I should have come to check on you."

"You needn't worry about me." She forced a smile. "I came to see how Harry's doing before I leave."

Quinn frowned and pulled out his pocket watch. "I've kept you past the lunch hour. I'm sorry." His eyes were red-rimmed, and his hair was tousled, as though he'd been running his hands through it.

"I was about to go in search of something to eat," she said. "Can I get you anything?"

"Thank you, but I don't think I'll be able to eat until I know Harry is all right."

She moved closer, noting the boy's pallor and the bruises marring his arms. "He's going to recover, Quinn. His body needs this time to heal, but he will wake up. You have to believe that." In her earnestness, she reached out to squeeze Quinn's arm.

The sorrow on his face tore at her heart.

"I pray you're right. I don't know how I'll live with myself if he doesn't."

It felt only natural for her to lean in and wrap her arms around him. If ever anyone needed a hug, it was Quinn. "Don't give up. Everyone's praying for him."

"Thank you." The look of gratitude he gave her made her insides hum. Their gazes stayed locked together for several seconds, long enough for the heat to climb into her cheeks.

A throat cleared behind them. Julia blinked and stepped back.

"Dr. Overmire," Quinn said. "Please, come in."

"Sorry to interrupt, but I need to examine Harry again." The thin man smiled. "If you wouldn't mind waiting in the outer room, I'll come and give you an update when I've finished."

"Certainly. Thank you." Tension rolled off Quinn in waves as he ushered Julia out of the room.

She bit her lip. How could she leave now? What if the doctor had bad news? Quinn would need someone here with him. She stopped by the waiting room door.

"I can stay a bit longer," she said. "I'd like to hear what the doctor says. If it's all right with you."

"I'd like that. Thank you."

"It helps to have someone with you at a time like this." For a moment, her thoughts flew back to the support Dr. Hawkins had shown her during the difficult days with Sam, both before his death and immediately afterward. She'd appreciated the man's solicitude, never guessing what a dark road it would lead her down.

"It does help. More than you know," he said. "Do you mind if we walk a little? I don't think I can sit in that waiting room."

"Not at all. I'd welcome a chance to stretch my legs."

They walked down the corridor to a small alcove where a window overlooked a courtyard. Quinn looked outside, one arm raised against the glass. A shuddering sigh rippled through his body.

Julia stood slightly behind him, unsure what to say to ease his obvious turmoil. She remained silent, hoping he would open up when he was ready.

"I hate hospitals," he said at last, without turning. "They bring me back to the worst time in my life, when my father was dying of consumption."

She murmured something sympathetic, feeling terribly inadequate.

"My father is the main reason I'm on this quest to reunite my family." His voice was so low she almost missed it.

Julia frowned. Hadn't his father passed away a long time ago? "How so?"

"Before he died, he made me promise to take care of the family. To step up and fill his shoes. And to keep everyone together." He bowed his head. "I've failed miserably in every possible way."

"Oh, Quinn. That's not true." She rubbed a hand down his arm.

"I'm afraid it is." He shook his head. "No matter how hard I worked, I couldn't provide enough money to keep my mother from losing her children. Not only aren't they together, they're on a different continent. And now because of me, Harry is suffering." Quinn's jaw muscles clenched. "All I ever wanted was to make my father proud, but I keep falling short."

Julia swallowed hard against the tears that were ever present. This man had no idea of his true worth. How noble and courageous he was. "You're doing your best. No one could ask for more than that."

"I doubt my mum would agree. Stuck in that workhouse. It's worse than the flat you were living in."

She could only imagine what the poor woman had gone through. But what Julia didn't understand was how his mother's situation would change once Quinn returned. "What do you intend to do if you manage to get all your siblings to come back with you?" she asked. "Surely they won't end up in the workhouse too."

His whole frame stiffened. "I have somewhere in mind," he said. "Once I get home, I'll be able to finalize the details."

"That sounds promising. Is it in London?"

"No, it's not." His gaze shifted away. "Let's head back, shall we? The doctor might be finished by now."

She frowned. Something about his tone put her on alert. There was a subtle tension and evasiveness to his answer, which led her to believe he was keeping something from her. But what?

As they walked back toward the waiting room, Julia tugged on Quinn's hand. "Try not to worry. I'm sure God has a plan for your family and that everything will work out as it's meant to."

He looked down at her, his expression guarded. But he gave

a tight smile. "Thank you, Julia. Your support means the world to me."

She opened her mouth to respond, but the doctor exited Harry's room and came toward them.

"Here's the doctor now," she said.

Quinn had never been so happy for an interruption. How could he explain his plans for his family when they returned to England? If he were to tell Julia about the earl's reward for bringing her home, she would think his only motivation for helping her was to get his own farm. What had once seemed like the promise to a shiny dream now felt like a tarnished, guilt-laden secret.

"Mr. Aspinall?" The doctor lowered his clipboard. "I'm happy to report that Harry is improving. He's no longer unconscious but is sleeping normally. He will be in a great deal of pain until the bruising subsides and the ribs start to heal. The good news is there doesn't seem to be any internal bleeding. I believe he should make a full recovery."

Quinn sagged and released a loud whoosh of air. "That's excellent news, doctor. Thank you so much."

The man studied Quinn. "I would be remiss if I didn't ask one pertinent question. Do you know who did this to your brother?"

Quinn frowned. He'd been so consumed by making sure Harry would recover that he'd almost forgotten the reason for his injuries. He gave a curt nod. "I believe it was Harry's employer."

The doctor's face darkened. "What that man did is a crime. I would advise you to think about getting the authorities involved and perhaps press charges."

"I'll consider it when Harry is feeling better."

Dr. Overmire nodded. "I'll look in on him again later tonight. If he continues to improve, I'd estimate about three more days before he can be released."

Relief wound through Quinn's system, yet the underlying tension remained. Though the news was good, Quinn would have to put his search for Becky on hold again until he could leave Harry. He only prayed Becky was doing better than her brothers.

When the doctor disappeared down the corridor, Quinn turned to Julia.

She was wiping tears from her cheeks. "I'm so happy for Harry. And for you."

"Thank you, Julia. I don't know how I'd have made it through this day without you."

Her brown eyes glowed. "I'm glad I could help." She rose up on her tiptoes to kiss his cheek, her soft lips lingering for a second longer than necessary.

Her scent, a mixture of lavender and vanilla, wrapped around him. Without thinking, he pulled her closer into a hug. Despite the warmth radiating between them, she shivered, then stepped back.

"I'll check in tomorrow to see how he's doing. Try to get some rest. You don't want to get ill yourself." Her cheeks were pink, and she averted her gaze.

Had he embarrassed her by his display of affection? *Get a grip, man. Remember your place.*

"I'd best be off. If I'm lucky, Mrs. C.'s cook will have saved me a plate." She gave a light laugh, likely an attempt to relieve the awkward moment.

"Will you be all right by yourself?" Quinn frowned. He really should see her home, but he wanted to be there when Harry woke up.

"I'll be fine. The streetcar stop is right outside."

"I'll talk to you tomorrow, then."

"I look forward to hearing from you." She smiled at him with so much warmth that his heart did a slow roll in his chest.

As she walked away, he stared after her. Then he squeezed his eyes shut. His feelings for Julia had gotten entirely out of hand. He needed to get his emotions under control before he did something foolish.

Like fall in love with a woman totally out of his realm.

CHAPTER 14

Three days later, Quinn whistled as he made his way down the corridor to Harry's hospital room. For once, circumstances might finally be turning in his favor. Harry was improving at a faster rate than expected. And for now, Quinn decided to make a concerted effort to put his worries aside and celebrate this minor victory.

The first time Harry had awakened, he'd managed to sip some water before falling asleep again. Then later on, he'd sat up and had some chicken soup. Much to Quinn's relief, with every bite of food, Harry's condition seemed to improve.

Today, Quinn expected Harry to be released, and he would take his brother to Mrs. Chamberlain's boardinghouse until he had fully regained his health. The dear woman, likely with some prodding from Julia, had insisted he bring Harry to her place to recuperate.

"I thought you didn't take males," Quinn had argued.

"Why, Harry's only a boy. I'd never turn away a child in need."

Her indignation had made Quinn want to laugh out loud. Instead, he kissed the woman's cheek. "You're a gem, Mrs. C. I don't know how I'd have gotten on without you."

She'd shooed him away with the edge of her apron, but not before Quinn had noted the smile teasing her lips.

Quinn entered Harry's hospital room, a brown package under his arm. Julia had helped him shop for some new clothes for his brother, seeing that the hospital staff had gotten rid of the ones he'd been wearing. The mere thought of Julia quickened Quinn's pulse. He looked forward to seeing her any moment now, since she'd insisted on coming to help him bring Harry home. Even though Quinn was perfectly capable of managing the trip on his own, he accepted Julia's offer solely for the chance to be in her company.

"Good morning, Harry. How are you feeling today?" Quinn removed his cap and stood at the end of the bed.

Sitting up against the pillows, the boy gave a faint grin. "Much better. Especially since Dr. Overmire says I can leave the hospital today."

"That's right. And I've brought you some new clothes for the occasion." Quinn handed him the package.

"Really?" Harry fingered the string surrounding it with awe. "I haven't had anything new . . . ever. I always got Cecil's hand-me-downs."

Quinn swallowed hard. "Well, open it and see what you think."

Harry tore off the paper and pulled out a plain cotton shirt, brown pants, new undergarments, socks, and a pair of shoes. Julia had also insisted on getting him a set of suspenders and a jaunty new cap.

"It's the least the poor dear deserves," she'd said.

Thankfully, Mrs. C. had sent word to the shopkeeper she frequented to give Quinn the best possible price on everything he bought.

Harry's hazel eyes glowed as he admired the sturdy footwear. "My very own shoes with no holes. Thank you, Quinn."

"You're welcome." Quinn's chest swelled with mixed emotions. Regret that his brother had lived without these simple necessities and gratitude to be able to bring Harry such joy. "You get dressed, and I'll see if the doctor left any instructions."

"Is Miss Julia coming today?"

Quinn suppressed a smile. It appeared Harry had developed a crush on Julia since she'd been here every day to see him.

"She said she would come. Apparently, she didn't think I could manage to get you home on my own." He winked at Harry, who laughed. "I'll pull the curtain around for you. Be right back."

Quinn exited the room, the lightness in his heart almost too much to bear. For the present, he would set aside his worry over Cecil and Becky and simply enjoy this time with his youngest sibling. Harry deserved all of Quinn's attention right now after the ordeal he'd been through.

"Quinn. I hope I'm not late." Julia hurried toward him, her skirt billowing around her calves as she walked.

Her brown eyes sparkled, and her cheeks glowed, likely a result of her walk in the fresh air.

"Not at all. Harry's just getting dressed. He loves his new clothes."

"I'm so glad." She clapped her hands together. "I can't wait to see how he looks in them."

"Thank you again for everything you've done for him. He's taken a real shine to you." Grinning, he leaned closer. "In fact, he might even have a tiny crush on you."

Julia laughed. "The feeling is mutual. I adore that rascal and will enjoy every moment nursing him back to health."

Before he could stop himself, Quinn reached out a hand to brush a stray lock of hair from her cheek. Her gaze met his and the laughter ebbed away, replaced by something more intense, a type of electricity sparking between them. Her lips parted. Quinn's breathing grew shallow, and all he could think of was kissing her.

"Miss Holloway. What an unexpected surprise." The male voice came from behind them.

Julia jerked away from Quinn. Her mouth fell open, and all color drained from her face. "Dr. Hawkins."

Quinn turned to see a distinguished-looking man of about forty. Though he stood a head shorter than Quinn, the confident manner in which he held himself made him appear larger. Judging by his white coat, he must be a physician on staff, which likely explained his poise.

When it became apparent Julia was not going to make introductions, the man offered Quinn his hand. "I'm Dr. Richard Hawkins."

"Quinten Aspinall." He looked the man in the eye. "You're a friend of Miss Holloway's, I take it?"

"You could say so." The man stared at Julia in an oddly familiar way. One that seemed terribly inappropriate.

A flash of heat seared Quinn's neck. Was this man a former suitor?

"Dr. Hawkins was Sam's personal physician," Julia said at last. "We . . . that is, he . . ." She shook her head, as though unable to find the right words.

"What Miss Holloway is trying to say is that the shock of Sam's death forged a bond between us as we helped each other cope with the devastation of that tragedy." The man smiled at Quinn in a rather smug fashion.

"It must have been terrible," Quinn said. "Losing a patient under such circumstances."

As he spoke, he glanced down at the man's hand and noted the wedding band there. Immediately, the muscles in Quinn's chest loosened. Dr. Hawkins was married. Quinn must have mistaken the tension between him and Julia. Still, something about this man rubbed him the wrong way.

"I'm here to check on a patient of mine," the man said. "But what brings you here, Miss Holloway? You're not ill, I hope."

Julia's lips trembled as she shook her head.

Was she afraid of him?

Every protective instinct came alive inside Quinn, and he moved closer to her. "She's here helping me bring my younger brother home, and I'm most grateful for her assistance." Quinn pasted on a smile.

"And how exactly do *you* know Miss Holloway?" The man's dark eyes glittered.

Julia clutched Quinn's arm, her face growing even paler, if possible. He didn't know if she was feeling faint or if she was trying to impart a message to him.

"Quinten and I met through the church," she said quickly. "We've been seeing each other for a while now." She squeezed his arm again.

This time, he was sure of her intent. For whatever reason, she wished this man to believe them to be a couple—a ruse Quinn didn't mind playing along with at all. He smiled down at her. "Meeting Julia is the best thing that ever happened to me."

The look of gratitude and relief on her face made Quinn feel like he'd slayed a dragon. "Well, we'd best get going. Harry will wonder what happened to us." He stared at the physician. "It was nice to meet you, Mr. Hawkins."

"It's *Dr*. Hawkins." The man's dark eyes hardened, then he turned to Julia. "We must get together soon and catch up."

Julia didn't meet his gaze. "I . . . I'm not sure that will be possible with my work schedule."

Hawkins's nostrils flared. "Then perhaps we'll run into each other again."

"Perhaps. Good day, doctor." Julia gave a slight nod and allowed Quinn to guide her down the corridor.

She walked beside him, looking straight ahead. Once inside the room, however, she sagged against Quinn, her whole body trembling. Quinn kept an arm around her waist for support.

"Thank you for going along with that," she said at last.

"I assume you had a good reason to mislead him."

She nodded. "I'll tell you about it later. Right now, let's get Harry home."

Back at the boardinghouse, Julia struggled to keep her nerves under control as she made the bed in the room down the hall from hers. How long could she put Quinn off before he asked her about Dr. Hawkins? She'd seen the questions in Quinn's eyes and knew he wouldn't let the matter drop. Julia blew out a frustrated breath. Of all the times to run into that man again. Yet, if she'd been alone, it could have been so much worse.

With effort, she turned her attention back to smoothing the

wrinkles from the quilt. After they had arrived with Harry, Mrs. C. had rushed the boy into the dining room, eager to feed him a good meal. With Julia as the sole occupant of the third floor, Mrs. C. had decided that Harry should stay there, somewhat removed from the rest of the boarders, where it would be quieter and more conducive to healing. Julia had volunteered to make up his room.

She certainly didn't mind sharing her floor or the small lavatory with Harry. It had felt a tad lonely being here by herself, but she hadn't wanted to complain, being so grateful to have such nice accommodations. By the time she was ready to move in with Mrs. Middleton, Harry would be stronger and hopefully be able to stay with Quinn at the YMCA.

She fluffed the pillow and moved to the window to open the curtains. Then, with nothing left to do, Julia forced herself to go down to the main level. If luck was with her, perhaps Quinn would have forgotten about Dr. Hawkins in his concern for his brother's comfort.

At the foot of the stairs, Mrs. C. stood talking with Quinn.

"Of course, Harry can stay as long as you need. He'll be no trouble at all."

Quinn looked up as Julia reached them. "I've asked Julia to accompany me to Peterborough. But we won't leave until I'm certain Harry is doing better. And that he won't be a burden."

"Whenever you feel the time is right, dear. For now, let's take one day at a time."

"I agree, Mrs. C.," Julia said. "In the meantime, I'll keep Harry company in the dining room. I'd love a cup of tea and a biscuit."

She walked into the room, where Harry sat in front of a large bowl. The rich scent of beef and onions hung in the air. Though still pale, the boy looked more relaxed, his eyes less haunted.

He lowered his spoon when he spied her. "Miss Julia, this is the best barley soup I've ever tasted."

"I'm glad you're enjoying it." She laid a gentle hand on his shoulder on the way to the sideboard, where Mrs. C. always kept a pot of tea ready. "Mrs. Teeter is an excellent cook. Wait until you taste her chicken potpie."

Julia chuckled at the boy's awed expression. "Don't eat too much now. Your stomach isn't used to such big portions. And you can always have more later."

The light left Harry's eyes. "At the farm, if I didn't finish my meal in five minutes, Mrs. Wolfe fed my dinner to the pigs. I started eating as fast as I could after the first time that happened."

Julia set the teapot down with a thud. "Well, no one here will take your food, love. You take your time and eat as much or as little as you like." She turned her head to hide the tears forming at what that poor child had been through. It made her problems seem trivial in comparison. At least she was a grown woman. This boy had been only seven years old when he'd come to this country, separated from his siblings and sent to live with a heartless beast of a man whose wife didn't sound much better.

Julia looked over at the boy's fair head as he slurped the rest of his soup and vowed to do everything in her power to make Harry's life better. To make sure he had a reason to smile every day.

If the boy affected her this way, she could only imagine the powerful emotions Quinn must be feeling. She had no doubt he would do whatever was necessary to protect his younger brother and keep him safe from any further harm.

Julia only hoped she could help in some small way to make that happen.

CHAPTER 15

The passenger train rocked back and forth as it chugged along the tracks. Seated in the sparsely populated second car, Julia swayed along with the rhythm. Lulled by the monotonous *click-clack*, she fought to keep her eyes open. Another symptom of pregnancy, she'd discovered, was the insatiable need for sleep. She'd never taken so many naps in her life.

Beside her, Quinn drummed his fingers on his thigh. It appeared his relief at Harry's recovery had been short-lived, replaced now by anxiety over Becky's fate.

Julia had prayed every night for this girl she'd never met. If Becky had been mistreated at her place of employment, Julia wasn't sure how Quinn would take it.

"So," Quinn said quietly about half an hour into their trip, "you were going to tell me about the man we met in the hospital. Dr. Hawkins, I believe his name was."

Julia stiffened on her seat, the hard back pressing into her spine. It had been several days since their run-in at the hospital, and she'd hoped Quinn had forgotten about him.

Apparently not.

She took a breath in preparation for the unpleasant conversation ahead. "Dr. Hawkins was Sam's physician. He came to the house quite often."

Quinn frowned. "I thought Dr. Clayborne was Sam's doctor."

"Dr. Clayborne oversaw Sam's physical therapy, but Dr. Hawkins took care of all his other medical needs. I . . . I worked closely with him in order to make sure I was giving Sam the best care possible."

"I see."

Julia dropped her gaze to her hands, which were clasped on her lap. "When I found Sam that terrible morning, Dr. Hawkins was the first person I called. After he'd dealt with matters, he could see I was terribly distraught and prescribed some medication to help my nerves. I was grateful to him for handling things and for taking care of me." She paused to consider her next words.

Quinn frowned. "Then why did you seem so afraid of him?"

Julia sucked in a breath. How could she explain her aversion to the man? A man Sam had trusted implicitly. "After Sam's death, Dr. Hawkins was very attentive. He checked in to see how I was doing and ask whether or not the medication was helping." She hesitated. "Unfortunately, he became a little more . . . friendly than I wanted."

Quinn's eyes widened. "He made advances to you?"

She nodded, looking away for fear he would see there was much more to the story.

"But he's married. I saw his ring." Outrage rang in Quinn's voice.

"Clearly that doesn't stop some men."

"I'm so sorry, Julia." His voice was low. "You shouldn't have had to deal with that. Especially at a time when you were grieving and vulnerable."

She nodded. "Thankfully, I had Dr. Clayborne to turn to. He was nothing but kind and respectful. Knowing I was out of work, he helped me get a job at the hospital. And he insisted I stay with him and his wife until I could find somewhere to live." She glanced over at Quinn. "If not for him, I don't know where I'd have gone."

"I'm glad you had one decent person to help you."

"And now I have you." She placed a hand on his arm. "An honorable man looking out for the best interest of his family." Julia often thought how wonderful it would be to have a partner like

Quinn to share all the challenges that lay ahead. Some nights, fear of the unknown kept her awake until the wee hours of the morning. Only her faith that God would take care of her allowed her to keep going. "Your siblings are lucky."

"I'm not so certain." He scowled. "I haven't exactly lived up to my father's expectations."

"Don't you think you're being too hard on yourself?"

Quinn turned serious gray eyes on her. "If anything, not hard enough."

"Well, while I'm around, I'm going to keep reminding you that you're doing your best. And that your best is more than enough."

Quinn could have stared into Julia's luminous brown eyes for the rest of the trip. Having her champion him as some sort of hero warmed the cold places in his heart. However, he couldn't allow himself to bask in her praise. Not until he had Harry, Becky, and Cecil all safely back home with their mother.

Maybe then the gaping void inside him would be filled.

Maybe then he could finally relax and simply breathe.

The train chugged to a halt, dragging Quinn's attention to the window. The Peterborough station slid into view, a low, brown-bricked building with black trim. An instant rumble of nerves shot through his stomach.

Please, Lord, let me find Becky without any problems, and please let her be all right.

As if sensing his thoughts, Julia squeezed his hand. "Let's go find your sister."

Quinn swallowed, his throat tight, and with a quick nod rose to escort Julia to the platform below. Once inside the station, he asked directions to Hazelbrae.

"It's called the Margaret Cox Home for Girls now," the clerk told him. "But it's right up the road to the left. The big house on top of the hill. You can't miss it."

A few minutes later, as they climbed the steep road, the majesty of the residence almost stole Quinn's breath. A far cry from the narrow Barnardo building in downtown Toronto, this house sprawled on a wide expanse of property. Some rich benefactor must have bestowed this land to be used for children. How else could a home for orphans afford such luxury?

As they reached the front door, Quinn stopped to wait for Julia.

"It's magnificent," she breathed. "I hadn't pictured anything so grand."

"Nor did I. I'm going to take this as a positive sign that Becky has had good care." He looked down at her. "Are you ready?"

"Ready."

"Right, then. After you." He held the door open for her to enter. She tilted her chin, gathered her skirts, and swept in the door.

Quinn blinked, certain he'd just witnessed Julia putting on her battle armor, and in that instant, he was very glad he'd agreed to let her do the talking. He tugged his waistcoat into place and followed her inside.

"Good day, ma'am," Julia said to the woman at the reception desk. Her aristocratic tone held exactly the right mixture of cheerfulness and steel, much like Lady Brentwood when she spoke to the servants. "We'd like to speak with the directress, if you'd be so kind."

The woman removed her spectacles, a slight frown wrinkling her brow. "May I ask what this is about?"

"It concerns one of the girls who was sent here."

The woman opened her mouth, most likely to argue, but Julia cut her off. "I understand your need for privacy and that you aren't able to give out certain information, which is why we wish to speak to the directress herself."

Quinn held his cap in front of him, willing himself not to fidget.

The woman's lips pinched together as she rose. "One moment and I'll see if Mrs. Whitaker has time to see you."

As soon as they were alone, Quinn let out a long breath. "What is your plan if she's not available?"

"We'll have to play it by ear." She turned to him, a mischievous twinkle in her eyes. "If all else fails, you might have to use your good looks to charm the lady."

He blinked at her. Was Julia flirting with him?

Footsteps sounded as the receptionist returned. "Mrs. Whitaker can spare five minutes. If you'll follow me, please."

Without waiting for them, she spun and headed back down the hallway.

Quinn gave himself a shake, pulling his thoughts away from this confident, flirtatious Julia and how pretty she looked today. He needed to concentrate on this meeting. His sister's well-being could depend on it.

The receptionist stopped in front of an open door and gestured for them to enter. Quinn waited for Julia to precede him into the room.

Behind a rather cluttered desk, a middle-aged woman rose. "Good afternoon. I'm Mrs. Whitaker, the directress." She looked at Quinn first, so he stepped forward.

"I'm Quinten Aspinall, and this is Miss Julia Holloway."

"It's nice to meet you, Mrs. Whitaker," Julia said with a charming smile. "You have a beautiful residence here."

A bit of the wariness left the woman's face. "Thank you. We're quite proud of it. Won't you have a seat?"

As soon as they did, Mrs. Whitaker looked at Quinn. "From your surname, Mr. Aspinall, I believe I can surmise why you're here." One brow rose. "You must be a relative of Rebecca Aspinall."

"Yes, ma'am. I'm her older brother." He paused. Admitting he was here to make sure his sister wasn't being mistreated wouldn't get him very far. "I've come to see how she's doing and to give her news of our mother."

"Your mother? Rebecca wasn't an orphan when she came to our organization?"

"No, ma'am. My mother was left a widow with four children to raise on her own."

Julia leaned forward on her chair. "Quinn went to work to help support the family, but for the last few years, he's been away at war."

Mrs. Whitaker murmured something sympathetic. "This war has been a terrible tragedy for both our countries."

"Indeed it has." Quinn straightened against the seat.

Julia glanced over at him, then focused back on the directress. "You can imagine Quinn's distress when he returned to England only to learn that his younger siblings had been sent to Canada. That, on top of his mother's ill health, was almost too much to bear." Julia took out a handkerchief from her handbag and dabbed at her eyes.

Quinn tensed. Julia was laying it on rather thick. Mrs. Whitaker seemed to be a clever woman, one who wouldn't be taken in by dramatics.

Before Julia could say anything more, he jumped in. "I've come to ask your help in finding my sister, ma'am. I need to know she's all right and to tell her I've found our brothers."

"You have? Were they also sent through Dr. Barnardo's organization?"

"They were."

"And the people in charge told you where your brothers were placed?"

Quinn hesitated. How could he answer this question without incriminating someone?

"I can't tell you how much seeing his brothers has eased Quinn's mind," Julia added quickly, as though she feared he might say something to jeopardize their mission. "Now, if we can just do the same for Becky, he'll be able to give his mother the good news that her children are doing well." She gave the woman a watery smile.

Mrs. Whitaker looked at her with a slight frown. "I'm sorry. I didn't get your connection to the Aspinalls."

Julia's mouth fell open, and she blinked. "Really? I thought for certain we told you—"

"Julia is my fiancée," Quinn interjected. He darted a quick glance at Julia, hoping she wouldn't appear too shocked. Though he hated telling an untruth, he hoped he would be forgiven in this instance, with the gravity of Becky's situation hanging in the balance.

Julia met his gaze, her cheeks growing pinker, then turned her focus back to the directress with a wide smile.

"Oh, I see. No wonder you're so invested in his family." Mrs. Whitaker beamed at them, then folded her hands on the desktop. "Normally, I'm reluctant to give out any information on our children, but I can see you're concerned about your sister." She released a sigh. "Let me assure you that Rebecca is doing very well. She has an excellent placement now, one that suits her in every way."

Now? The hairs on Quinn's neck rose. "What do you mean by 'now'?" he all but growled. Only the weight of Julia's hand on his arm kept him from jumping out of his chair.

"Nothing to worry about, Mr. Aspinall." She twisted a pen through her fingers. "Rebecca had a bad fit with her first placement and returned here for several weeks until we found a more suitable home for her. That was about four years ago. Now she's working for one of the most prestigious families in Peterborough." She gave a laugh that was a touch too loud.

Quinn wanted to slam his hand on the desk and force the woman to give him the information he needed. But losing his temper would eliminate every chance of gaining the directress's cooperation. At any rate, he'd learned Becky was living in Peterborough, which meant he wouldn't have to travel to another destination. That much, at least, was good news.

"How wonderful," Julia said. "Mrs. Whitaker, I hope you understand how much it would mean to see Becky in person. Would you be able to arrange that for us?"

The woman looked from Julia to Quinn. "I can't guarantee anything, since it will be up to her employer, but I could contact them and let them know of your situation. Perhaps on Rebecca's next afternoon off, she might be able to meet with you."

Frustration screamed through Quinn's tense muscles. "Her next day off? When would that be?"

"Now, Quinn." Julia squeezed his arm a tad roughly. "Mrs. Whitaker is doing her best to help. Why don't we give her a moment to place the call?" She rose and looked at the directress. "We'll wait outside to give you some privacy."

"Thank you." Mrs. Whitaker inclined her head and reached for the candlestick telephone on her desktop.

With little choice, Quinn got to his feet and followed Julia into the hall. He pushed his fingers through his hair as he paced the narrow corridor, not caring if he looked like a wild man.

Julia gave him a stern look. "Don't lose your patience, Quinn. Not when we're so close to our goal."

"How can you say that? I doubt Becky's employer will allow us to see her. And then what will we do? It's not like a farm. I can't just waltz into their house and look for her."

She came a step closer and stared into his eyes. "Then we will leave it up to God. I know He's watching out for us. Everything will work out as it's meant to."

Quinn envied Julia's faith, her absolute conviction that all would be well. If only he could be so certain. He forced himself to calm down and think logically about their next step. "What if we can't see Becky today? Are you sure you don't mind staying in Peterborough overnight?" At least he'd had the foresight to suggest she bring a change of clothes, just in case.

Julia hesitated for a second, then smiled sweetly. "That depends. Are you offering to pay for your fiancée's hotel room?"

Heat blasted up Quinn's neck. He'd forgotten about his fib. "I'm sorry. I don't know why I said that, but—"

"It's all right. I don't mind her thinking we're a couple."

"You don't?"

Her cheeks grew rosy, but she didn't look away. "Any girl would consider herself fortunate to be marrying you."

Quinn swallowed. How he wished they were somewhere else at this moment. Somewhere more private, where he might give in to the urge to kiss her and show her how much he truly admired her.

The door opened and Mrs. Whitaker walked toward them, smiling.

"Mr. Aspinall, I have good news. When Mrs. Sebring learned

Rebecca's brother was here from England, she insisted on you coming to see her tomorrow. They've arranged for Rebecca to have the afternoon off so you'll have time to visit. Isn't that generous of them?"

Relief flooded his body, and Quinn managed a genuine smile. "It is indeed."

She handed them a piece of paper. "Here's the address. Be there at one o'clock. Rebecca will be expecting you."

CHAPTER 16

Julia looked up at the sign on the redbricked building in front of them. The Oxford Hotel appeared to be an eminently respectable establishment. Then why did she feel so nervous about staying there? Perhaps it was because she'd be posing as Quinn's fiancée. A turn of events she found rather unsettling since the idea of having him as her partner and protector appealed to her far more than it should.

"Does the place not suit you?" Quinn's voice jarred her from her thoughts. "If it doesn't, we can always find another hotel."

"It looks lovely." She smiled. "I hope it's not expensive." She'd gotten so used to living in poverty over the past months that her former luxurious lifestyle was no more real than the wisps of cloud drifting overhead. Yet this man, a servant in her uncle's estate, now had more money than she did.

"Don't worry. I have enough funds to cover the cost and to treat you to a nice dinner as well." Quinn's grin lit his gray eyes, creating appealing crinkles at the corners.

It was good to see him in better spirits. The fact that he was going to see his sister tomorrow must have finally sunk in. Still, a meal in the hotel would probably be pricey.

"A fancy dinner isn't necessary," she said quickly. "I'd be fine with a sandwich."

"Nonsense. It's the least I can do to thank you for coming with me." Quinn opened the door and waited for her to enter the lobby.

In no time, he'd arranged for two rooms on the second floor and had escorted Julia to her door. "I'll be in the next room if you need me. Would an hour give you enough time to freshen up before dinner?"

"That would be perfect."

"Good. I'll see you then."

Once Julia had entered her room and locked the door, she heard Quinn's retreating footsteps.

She took a moment to look around the elegant space that contained a large bed, a dresser with a washstand, and a Tiffany lamp on the night table. The plush carpeting beneath her feet gave the room a definite feel of luxury. She sighed as she set her bag down, thankful Quinn had insisted she bring a small overnight case. From his experience with finding his brothers, he'd learned these matters weren't always settled as quickly as he hoped.

Julia removed her hat and set it on the dresser, fatigue suddenly weighing her down. She climbed onto the bed to rest for a minute, sinking into the comfy pillow and mattress. What a far cry from the horrid bed in Mr. Ketchum's building. She still couldn't believe how fortunate she was to have escaped her landlord's grasp. And all because of Quinn.

A loud rapping noise brought her out of sleep.

"Julia? Are you all right?" Quinn's deep voice sounded through her door.

"Y-yes. I'm fine. Sorry, I must have dozed off." She pushed off the bed, her head suddenly spinning. How had an hour passed so quickly? "Give me ten minutes and I'll be ready."

"No need to rush. I'll wait for you in the lobby."

Julia used the lavatory down the hall and washed her face and hands. Back in her room, she re-pinned her hair and smoothed out the wrinkles in her dress. She wished she had a better outfit, one more suited to eating in the dining room, but her day dress would have to do.

She picked up her handbag and the room key and went to find Quinn.

The lobby was abuzz with patrons, but Julia easily spotted him. He stood by the dining room entrance, posture erect, hands clasped behind him. Julia stifled a smile at his servant's stance, which must be second nature to him. Yet to her, it embodied a watchfulness and protection that made her feel safe.

She paused at the foot of the stairs, memories stirring of her and Amelia racing through the halls of Brentwood. Once, in trying to keep up with her cousin, Julia had slipped on a carpet that slid from under her, and she would have fallen if a certain valet hadn't caught her by the elbow and steadied her.

"Careful, miss. Those floors can be hazardous."

She remembered being breathless from her dash and looking into the handsome young man's face, his serious demeanor belied by the twinkle in his eye.

"Thank you." Her face had turned warm, and she'd hoped he thought it from the exertion of running, not from being flustered by his touch.

Now, as she caught Quinn's intense gaze on her, the same heat crept into her cheeks. She lifted her chin and headed toward him, chiding herself for her foolish fantasies. Back then, she'd been a silly girl, mooning over a servant, yet the same impossible class structure still remained. She laid a palm over her abdomen to remind herself of the other important reason why a romance with Quinn was simply not an option.

A far more insurmountable reason, to be sure.

Quinn looked up to see Julia coming toward him, and his pulse sprinted to life. Her cheeks bloomed with color, and her eyes glowed as brightly as the chandelier above them.

"Julia. You look lovely and well rested." He held out an elbow to escort her into the dining room. "I took the liberty of reserving us a table."

"Thank you. I think I could eat an entire roast right now."

Quinn laughed. "That I'd like to see."

The maître d' led them through the crowded room to their table, where Quinn pulled out a plush velvet chair for Julia. Each round table had a small lit candle in the center and a vase with a long-stemmed rose. White-and-gold china plates shone in the flickering light. Murmurs of intimate conversation and the clinking of silverware lingered in the air, punctuated every so often by a burst of laughter.

Julia opened the menu to scan the entrées. Trying to control his pulse rate, Quinn couldn't seem to focus on the words. He set the menu aside. "Your mention of roast beef has made me crave the prime rib," he said. "What do you fancy?"

She glanced up. "The fried chicken and mashed potatoes sounds delicious."

"Indeed. That was my second choice."

The waiter arrived to take their order and brought a basket of bread. As soon as he left, Julia lifted the napkin from the warm rolls. "Do you mind if I start on one of these?"

"Not at all. I'm glad you don't want to wait."

She passed him the basket with a shy smile.

It suddenly felt to Quinn like they were on a real date. Did she feel it too? Judging from the quick glances she was giving him and the way she kept biting her lip, Julia appeared somewhat nervous. Perhaps it would be better to keep the conversation casual, pretend as though the tension between them didn't exist. He certainly didn't want to make her uncomfortable.

"What do you miss most about England?" Quinn asked as he buttered a roll.

Her shoulders relaxed. "I suppose it would be the rain."

He laughed. "Really? You miss feeling soggy?"

"In a way, yes. I loved walking over the grounds at my uncle's estate in the rain. Seeing the green of the grass and the mist over the moors. Smelling the freshness in the air." Her features softened, her gaze far away.

Perhaps she was homesick after all. And perhaps Quinn could use this moment to remind her how perfect it would be for her to come back to England with him. "Ah yes. That's a smell I've yet to experience over here. And I do love the coziness of a fire in the hearth when it's raining."

"Me too."

"I miss good English home cooking, scones and cream, and the tea . . . It's just not the same here. I'll be glad to get back—"

"I know what you're doing," she said quietly. "You're trying to make me remember all the things I miss back home so I'll want to go with you."

He set his bread down, one brow quirking up. "Did I succeed?"

Her attempt to look annoyed failed when her lips twitched. "Almost."

He laughed out loud. "I'm warning you now, Miss Holloway, I intend to keep pestering you until you buy that ticket."

She ducked her head, avoiding his eyes.

Why did he get the feeling something had changed? Up to this point, he'd believed that money was the sole issue keeping her here, but now he sensed something else was amiss.

The waiter arrived with their food, ending the conversation. Perhaps it was just as well. He didn't want to push too hard. Best to change the topic. "Tell me about your parents. What was your life like before you came to Brentwood?"

She swallowed a forkful of mashed potatoes and took a quick sip of water.

"Only if you don't mind talking about it," he said, suddenly aware that perhaps it was too painful a subject.

But she shook her head. "I don't mind. I had a lovely childhood. Being an only child, I was spoiled, of course. Especially by Daddy."

"I'm sure you were. Quite a different experience from our house with four children." He dug into the prime rib, savoring the tender meat that fairly melted on his tongue.

"I would have envied your family. I used to pray for a brother or sister." Julia attacked the chicken like she'd been deprived of food for several weeks, then patted a napkin to her mouth. "I noticed there's a sizable age difference between you and your siblings. Were you very close with them despite being older?"

"As close as possible given the circumstances. Becky was only ten when I left home to seek employment after our father died. I sometimes wonder how different things might have been if my dad had lived." A wistful feeling filled his chest. "I'm sure I would have been more involved in their lives."

"It sounds like you did your best to keep in touch."

"I did what I could." Quinn lowered his fork. "I still can't help but wonder why Mum never told me how dire her situation had become. If she had, I could have figured out some way to get more money."

Julia reached over to pat his arm. "Don't you think it's time you let go of the guilt?"

"Perhaps." He sat back, his stomach suddenly in knots. "I keep thinking if I can get Becky and the boys back home, I might finally be able to put the past behind me, once and for all."

"I truly hope so. You deserve to have peace of mind after all you've been through."

In that instant, with her gazing at him with those expressive brown eyes as if he were some type of hero, Quinn dared to hope he could achieve everything he desired.

A waiter came by to refill their water glasses, and Quinn focused on his meal, pleased to see Julia seemed to be enjoying her food as well. As they continued eating, the conversation turned to less emotional territory, which allowed Quinn to relax.

At last, Julia sat back with a contented sigh and laid her napkin over her plate. "That was delicious."

"You must have been starving. You ate every bite."

Her cheeks turned pink. "I hope I didn't embarrass you. My aunt always scolded me for eating too much whenever we were in public. She made Amelia and me eat before we went out to any of the balls."

"Don't be silly. I'm glad you enjoyed it."

The waiter appeared again. "May I clear your dishes?"

"Yes, of course." Julia moved to one side to allow him access.

"Would you care for any dessert, miss?"

"No, thank you," she answered a bit too quickly.

Quinn frowned. He'd seen her eying their neighbor's dessert earlier. Was she concerned about him spending more money on her? "I would love a slice of chocolate cake," he said. If memory served from his time at Brentwood, chocolate used to be one of Julia's favorites.

"Very good, sir."

"Oh, and could I trouble you to bring two forks?" He winked at Julia. "I think I might have to share."

Harriet untied her apron with a heavy sigh and hung it on the hook in the kitchen. She looked around the room, and once she was satisfied that everything was ready for Mrs. Teeter in the morning, she glanced at the clock on the wall. Eight thirty. Would young Harry be asleep, or would he be lying awake, lonely in a strange house with Julia gone?

She took a jug of milk out of the icebox and poured a small glass. Then she lifted the cookie tin from an upper shelf, picked out two gingersnaps, and wrapped them in a napkin. She would check on the lad and make sure he wasn't in too much pain. If he was asleep, she'd leave the treat on his night table for when he woke.

After climbing the staircase, she paused outside his room on the third floor and knocked softly on the door. When there was no reply, she opened it and peered inside.

The lamp on the night table illuminated the room with a soft glow. Harry lay against the pillows, his eyes shut, the lashes creating dark shadows on his cheek.

Her throat tightened at the sight. Such a beautiful boy. One who deserved to be safe and loved, not beaten and abused. She swallowed hard and walked quietly to the bedside, searching his face for any sign of pain. Faint lines creased his forehead, and the skin around his eyes was taut, not exactly relaxed.

She set the glass and the cookies on the table, then took a seat on a chair in the corner. Somehow the thought of going to her quarters on the first floor, so far away from the child who might need her in the middle of the night, didn't sit well. Even though Mabel had offered to stay on the third floor while Julia was away and had moved two doors down, the lad didn't know her very well. Harriet would stay here a spell until she was certain he would be all right.

A moan woke her some time later. She jerked awake and blinked, rubbing at the stiffness in her neck.

Harry was thrashing about under the covers.

She rushed to his side, laying a hand on his shoulder.

A scream erupted from the boy, and he curled into a tight ball.

"It's all right, Harry," she said. "You're having a bad dream."

But the boy didn't move, except for the trembling of his body under the sheets.

Shock flooded her system. The child was terrified—*of her*.

"Harry, love. It's Mrs. Chamberlain. You're safe here. No one is going to hurt you, I promise."

Harry kept his eyes shut tight, his breathing erratic.

"I brought you some milk and cookies in case you were hungry. Or in case you couldn't sleep. I know it often helps me." She kept her voice at a near croon, like she was trying to coax an anxious kitten out from hiding. "Are you in pain, dear? Can I do anything for you?"

Please, Lord, let him trust me. Help him to know I mean him no harm.

The bedclothes shifted, and one eye opened. "Mrs. C.?"

"Yes, love. You're at my boardinghouse, remember?"

The lines in his forehead disappeared, and he moved the blanket farther down. "I was dreaming that I was back at the farm. Hiding from Mr. Wolfe . . . but he found me." His voice was a mere whisper.

"Well, you're not at the farm. You're safe and sound here."

He studied her. "Did you say there were cookies?"

Harriet chuckled. "I did indeed. Do you like gingersnaps?"

Harry grimaced slightly as he sat up. "I love them."

"Good." She handed him the napkin and helped him unwrap the treat. He took a large bite and smiled.

She sat back down, waiting patiently as he ate both cookies and drained the glass of milk. When he'd finished, she took the napkin from him. "I hope you can sleep better now, dear, with no bad dreams to trouble you." She couldn't resist reaching out to rest a hand on his tousled hair.

He looked up at her with serious eyes. "Mrs. C., are you sure I don't have to go back to the farm when I'm better?" He bit his bottom lip, frowning.

Harriet clenched her teeth together, working to contain her emotions before she spoke. "No, lad. You never have to go back there again. Your brother is making sure of that."

A slow smile emerged. "Quinn's going to look after me now?"

"I'd bet my last shilling on it." She pressed a kiss to the top of his head. "Now, try to get some rest. If you're feeling better tomorrow, I'll teach you a card game I think you might like."

He lay back against the pillows. "Good night, Mrs. C."

"Good night, Harry. Would you like the lamp on or off?"

"On, please. If that's all right."

"Of course it is. And Mabel is right down the hall if you need anything."

"Mrs. C.?"

She paused at the door. "Yes, dear?"

"I wish I had a grandmother like you."

Harriet squeezed the door handle, unable to say a word. At last, she summoned a smile. "Good night, love. Sweet dreams."

And as she closed the door behind her, Harriet felt in her very bones that God had brought this boy to her for a purpose. A purpose she was determined to figure out, no matter how hard it was to face the truth.

The dining room gradually emptied until only one other couple remained at the far end of the restaurant. Julia couldn't remember when she'd had a more wonderful time.

When they couldn't extend their meal any longer, Quinn paid the bill and escorted Julia up the main staircase. As they approached their rooms, Julia's palms grew damp, her heart beating a strange rhythm. Sharing the cake with Quinn had been a very intimate experience, leading her imagination down a path she had no business traveling.

At one point, when the waiters were nowhere near, he'd reached over with his thumb and wiped some chocolate icing from the corner of her mouth. His hand had lingered against her cheek, and his eyes had darkened in intensity, robbing Julia of air. In that instant, she'd gotten the distinct impression that Quinn wanted to kiss her, and to her shock, she realized she would have let him.

Now as they approached their rooms, Julia's nerves tingled with awareness. The brush of his leg against hers, the tightening of his arm muscles beneath her hand, the heated glances he kept giving her all combined to throw her off balance.

This attraction, although thrilling, could prove dangerous and was not something she could afford to pursue. She had to remember he was her uncle's servant and she a fallen woman.

Yet, despite every warning bell in her head, she couldn't deny the longing to experience the thrill of his kiss. Just once.

They came to a stop at her door.

Quinn smiled at her. "Thank you for having dinner with me," he said. "I enjoyed our time together very much."

"As did I. It's been a long time since I've had such a fine meal—with such fine company. Thank you, Quinn."

He took her hand. "If I had the means, I'd give you everything you ever wanted, just to watch your face light up." He raised her hand to his lips, his gaze never wavering.

Julia's pulse rate grew rapid, her breathing shallow. She couldn't seem to tear her eyes from his.

Then slowly he moved toward her. "Julia." Her name was a

whispered caress against her cheek. "Do you know how beautiful you are?"

She shook her head, afraid to break the spell he'd cast. Afraid he would kiss her, yet terrified that he wouldn't. When he slowly lowered his mouth to hers, her lids fluttered closed on a sigh. He tasted of chocolate and cream. His arms came around her, pulling her against his chest, where she could feel his heart beating wildly beneath her palm.

As his kiss grew more intense, the blood surged in her veins. She couldn't seem to feel her legs, as though her feet had left the carpeted floor. She was floating, weightless, with only Quinn's lips keeping her from drifting away.

Then, abruptly, he broke the embrace and stepped back, allowing a rush of cool air between them. "Forgive me, Julia. I should never have presumed to take liberties with you."

She blinked. "You did no such thing."

He scrubbed a hand over his face. "Then why does it feel like I've committed a crime?"

A crime?

She winced. "Because you can't forget our social positions. Despite our change in circumstances, it still feels . . . forbidden."

The lines on his forehead eased. "Exactly."

"We're not in England now," she said softly. "In this country, those types of social restrictions don't exist—at least not that I can tell."

Quinn shook his head. "Your uncle is still my employer. He wouldn't look kindly on this." He sighed. "It's probably best not to start something we can't continue."

In the aftermath of his kiss, she wanted to argue with him, tell him it didn't matter what her uncle thought, but in truth, Quinn was right. Despite their attraction, a relationship between them simply wasn't feasible. Soon Quinn would be headed back to England, and she would be staying here to give birth to her child. A life-changing event that would force her to make some serious decisions about her future.

"You're right, as usual. We should forget this ever happened." She swallowed a rise of disappointment that threatened to choke her. "Good night, Quinn."

"Good night, Julia. Sleep well." And with a last sorrowful smile, he walked away.

CHAPTER 17

At precisely one o'clock the next afternoon, Quinn helped Julia out of a cab in front of the Sebrings' house—though *house* was not an entirely appropriate word for the building in front of him.

He stood for a moment to take in the sheer magnificence of the property. Other than Brentwood, Quinn had never seen the likes of it. Three stories of whitewashed walls rose above them, punctuated by black-shuttered windows and framed by an ornate iron fence that surrounded the perimeter. Tall white columns guarded the impressive double-door entrance.

Was Becky really living in such luxury?

Quinn couldn't help comparing this place to Harry's bed of straw in the Wolfe barn. How vastly different his siblings' experiences were. He could only be grateful Becky had fallen into such good fortune. At least one of his siblings had come out ahead. Or so it appeared. As long as this outer luxury wasn't masking other evils within.

He took a moment to picture his younger sister as he had last seen her, her reddish-brown hair in two plaits, a white pinafore over her cotton dress. She'd had tears streaking her freckled cheeks as she clung to Quinn's waist, begging him not to leave, ripping his already-breaking heart in two. It had been Mum who finally pried her loose. Becky had buried her face in Mum's apron, while

Cecil had shaken Quinn's hand. Harry's bottom lip had quivered as he tried desperately to imitate both his older brothers' stoicism.

Julia nudged Quinn's arm. "Come on. They'll be waiting."

"Right." He tugged his jacket into place.

"Are you sure you don't want to visit with Becky alone? I don't mind waiting out here."

He took her hand in his. "I'm delighted to have you with me. You steady me, Julia. Without you, I'm likely to do something daft, like kidnap my sister."

She stifled a laugh. "Okay, then. I'll make sure you don't give in to any mad impulses."

"Thank you." He was glad that despite the blunder he'd made kissing her last night, they'd managed to avoid any awkwardness today. Yet, try as he might, he couldn't help reliving the intensity of their embrace, the exquisite softness of her lips, the rightness of her in his arms.

They walked up the flagstone path to the grand front doors, which were painted a deep red and sported an inlay of stained glass.

A woman in uniform answered Quinn's knock. "Please, come in," she said once they introduced themselves. "Mrs. Sebring apologizes that she's not here to meet you, as Thursday is her afternoon for tea at the bridge club. Rebecca is waiting in the parlor for you."

"Thank you." Quinn rubbed his hands together, his throat suddenly dry. How would this reunion with his sister go? Would it be as strained as the one with Cecil, or would Becky be happy to see him? Eager to come home with him?

"Quinn? Is it really you?"

A young woman appeared in the hall. She wore her now-chestnut hair in a soft puff on top of her head with a few loose tendrils framing her face. How different she looked from the wisp of a girl he'd left behind in their one-room flat in London. This woman, in her tidy white blouse and navy skirt, was tall and comely, her green eyes and freckles the only features he remembered.

"Becca?" His childhood name for her slipped out as he stared at her.

With a sob, she flew toward him and threw herself into his arms. "I can't believe you're here. I thought I'd never see you again." She buried her face in the wool of his jacket, her body shaking with the force of her emotion.

Quinn tightened his arms around her and just breathed. *Thank you, Lord.* The stranglehold of fear that had held his heart hostage for so long loosened its tenacious grip. His three siblings were alive and well, doing the best they could. How he would eventually get them all back to England was a problem that could wait for another day. Right now, he simply wanted to enjoy getting to know his sister again.

At last, Becky moved away to blow her nose, then smiled up at him. "You look as handsome as ever." Her gaze moved past him to Julia. "Who is this? Your wife?"

Heat streaked into Quinn's face. "This is a good friend, Julia Holloway. Julia, this is my sister, Becky."

Julia moved forward to grasp Becky's hand. "It's lovely to meet you. Quinn has told me so much about you."

Becky's brows rose. "He has?"

"Yes . . ." Julia trailed off and bit her lip.

"Just how long have you known my brother?" A mischievous twinkle lit Becky's green eyes, a look Quinn remembered all too well from their childhood, which usually resulted in one of them getting their ears boxed by Mum.

Quinn stepped forward to take Becky's arm and steer her toward the nearest room, hoping it was the parlor. "I met Julia at Brentwood Manor when she was only thirteen, but we've only recently renewed our . . . acquaintance." He let it go at that for the moment. Most likely Becky would assume Julia was a maid at the estate, which was fine by him. No need to explain their complicated history.

He scanned the room with its elegant sofas, wing chairs, and a marble fireplace. A silver tea service, a large pitcher, and an array of small pastries sat on a low table.

"Please sit down," Becky said. "Mrs. Sebring ordered refreshments for your arrival." She lifted the teapot. "Would you like tea or prefer lemonade?" The subtle trembling of her hands betrayed her nerves.

"I'd love some lemonade," Julia said brightly.

Quinn frowned. "It's all right, Becky. You don't have to serve us." Perhaps her situation wasn't as rosy as she'd like him to believe. "Is everything going well? Are you being treated fairly?"

Immediately her face brightened. "Oh yes. The Sebrings are lovely to work for."

"That's good to hear." Quinn rose to pour his own drink.

Becky handed Julia a glass. "So what are you doing in Canada, Quinn? The last I heard you were set to join the war."

He straightened, cup in hand. A warning look from Julia made him bite back his immediate response. "I did serve in the war, and thankfully survived with only minor injuries." He crossed the room to his chair but remained standing. "When I went to see Mum after I got back, she finally admitted she'd sent the three of you to Dr. Barnardo's Homes."

Becky's gaze faltered, settling on the table in front of her. "She had to, Quinn," she said. "We had nothing to eat, no heat in the flat. When we were evicted, Mum didn't know what else to do. She thought we'd be better off in a place with a warm bed for each of us and three meals a day." Becky sighed. "She promised she'd come get us once her situation turned around, but I guess it never did."

Quinn set his cup down, his stomach too tense to tolerate anything in it. "You must have been terrified when they said you were being sent to Canada."

"Not terrified. Anxious, maybe. Part of me looked forward to traveling, to seeing another part of the world. Cecil and Harry thought it would be exciting." She smiled sadly. "Cecil even pretended he was going off to war, like you."

Quinn flinched, not wanting to envision them boarding the ship, filled with a desperate hope for a better future. "Did you even get to say good-bye to Mum?"

"No. They said there wasn't time since the boat was leaving

soon." Her bottom lip trembled. "We tried to make it a grand adventure."

"But it wasn't so grand, was it?"

"No." She smoothed her skirt down with jerky movements of her fingers.

Quinn came to sit beside her and took her hand in his. "I understand you left your first placement. Did they hurt you, Becca?"

A world of pain came into her eyes, swirling amid the tears that bloomed. But she shook her head and pulled her hand away. "That's over now, and I'm happy here. Let's leave it at that." Becky looked over at Julia, then back to Quinn. "I still don't understand why the two of you are here."

He frowned. "I came to find you, Cecil, and Harry and bring you home. Why else would I be here?"

A variety of emotions flitted across her features. "Did you find our brothers? I haven't seen them since I left Halifax five years ago." She blinked rapidly, still holding back tears.

"Yes, I found them." Quinn rose from the sofa and walked to the fireplace, contemplating his next words. He didn't want to ruin their visit with the brutal truth of Harry's situation. "Cecil seems content on the farm where he's working, and Harry . . . well, Harry wasn't as happy with his post, so he came with me." He turned back to face her. "He's staying with some people I know in Toronto while I'm here."

"Is he all right?" Lines creased Becky's forehead. "I hated leaving him, even though Cecil was with him. He was so little and so scared." She swiped at a tear on her cheek.

"He's fine now that I've got him away from that farmer." He focused his attention directly on his sister, needing her to know how important his next words were. "The thing is, Becky, Mum's not doing so well. She's in the infirmary at the workhouse and very weak. I promised her I'd bring you and the boys back home with me. It might be the only thing that saves her."

Becky lowered her head, avoiding Quinn's eyes, and his stomach dropped. He thought she'd be eager to leave, overjoyed to be going home. But from the expression on her face, he wasn't at all sure of her response.

"You will come with me, won't you?"

She twisted her hands together on her lap. "I suppose I could ask for some time off to go back for a visit."

"A visit?" Quinn surged forward. "You mean you want to come back to live here? So far away from your home and your family?"

Becky looked up at him sorrowfully. "My home is in Canada now, Quinn. The only thing waiting in England is more poverty, more suffering. At least here I have a good position and a lovely home to live in."

"You're only a servant to these people," he said, unable to stop his voice from rising. It was one thing for him to be a valet, but he wanted better for his sister.

"Quinn." Julia crossed the room to his side. "Give Becky a chance to explain herself."

Quinn took in a breath and nodded.

"Go ahead, Becky," Julia prompted gently.

"The Sebrings have treated me like one of the family. They pay me more than my contract stipulates and they don't overwork me." She glanced at Quinn.

"All right," he said slowly. "So your employers are nice, and you've grown . . . fond of them?"

"Yes." Her features brightened. "I truly love my job here. I doubt I'd ever find one I like better back in London."

Quinn fought the anger rising in his chest. How could she so blithely turn her back on her family and her homeland? More importantly, didn't she care that their mother might be dying? "How can you do this to Mum?" he bit out.

Becky jumped to her feet, twisting her hands in front of her. "Quinn, please try to understand. . . ." She pressed her lips together. "There's something else. A more important reason I want to stay."

He stared at her, shaking his head. "What else could keep you from your family?" He hated the bitterness in his voice and the way Becky's eyes shone with hurt.

"Rebecca? Is everything all right?" a deep voice asked.

Quinn turned to face the door, where a slim young man stood in the opening, his face filled with concern.

Becky rushed forward. "Ned. Yes, everything's fine. Please, come in."

He grasped her hand and tucked it under the crook of his arm, smiling down at her. At the adoring look she gave him in return, it all made sudden sense. Becky had a beau.

The pair moved into the middle of the room, Becky hanging on the man's arm like he were a life preserver amid a stormy sea.

Quinn looked over at Julia, who gave a slight shrug.

"Quinn, Julia, this is Ned Patterson," Becky said. "Ned, this is my brother Quinn and his friend Julia."

Ned stepped forward, his hand outstretched. "It's a pleasure to meet you, sir. I'm so happy Rebecca has made contact with her family at last." He pumped Quinn's hand eagerly.

Quinn assessed the lad with what he hoped was an objective opinion. Ned was appealing enough, with thick brown hair, blue eyes, and an easy smile. Though wiry in stature, he appeared well-muscled, as if no stranger to hard work. "Nice to meet you, Ned. Do you work for the Sebrings as well?"

Ned frowned slightly and gave Becky a questioning look.

"I haven't had a chance to tell them yet," Becky said quickly, her cheeks reddening. She wound her arm more firmly through Ned's and tilted her chin. "Ned is my fiancé. We're getting married in September."

CHAPTER 18

Julia held back a gasp at Becky's bold declaration and immediately glanced over at Quinn. The look of shock on his face mingled with an expression of hurt.

Oh, Quinn. You certainly didn't expect this.

Julia stepped toward the couple. "Please accept my congratulations," she said a bit too brightly in a vain attempt to ease the tension.

"Thank you," Becky responded with a wary smile. "We're very excited."

Beside her, Ned beamed. "I'm a lucky man." He turned to Quinn. "I want you to know, sir, that I love Rebecca very much and will do everything in my power to give her a good life."

Quinn just shook his head, his eyes taking on a hint of panic. He raked his fingers through his hair as he paced away from them.

Julia's muscles stiffened in anticipation of Quinn's next actions.

He whirled back around, color high in his cheeks. "Becca, you're not even eighteen yet. What is the confounded rush to marry?"

Becky blinked and clung harder to Ned. "We love each other and want to be together. Besides, I'll be eighteen next month, and my contract will be completed."

Ned shifted his weight. "I've been saving for a place of our own for a while now, and I should have enough by the fall." He smiled down at Becky. "We'll have our own little chicken farm. Maybe a cow and a horse too." He focused back on Quinn. "Over time, I hope to be able to expand, and then—"

"Is this what you really want, Becky? To be a farmer's wife?" Quinn waved a hand around the room. "To go from living in a fine house like this to tending chickens?"

Julia cringed. Did he realize how insulting he sounded?

Becky lifted her chin. "I'd trade this lifestyle in a minute to be Ned's wife." She moved toward her brother. "It's all I've wanted for a long time now."

Quinn's shoulders sagged then, as though realizing he'd lost a battle. The light in his eyes faded, and he turned away from the happy couple.

Julia's heart went out to him, sensing his keen disappointment like it was her own. He'd traveled so far with one goal in mind, and at every turn, his efforts were thwarted.

"Why don't we sit down and talk? You could tell us how you met." Julia forced a smile as she took a seat in a wing chair.

Becky and Ned moved to sit on the sofa, but Quinn remained standing by the fireplace.

"Ned worked on the first farm where I was sent." Becky's features softened. "He rescued me from a bad situation there. Brought me back to Hazelbrae. I don't know what would've happened to me if it weren't for him."

The younger man's ears reddened. "I only did what any decent person would." He raised Becky's hand to his lips. "I'm just grateful to God for bringing Rebecca into my life."

"And I thank God every night for you," Becky said softly.

Ned bent and dropped a kiss on her lips.

Julia's throat tightened. How would it feel to have the love of such an upstanding man? Against her will, her gaze captured Quinn's profile as he stared into the fireplace. His jaw was taut, his forehead tense.

Perhaps she could salvage something of this meeting for Quinn's sake. Julia leaned toward the couple, then turned to Ned. "Right before you arrived," she said, "Quinn was telling Becky that their mother's health is failing and how he hoped to take Becky and his brothers home to see her. Becky thought she might get away for a bit of a holiday."

Quinn shot her an unhappy look over his shoulder. Julia raised a brow in silent warning. If a quick visit was all Becky could manage, he might have to accept that it was better than nothing.

Becky frowned and turned to her fiancé. "What do you think, Ned?"

Ned's forehead furrowed. "Will the Sebrings allow you to go?"

"I think so. They mentioned they would give me some time off if I ever needed it. Besides, my contract will soon be over."

"And the money for your passage?"

"I'll take care of that," Quinn added quickly, coming to join them.

"When would you be leaving?" Ned put an arm around Becky, as if wanting to keep her by his side, the mere thought of her leaving unbearable.

"As soon as I can get everyone together." Quinn ran a hand over his jaw. "Cecil is resisting the idea. Harry needs more time to regain his strength, but maybe three weeks from now we'd be ready."

Becky exchanged a meaningful look with her fiancé, then turned to Quinn. "I'll give it serious consideration. Let me speak with the Sebrings and I'll get back to you. I promise."

Quinn hesitated, then at last he nodded. "I suppose that will have to do."

"Do you have a telephone here?" Julia asked.

"Yes, of course," Becky said. "Let me write down the number for you." She rose and walked to a nearby table.

"We'll give you a call next week," Julia said when Quinn didn't add anything. "Maybe by then we'll all be in a better place to make some definite plans."

Becky came back with a pencil and paper. "Are you going back to England too, Julia?"

Julia's stomach clenched, suddenly realizing her error. She hadn't meant to give Becky the impression she would be joining them, and she certainly hadn't planned to let Quinn in on her decision just yet.

Quinn was looking at her now with such a hopeful expression that she couldn't meet his gaze. "My plans are somewhat . . . tentative at the moment. I had been considering accompanying Quinn home so I could visit my uncle." She paused. "However, I'm about to start a new job and fear the timing isn't right."

Quinn's eyes narrowed, his mouth a tight line.

Becky handed Julia the paper. "Well, as you said, we'll see how things stand in a week or two." She gave a strained smile. "In the meantime, if you tell me where I can reach Mum, I'll write her a letter and tell her about my engagement. Maybe that will give her a lift."

"Wouldn't it be wonderful," Ned said, "if your mother regained her health and could make the trip here to attend the wedding?"

"It would, though it doesn't sound too likely." Becky's half-hearted response belied her words.

Julia tucked the phone number into her pocket. What was the issue between the girl and her mother? It was obvious she wasn't excited about going home to see her or for her mother to come here. Perhaps Becky resented Mrs. Aspinall for putting them into the orphanage.

Becky rose from the sofa and smoothed her skirt. "It's been so good to see you, Quinn. It's like having a taste of home right here." She clasped her hands together. "But I promised Ned I'd go into town with him today."

Quinn strode across the carpet, his expression thunderous. "I thought you were spending the afternoon with me." His scowling demeanor didn't fool Julia. Hurt swirled in the depths of his eyes. Yet how could he not understand that Becky was in love and that matters of the heart overruled everything else? Even a brother she hadn't seen in years.

"I . . . I'm sorry, Quinn," Becky said softly, "but there's really not much more to say for now, is there?"

At the defeated look on his face, Julia wanted to wrap him in a hug and tell him everything would work out.

Instead she rose and held out her hand to Becky. "It was lovely to meet you, Becky. And you as well, Ned. I hope to see you again."

Then she walked out into the hall to give Quinn a moment to say his good-byes, praying she could find the right words to comfort him on the train ride home.

Harriet attempted to ignore the arthritic pain attacking her knees in spite of the padding on the church kneeler. Granted, the kneelers probably weren't meant for hours of use without moving. But Harriet was determined not to leave until the good Lord provided her with some sort of answer, or at the very least, some small measure of peace.

Ever since Quinten had come into her life, Harriet had been plagued by events from her past. Emotions she'd thought safely tucked away had once again risen to the surface, refusing to stay buried. Now with young Harry staying under her roof, the demons within were becoming even harder to quiet.

God must have a reason for bringing this family to her. If only she could figure out why, perhaps she could resume her peaceful life.

She squeezed her eyes shut, but nothing blotted out the image of Harry's battered body from her mind. The angry bruises, the swollen rib cage. What twelve-year-old boy deserved that?

And for that matter, what fifteen-year-old girl deserved to feel desperate enough to take her own life?

"Harriet?" A booming voice echoed over the silence of the space.

Her eyes flew open.

Geoffrey crossed in front of the altar, concern radiating from his face.

She blinked and only then realized her cheeks were wet.

"Is everything all right?" He stopped in front of her pew.

With a nod, she swiped the back of her hand across her cheeks. "I guess I got carried away with some overly zealous praying." She held out a hand. "Help me up, will you? I think my knees are fused to this bench."

He came into the pew and gently assisted her to her feet. "How long have you been here?" he asked.

"I don't really know. I've lost track of the time. An hour or two maybe."

"Then I think you'd better come with me, young lady." He took her hand and steered her toward the hall beyond the sanctuary that led to his office.

"Young lady?" she huffed. "I think you need your prescription glasses changed."

He laughed but held her hand tighter.

In his office, the lamp on his desk sent a yellow glow over a pile of papers and books. Obviously, he'd been in the middle of something, likely writing his sermon for Sunday.

"I don't want to interrupt your work," she said. "I'll just head home."

"Not before a conversation. Now sit." He pointed to the chair across from the desk.

Because her knees still ached and her legs were shaky, she obeyed. For once without argument.

Instead of going behind the desk, Geoffrey dragged a chair over beside her. He sat down and took her hand in his. "Now, tell me what has you so rattled."

"What makes you say—"

"I've known you for almost thirty years, and I can count on one hand the number of times you've come to the church midweek. Never mind that you were here praying nonstop for hours."

She looked away from his probing gaze. How could she begin to describe the ghosts that haunted her? She took in a shuddering breath. "I . . . I don't know where to start."

"Does this have anything to do with Quinten and his brother?"

She sniffed, and Geoffrey passed her a handkerchief. How did the man always seem to know her thoughts? "I suppose it does."

He sat quietly, waiting for her to elaborate. Silence was one of his best tools to get people to open up.

Finally, she released a long breath. "You should see the bruises on wee Harry's body. To think a grown man took out his anger on a boy in such a vile manner . . . The brute should be behind bars."

"I agree," he said solemnly. "No one has the right to hurt a child." He paused. "Is that what you were praying about?"

"If you must know, I was asking the Lord to take away this dreadful resentment. This unsettled feeling I can't shake since—well, since Quinten started talking about Dr. Barnardo's Homes and Hazelbrae."

"Seems he's brought a lot of unresolved anger to the surface."

"Not just anger." Her voice faded to a whisper. "Horrible, debilitating guilt."

His brows rose above his glasses. "What do you feel guilty about?"

"About staying silent all these years." She shuddered. "I never did anything after Annie died. What if I'd fought to have the man who abused her brought to justice? Or at least told someone about the type of exploitation we endured? Maybe it would have stopped the mistreatment. Maybe children like Harry wouldn't still be suffering today." More tears brimmed her lashes.

"Harriet, you can't take the blame for everything that's gone on in the organization for the past forty years." He squeezed her hand.

She shook her head. "I was a coward, Geoffrey. Plain and simple. After Annie's death, I kept quiet, too afraid that if I made a fuss, I'd be punished as severely as she was."

"No one would have believed the word of a twelve-year-old girl, Harriet."

"But what about later? When I was older? I could have gone back as an adult and made sure the conditions were better." She rose from the chair and walked to the small window overlooking the church grounds. "Instead, I buried my head in the sand. Eased my conscience by telling myself I was helping other immigrants with the Newcomers Program." Her voice became shrill. "And all along, little children were dying."

"And you think you could have single-handedly changed that?" He came up behind her. "Even you, my dear Harriet, are not that formidable." The gentle weight of his hand on her shoulder brought her a measure of calm.

"I don't think I can remain silent any longer." She turned to look at him. "I have to do something, but I'm not sure where to begin."

Geoffrey stroked his chin. "We could start by paying a visit to the director of the boys' home. There's a chance the man isn't aware of the true extent of what's going on."

"We?"

He smiled. "You don't think I'd let you take on the establishment by yourself, do you? Besides, having a member of the clergy with you might strengthen your claim."

Her throat tightened. This man had been her ally and best friend for so long now. Never once had he let her down, always by her side when she needed him. And now he was willing to go into battle with some potential hard-necked bureaucrats for her.

She leaned over to kiss his cheek. "Thank you, Geoffrey. That means a great deal to me. Perhaps bringing this issue to light will lay my demons to rest once and for all."

"I'd slay any demon for you, Harriet." And with that, he pulled her closer and kissed her on the lips.

For a split second, she froze, the air stalling in her lungs. Had he meant to kiss her cheek and missed?

Then, before she could react, he stepped back. But instead of seeming embarrassed, he searched her face, his expression earnest. "I've wanted to do that for a long time now," he said softly. "I hope I haven't shocked you."

"As a matter of fact, you have." She couldn't stop the heat from rising in her cheeks. Because as much as he surprised her, it wasn't exactly an unwelcome development. One she'd daydreamed about lately, although she wasn't quite sure why.

He brushed a finger down her cheek. "Don't you think it's time we took our friendship—our very long friendship—to the next logical step?"

She shook her head. "I don't know. I rather like our relationship as it is. What if a romance ruins everything?" She was still a coward, no two ways about it. "I couldn't take losing you. . . ." Her voice quavered.

Geoffrey enfolded her hand in his. "That will never happen. No matter what, you're stuck with me."

She attempted a smile, but the cold ball of fear in her belly would not dissolve.

He patted her hand and rose. "No pressure, my dear. In the meantime, let's put a call in to Dr. Barnardo's."

Her shoulders slumped with relief at the reprieve. "Yes, let's do that."

CHAPTER 19

Quinn leaned his head back against the seat of the train and closed his eyes. What a colossal disaster this day had been. Instead of coming closer to fruition, his dream of reuniting his family was growing dimmer by the moment.

First Cecil, now Becky.

It was clear his sister had no desire to return to England. Her promise to see if she could get time off was likely a stalling tactic. Did she care so little about their mother's health that she wouldn't at least try to help?

He blew out a long breath, trying to rid himself of the frustration building within him.

And then there was Julia. She'd let it slip that she probably wasn't coming with him either. He should be furious with her for misleading him—whether by accident or on purpose he didn't know. But he was more hurt than angry. He thought they'd been growing closer and that their mutual attraction might tip the balance in his favor—no matter what he'd said last night about their not being able to be together.

Now he'd lose the opportunity to obtain his own piece of land and a home of his own. But really, what did it matter if there was no family left to live there? Quinn might as well keep his position as the earl's valet and his room in the servants' quarters. However, if he didn't find somewhere else to live, a place where his mother could stay also, she would have to remain in the workhouse. And where would Harry go? Quinn couldn't subject him to his mother's horrid living conditions. The workhouse might even be worse than the Wolfe farm.

Quinn fingered the key in his pocket, trying not to let the weight of his disappointment crush him. Trying not to imagine what his father would think of him now. The man certainly would be disillusioned with Quinn for failing to keep his promise.

For failing his family and failing himself.

What had made Quinn think he could sail to Canada, round up his siblings like a flock of sheep, and herd them back to England without so much as a bleat of protest?

He was an idiot, clinging to a dream for the future that clearly no one else desired but him.

Movement stirred the air around him. He opened his eyes.

Julia had crossed to sit on the seat beside him. "I can tell by the wrinkles on your forehead that you're not asleep."

He shrugged. "My mind's too agitated to sleep."

"Try not to worry," she said. "Everything will work out in time. I know it will."

"How can you say that?" Bitterness burned on Quinn's tongue. "I was a fool to think Becky would jump at the chance to return home and help care for our mother. How could I have been so wrong? About her? About Cecil? And about . . ." *About you?*

"About what?" she prompted.

"Just . . . everything." He turned to stare blindly out the window, barely noticing the landscape that whizzed past them.

"You mustn't lose hope now." Julia's slim fingers wrapped around his hand. "This quest has been a huge undertaking. Can't you simply be happy for the progress you've made so far?"

Warmth spread up his arm. Could she feel the jump of his pulse at his wrist? He summoned the courage to look at her, only to find her brown eyes beseeching him.

"Think about it," she continued. "You could have come all this way and never found any of your siblings. Or you could have learned they had died. At least you've found them and know they're all right." Moisture swam in her eyes. "That qualifies as a miracle in my book."

Quinn swallowed hard and looked away, afraid she'd see too much. She was so good, so kind. Always believing the best in everyone. Believing that every circumstance, no matter how horrible, had a hidden blessing.

"Did you ever plan to come back to England with me?" he asked at last. "Or did you only say that to keep me from hounding you?"

She removed her hand from his with a soft sigh. "For a while, it was a lovely dream to imagine returning to my former life. However, I've come to realize my future is here now."

He stiffened against the seat as the train rounded a bend. "But your uncle wants you back. You could live with him and your aunt and cousin indefinitely. Do whatever you wish with no worries about money or how to survive."

"That's not entirely true." Her brow puckered. "Uncle Howard would have certain expectations if I returned. He'd want me to jump back into society, attend all the balls and galas, the boring ladies' teas. And he'd continue to try to pick out a suitable husband for me." She shook her head. "I was silly to even entertain the idea."

"Is your independence so important that you'd rather live in a country where you don't know anyone? So important you'd cut all ties with your family?"

A pained expression darkened her features. "I'm not the first person to move far from home, Quinn. It happens all the time. And the reality remains that I lost my true family a long time ago." She let out a shaky breath. "Don't think I'm not grateful to Uncle Howard for taking me in. But I need to live my own life now. One he wouldn't approve of."

Quinn shook his head, exasperation leeching through him. "I still don't understand. What exactly won't he approve of?"

She bit her lip and looked down at her lap. "For one thing, he wouldn't agree to my pursuing a career. He deems working for a living beneath his family. And any future husband Uncle Howard would choose for me would be of the same mindset. Here . . . well, there's a freedom I wouldn't have at Brentwood."

Quinn held back a snort. Freedom was a wonderful concept in theory, but was anyone ever truly free? Quinn hadn't known freedom since the day his father died and he'd been clamped with the shackles of responsibility. He supposed it might almost be worth leaving one's family behind for a taste of such liberty. However, he could never imagine walking away. And he could never abandon his mother or any of his siblings for his own sake.

"I'm sorry, Quinn," Julia said. "I never intended to mislead you. You made me begin to believe I could go home again." She sighed. "But for many reasons, that just isn't possible."

The sudden tightness in his chest gave him pause. It wasn't only because he'd lose the farm if she didn't come with him. It hurt that she could so easily let him go. He thought they shared a bond, something more than mere friendship. And though there were many obstacles to keep them apart, his foolish heart refused to listen.

"What about that kiss last night?" he demanded. "Did it mean nothing to you?" The moment the words burst forth, he almost wished he could leap out the window, if only to escape the disapproving glare of the lady across the aisle.

What had happened to his pride? His self-respect?

"Of course it did," she said in a low voice. "It was the most wonderful moment of my life."

A crazy surge of hope rushed through his veins. "Then how can you not want to see where our relationship might lead?" Even though last night he'd dissuaded her of a possible romance, now it didn't seem to matter. The force of emotion that surged through his body made him believe they could overcome any impediment to be together. He laced his fingers with hers. She jumped a little but didn't pull her hand away, giving him the courage to continue. "I want to be with you, Julia. To spend every day together. Walk the grounds of Brentwood with you on my arm."

The sorrow on her face halted his ramblings.

"Don't you see, Quinn? If I return to Brentwood, I won't be

allowed to speak to you except to issue you orders." She squeezed his fingers, her expression earnest. "But in Canada, our stations don't matter." She raised her hand to his cheek. "You could stay here with me."

Her luminous brown eyes drew him in like a riptide. He hardly cared if he drowned in the process. Oh, how he wished that staying was an option. That nothing else existed except Julia and the softness of her lips. The intoxicating scent of lavender that surrounded her. But he shook his head before the temptation to say yes grew too great. "You know I could never leave my mother alone. Even if I can't persuade my siblings, I have to go back. I'm all she has left."

Sadness filled Julia's eyes, but she nodded. "I understand."

Gently, he brushed his thumb over her palm. "Let's not dwell on all that right now. We have some time before any hard decisions must be made. Can we agree to simply enjoy the remaining time we have left together?"

"I'll take whatever time I have with you, Quinten Aspinall," she whispered. "You're the best man I've ever met."

Quinn's chest expanded. When she looked at him that way, he believed he could sprout wings and fly all the way to England. It took everything in him not to kiss her lips right then and there, with all the other passengers in the car looking on.

Instead, he leaned back in his seat, his heart thumping as loudly as the train over the tracks.

Lord, I don't know why you've led me down this path. I pray you know what's waiting for me at the end of this journey and that I'll be able to live with my choices.

Julia hung her shawl on the hook in the boardinghouse foyer. Quinn entered behind her, saying he wanted to check on Harry before he headed back to his room at the Y.

After their intense conversation on the train, Julia found herself feeling out of sorts, unsettled.

"*What about that kiss we shared?*" His question had jarred her with its forthrightness. But more worrisome was the way she'd wanted to melt into his arms again, feel the thrill of his lips on hers once more and show him exactly what the kiss had meant to her. To do so, however, would have been the most selfish act in the world.

And what sort of madness had made her ask him to stay in Canada? She must have been out of her head, because even if he was willing to forsake his family to be with her, there still loomed the matter of the illegitimate child she carried.

"There you are." Mrs. C. bustled into the hallway, smiling. "How did you make out in Peterborough?"

Quinn's jaw muscles tightened as he removed his cap.

"Quite well," Julia jumped in. "But I can tell you about it later. I think Quinn is eager to see Harry."

"Oh, of course. He's upstairs resting."

Quinn frowned. "Is he no better, then?"

"Actually, he's much improved. Mrs. Teeter's soups have shored up his strength. But I'm making sure he gets as much rest as possible."

The lines across Quinn's forehead relaxed. "That's good to hear. I'll go up and say hello if it's all right with you."

"Certainly. I'll put on some fresh tea." Mrs. Chamberlain headed off to the kitchen.

Quinn paused at the foot of the stairs to give Julia a long look. "Are you coming? Harry will want to see you too. Probably more than me."

She laughed, her tense shoulder muscles loosening. "I'll see him later. I thought you might like some time alone with him. To tell him about your visit with Becky."

He stepped toward her and took her hand. "You are the most thoughtful woman I know, Julia Holloway."

Heat spread into her cheeks at his warm regard. "Go on with you, then. Tell Harry I'll be up soon."

Quinn's steadfast gaze held hers until she could scarcely breathe. What was wrong with her? No man had ever affected her this way.

He kissed her hand, then released it and turned to climb the stairs.

Julia stayed below, watching until he was out of sight, her pulse still racing from his touch.

She'd never met a finer man. A true gentleman. One who put the needs of his family ahead of his own happiness.

A strange fluttering sensation hit her abdomen. Julia pressed her palm against her stomach. Could it be her baby moving inside her? This was the sign she needed to remind her why she had to forget about her attraction to Quinn. After all, what would he think of her when he learned she was with child?

Never mind, little one. We'll be all right no matter what.

"Julia, would you mind opening the doors, please?" Mrs. Chamberlain stood in front of the parlor with a tray in her hand. "Someone must have closed them without thinking."

Julia rushed to open the pocket doors, then followed her inside.

Mrs. C. set the tray down on the table and straightened. "I'm glad you're back, dear. Mrs. Middleton telephoned this morning to say she expects to be released from the hospital tomorrow. I told her you'd likely be back in time to help her get home."

Julia clasped her hands together as she took a seat on the sofa. The timing couldn't be better. She needed the distraction of starting her new position. Needed to forget any ridiculous fantasies of romance and get back to reality. "Thank you, Mrs. C. I'll go over first thing tomorrow." She gave the woman a sad smile. "It looks like I'll be moving out."

"It appears so." Mrs. C. set down the teapot. "I'll miss your company, Julia dear, but I'm sure you'll be very happy in your new job. Remember, though, you're welcome back here anytime."

Julia rose to kiss Mrs. C.'s cheek. "I'll never forget your kindness to me when I was in need."

"It was my pleasure. And if I can do anything to help, just name it."

Julia paused, then nodded. "Actually, there is one thing. If a man named Dr. Hawkins comes looking for me, please don't tell him where I've gone."

Instead of going straight back to the Y after seeing Harry, Quinn found himself walking south toward Lake Ontario. Something about the sound of gentle waves lapping against the shore soothed him. When he reached the water, he found a large rock overlooking the shoreline, climbed to the flat top, and sat down.

He raised his head to stare up at the multitude of stars hovering over the water and simply breathed in the magnificent sight. It occurred to him that he'd failed to fully appreciate the beauty of this country. In truth, Canada could give England a run for its money, especially with the vastness of the land and the boldness of its terrain. The various train rides Quinn had taken since his arrival had shown him that.

Now, in the darkness of night, the land gave Quinn a sense of peace and belonging. A feeling that no matter where in the world he traveled, God was with him.

Even if He didn't answer his prayers exactly as Quinn would have liked.

He picked up a stone and tossed it out into the water, taking pleasure in the way the soft ripples captured the moonlight. If he were a painter, he'd have loved to capture the image on canvas.

It occurred to Quinn that this was the first time he'd simply stopped and lived in the moment. For once he wasn't plotting his next move, trying to coerce everyone into falling in line with his plans. For now, he let himself simply . . . be.

Maybe Julia had been right earlier. Instead of concentrating on his failures, he should be counting his blessings. All three of his siblings were alive and, for the most part, doing well. He'd had the chance to see each of them in person, give them a hug, and tell them how much he missed them. And he'd managed to get Harry out of a bad situation. Even if nothing else came of this journey, Quinn would be forever grateful for that.

He hoped if his father was looking down on them, it would be enough for him as well.

Quinn lifted his face again to gaze at the sky. "I've tried my best, Dad. Worked myself to the bone to provide for Mum and the kids. But it seems their fate is out of my hands now. I suppose we'll have to wait and see what God has in store for us."

The wind picked up, blowing Quinn's hair across his forehead. What a beautiful night. A night meant for romance. His thoughts inevitably turned to Julia, the one bright light in this whole episode.

She continued to surprise him at every turn. She was charming, level-headed, kind, and compassionate. And she possessed a type of unassuming beauty that could bring a man to his knees.

He drew in an unsteady breath.

Lord, I think I'm in love with her, but I don't know what to do about it.

When he'd begun this journey, his sole purpose in finding Julia had been for his own selfish benefit, namely to gain his own piece of land. But the more he came to know her, the less he cared about that. Now, after they'd shared that amazing kiss, the main reason he wanted her to come back to England was to have more time with her. The mere thought of leaving here and never seeing her again made his heart squeeze with sorrow.

With a sigh, Quinn climbed down, dusted off his pants, and started the walk back to his room, vowing to do his best with the time that remained to change Julia's mind.

Because going on without her now seemed unbearable.

Once Quinn had left the boardinghouse, Julia finished her tea and headed upstairs to bed. Despite being weary to the bone, she'd promised Harry to come up and see him, and she wouldn't disappoint the boy. She stopped outside his room and listened for any movement within. After several seconds of silence, she inched the door open and peered inside. The bedside lamp was on, providing her enough light to see Harry sitting back against the pillows, staring into space.

His face brightened as she entered the room. "Miss Julia."

"Hello, Harry. How are you feeling?"

"Much better now. How was your trip?"

"Very nice." She moved to the chair beside his bed. "I met your sister. She's a lovely girl."

A shadow dimmed Harry's features. "I miss Becky. It's been so long that I almost don't remember what she looks like."

"Oh, honey. Don't worry. I'm sure you'll see her again soon."

Harry nodded, then looked up with a smile. "Quinn says she might come back to England with us. I hope she does. And Cecil too. That way we can be a real family again."

Gazing into his expectant face, Julia wished she could do something to ensure his wish came true. That the dear boy would be back with his mother and the rest of his loving family once more. After everything he'd been through, he deserved that stability and happiness. "I hope so too," Julia said softly.

Harry raised wide eyes to hers. "What about you, Miss Julia? Are you coming with us?"

Julia blinked. "Oh, I . . ." With all her heart, she wished she could say yes, but to give him false hope would be cruel. "Actually, I don't think so, love. You see, I'm about to start a new job. Which is another reason I wanted to talk to you tonight." She did her best to ignore his crestfallen expression. "I'm going to work for an elderly lady who needs a companion. But it means I have to live in her house with her." She softened her features. "I'll be moving out tomorrow."

Harry stared at her. "I don't understand. I thought you were coming to England with us so your uncle would give us a farm to live on."

Julia frowned. "I think you misunderstood, honey."

"No, I didn't." He shook his head, his mouth set in a petulant line. "Quinn told me your uncle is giving us a farm because he's so happy Quinn is bringing you home. And we're all going to live there together. Me and Cecil are going to teach Quinn how to grow crops."

Julia stiffened on the chair, suddenly recalling Quinn's odd response when she questioned him about where he and his family would live. His evasive manner. His unwillingness to explain. *"I have somewhere in mind. Once I get home, I'll be able to finalize the details."*

Was this the reason he wouldn't talk about it? Had Quinn made some sort of bargain with her uncle? Bring Julia home and you'll get a farm?

"When did Quinn tell you this?" Julia attempted to keep her tone casual.

Harry shrugged. "In the hospital, I think. Before you went to see Becky."

Before Quinn knew Julia wasn't going back. Her mind raced, trying to piece together her interactions with Quinn in light of this new information.

She rose on shaky legs and crossed to look out the narrow window in an effort to gain control of her emotions. She wouldn't let Harry bear the brunt of her outrage at Quinn's betrayal.

And betrayal it was—on the deepest of levels. Now every action she'd deemed so noble took on the taint of selfishness. Quinn didn't care about her; he only wanted to use her for his own gain. No wonder he was so insistent she forgive her uncle and return home to make amends.

She pressed a trembling hand to her mouth. How could she have been so naïve? Again.

"Miss Julia?"

She swallowed hard. With Herculean effort, she forced a smile to her lips and turned around. "Yes?"

"Would you read to me?" He held out the book that she'd been reading to him before she left for Peterborough.

She exhaled and nodded. "Of course I will."

There was nothing she could do about Quinn tonight, and with her new job starting the next day, dealing with his deceit would have to wait for a more opportune time.

But one way or the other, she would get to the bottom of Quinn's deception. And then she'd let him know—in no uncertain terms—exactly what she thought of his duplicity.

CHAPTER 20

The taxi pulled to a stop in front of a stately white-brick house. While Julia paid the fare, Mrs. Middleton opened the door and stuck her cane out in front of her. Julia hurried around to assist her.

"Just leave the bags on the walkway and I'll come back for them later," Julia told the driver.

"No need, miss. I'll bring them up to the porch."

"Thank you." She gripped Mrs. Middleton by the elbow, and they slowly made their way to the front door.

The trembling in the older woman's limbs proved she was still plagued by weakness.

After pulling a key from her handbag, Mrs. Middleton unlocked one of the double doors, which creaked as it swung inward. "Ah," she said as she entered. "It's good to be home." She took a few steps into the foyer.

Julia looked around the interior. Though dated, the stately home boasted an old-fashioned elegance that time couldn't dim, from the polished wooden staircase to the flocked green wallpaper that graced the hallway.

"What a lovely house," she said.

"She's a bit tired-looking, I'll admit," Mrs. Middleton said. "But it's always been home."

Julia's gaze flicked up the grand central staircase. Mrs. Middleton needed to rest before she tackled that climb. "Let me get you comfortable. Where would you like to sit?"

"The parlor will do for now." Mrs. Middleton pointed to the French doors on the right. "I hope Allison made a fire in here. It gets chilly, even in the summer." She headed into the parlor, Julia following behind.

The pale blue room was crowded with furniture of every description. Each corner held a table or a bookcase, a chair or an ottoman. As Mrs. Middleton had hoped, a small fire graced the hearth.

Julia helped the woman into a chair near the warmth and pulled a knitted afghan from the ottoman to drape over her lap. "Are you comfortable for a minute while I bring in the bags?"

"I'm fine. These old bones are happy to be back in my familiar seat."

Julia hurried out to the porch where Mrs. Middleton's bag, as well as Julia's case, sat on the top step. She brought them into the foyer and returned to the parlor.

A woman in a black dress with a white collar stood in front of Mrs. Middleton's chair. The housekeeper, most likely, Julia surmised.

"It's grand to have you home, ma'am," the woman said. "The place hasn't been the same without you. If I'd known you'd arrived, I would have met you at the door."

"Thank you, Allison. It's good to be back at last." Mrs. Middleton looked over. "Oh, here she is now. Julia, please come and meet my housekeeper, Mrs. Banbury. This is Julia Holloway. I've hired her as my live-in companion. She will take the room across from mine."

"Nice to meet you, Mrs. Banbury." Julia gave the woman a wide smile.

The servant only nodded, her expression less than friendly. Then she turned back to Mrs. Middleton. "I'll have Mrs. Neville prepare your favorite dish for the evening meal. In the meantime, I'll make up the guest room."

"Thank you, Allison."

"Is there anything else for the moment?"

"No, that will do for now. I believe I may need to lie down for a while."

Julia moved toward her. "I'll help you upstairs if you're ready."

With a grunt, Mrs. Middleton pulled herself out of the chair.

Before they started up the main staircase, Julia retrieved the woman's bag. Again, the process was slow, and Mrs. Middleton was breathing heavily by the time they reached the room she indicated was hers.

The housekeeper had been busy, it seemed. The windows were open, allowing a slight breeze to stir the curtains. A large bed with a white iron headboard dominated the room, and a vase of fresh flowers sat on the dresser.

Julia helped the woman to lie down, and spread a light blanket over her. "I'll check on you later. Have a good rest."

Mrs. Middleton settled back against the pillows with a sigh. "Welcome to my home, Julia. I hope you'll be happy here."

She smiled. "I'm sure I will."

But as she closed the bedroom door behind her, her thoughts turned to Quinn. Soon, she would have to confront him about his dealings with her uncle. She'd give herself a few days to get settled first, and hopefully by the time she saw Quinn again, she'd be in control of her emotions and able to have a reasonable conversation with him.

Quinn trudged along the sidewalk on his way to the boardinghouse, trying to ignore the way his damp shirt clung to his skin. The intense heat of the summer was one aspect of the city he still hadn't grown accustomed to, and today it was making him more than a bit irritable.

It had been three days since Quinn and Julia had returned from Peterborough. Three days since Julia had moved in with Mrs. Middleton. Yet it felt more like three years. He missed her warm smile, the amber flecks in her brown eyes, the way her face lit with enthusiasm at every new sight she encountered. He missed sharing his thoughts with her, knowing she'd listen and sympathize with him. Or perhaps even suggest a different course of action.

Now, as he approached Mrs. Chamberlain's front door, Quinn missed the thrill of anticipation he used to experience, knowing she was inside. Somehow the boardinghouse didn't hold the same appeal without her.

Even Harry agreed.

As the boy's health improved, he was becoming restless, unused to lying around with nothing to do. And he complained about Julia not coming to visit him. "Julia brings me cookies," he whined. "She reads to me and plays cards with me."

Apparently, Quinn didn't quite measure up in the visitor department.

"You know Julia has a new job," he'd reminded Harry. "I'm sure when she has some time off she'll come 'round."

"Or maybe when I'm better, you could take me to visit her." Harry's face had brightened, his eyes pleading.

"We'll see." But Harry's comment had given Quinn pause. Quite innocently, the boy had let it slip that he still wasn't fully recovered. Which only reinforced Quinn's goal for today.

He planned to speak with Mrs. Chamberlain, get her opinion on Harry's prognosis, and ask her what she thought they should do next. He didn't want Harry to become a burden. Yet Quinn's room at the YMCA had room for only one cot. If need be, Quinn could make a pallet on the floor for himself and give Harry the bed, but that arrangement wouldn't do for long. Perhaps Mrs. C. would have another alternative.

Quinn knocked on the door and shifted from one foot to the other as he waited.

Today he would also ask to use Mrs. C.'s telephone to contact Becky and find out what she had decided regarding coming back to England.

He'd checked into the schedules for ships leaving Halifax for England, and there was one leaving at the end of July. The daunting task of getting all three of his siblings, as well as Julia, on that boat weighed heavily on Quinn. Only his faith allowed him to believe it could be possible. Surely, God hadn't brought him this far to let him return empty-handed.

"Hello, Mr. Aspinall." Barbara Campbell, one of the boarders, opened the door with a smile.

"Good morning, Miss Campbell." He removed his cap. "How are you today?"

"Very well, thanks," she said with a grin. "You must be here to see that adorable brother of yours."

"That's right." He moved into the foyer. "But I'd like a word with Mrs. Chamberlain first, if she has a minute."

Barbara rested a hand on her hip. "Sure thing. I'll get her for you. You can wait in the parlor."

A few minutes later, Mrs. C. entered the room. "Good morning, Quinten. What can I do for you?" Today, she looked different. All dressed up, as though ready for church.

"You look like you're heading out somewhere," he said.

"I am. But I have a few minutes to spare." She indicated the sofa. "Sit down and tell me what's on your mind."

He perched on the edge while she took her usual chair.

"I wanted to get your opinion about Harry," he said. "Whether he's well enough to move in with me at the Y."

"He's doing quite well, but surely there's no rush. We all love having him here."

"You're sure he's not a burden? I don't want to add to your workload."

"Nonsense. Harry is a delight."

"Even without Julia to help care for him?" Quinn fought to keep his tone neutral, though his neck heated under his collar.

"We all miss Julia, of course," Mrs. C. said. "But the other girls are pitching in to make sure Harry is well looked after. In fact, Mabel stayed on the third floor so Harry wouldn't be alone."

"That's kind of her. Be sure to thank her for me." Quinn hesitated, attempting to appear casual. "Speaking of Julia, have you heard from her since she moved out?"

"Just once. She called to check on Harry."

"Did she say how she's managing in her new post?"

"She likes it quite well so far. Especially her spacious bedroom in Mrs. Middleton's mansion."

"Mansion?" Quinn's head shot up. He'd pictured a little cottage-style house, one befitting a lonely widow. "Is Mrs. Middleton a wealthy woman?"

"I wouldn't say wealthy, though she's hardly a pauper. The Middleton mansion has been handed down through the family for three generations. In any case, Julia seems content there."

Quinn swallowed and loosened his collar. Why wasn't he happier for her? He should be thrilled she landed the perfect job working for an independent woman of means. But part of him wished she missed him—at least a little.

"Getting used to Mrs. Middleton's eccentricities will be a bit of a challenge; however, Julia is more than capable of handling it. I have no doubt they will both settle into a mutually beneficial relationship."

Which meant Julia would have no incentive to return to England. Quinn let out a sigh.

"Is something wrong?" Mrs. C. studied him.

"Of course not. Julia deserves to be happy." Mentally switching gears, he leaned forward. "Mrs. C., is there anything I can do to repay you for all your kindness? Any work you need done around the house?"

"Not at the moment." Her eyes narrowed. "But there is one thing you could do."

"Name it." Quinn itched to have something physical to do to keep busy. To keep his mind from dwelling on circumstances he couldn't control.

"Reverend Burke and I have an appointment with Mr. Hobday at Dr. Barnardo's today. We want to talk to him about the harsh conditions some of the children are living in and demand he send more inspectors to check on them." She paused, one brow raised. "We could use your testimony added to ours."

Instant tension seized Quinn. The thought of facing Mr. Hobday again was not something he looked forward to. Especially since Quinn had not only interfered with Harry's position, he'd removed Harry from the farm altogether. Would Mr. Hobday be aware of this? Or would Mr. Wolfe have been too ashamed to report the boy's absence?

However, despite dreading the encounter, the thought of other boys—or worse yet, young girls—receiving such horrendous treatment at the hands of their employers made Quinn's stomach clench. He owed it to Harry to report the incident to someone who could perhaps make a difference.

Besides, Quinn owed a huge debt to Mrs. Chamberlain for helping both Julia and Harry in their time of trouble. It was the least he could do for her. "I suppose, if you think it will help . . ."

"I'm sure it will."

"Then I'd be happy to come with you." He held back a sigh. It's not as if he had anything else on his schedule for today. Like seeing Julia.

"Wonderful. Reverend Burke will be here in twenty minutes."

Quinn dredged up a smile. "Long enough for me to say a quick hello to Harry."

Half an hour later, in the back seat of Rev. Burke's Model T, Quinn gripped the doorframe with white-knuckled intensity. How did a pastor afford his own automobile, anyway? And where had he learned to drive like a madman?

When the automobile bounced over a rut in the road, Quinn barely kept from banging his head on the roof. He breathed a sigh of relief when the man pulled up to the curb and set the brake.

Rev. Burke hurried around to help Mrs. Chamberlain out of the passenger seat, then waited while Quinn unfolded his frame from the cramped rear seat and climbed onto the sidewalk.

Mrs. C. smoothed out her skirt. "Let's hope Geoffrey's collar will add a certain credibility to our visit. That, along with your witnessing Harry's abuse firsthand, should be enough to convince the man to take action."

"We can only hope and pray, my dear." Rev. Burke patted Mrs. C.'s arm as he led her up to the front door.

"Good day," Rev. Burke said to the receptionist. "We have an appointment with Mr. Hobday. Reverend Burke and Mrs. Chamberlain."

The woman eyed Quinn. From her scowl, Quinn determined that she remembered him and his persistence. "Is this man with you?" she asked.

"Oh yes, forgive me," Mrs. C. said. "This is Mr. Quinten Aspinall."

"We've met," she said tersely.

"Hello, Mrs. Allen." Quinn doffed his hat. "Lovely to see you again." He doubted his tight smile fooled the woman.

She rose from her chair. "Please follow me."

Once again, Quinn followed her to the director's office, this time joined by his two companions.

Mr. Hobday looked up from his desk and removed his spectacles. When he spotted Quinn, he frowned. "To what do I owe this honor?" His expression said it was anything but an honor.

Rev. Burke stepped forward. "Good day, sir. We have an important matter to discuss with you."

Mr. Hobday glanced warily at each of them, then nodded. "Please have a seat."

Mrs. C. took a chair, her purse perched on her lap. "Mr. Hobday, as superintendent of this home, we want to talk to you about the children and some of the situations they are living in."

Rev. Burke cleared his throat. "First, let us begin by saying that we appreciate the tremendous job you are doing and how difficult it must be to bear the burden of such a responsibility."

"Thank you." Mr. Hobday lifted his chin. "I'm glad you understand the daunting task I face each and every day."

"Indeed. However, we do have a concern about the conditions some of the children may be experiencing." The minister turned to look at Quinn. "Conditions Mr. Aspinall's brother, Harry, found out the hard way."

Mr. Hobday's features tightened as he focused on Quinn. "It appears you were successful in locating your siblings. Or one of them at least. I received a letter this morning from Mr. Wolfe stating that Harrison has left his post and is in breach of his contract."

Heat blasted through Quinn, and he scowled. The utter nerve of the man to complain. "If anyone is in breach of a contract, it's Mr. Wolfe. Unless physical violence is condoned by your organization." He glared at the superintendent.

A shuttered look came over the man's face. "At times, the farmers find it necessary to use punishment to temper undesired behavior. If you recall, I did warn you about the potential consequences of your search."

Quinn curled his hands into fists, fighting his rising temper. How could this man be so glib about the type of violence Harry had endured? "You said the farmer would be annoyed. Not that Harry would be beaten within an inch of his life."

The color drained from Mr. Hobday's face, his lips pressed into a grim line.

Rev. Burke leaned forward. "We're not blaming you, Mr. Hobday, but we hoped that by bringing the matter to your attention, we could find a way to rectify the situation and ensure the other boys in your care are safe."

Mr. Hobday looked at Quinn. "I'm sorry about your brother. Believe me, in no way do I condone that type of treatment." He paused. "How is Harry doing?"

"He's improving slowly, after a stay in the hospital."

"Hospit . . ." The man swallowed.

Quinn shook his head. "That's not the worst of it. Harry was half-starved to begin with, living on a bed of straw in the barn."

Mr. Hobday closed his eyes, his hands folded on the desktop. On a loud exhale, he opened his eyes. "I'm terribly sorry," he said again. "That is not how we want our boys to live. We brought them to Canada for a chance at a better life, not for mistreatment."

"Then, what are you prepared to do to ensure this isn't happening to others under your care?" Mrs. Chamberlain asked. Her chin jutted out, her features hardened.

Quinn had never seen her this way. Unforgiving, confrontational. Harry's problems had no doubt brought back all the pain of her own childhood, as well as her sister's tragic fate.

Mr. Hobday's expression remained sympathetic. "Unfortunately, there's not a lot I can do other than lobby for more funds to hire additional inspectors. The few we have are hard-pressed to get in their yearly inspections."

"And clearly those visits are useless." Mrs. C. bristled. "Do they even interview the children themselves to ask how they're being treated?"

"They do, however, the boys rarely say much. Only a few ever speak of harsh conditions, and when they do, the inspectors give the farmers recommendations."

"Does anyone follow up on these recommendations to ensure they're being implemented?"

Mr. Hobday shook his head. "Not until the next scheduled inspection."

"Then you need more frequent visits to the farms." Mrs. C. fairly quivered with indignation.

"Again, Mrs. Chamberlain, it's a matter of funding. Unless you have an idea as to how to accomplish this on our limited budget . . ."

"What if I told you we did?" Rev. Burke said evenly.

The man's brows rose. "Go on."

"I believe I could get a team of volunteers together who would be willing to help with these inspections. Some clergy, some laypeople."

Mr. Hobday shook his head. "That wouldn't work, I'm afraid. We couldn't have a bunch of random people with no authority invading the farmers' domains."

"I see your point. But what about clergy? Surely there could be no objection to a minister paying the boys a visit? There would be authority in the position, and the children might feel more comfortable talking to a pastor rather than a man in a business suit."

Mr. Hobday stroked his chin. "That might be acceptable. But how would we find these clergymen and organize their visits? I do not have the time nor the manpower to do that myself."

"I understand." Rev. Burke nodded. "And I am willing to take this on. I'm sure Mrs. Chamberlain, as well as some of my other parishioners, would be happy to volunteer their time to organize such an undertaking. Perhaps once we have a list of willing participants, we could meet with your administrator here and work together to set up a schedule."

Mr. Hobday studied them. "It's definitely worth a try. And if it won't cost us any more, I can't see why anyone would object." The director rose. "Let me propose it to the other board members while you begin contacting the clergy. We'll be in touch and go from there."

Rev. Burke rose as well, stretching out his hand to the director. "That sounds like a good place to start. Thank you for listening to our concerns."

Mr. Hobday shook the minister's hand. "And thank you for the information. I assure you I'll do my best to rectify the situation. We are committed to keeping Dr. Barnardo's dream alive and maintaining the level of quality he always insisted upon."

"Really?" Mrs. Chamberlain's voice was laced with disbelief. "Tell me, sir, did you ever meet Thomas Barnardo?"

The man frowned. "No, unfortunately he passed away before I had the privilege. Why do you ask?"

"Because many years ago, I was one of his orphans. I lived in one of his homes in London, and yes, the man had good intentions. But once the children left his residence, he often had no idea what was happening on the other side of the ocean. I only wish I'd had the courage to do something about it a lot sooner." She inclined her head. "Good day to you, sir. Be assured you will hear from us again."

The man blinked, seemingly unsure how to respond to her heated words.

Quinn started to follow them out, but the director stepped forward.

"Mr. Aspinall. A moment, if you will."

Quinn stiffened. "Yes?"

"May I ask what you intend to do now?"

Quinn regarded him coolly. "If you're asking whether I am going to press charges against the man who beat my brother, I'd like nothing better than to see the cretin behind bars. However, I have no real evidence other than Harry's testimony, and I'll not put him through the horror of reliving the experience again."

"I understand." Mr. Hobday stroked his chin. "What I meant is, what do you intend to do about Harry? He is still bound by his contract. When he is recovered, he will have to return for a new placement."

Quinn's chest muscles tightened, and he fought to contain the anger that crept into his voice. "Harry may never get over the trauma of his assault, and I certainly won't subject him to the possibility of it occurring again. I intend to take my brother home." He pinned the man with a hard stare. "Now I must ask what you intend to do in light of my plans for Harry?" He held the man's gaze, his challenge unmistakable. If Mr. Hobday desired, he could create a lot of trouble for the Aspinalls.

The man paused for a moment, then walked back to the desk. He pulled a sheet of paper from the blotter and went over to toss it in the fireplace. "I believe Mr. Wolfe's correspondence must have gotten lost in transit. By the time another letter reaches our office, I won't have any idea how to find Harry." He gave Quinn a pointed look.

"Good." Quinn put on his cap and nodded. "Just make sure you never send another boy out to that man's farm again."

Mr. Hobday's features turned grim. "On that you have my word, sir."

"Thank you. I trust you'll do your best to ensure no other boys suffer a similar fate. Good day."

CHAPTER 21

"There's a man at the door for Miss Holloway." The housekeeper stood in the dining room doorway, her face twisted in a grimace as though the mere thought of Julia speaking to a man was an unpardonable sin.

Julia set aside her bowl of oatmeal, her heart thumping. With the issue of her uncle's farm ever-present on her mind, she had sent word via Mrs. Chamberlain that she wished to speak with Quinn. Though she hated confrontation, this was not a subject she could avoid. She needed to settle the matter once and for all.

Mrs. Middleton lowered her cup. "Did the man give a name?"

"A Mr. Aspinall, ma'am." The housekeeper shot Julia a sour look.

"He's a friend of mine from back home," she said, rising from the table. "Do you mind if we use the parlor for a few minutes, Mrs. Middleton?"

"Not at all. But I'd like to meet this young man if you don't mind."

"Of course."

Julia moved past the housekeeper into the hall, smoothing any stray hairs as she walked. Her pulse rioted through her, and she had to force herself to walk sedately.

It had been over a week since she'd last seen Quinn. A week since she'd learned of his duplicitous reasons for wanting her to go back to England. And she still hadn't sorted through all her feelings about the issue. Part of her held out hope that Harry had misunderstood what Quinn had told him. Until then, she would give him the benefit of the doubt and hear his side of the story.

She paused before entering the foyer and took a calming breath. Then she lifted her chin and moved forward.

Quinn stood inside the front door.

"Hello, Quinn," she said.

His whole face lit with a smile. "Julia. It's good to see you. You look beautiful, as always."

"Thank you." Her cheeks heated, though the compliment didn't sway her as it once would have. "Can you come in for a minute?"

"Of course, as long as it won't interfere with your duties."

"I believe I can spare her for a few minutes." Mrs. Middleton hobbled forward on her cane.

"Mrs. Middleton," Julia said. "This is Quinten Aspinall."

"Lovely to meet you." Quinn gave a bow. "Thank you for giving Julia this position. Knowing she has somewhere decent to live is a great relief."

The elderly woman gave him an appraising look. "I was happy to do so since Julia's presence here allows me to continue living in my home. Now, if you'll both excuse me, I'll be in my study, catching up on some correspondence."

"Thank you, ma'am." Quinn bowed once more.

The sound of the cane echoed through the hall as she walked slowly away.

"Please, come in." Insides churning, Julia led Quinn into the parlor, searching for some sort of normal conversation before broaching the difficult topic that weighed on her heart. "How is Harry doing? I'm sorry I haven't been able to get over and see him."

She took a seat on the sofa, somewhat surprised when Quinn sat down beside her. She shifted slightly away so she could see him better.

"He's much improved," he said, "and dying to see you. I couldn't tell him I was coming here today or he would have insisted on tagging along. I didn't know if your employer would appreciate that." He gave a warm chuckle.

"She wouldn't have minded, I'm sure."

Quinn laid his cap on his knee. "This position must agree with you. You're positively glowing."

Julia fought the instinct to cover her abdomen. Wasn't that a term applied to pregnant women? Though she'd let out the seams in her skirts, she didn't think she could be showing already. She managed a stiff smile. "So far, I'm quite content here. Mrs. Middleton has been very kind." It was true. Other than the hostile housekeeper, who apparently disliked anyone hailing from England, Julia had not one complaint.

"I'm glad." Yet there was a hint of wistfulness in his voice. "Before I forget, a letter came for you today at the boardinghouse. Mrs. Chamberlain asked me to deliver it to you." He pulled an envelope from his jacket and handed it to her.

Scanning the penmanship, she frowned, then stuffed it in her pocket. "Thank you. I'll read it later." She fought to put all distractions aside except for the issue she needed to discuss. "You're probably wondering why I asked to see you."

"I am, but before we get into that, I must tell you my news." A smile creased his cheeks. "Becky has agreed to come back to England with us. Only for a visit, but it will have to do. For now, anyway."

"That's wonderful." And it was. Despite everything, Julia still wished the best for Quinn's family.

"Now all I need is for Cecil to agree. I'm going to see him again before we leave. Which is another reason I was glad you asked me here." He hesitated, rubbing his palms on his pant legs nervously. "I wanted you to know that if Harry continues to improve, I plan to leave for England at the end of the month."

"I see." She should be relieved to know he would soon be gone, but she couldn't shake the wave of sadness that engulfed her. "That leads me to the matter I asked you here to discuss."

Quinn frowned. "From your expression, it must be something unpleasant."

"That will depend on you." She squared her shoulders. "Harry told me that when you return to England, you and your family will be living on a farm." She pinned him with a pointed stare. "A farm my uncle is apparently going to give you in return for bringing me home."

The color drained from Quinn's face, but he didn't flinch or look away.

"Is this true? Or did Harry misconstrue what you said?" She held herself very still, awaiting his response.

Please let him have misunderstood.

Quinn closed his eyes briefly, then let out a slow breath. "It's true. Although it's a moot point now."

Disappointment rushed through her with astonishing force. "Why? Because you couldn't coerce me into returning with you?" Despite her best efforts to contain her emotions, sarcasm seeped into her words.

"Please let me explain. It's not as diabolical as you make it sound."

She lifted her chin. "By all means."

He exhaled and ran a hand over his jaw. "When your uncle first requested my help to locate you, I wasn't exactly enthusiastic about the idea. I figured I would have enough to worry about trying to find my siblings." He shrugged. "In order to sweeten the pot, his lordship offered me one of his tenant farms if I managed to bring you back with me."

Julia's breakfast soured in her stomach. Hearing him admit it aloud was somehow worse than her imaginings. Now every encounter they'd had since he first saw her scrubbing floors in the hospital was ruined. Tainted by his ulterior motives.

The sting of tears bit at the back of her eyes. Was every man in her life destined to let her down?

Desperate to put some space between them, she pushed up from the sofa and moved to the far side of the room, facing away. She couldn't bear to look at him right now. Not with her emotions so raw.

Soft footsteps came up behind her.

"Julia." His tortured whisper sent shivers down her spine. "I admit that at first the idea of gaining a home for my family was a huge incentive. But the more I came to know you, the more I came to care for you, and the farm simply faded in importance." He moved closer.

She held herself rigid, willing him not to touch her.

"All I wanted—then and now—is your happiness. I hope you can believe that."

"How can I believe anything you say now?" Her voice quavered, and she berated herself for her weakness.

Quinn gently turned her to face him, a plea evident in his eyes. "Because you know my heart. Have I done anything underhanded to persuade you to come with us?"

Her chin quivered, but she couldn't seem to form an answer.

"Did I try to dissuade you from taking this job?" he continued. "A job that would enable you to stay in Canada?"

"No." She dropped her gaze to his vest, confusion twisting her stomach into knots.

A storm of emotion passed over his features. "I can't deny that I still want you to come back with us, but that has nothing to do with the farm and everything to do with my feelings for you."

Before she could utter a word, he pulled her into his arms and kissed her. A thousand sensations passed through her at once. Shock, pleasure, and then anger. How dare he try to confuse her by kissing her again? She wrenched herself away from him.

Right away, he held up his hands. "Forgive me. That was . . ."

"Unconscionable?"

"Yes." He hung his head. "I couldn't think of any other way to show you how I feel. How the thought of leaving here and never seeing you again is unbearable." When he raised his head, abject misery swirled in his eyes. "But once again, I'm being selfish. Not considering what you want." He took a tentative step toward her. "Did I misread the attraction between us, Julia? If so, please be honest with me."

She stared into his eyes, now the color of warm pewter. Despite everything, she couldn't lie. "I can't deny the connection between us, but as we discussed after our trip to Peterborough, it will do us no good to pursue it. My life is here now."

"Why is that? Is it really due to the lack of freedom back home? Or is there something else keeping you here?"

She almost laughed out loud at the ludicrousness of his question. Being unwed and pregnant meant she would be a pariah, shunned by society no matter where she lived, especially in England. At least here, she could remain anonymous. She released a weary sigh and stepped away from his nearness, her shoes sinking into the thick area rug. "There are reasons I can't disclose. Extremely personal ones that dictate I must remain here."

In the ensuing silence, the distant toll of a church bell could be heard.

"If you have a problem, I'd like to help," he said quietly.

"Please don't press me on this, Quinn. You'll only make matters worse." She held his gaze with a determined stare of her own.

At last, he let out a long breath. "Very well. If this is what you want, I will respect your decision." He gave her a long look. "But don't ask me to like it, because I never will." Without another word, he shoved his cap on his head and strode out of the room.

After Quinn left, Julia sat in the parlor, absorbing the depressing fact that she might never see him again. Within a matter of weeks, he would be heading back to England. And he wouldn't be returning.

Her heart already felt shrunken in her chest. Had she made a terrible mistake? Should she have revealed her real reason for staying and given Quinn the chance to decide how he felt about it? She ran a hand over her tired eyes. In the end, what difference would it really have made?

She shifted on the sofa, a crinkling sound alerting her to the letter in her pocket she'd forgotten about in all the turmoil. She drew it out and frowned. There was no postage, indicating it had been hand-delivered by someone in the city. A sense of dread rolled in her stomach.

She pulled out the letter and unfolded it.

My dearest Julia,

If I didn't know better, I'd think you've been trying to avoid me. Perhaps you're embarrassed about our relationship. I hope that's not the case, because I haven't been able to get you out of my thoughts since our time together.

And I don't for one second believe you're serious about that Aspinall character. I think you were only trying to protect yourself because I'm still married. I suppose I can't blame you for that, but you should know that my circumstances have changed, and I need to speak to you about it.

Please meet me at the military hospital tomorrow afternoon at three o'clock. I think once you hear my news, you'll be as pleased as I am.

With great affection,
Richard

Julia crumpled the paper into a tight ball, holding in a scream. She only prayed no one had told him the location of her new residence or she'd never feel safe here again.

"I take it Mr. Aspinall has left." Mrs. Middleton entered the room, her features pinched with what looked like a disapproving frown.

Julia shot to her feet, stuffing the balled-up letter into her pocket. "I'm sorry. I thought you were still busy with your correspondence." She rushed to take the woman's arm. "Do you need anything?"

Mrs. Middleton pointed to her armchair.

Julia helped her settle there, placing a woolen blanket over her knees. "Would you like some tea? Something to eat?"

"Sit down, child. We need to have a chat." The woman's grim expression made the nerves jump in Julia's stomach.

She sat across from her and folded her hands on her lap.

"If you recall, I asked you only one question when I agreed to hire you, and that was if the father of the child was in the picture. You assured me he was not."

"That's right." Julia frowned. What did she . . . ? "Oh, no, Mrs. Middleton. Quinn is not the father. He doesn't even know about—" she lowered her voice, in case a certain nosy housekeeper was listening outside the door—"the baby."

"Then perhaps we have another problem." Mrs. Middleton's piercing gaze made Julia squirm. "Mrs. Banbury said she saw you kissing Mr. Aspinall in this very room."

Heat burned in Julia's cheeks. "I'm so sorry, ma'am. I never expected Quinn to do that."

Mrs. Middleton tilted her head. "Then what exactly is the nature of your relationship with him? It seems more than mere friendship to me."

Julia's stomach plummeted. It was only natural that Mrs. Middleton would question her morals. After all, she was unmarried and expecting a baby. Shame moved through her like a flash flood. "We've only shared a kiss. That's all. Quinn would like it to be more," she admitted. "But for a variety of reasons, that's not feasible. This baby being one of them." She laid a palm over her abdomen. "Besides, he's going back to England in a few weeks. I doubt I'll ever see him again." Her bottom lip trembled, betraying her.

Mrs. Middleton studied her. "So, you're telling me this relationship won't interfere with your job?"

"Absolutely not." Of that, Julia was certain.

Mrs. Middleton waited, then banged her cane on the floor. "Fine. From now on if you wish to entertain visitors, you will do so on your day off. Which is Monday, by the way. And no more kissing in the parlor."

"You have my word." Julia held her breath, waiting for some other condition to her staying on.

Instead, Mrs. Middleton leaned closer, softening her voice. "For the record, my dear, if this man truly is your friend, I think you owe him the truth of your situation. From my experience, it's always best to be up-front with the people closest to you and let God take care of the rest."

CHAPTER 22

A few days later, Julia stood beneath the oak tree on the corner of the church property, seeking relief from the hot sun. It was a quiet Monday afternoon, and in the heat of the midday, not many people were out walking. The church itself stood as a silent sentinel, empty of worshipers for the time being.

Yesterday morning, when Julia and Mrs. Middleton had attended service here, Julia had encountered Mrs. Chamberlain with Quinn and Harry. Harry had been enthusiastic to see Julia again, and it had done her heart good to see the improvement in the lad.

However, the awkwardness between her and Quinn had left Julia with a huge knot of regret in her stomach.

She'd had a few days to process all the things he'd told her during their last conversation. And when all was said and done, Julia believed him. Believed that the farm might have started out being his initial motivation to find her, but that his growing feelings for her had made him rethink the situation. The fact that he cared for her was evident. Not even he could be that great an actor. And in the end, he'd left without trying to convince her to come home or to coerce her to disclose the reason why she needed to stay. Overall, Quinn had treated her with nothing but respect.

Well, except for stealing that last kiss.

The more she considered Mrs. Middleton's advice, the more she came to believe that the woman had a point. Maybe Quinn should know the truth. She'd discovered his secret, and they'd gotten through that. And as scary as it would be to tell him, perhaps he deserved to know hers. That way, nothing would remain unsaid between them.

When the service had ended and the congregation filed out into the vestibule of the church, Julia followed Quinn outside.

"I have something I need to tell you," she'd whispered. "But not with so many people around. Could you meet me here tomorrow around two o'clock?"

He had frowned, glancing over in Harry's direction, but at last he'd nodded. "Very well. Two o'clock."

Now, after pacing the walkway for twenty minutes, Julia looked up at the clock tower. Ten minutes past two. Perhaps Quinn had decided not to come after all. Part of her hoped he wouldn't, since it would save her from having to see the shock and disappointment on his face when she told him about her pregnancy.

She blew out a long breath. She'd better get used to being the object of people's disgust, for once everyone learned of her condition—which was becoming harder to conceal by the day—it would become an all-too-common reality.

"Hello, Julia."

She whirled around to see Quinn standing on the sidewalk. Her heart leapt at the sight of him, so solid and familiar. His serious gray eyes studied her, as if he might be able to determine what she was about to disclose.

"Quinn. I thought maybe you weren't coming after all."

"The walk took longer than I anticipated. I decided to forgo the streetcar today."

She wanted to ask why but pressed her lips together. He was here now, that was all that mattered. Best to get the conversation over with.

"I thought we could sit on the garden bench." It was tucked far enough out of the way that any pedestrians wouldn't notice them there.

Quinn followed her across the short span of lawn to a spot near the rectory where roses, dahlias, and an assortment of wildflowers grew in profusion. Apparently, the garden had belonged to the minister's wife, and ever since her death, he'd kept it up in her memory.

Julia took a seat. Quinn sat at the opposite end of the bench, putting as much space between them as possible. She lifted her chin, not wanting him to see how much that hurt. The last time they'd been together, he couldn't sit close enough to her. But perhaps given the nature of the impending conversation, it was for the best.

A pair of squirrels dashed across the lawn and up the tree trunk, causing the leaves to rustle.

"What is it you wish to say, Julia?" Quinn faced forward, looking out at the street.

This was it. Time to bare her soul. She ran her tongue over her dry lips. "I didn't like the way our last conversation ended," she said slowly. "After all you've done for me, I owe you a better explanation for my actions." She paused to glance over at him, willing him to look at her, but he continued to stare straight ahead. "The truth is, I've been keeping something from you, something I've dreaded having to tell you." Her heart beat too quickly in her chest. She inhaled deeply, but no amount of air would help.

He turned to look at her. "You needn't be afraid to tell me anything."

The affection and longing in his eyes threatened to undo her tightly held control. "I *am* afraid," she said, "because once you know, you'll never think of me the same way again." She swallowed the lump forming in her throat, determined to get through this without resorting to tears.

"Why don't you let me be the judge of that?"

"Very well." She twisted her clammy hands together on her lap. "The reason I can't go back to England, and why I can't entertain any sort of relationship with you, is because . . ." She exhaled, her heart pounding. "I'm pregnant." The words seemed to hang in the air. She gazed down at the grass beneath her feet, unable to bear the shock that must be evident on his face.

After several long seconds, she turned to look at him.

He stared at her, looking as though someone had just punched him. "You're pregnant?" A host of emotions raced across his features—shock, anger, and then hurt.

She nodded. "Almost five months along."

A few beats of silence ensued, broken only by the twitter of some nearby birds.

"Wh-who is the father? Was it Sam?"

Julia hung her head. "No."

"Then who else—" He stopped abruptly. "That doctor. The one you were so frightened of. Is it him?" Disbelief rang in his voice.

She nodded again, her throat too tight to form a reply.

Quinn jumped up from the bench and began to pace the lawn. "Did that cretin force himself on you?" Rage leapt behind his eyes. He looked like a wild man, bent on revenge.

She gripped her fingers together. It was imperative to keep control of her emotions. No matter what, she had to keep Quinn from seeking retribution on her behalf.

"It was my fault for trusting him." Julia released a shaky breath. "He'd never given any indication. . . ." She paused. That wasn't entirely true. In hindsight, when she recalled several of their conversations, she recognized times she'd ignored comments that no married man should have uttered. She'd learned too late that just because she viewed Dr. Hawkins as a father figure didn't mean he felt the same. "I never imagined he would take advantage of me that way." A shudder rippled through her as unbidden memories surfaced. The man's hands on her body. His lips assaulting her face and neck. Even the amount of medication she'd been on couldn't make her forget those horrid sensations.

"Why don't you tell me exactly what happened?" Though his voice was low, tension emanated from him.

She hesitated, her stomach churning. The last thing she wanted to do was relive the experience, but she owed him the truth, as much as she could remember.

"The day after Sam died, I was still distraught, despite the pills

Dr. Hawkins had given me." She took out her handkerchief from her handbag, certain she would need it. "Sam's cousin ordered me to pack my bags and leave the premises. I told him I had nowhere to go, but he didn't care. He said his solicitor would be by the next day to make sure I'd left." A soft breeze ruffled Julia's skirt and lifted her hair from her neck. "Dr. Hawkins came to see how I was doing and found me beside myself—nearly hysterical, I'm ashamed to say. I didn't know what I was going to do. Sam still owed me a month's wages, and without it, I had very little to live on." She twisted the handkerchief between her fingers. "Dr. Hawkins tried to comfort me. Gave me another pill and insisted I drink some brandy to calm my nerves." She shrugged. "I figured since he was a physician, I could trust his judgment, so I did as he said."

Quinn paused in front of her. "Pills *and* liquor? What was he thinking?"

"He seemed so caring, like he truly understood what I was going through. I remember sobbing on his shoulder . . . and then not much else after that." Her account wasn't one hundred percent accurate, but Julia didn't wish to impart any of the more sordid details she could recall. She sucked in a breath. "When I vaguely realized what was happening, I wanted to do something. Scream for help. Anything. But it was as if my bones had turned to jelly. I couldn't even speak, let alone fight him off." Tears leaked from the corner of her eyes. She blotted them with her handkerchief. "I should never have taken those pills. I should have recognized his true intent earlier."

"That's not true. He took advantage of you, Julia. He should be arrested and lose his license to practice medicine." Veins stood out in Quinn's neck, and his fists were clenched.

Julia swallowed hard, forcing back the tears. "I don't remember much of anything until I woke up the next morning. I felt terrible. My head hurt, my mouth was dry, and I was sick to my stomach."

"Were you alone?"

"Yes. I got cleaned up and started packing. Before I was done, the solicitor came to the door, telling me I had to vacate the premises.

He waited until I had all my belongings together and escorted me off the property."

"What did you do then?" Quinn stood above her, his figure casting a shadow over the bench.

"I went to see Dr. Clayborne." Her mouth curved slightly at the memory of his kindness. "He took me home to stay with his wife and infant daughter. They let me live there for a few weeks until I got my bearings." She sighed. "You know the rest of the story."

Julia sagged back against the wooden bench. She felt deflated, now that her secret was out, yet relief eluded her.

If only she could really know what Quinn was thinking.

Pregnant!

Quinn strode over to the nearby tree and stared blindly across the street in an attempt to process all Julia had told him.

She'd been assaulted and was now expecting Dr. Hawkins's baby. No wonder Quinn had gotten such a bad feeling from the man when he met him.

Quinn took a few breaths until he felt calmer, then turned to face Julia, noting for the first time her expanding waistline. How had he not noticed it before? "The day at the hospital with Harry," he said, "was that the first time you'd seen him since the . . . incident?"

She nodded.

A muscle tightened in his throat. "So that's why you pretended we were a couple."

"Yes." She raised tortured eyes to his. "I knew he'd been trying to find me, and I hoped if he thought I was with someone else, he'd leave me alone."

"He doesn't know about . . . ?" The words lodged in his throat.

"No." She lifted her chin. "And if I have my way, he never will."

Quinn stared at her, unblinking, his jaw tight. A thousand questions overwhelmed him, but he forced himself to slow his racing thoughts, mindful of the delicate nature of the situation.

He returned to the bench and resumed his seat. They sat in

silence until he took in a deep breath and turned toward her. "Did you ever consider going to the authorities?" he asked.

She lowered her head, fiddling with the fringe on her bag. "When I was safe at Dr. Clayborne's, I did consider it." She paused, seeming to search for the right words. "But I realized it would be difficult to prove. It would be his word against mine. And who would believe me, a foreigner with no credentials, over a well-respected physician with deep ties to the community?" She shook her head sadly. "No one."

A primal urge to scream rose in Quinn's chest at the unfairness of the situation. Where was justice in all this? Why did a man like Hawkins get to walk away from his crimes free and clear, while Julia would feel the repercussions for the rest of her life? He huffed out a frustrated breath. "I understand. Though I don't like it. Not one bit. That miscreant should be in prison for what he's done."

He closed his eyes, trying to block out the ugly truth. When he opened them again, he dared voice the other question rattling around in his head. "Are you going to keep the baby?"

Julia hesitated. "I hope to. Mrs. Middleton has agreed to let me stay with her as long as I can do my job. She seems to think I could still perform my duties and that the maid and even Mrs. Neville, the cook, would help out with the baby if need be."

A mixture of respect and despair wound through his system. Of course she would want to raise her child, no matter who the father was. That spoke to the type of woman Julia Holloway was. One who knew the value of family and how it felt to be parentless.

Unfortunately, it did little to ease his pain, only solidifying the fact that her future would follow a very different path than either of them had imagined. A path that, for the foreseeable future, he couldn't see intersecting with his own.

Perhaps down the road, when he had his family settled, he could consider returning to find her, but how long that would be he had no idea. And it wouldn't be fair to put both their lives on hold for a whisper of a possibility.

Quinn rose stiffly from the bench, a terrible ache permeating his chest. How did he say good-bye, knowing that this time it was likely for good? "Thank you for telling me this, Julia. I know how hard it must have been. And I understand now why you feel the need to stay here." Coming home pregnant and unmarried would only prove the earl's worst fears had been correct.

Julia rose with him and reached out to grasp his arm, a hint of panic flashing over her features. "Quinn, please don't say anything to my uncle about the baby. I'll write to him and let him know."

He gave a brief nod. "Very well." With supreme effort, he attempted to corral his emotions behind a neutral façade until he could examine them later in private. He forced himself to look directly into her luminous brown eyes. "I wish you nothing but the best, Julia. You deserve it."

Pain twisted her features, tears welling in her eyes once more. "I'm so sorry, Quinn. I never meant to hurt you. I hope you believe that."

He released a breath, closed his eyes again for a brief moment, then nodded. "I believe you. I never wanted to hurt you either. It's just a shame that . . ." He shook his head. "It's just a shame is all."

A silent tear spilled down her cheek.

His heart squeezed with the unfairness of the turn their lives had taken. But there was nothing he could do about it. In a few weeks he'd be on a ship to England, and in a few months she would have a baby. "Good-bye, Julia. Take good care of yourself."

"Good-bye, Quinn. And thank you for everything. I'll never forget your kindness." She stepped away from him, pressing a handkerchief to her mouth.

His eyes misted over. "I'll be praying for you and for the child. Always." He gave her one more heart-wrenching look, then spun on his heel and walked away.

CHAPTER 23

Two days later, Quinn and Harry took the train back to Elmvale to pay Cecil another visit. One last-ditch attempt to get him to see reason and come home with them. For most of the ride, Harry kept Quinn occupied with an ongoing commentary on the countryside, the passengers, and anything else that piqued the boy's interest. Quinn didn't discourage the constant ramblings, since it allowed him to think of something other than Julia.

Quinn had gone over and over her situation for the past forty-eight hours to no avail. He couldn't seem to rise above the devastation he'd felt upon learning she was carrying another man's child. Granted, the circumstances of the baby's conception were not Julia's fault. But he couldn't get over the fact that any relationship with Julia would require him to be a father to that wretch's offspring. What did it say about Quinn that the very thought terrified him?

He'd always prided himself on being nonjudgmental, of being able to see people with compassion, through a Christian lens. Yet now Quinn found himself floundering and couldn't deny that fear had him by a chokehold. What if he resented the child's existence and couldn't give it the love it deserved?

He scrubbed a hand over his stubbled jaw. Despite his love for Julia, no matter how he looked at the situation, he couldn't seem to come up with a solution for them to be together.

When the train pulled into the Elmvale station, Quinn and Harry got off and headed to the livery to rent a cart and horse. The long distance to the Sherman farm would have been too much for Harry to handle, especially in the intense July heat. And at least when the horse reached a good trot, it gave them a slight breeze. Along the way, Harry pointed out every house and barn they passed, and Quinn had to keep reminding him they had a fair distance to go yet.

Finally, almost an hour later, hot and dusty from the ride, Harry tugged on Quinn's arm. "There's another farm, Quinn. Is that it?"

Quinn brought the horse to a slow stop. "Looks like the right one. We'll need to take a back route to get to the barn. And that means walking the rest of the way."

Thankfully, Harry didn't question Quinn's statement. They climbed down and he tied the horse to the mail post, then they continued on. All the while, Quinn kept a sharp watch on the boy, making sure he wasn't overdoing it. When Harry had learned Quinn intended to pay Cecil another visit, he'd begged Quinn to take him with him. Quinn had weighed the decision from every angle and finally allowed him along, hoping that seeing Harry would be the factor that swayed Cecil to come back with them.

Quinn made sure to avoid the farmhouse and headed straight for the barn. If they were fortunate, they would catch Cecil there. Alone.

"I hope his farmer is nicer than mine," Harry said as Quinn guided him around the rear of the building.

"I do too." Quinn stopped at the open door. "Wait here until I see if he's inside." He gestured to a wood stump, and Harry sat down. "I'll be back soon."

Quinn peered around the door and was met with an unnatural silence. All the animals must be out in the pasture. If that was the case, then probably Cecil would be too. Quinn walked down the main aisle. A quick search indicated the barn was empty.

He returned to Harry. "He's not here. Come on, let's check the fields."

Quinn led Harry into the closest pasture and, keeping to the outer perimeter to avoid detection, they made their way to where a group of cattle were grazing.

Halfway there, Harry stopped and bent low over his knees.

"How about a ride, lad?" Quinn asked.

Harry's face brightened. "Sure."

"Hop on, then."

The boy climbed onto Quinn's back and flung his arms around his neck.

"All right now, you keep a lookout for people."

"I will." Already the boy sounded better. Well worth the extra weight under the very warm sun.

"I can see horses," Harry said once they'd crested a hill. "And someone riding one."

Instant tension seized Quinn's gut. *Please let it be Cecil and not one of the other farmhands.* He stopped and squinted against the glare. From the man's slight frame, it could very well be their brother.

Nothing to do but continue on and hope for the best.

When the man spotted them approaching, he pulled his mount to a halt. Then, slowly, he slid from the saddle and pushed off his hat, which swung from a string around his neck.

Cecil.

Thank you, Lord. Now if you could just help us change his mind . . .

"It's him, Harry." Quinn bent low so the boy could jump off. "Why don't you go and surprise him?"

Clutching his side, Harry moved forward, smiling despite the obvious pain. "Cecil! It's me, Harry."

Cecil started running toward them. When he reached Harry, he swooped the boy up into a hard embrace, burying his face in Harry's neck.

"Careful of his ribs," Quinn called as he neared the pair. "He's injured."

Cecil broke away, set Harry down, and wiped his eyes. "How'd you get injured?"

Harry's smile faded.

Quinn laid a hand on the younger boy's shoulder. "A hazard of the job." He gave Cecil a pointed look.

Cecil's face darkened, and he turned his head to scan the fields around them, as if Quinn had reminded him of the potential danger. "We can't talk here." He grabbed the horse's reins. "I have to ride out to the train station to pick up some supplies on the next freight. I'll hitch up the wagon. Meet me on the road, and we'll talk on the way there."

Quinn nodded. "Right. We'll wait by the mailbox." He didn't need to explain the situation to Harry. The boy's grim expression said it all.

Ten minutes later, the rumble of a wagon sounded on the road. Upon spying Cecil at the helm, Quinn and Harry stepped out from behind the cart, where they'd been trying to stay out of sight.

Quinn approached the wagon as it slowed. "I rented this cart and horse from the livery in town," he told Cecil. "I'll tie the mare to the back of the wagon. She's pretty docile, so it shouldn't be a problem."

Cecil nodded.

Quinn helped Harry onto the bench seat, then went to secure the horse behind them.

When he came back, Cecil had his arm around Harry. He made a strange noise that sounded suspiciously like a sob and pressed a kiss to Harry's hair. "I never thought I'd see you again, Harry lad. I'm so sorry I couldn't keep us together. I tried my best, but they wouldn't listen."

Quinn hauled himself up onto the bench. "It wasn't your fault, Cec. You had to go where they sent you."

Cecil raised his head and swiped his elbow across his face. He met Quinn's stare, gave a brief nod, then ruffled Harry's hair. "So, you found Harry and managed to get him away from his farm?"

"I certainly wasn't going to leave him there under those conditions."

"Quinn took me to the hospital, and the doctors fixed me up right fine." Harry grinned.

"Glad to hear it." Cecil smiled, then shot a look behind him. "We'd best get going." He clucked to the horses, and they started off down the road.

They traveled in silence for several miles until at last Cecil relaxed. His shoulders dropped a few inches, and he let out a long breath. "Is there a reason you came here other than bringing Harry to see me?" He shot Quinn a wary glance.

"I found Becky," Quinn said quietly. "She's working for a family in Peterborough."

Cecil's eyes widened. "Is she all right?"

"She's fine." Quinn paused. "In fact, she's getting married in a few months."

"Married?" Cecil whistled. "Imagine that."

"And we're going back to England soon," Harry piped up. "Becky's coming with us."

The wagon bounced and jostled them, almost unseating Harry, who winced.

"Watch the holes if you can. Harry's ribs can't take the bouncing."

"Sorry." A muscle in Cecil's jaw ticked. "Is that why you came, then? To pressure me into going with you?" He stared straight ahead at the road before them.

"Not to pressure you. To appeal to your conscience. We're all going back for Mum's sake. Even Becky's making time, despite her upcoming wedding." Quinn attempted to push back his frustration. It would serve no purpose to rile Cecil. "You could do the same. Come back for a visit and then return here, if you're so determined to stay."

"Please, Cecil." Harry tugged on his sleeve. "We'd all be together again. It would make Mum so happy."

The train station came into view, and Cecil slowed the horse's gait. "When?"

"There's a ship leaving Halifax at the end of the month. I aim to be on it."

"So soon?"

"I only pray we're in time and that Mum lives long enough to see us all again."

Cecil's thin frame stiffened. "I'll hand it to you, Quinn. You have manipulation down to an art."

Irritation spiked in Quinn's chest. "This is not about me."

"Of course it is." Cecil's eyes flashed. "It's all about you needing to prove yourself. To make everything perfect. Like you've been trying to do ever since Dad died." He pulled the reins sharply. "But life isn't perfect, Quinn. Not even close."

Quinn clamped his lips together to keep from arguing. Nothing he said right now would help matters. Instead, he counted to ten as his brother reined in the horses behind the station.

"You're right, Cecil. Nothing is perfect." He withdrew a piece of paper from his pocket where he'd had the forethought to write down the boardinghouse address and phone number. "You can get a message to me or Harry here. I'll be praying you change your mind." He stood and jumped lightly to the ground.

"Please come," Harry said. "It won't be the same without you." Then he flung his arms around Cecil's neck, hugging him hard, before accepting Quinn's assistance off the bench.

Cecil sat in the wagon for several seconds before he climbed down and tied the horses to the post. "I'll give it a good deal of thought. That much I can promise you. And if Mr. Sherman agrees to give me the time off, I'll consider making the trip."

"Thank you." Quinn stood looking at his brother, very aware of how little he really knew him anymore. He longed to pull him into a tight embrace, but an awkward silence developed between them instead. Quinn straightened his posture. "Take care of yourself, Cecil."

The shrill sound of a train whistle pierced the air. The ground beneath them began to vibrate.

Cecil stepped away from the wagon. "Have a safe trip, and if you don't hear from me, give Mum . . . and Becky . . . my love." He reached out a hand and once again mussed Harry's hair. Then he turned and jogged over to the platform to meet the approaching train.

CHAPTER 24

"Will you be coming to church this morning?" Mrs. Middleton asked Julia the next Sunday as she cut into her poached egg.

Julia's hand stilled on her fork. How she wished she could attend, but with her ever-expanding belly, someone was bound to notice her condition, and she did not want to take the chance. "I don't think so. But thank you for asking." She patted a napkin to her mouth. "I'm sure Mrs. Banbury will go with you, if you'd like."

"I expect she will. But I prefer your company." Mrs. Middleton winked at her.

"I enjoy going with you too. However, until the baby comes, I feel it would be best to stay out of the public eye as much as possible. I wouldn't want to cause you any undue criticism or mean-spirited gossip."

"Balderdash." Mrs. Middleton set her teacup down with a clank. "No one would dare say anything to me or risk being on the receiving end of my wrath."

Julia reached over to lay her hand on the woman's arm. "Your support means the world to me. But you needn't fight my battles."

"Very well, my dear." Mrs. Middleton rose. "Any word from that young man of yours?"

A stab of pain ripped through Julia at the mere mention of Quinn. *He's not my young man*, she wanted to say. Instead, she shook her head. "I don't expect to hear from him again."

"Hmph." The woman hobbled toward the door. "From what you'd told me about him, I thought the lad would have had more sense." She glanced at Julia with a sympathetic look. "Enjoy a wee rest while I'm out. You deserve it."

Julia managed a smile. The more she was around the feisty widow, the more she liked her. She had an unconventional attitude, combined with a sharp wit and a wicked sense of humor. Secretly, Julia liked to pretend Mrs. Middleton was the grandmother she'd never known. Though even a grandmother might not have accepted her scandalous condition as easily.

Julia lingered in the dining room over another cup of tea until she heard the front door close, signaling the women's departure. Then she rose and went into the parlor, where her Bible awaited her. She might not be able to attend services, but she could still spend the hour in prayer.

Though Julia did her best to keep her focus on scripture, her mind inevitably wandered back to Quinn. Had he convinced Cecil to return to England? Was he still in town, or had they all left for Halifax? If Harry was well enough, there would be no need to stay in Toronto until the last minute, and Quinn would likely want to get to Halifax in plenty of time to secure their passage.

A well of hurt arose at the idea that he might have left the country without seeing her one last time. But what else did she expect once he'd learned the truth? Deep down, she'd hoped he would be able to overlook her pregnancy and understand why she chose to keep it a secret. Even though it had seemed he didn't blame her for what happened, his silence spoke volumes.

A loud knock echoed through the quiet of the large house.

Julia jumped, knocking the Bible from her lap. It landed with a soft thud on the carpet. She glanced at the clock on the mantel. Too early for Mrs. Middleton to be home, for she always enjoyed fellowship in the church hall after the service. Besides, the woman wouldn't knock on her own door.

Could Quinn have had a change of heart and come to see her after all? Julia's pulse sprinted with hope as she retrieved the Bible and set it on the table. Then she smoothed her skirt and hurried to answer the door.

But when she pulled it open, the feeling of anticipation evaporated faster than drops of water on a hot griddle. Instead, her mouth fell open, and her legs threatened to buckle.

Richard Hawkins stood on the porch, impeccably dressed as always in a suit and tie. His stern features softened slightly when he saw her. "Julia. Thank the heavens, I've tracked you down at last."

Her hand flew to her throat, and without thinking, she retreated a few steps.

He took advantage of her surprise to push his way into the house. "You didn't meet me at the hospital as I asked in my letter. I've been frantic not being able to reach you. There's so much I need to say to you." He paused to gentle his voice as he turned to face her. "Julia, ever since our time together, I can't get you out of my mind. I want you to know how special you are—" His gaze strayed to her abdomen then, and he froze. His face hardened, his eyes narrowing.

Julia shoved her trembling hands into her apron pockets, hoping to disguise the swell, but it was too late.

"You're with child," he hissed. "Several months along, from the look of it."

Her mind scattered, all forms of rebuttal escaping her. *Dear Lord, help me. What do I do now?*

Perspiration beaded on her forehead, one cold droplet sliding down her neck. With no other viable option, she did the only thing she could think of. She jutted her chin out. "I may have put on a few pounds, thanks to the cook's enticing menu, but I hardly believe that warrants such a comment." She edged toward the front entrance, but he reached out to snag her by the arm.

"Come now, Julia. I'm a physician. You can't fool me."

Panic gripped her airway as she realized just how alone they were. Everyone else was out at church. Even Mrs. Neville. She glanced toward the open door and tried to estimate her chances of making it outside without injury.

"How dare you keep this from me?" Spittle formed at the corner of his mouth. "I have a right to know I'm going to be a father."

She backed away from him. "You're wrong."

"I don't think so. The night we were together, it was abundantly clear that you were an innocent, and I doubt you've been with anyone since."

Bile rose in her throat. Her first impulse was to tell him it was Quinn's baby. But her tongue wouldn't cooperate, refusing to drag Quinn into her shame.

Her cheeks heated. Tears burned the back of her eyes. What would Richard do now? Would he try to take the child from her? He was a respected doctor, a man with power and influence in the community. The very reason she had never accused him of assaulting her, fearing his word would hold far more weight than hers.

She backed up further until the sharp edge of the wall's wainscoting stabbed her hip.

"Julia." He sighed, trying to regain control of himself. "You needn't look so terrified. I came here to tell you the good news—that after a great deal of consideration, I have decided to divorce my wife. Soon I will be free to marry you. You must admit the timing has to be fate." He bent and splayed his fingers over her abdomen. "I've always wanted a son. Something my present wife couldn't give me."

Nausea churned in Julia's stomach at the feel of his hands on her. Her whole body began to rebel, shaking uncontrollably, but she pulled herself up and summoned the last remnants of courage. "I want you to leave. Now," she said in a loud voice.

He jerked upright and stared. "I'm not leaving without you. Go and pack your things. You're coming with me." He grabbed her by the elbow and began to propel her toward the staircase.

"I'm not going anywhere with you." She grasped the newel-post, digging her feet into the carpet in an attempt to thwart his progress. Fear tasted metallic on her tongue. Mrs. Middleton wouldn't be home for almost an hour. When she returned, she'd find Julia gone and would think the worst. That despite her kindness, Julia had run off—

"Take your filthy hands off her." A deep voice thundered through the hallway.

Julia's legs went weak. *Quinn!*

Richard whirled around. "This is a private matter. None of your concern."

Quinn charged forward, fists clenched. "You have no right to put your hands on Julia. Especially after what you've done to her."

Richard eyed him and released Julia's arm. "I have every right. I am the father of this child, and I intend to marry her."

Julia gave a strangled cry, her eyes glued to Quinn. She shook her head, silently begging him not to believe it. She would never marry Richard. She'd give up the baby first before she let him near her child.

The veins in Quinn's neck stood out, evidence of the temper he was working hard to suppress. Julia feared that at any moment he would attack Richard in a misguided attempt at revenge. But violence wouldn't solve anything and would only get Quinn in trouble with the law.

"Julia is not going to marry you," Quinn said tersely, towering above the shorter man. "Because she is marrying me." He stared at Richard without blinking.

Julia gasped. What on earth made him say that?

Richard's eyes narrowed on Julia. "Is this true?"

She quickly moved to Quinn's side, her heart thudding loudly. "I told you the day we met in the hospital that Quinn and I are together." The white lie rolled easily off her tongue. She'd do anything to protect her baby. Never would she allow her child to be raised by such a man. "We have nothing further to say to each other, Dr. Hawkins. And if you contact me again, I'll . . . call the constable."

Quinn draped a protective arm around her, his upper body as inflexible as granite.

Red splotches marred Richard's face. "You're bluffing. I am the father of your child. I'd bet money on it."

Julia willed her gaze to remain steady, neither confirming nor denying his claim.

"You are a married man," Quinn practically sneered. "You have no right to stake a claim on another woman. Now leave and don't return." He grabbed hold of Richard's arm and forced the man toward the doorway.

Richard twisted back to glare at Julia. "You haven't heard the last of this." The iciness of his voice matched the coldness in his eyes. "I'll find a way to prove that's my child, and when I do, there'll be hell to pay."

It took every ounce of Quinn's control not to smash his fist into Hawkins's detestable face. Make him pay for what he'd done to Julia. Instead, he gritted his teeth, shoved the blustering oaf out onto the porch, and slammed the door. Congratulating himself that he hadn't lost control, he took a minute to calm himself before going in to face Julia.

After much reflection and self-recrimination over the past week, Quinn had come to apologize to Julia for the way he'd reacted to the news of her situation. Once the shock and disappointment had faded, he'd been able put himself in Julia's shoes, trying to imagine how lost she must be feeling, about to face motherhood alone. He knew then he had to try and make amends.

It never occurred to him that the cad who had taken advantage of Julia would be bold enough to come after her again. Seeing the man's hands on her, all Quinn's protective instincts had roared to life, and he'd blurted out the lie before he'd had time to think it through.

Lord, forgive me and help me rectify the situation with Julia.

He strode over to where she stood trembling in the hall, her eyes wide.

"Are you all right? He didn't hurt you, did he?"

"No. I'm fine." Yet her breathing was shallow, her face too pale.

"Come and sit down."

He led her into the parlor to the sofa, then went to get her a glass of water.

Once she had drained half the glass and a bit of her color had returned, he took a seat across from her.

"Thank you," she said quietly as she fingered the glass. "You didn't have to do that."

"I couldn't stand watching that man put his hands on you as if he owned you." He clenched his molars together and mentally counted to ten.

"Why are you here, Quinn?" Her soft question was laced with hurt. Or was it regret?

He released a long breath. "I felt bad about the way I reacted the other day." He leaned over his knees, his gaze sliding to the carpet. "I did a lot of thinking afterward, and I realized I hadn't considered how hard this must be for you. Having a man you trusted abuse you, facing an unknown future, raising a child alone—that would be enough to break most people."

Silence. He raised his head to look at her.

Julia's forehead had puckered, and tears brimmed in her brown eyes.

With a sigh, he moved to sit beside her on the sofa. He took one of her hands in his, and when he looked down into her misty eyes, he could no longer deny the truth. No matter the horrid circumstances, no matter that she carried another man's child, he was in love with this woman. "Can you forgive me for being so judgmental?"

"There's nothing to forgive." A tear slid down her cheek. "I hated thinking that you despised me."

"I could never despise you, Julia." He gave her a rueful smile. "However, I won't deny I was disappointed."

Her gaze faltered.

"Not in you. Never that." He lifted her chin. "I was disappointed because I wished the baby was mine."

"Oh, Quinn." More tears spilled over.

He took out his handkerchief and gently wiped her cheeks.

Though he hated to distress her any further, a harsh reality had to be faced. "I hate to add to your troubles, but there's something we need to address. Hawkins is going to continue to harass you. He's convinced the baby is his, and I suspect nothing will stop him from attempting to gain control."

She laid a protective hand over her stomach. "What am I going to do? I will never marry him. And I won't let him take my baby." Panic flashed over her features.

"I won't allow that either." He put an arm around her, pulling her against him. All the while, his mind raced with what he could do to protect her. "Come to England with me. He won't be able to bother you there. And once you explain the circumstances, I'm certain your uncle will take you in."

The flames crackled as a log fell over in the hearth.

She sniffed into her handkerchief. "I can't do that, Quinn. I can't bring shame to Uncle Howard's good name. You know how his peers value their reputations. He would be ostracized because of me."

Quinn wanted to argue with her, but deep down he knew she was right. He'd witnessed the English nobility's snobbery firsthand. The only way to save face would be . . .

He sucked in a breath. "I believe I've already devised the solution," he said. "That is, if you're willing to consider it." This had to be done properly, or she might refuse to listen.

Once again, he took her hands in his. "If we were to marry before the baby is born, the child would be considered mine."

"You can't be serious?"

"I'm very serious."

"No, Quinn, I couldn't . . ." Julia bit her bottom lip. "It wouldn't be fair to you."

Not fair to *him*? How was any of this fair to *her*?

"Besides," she said, "you're leaving for England soon. And you have your family to think about. They must be your priority."

He ran his thumb gently over her hand and waited until she looked at him. "I could give you my name and my protection before I go. Or you could come with me . . . as my wife. Your uncle need never know the circumstances of the child's conception." He squashed the niggle of doubt that he might not be able to love Julia's child as he should. With no way to determine that for certain, he would have to pray for God's grace on the matter.

The more he thought about it, the more certain he became. Marriage was the right thing for both of them.

Slowly she disengaged her hand from his. Then she rose and crossed to the window that looked onto the front yard.

Quinn forced himself to remain quiet, to give her time to think, to weigh her options. If she thought about it logically, she would have to see the perfection of this solution.

Suddenly, it dawned on him how advantageous this could be for him as well. They could marry and go back to England, with his siblings. The earl would give Quinn the property he'd promised him, one with enough room to house him and Julia and the babe, as well as his mother and Harry and perhaps even Cecil, if the lad ever came to his senses. This whole situation might turn out to be a blessing in disguise.

At last, Julia turned back to him. A wreath of sadness shrouded her features. "You'll never know how much I appreciate your offer, Quinn." She sighed. "However, I can't allow you to sacrifice your life for me."

She looked so beautiful, her fair head framed with light from the window behind her. If only she'd accept his help. "I wouldn't consider it a sacrifice, Julia. I care about you a great deal." He hesitated, then, in a moment of utter surrender, allowed his defenses to fall away. "I might even be falling in love with you," he said quietly. "So, you see, it would be no great hardship to marry you."

Julia stumbled back a step. She pressed one hand to her mouth but nothing could contain the well of emotion rising through her.

Quinn might be in love with her?

How was that even possible after everything he'd learned about her? Her mistakes? Her pregnancy? Tears pushed at the corners of her eyes. That he would do something so noble to protect her and give his name to her child, well, it was beyond anything she deserved.

But love? She wasn't at all sure how she felt about that. Her breath skittered in her lungs, and nerves rioted through her stomach. She swallowed and attempted to formulate an adequate response to his declaration. Still, no words would come.

She raised her head and found his warm gray eyes watching her intently.

"Julia, please don't think I'm saying this solely to sway your decision. I just didn't want to leave things left unsaid between us." His lips twitched into a half smile. "And even if it will pain me, I want you to be honest too."

"Oh, Quinn," she whispered. "I don't know what to say."

Her legs began to tremble, forcing her to sit on the sofa. Confusion reigned as her mind wrestled with her heart, but she couldn't seem to reconcile the two. What *did* she feel for Quinn? She was attracted to him, no doubt about that. In addition, she admired many things about him—his intelligence, his loyalty, his determination. She might even be sliding toward love herself, though it was much too soon to say for certain.

He came to sit beside her, his nearness providing a distraction to thinking logically.

"It's all right, Julia. Love doesn't always happen at the same time. We could wed in name only until the baby comes. Then once your situation is secure and the baby is legally mine, we could determine whether or not to continue the marriage."

"Why would you want to do this? There is no benefit to you in this union."

His lips tightened. "Perhaps you're not used to someone simply wanting to do the right thing. I cannot in good conscience leave you here at the mercy of that cad. If I can't be here physically to protect you, then at least you'd have my name." His eyes begged her to believe him.

Yet there were still several important issues looming between them. Issues she couldn't ignore.

"What about the fact that our marriage would never be sanctioned by my family or anyone else in English society?" The thought of disappointing her uncle again was too overwhelming to consider. Coward that she was, she'd rather stay in Toronto.

He took her hand in his, heat from his fingers surrounding her. "We can face those obstacles when the time comes. Together."

Julia's air whooshed out. Her head spun with everything that had happened in such a short space of time and the emotional turmoil that accompanied it.

Quinn leaned closer, his warm breath stirring the ends of her hair. "Will you marry me, Julia?"

Her hand fluttered to her throat. She looked up, and when she met his soft gaze, she couldn't find the strength to turn down everything he offered.

But she needed to be sure she was doing the right thing. She gave him an apologetic look. "I need more time to make such a decision. Can I give you my answer tomorrow?"

He tried and failed to mask the hurt that crept into his eyes. But he managed a slight smile. "Of course. Until tomorrow, then."

CHAPTER 25

After a sleepless night of wrestling with Quinn's proposal and the fear of Dr. Hawkins returning for her, Julia took advantage of her day off to make an appointment with Rev. Burke. Though the thought of baring her soul and exposing the very personal details of her pregnancy to the upright man made her cringe, she found she craved an unbiased opinion of her situation. She hoped Rev. Burke could help her sort through her conflicting emotions about Quinn and what a marriage in name only would mean, legally and morally.

As she knocked on the rector's office door, Julia's heart beat too fast in her chest. She wet her dry lips and tucked several strands of hair into place while she waited.

"Julia, my dear, please come in." The minister's gaze strayed to her expanding midsection for a brief second, but then he stood up and smiled. "It's lovely to see you again."

"Thank you for making time for me, Reverend. I wouldn't have pressed, but I have an important decision to make, and I need your advice in order to do so."

"Well now, I'm honored you think so highly of my opinion. I'll certainly do my best."

Julia sat on one of the guest chairs, while Rev. Burke resumed his seat behind the desk.

The lingering smell of tobacco hung in the air, bringing a measure of comfort to Julia. It reminded her of her father sitting in his armchair on a Sunday afternoon, smoking his favorite pipe. What would he advise her to do now if he were here?

A beam of sunlight filtered through the window and danced across the wooden desk's surface, where a ledger sat open.

"Just balancing the church's accounts." Rev. Burke closed the book with a chuckle. "Now, how can I help you today?"

The simple question brought a lump to her throat. She twisted her hands together on her lap. "I have a story to tell you. Which leads up to the difficult decision I have to make."

"Go ahead. I'm a good listener." His gentle invitation went a long way to ease Julia's nerves.

She took a deep breath and then briefly relayed the story of Sam's death and Dr. Hawkins's betrayal. Other than a flicker of his eyelids once or twice, the minister showed no emotion. Until she told him that she was expecting a child. Then his face filled with sympathy.

"I'm terribly sorry, my dear. That is a heavy burden to bear."

Her throat tightened. "Thank you for saying that. I've been feeling so guilty about the whole situation. Guilty that I didn't try harder to stop him." She opened her bag to retrieve her handkerchief.

"I believe the medication and alcohol may have had something to do with that." Rev. Burke folded his hands on his desktop. "The man not only violated your trust, he violated the oath he took as a physician. You are not to blame for his vile actions."

Julia sat in silence, pressure mounting in her chest. Quinn had said something similar, yet shame continued to eat at her. "Why can't I stop feeling responsible, then?" she whispered. "Not only about this, but about Sam too." She sighed. "After he died, I was devastated. I felt I should have paid closer attention. Should have noticed his mood had slipped." She shook her head. "In the days that followed his death, I truly didn't care if I lived or died. Maybe I felt I deserved what happened to me." She dabbed the handkerchief to her eyes.

Rev. Burke came around the desk and pulled up a chair beside her. "My dear girl, I have dealt with many suicides over the course of my career, and in every case, someone feels exactly as you do. That it was their fault their loved one died. That it had been their responsibility to prevent it. The reality is that if someone really wishes to harm themselves, only God himself can prevent it."

Emotion welled up inside her until a flood of tears let loose. She held the hanky to her mouth to stifle her sobs. Why had all these bad things happened to her? What had she done to deserve such tragedy in her life?

Rev. Burke remained silent, patting Julia's back until her weeping turned to sniffles. Then he exhaled softly. "Have you brought your situation to the Lord, Julia? Have you asked Him to release you from your guilt?"

She shook her head. "I didn't feel worthy to even ask."

And therein lay the heart of her problems. She didn't feel worthy to ask anything of God, didn't feel worthy of Quinn's love or his protection, and she certainly didn't feel worthy to be this child's mother. She had disgraced her family and herself.

Rev. Burke gave her a long look. "Everyone is worthy of forgiveness, Julia. No matter how great or how small the sin. As long as you repent with a clean heart and try your best to live a better life."

"I do repent, Reverend. I want to live my life in accordance with God's will. I want to give my child a good life. Be a good mother." Fresh tears spilled down her cheeks.

"And so you shall. I'm certain of it." He patted her arm. "Why don't we pray together?"

She wiped her face and nodded. "I'd like that," she whispered.

He bowed his head. "Lord Jesus, we come before you with humble and contrite hearts, knowing we are sinners, asking for your help to live a life that is pleasing to you in keeping with your commandments. Give us the grace and strength to do so." He opened one eye. "Julia, would you care to add your own words here?"

"All right." Julia clasped her hands together and bowed her head, allowing her heart to open and the words to flow. "Lord, I ask your forgiveness for my many mistakes. First, for hurting my uncle by the callous way I left home. For failing Sam in his time of need. And for the part I played in my pregnancy, unwitting though it may have been. I also ask for your help to forgive the man who betrayed me." She paused to take a breath. "And I thank you, Lord, for this precious life within me. No matter how this child was conceived, no matter the problems involved, I believe this baby is a gift." Tears trembled in her voice. "Help me to be a good mother and to do what's right for everyone involved. Amen."

"Amen." Rev. Burke cleared his throat and glanced over at her. "That was beautiful, Julia. I believe you spoke from the heart, and as such God has forgiven your sins. And I trust the Lord will help you make your decision."

A tremor ran through her body, and as it faded, a sense of peace descended. She clutched the minister's hand, more tears welling, this time tears of gratitude. "Thank you so much, Reverend Burke. This is just what I needed."

"I'm so glad I could help." He tilted his head to study her, his gray hair falling over his forehead. "Tell me, is this decision about whether or not to keep the child?"

She wiped away the last of her tears. "Oh no. That one was easy. I couldn't bear to give up my baby." A breath shuddered through her. "But now that Dr. Hawkins has become aware of my condition, I fear he won't stop until he gets custody." She bit her bottom lip and quickly relayed Quinn's offer of protection, a marriage in name only.

When she finished, the minister sat back, stroking his chin. "That's quite a noble gesture on his part. How do you feel about it?"

How indeed? If she could figure that out, she might know what to tell Quinn.

"I'm honored and grateful that he would consider doing this, since it might be the only way to keep my baby safe. But on the other hand, I feel terrible, burdening Quinn with my problems." She inhaled and released a slow breath. "If I do decide to marry him, I would want a civil ceremony and treat it like a business contract. One that could be dissolved after the baby is born—if that's what we decide is best."

One of the minister's brows rose.

Her stomach dropped. "Have I shocked you?" she asked. The last thing she wanted was to offend the kind man.

He shook his head, chuckling. "It would take a lot more than that to shock me, my dear. This wouldn't be the first marriage undertaken for a similar reason. You seem to be looking at the situation in a logical manner. However, what if one of you wants to continue the marriage and one doesn't?"

Her pulse fluttered at the idea of Quinn becoming her husband in every sense of the word—an idea almost too scary to entertain. "I'm certain Quinn would respect whatever I decide." She glanced over at the minister. "Do you think it would be terribly selfish of me to marry Quinn?"

Rev. Burke pursed his lips. "He wouldn't have made the offer if he hadn't meant it. And wanting to protect your baby isn't selfish. It's a mother's prerogative." He smiled. "As long as both of you are honest about your expectations of the arrangement, I think it should be fine."

The tension in her neck suddenly eased. If this godly man didn't see this union as an abomination, then perhaps she could accept Quinn's proposal after all. Perhaps this was God's way of telling her it was all right. She grasped the minister's hand and squeezed. "Thank you, Reverend Burke. I think I know what to do now."

Quinn waited in Mrs. Middleton's parlor for Julia to appear, trepidation making him jumpy. After almost twenty-four hours of uncertainty, she'd left word that she wanted to see him. Would she consent to marry him and let him protect her and the child? Or had his declaration of love frightened her off?

Quinn paced the room, hating feeling so nervous. His palms were sweaty, and his collar felt two sizes too tight.

Footsteps alerted him to Julia's arrival. His gaze snapped to the door.

Dressed in a high-necked blouse and loose-fitting apron over her skirt, she entered the room, head held high. Her brown eyes were large and serious. Yet she wore a hint of vulnerability that made the need to protect her roar in his ears.

With extreme effort, he reined in his impatience, vowing to give her time to inform him of her decision. "Hello, Julia."

"Quinn, thank you for coming. I wasn't sure you'd get my message."

"I did. But even if you hadn't called, I planned on coming by this evening anyway."

She ran a hand down the side of her skirt. "Shall we sit down?"

"Of course." He followed her to the sofa. "I presume this means you've made your decision?"

"I have." She folded her hands in her lap. After several seconds, she lifted her eyes to his. "I have decided to accept your offer, but I wish to clarify the terms."

His joy was immediately squashed. She sounded like a solicitor proposing a business investment. "What terms are those?"

One fair brow rose. "I think we need to define what a marriage 'in name only' constitutes. And stipulate what happens if one of us wishes to end our arrangement."

"I see." Quinn did his best to hide the disappointment rushing through him. He'd hoped for a bit friendlier union, nothing so clinical, but in the end if he could protect her, he'd take his chances and pray for the Lord to guide their way. "I suppose we could write up an agreement."

She blinked. "I didn't mean anything that formal. I just . . ."

"A verbal agreement, then?"

The lines in her forehead eased. "That will do. I know you're a man of your word and that you'll stand by what you say."

"Thank you for that." He studied her face, the way she bit her lip giving evidence of her nerves. In fact, she looked more than nervous. Terrified would better describe it. That sudden realization instantly calmed his own anxiety. He needed to let her set the terms that would make the situation easier for her. "Why don't you begin?" he said. "How would you like our—" he hesitated—"partnership to look?"

"Well, first of all, I would want a civil marriage performed by a magistrate. It seems more in keeping with what we are doing."

Objections lodged in his throat. He'd always envisioned being married in the church, with a minister as officiant. However, he could be flexible. "Go on."

"Obviously, we would keep separate rooms." A blush spread over her cheeks and up to the tips of her ears. "Then, once the baby arrives and you are named the father, we will revisit our arrangement to determine whether or not we wish to continue."

Despite his best efforts, Quinn couldn't hide his frown. This was sounding worse by the moment.

"Is something wrong?"

"It all seems so impersonal. Not at all roman—" He bit his lip, instantly realizing his error.

"Romantic? That is exactly what I don't want." Her brow furrowed. "This will be a business arrangement. A contract between two parties."

"What if I want to keep my commitment and be a true father to the child?"

She looked around in confusion, a hint of panic on her face. "I hadn't considered that. I assumed we'd end the marriage and continue with our own separate lives." Her forehead crinkled, and she twisted her hands together.

He reached over to cover one of her hands with his. "You see my point. Every contingency can't be planned in advance. You need to trust, Julia. Trust God to walk this journey with us. And to show us the right path to take."

"I'm trying, but it's hard."

"Then trust me when I say that I will always honor your decision. If you decide to end our agreement, I will abide by your wishes." He tipped her chin up to make sure she was looking at him. "I will never go back on the vows I make to you. It will be up to you to make the move to end our marriage."

Her bottom lip quivered, but she gave an almost imperceptible nod.

"Then, Miss Holloway, I will ask again. Will you marry me and allow me to protect you and your child?"

Moisture rimmed her eyes, but her gaze did not falter. "Yes, Quinn," she whispered. "I will marry you."

Relief and something warm spread through his chest. He raised her hand to his lips. "Thank you. I will see to the arrangements and let you know what is required."

Nodding, she gave him a trembling smile.

Not exactly the romantic betrothal he'd envisioned, but it would have to do for now.

Thankfully, he was a patient man.

CHAPTER 26

Julia's knees shook as she followed Quinn into the courthouse three days later. These were no ordinary wedding jitters that had beset her. These nerves took jitters to a whole new level. Was she really about to marry Quinn?

Inside the main door, she paused. Despite the intense July heat, she wore a heavy woolen shawl over her dress to conceal her expanding belly from anyone who might see them. The stuffy air inside the building offered no relief from the warm temperatures, and since she could see no windows save an enormous stained-glass one above a split staircase, she doubted the air would be any cooler inside.

Standing in the main hall, she removed the shawl and folded it on her arm in front of her.

Quinn turned and stared, scanning the length of her satin ivory dress. "You look beautiful, Julia."

Heat rushed into her cheeks. "Mrs. Middleton gave me this gown and altered it to fit." Her gaze slid to the ground. How could he not be mortified to be marrying an obviously pregnant woman? Though perhaps she was being overly sensitive, because the design of the dress did manage to disguise her condition to a great degree.

Julia had been surprised at Mrs. Middleton's offer, since she had been a bit taken aback by Julia's sudden wedding. However, she'd been relieved to find out that Julia intended to stay on in her employ for the foreseeable future while Quinn traveled to England and, of course, that such a marriage would offer Julia protection. And when Julia mentioned she had nothing to wear for the ceremony, the gruff woman insisted on giving Julia one of her gowns. Thanks to the woman's skill with a needle, Mrs. Middleton was able to alter the garment to fit Julia's ever-increasing middle and still allow her to breathe comfortably.

In the days leading up to the ceremony, Julia had been plagued with doubt and almost changed her mind several times. What if Quinn became too attached to her during this mock marriage? What if she became accustomed to having a husband and Quinn decided it had all been a colossal mistake? There were so many ways this could lead to disaster. Yet each time, with no other alternative in sight, she'd resigned herself to going through with their plan.

As though sensing her disquiet, Quinn gave her an encouraging smile and wrapped her hand through his arm. She wished she could be as poised as he appeared to be.

They made their way down several hallways to Courtroom B, where a justice of the peace would marry them.

Quinn paused outside the door. "Please try to relax, Julia. Even if the circumstances aren't perfect, I'd like you to have some fond memories of our wedding day." He bent and pressed a soft kiss to her cheek.

Instead of easing her nerves, her stomach knotted. She certainly didn't deserve a man as fine as Quinn or the sacrifice he was making. Her hand fluttered over her belly. But then again, maybe this little one did.

Lord, I know I don't deserve your favor, but please help me get through this. And if this is not the right thing for Quinn, please give me a sign and I'll release him from his promise.

They entered the courtroom and waited for the official to call their names. When he did, they both moved toward the large desk at the front of the room.

A robed magistrate appeared and came to greet them. Quinn stepped forward and gave him their marriage license. Quinn had been concerned that since they weren't Canadian, they might not qualify for a license, but he'd been relieved to learn they did.

The man scanned the document, then smiled at them. "Welcome. If you're ready, let's begin. Do you have any witnesses?"

"No, sir," Quinn said. "We hoped you might have someone that could fulfill that duty."

"Certainly." The man turned to a woman near the side door. "Vivian, call Theresa in, please. We'll need you both as witnesses."

As soon as the two women returned, the official took his spot and nodded to them. "If you're ready, please join hands."

Julia inhaled and placed her hand in Quinn's, hoping he wouldn't notice its clamminess.

The official opened a book and began to read. "We have come here today to join—" he peered at the certificate—"Julia Holloway and Quinten Aspinall in marriage. Quinten and Julia, do you solemnly declare that you do not know of any lawful impediment why you may not be joined in matrimony?"

Quinn glanced at her and nodded. "We do," they said in unison.

The magistrate looked at Quinn. "Quinten, do you take Julia to be your wife, to have and to hold, for better or for worse, in sickness and in health, and forsaking all others, keep only unto her so long as you both shall live?"

Quinn gazed deeply into her eyes. "I do."

Julia swallowed, her hands trembling.

Quinn turned to the officiant. "I'd like to add something here, if I may."

The man's eyebrows rose. "Go ahead."

Quinn turned back to Julia, his gray eyes darkened to pewter. "Julia, I know this is not exactly the wedding of your dreams. But I promise to be a good husband and give you the best possible life I can. For as long as you need me."

Her throat tightened with the threat of tears. How like Quinn to make sure she knew that he would include her in every decision regarding their future. Blinking, she forced her lips into a smile. "And I will do my best to never let you regret this moment."

Time seemed to stop as their gazes locked, and Julia wished that their circumstances could be different.

Then the official cleared his throat. "Let's continue, shall we?" He pushed his glasses up the bridge of his nose and led them through the rest of the vows. When they finished, he looked up. "Is there a ring?"

Julia opened her mouth to say no, when Quinn pulled one hand free and rifled in his jacket pocket. He pulled out a plain silver band.

"I got this yesterday. I hope you like it."

Julia swallowed and nodded. She needed the visual proof that she was a married woman. It would go a long way to restoring her respectability in the eyes of society. How thoughtful of Quinn to think of it.

The magistrate pointed. "Place the ring on her finger and repeat after me. With this ring, I thee wed."

Quinn slid the ring onto Julia's finger and repeated the line, his voice husky.

The officiant closed his book and rocked back on his heels. "Quinten and Julia, insomuch as the two of you have agreed to live together in matrimony and have given each other these vows, I now pronounce you to be husband and wife."

The two witnesses murmured something inaudible.

Sudden tears burned at the back of Julia's eyes. Despite the fact that they weren't saying vows in a church, the solemnity of the occasion sank into the hollow spaces inside her, ones that had been empty for so long. She was married now. She belonged to someone.

That thought anchored her, steadied her, and gave a sense of peace she hadn't felt in a very long time.

Quinn's heart jackhammered in his chest as he stared into Julia's beautiful eyes. She'd worn her hair up, a few pink flowers woven through the blond strands.

"If you wish to kiss your bride, you may do so." The magistrate's voice echoed in the room.

Quinn's chest filled with so much emotion he feared it would burst. Julia was his wife. She and her child belonged to him. He gave a light laugh, the tight muscles in his shoulders loosening. "I would indeed, sir."

He turned back to Julia and raised a brow, asking permission. Her cheeks reddened, but she nodded.

Then he bent toward her and sealed their union with a tender kiss. Though he would have liked to linger, he held himself in check, not wishing to distress her.

Once they had signed the register, the justice of the peace gathered the papers and smiled. "Congratulations. I wish you both the very best."

"Thank you, sir." Quinn pressed a few dollars into the man's hand. A bit extra for making the ceremony go so smoothly.

Somewhat dazed, he took Julia by the hand and exited the courtroom. As they walked in silence down the wide corridor toward the main entrance, Julia seemed as unsettled as he felt. Perhaps she was struggling with their new status, trying to determine how they would go forward as a married couple. Even if it was in name only, they would have to give the pretense of being a legitimate couple.

"Where to now?" he asked. "Would you care to go out for dinner?" Quinn glanced at Julia, prepared to let her take the lead on this. He'd hoped she might enjoy some sort of celebration to mark the occasion and had made note of a nearby restaurant within walking distance in case she agreed.

"Mrs. Middleton gave me the rest of the day off, so I'm not needed there." She smiled. "I'd love to have dinner with you."

Satisfaction spread through Quinn's system. For now, he would pretend that Julia actually loved him and that theirs was a real marriage with their whole lives ahead of them. Because if Quinn had his way, this marriage would one day turn into the real thing. In the meantime, he would be patient, show Julia the kind of man he was, and pray that God would allow her feelings to grow to match Quinn's.

When they arrived at the restaurant around the corner, a rather fancy place with white tablecloths and candles, the savory aroma of beef and potatoes mingling with a hint of apple and cinnamon made Quinn's mouth water. He realized in all the excitement over the wedding, he hadn't eaten, and now his stomach complained rather loudly.

The maître d' greeted them and escorted them inside.

Quinn ushered Julia to the table, which was fit for a feast with china plates, crystal goblets, and silverware. A vase of fresh flowers adorned the middle of the table, giving the room a lovely scent.

Quinn seated Julia and took a chair beside her. Since it was still fairly early for the dinner crowd, they had the dining room to themselves. A brief sojourn of privacy.

The waiter arrived with a bottle of sparkling cider, compliments of the maître d', who had insisted on gifting them with the beverage once he learned of their marriage. With a flourish, the waiter poured two glasses and set the bottle on the table.

"I'll be back in a few minutes to take your order." He bowed and scurried off to the kitchen.

Quinn lifted his glass. "To my lovely bride. May today be the beginning of a wonderful life ahead."

Julia raised her glass to his, then took a sip, but didn't return his smile as he'd hoped. Instead, shadows lurked in her eyes. "You don't have to pretend this is real, Quinn."

He set down his glass. "It's as real as it gets, love. You and I are husband and wife. I think that deserves a celebration." He boldly brushed a quick kiss over her lips, wishing that simple act could convince her that everything would be fine.

She stared at him, the hint of a smile softening her features.

"Now, let's try to relax and enjoy our dinner. And not worry about anything else."

She laughed then and nodded. "You're right. This is our wedding day after all."

With that, Quinn's tense muscles loosened. Julia was nothing if not resilient. She just needed a little time to adjust to this new phase of her life. And Quinn would do everything in his power to ease the transition.

The meal passed in pleasant conversation. As if by mutual consent, they avoided any contentious subjects and spoke only of the good times they remembered from back home. Quinn did his best to regale her with humorous stories from his life as a valet, which kept her laughing through most of the meal. Several times he caught himself about to reach for her hand or kiss her but thought the better of it and held back. He didn't want to make her feel uncomfortable, constantly wearing his heart on his sleeve.

The engaging company and the good food soon had Quinn feeling lighter than he had in weeks. The daylight started to fade and the flicker of candles cast a homey glow around them. If only he could remain in this moment, he would be a very happy man.

Once the waiter had cleared the table, Julia rose from her seat. A grimace wrinkled her brow.

"Are you feeling all right?" Quinn asked.

She gave a slight shrug. "I get a wee bit uncomfortable sitting in the same position for too long. Would you mind if we head back to Mrs. Middleton's?"

Though he hated to put an end to their evening, he nodded. "Of course. I'll get us a taxi." While Julia visited the ladies' room, he paid the bill and asked to use the telephone.

Only then did he realize that it was his wedding night and he had no idea where he'd be sleeping.

CHAPTER 27

Seated beside Quinn in the back of the taxi, Julia twisted the new band on her finger, unable to fully grasp the fact that she was now a married woman. A few simple words, a ring, and a signature, and her life had changed forever. For better or worse, she couldn't know.

Now, the closer they got to Mrs. Middleton's, the more nervous Julia became as her new reality set in. She'd never found the courage to broach the topic of the wedding night . . . and beyond . . . with Quinn, and she had no idea what he was thinking. How did he intend for them to act until he was ready to leave Toronto? For all intents and purposes, they should at least appear to live as a true married couple so there could be no question as to the validity of their union, should anyone have cause to question them.

When the taxi stopped in front of the house, Quinn pulled out money to pay the fare. Then he helped her out and walked her to the door.

Julia's feet had swollen over the course of the day, and now her shoes pinched the sides of her feet. In addition, the dress that had fit fine earlier now cut off her circulation at her middle. She couldn't wait to get upstairs and change.

"May I come inside for a minute?" Quinn asked as she opened the door. "I'd like to discuss something with you." His expression seemed tense, a contrast to the ease of the rest of the evening.

Julia held back a sigh. The comfort of her nightclothes would have to wait. "Certainly. Why don't we sit in the parlor? Mrs. Middleton is likely in bed by now."

Julia removed her hat and gloves while Quinn set his hat on a hook by the door. Then, without a word, they entered the parlor, lit only by the remnants of a fire in the hearth. Julia snapped on one of the table lamps and sank onto the sofa.

Quinn hesitated for a moment, then came to sit beside her.

She turned to him. "What is it you wish to discuss?"

His gray eyes appeared almost the color of charcoal in the dim room. A slight furrow appeared between his brows. "I wondered if you'd given any thought to our living arrangements while I'm still in Toronto. More specifically, where you thought I should sleep tonight?"

Instant heat flooded her cheeks. "I assumed we'd go back to our respective rooms . . . but since it's our wedding night, that wouldn't seem right, would it?"

"Not really. People will expect us to live under the same roof." Even in the shadows, his complexion grew ruddier.

"I see your point." She bit her lip. "I did think of asking Mrs. Middleton if you could stay in one of the guest rooms, but I lost my nerve." Seeing how adamant the woman was about no romance under her roof, she feared the question might put her off keeping Julia as an employee.

Quinn frowned. "I should have planned this more carefully and booked a room at an inn. I'm sorry I didn't do a better job."

She looked down at her hand and fingered the silver ring, then raised her eyes to his with a soft smile. "From where I stand, I think you did just fine."

He took her hand, running his thumb over the metal band. "If I'd had the funds, I would have done a lot more."

"I don't need anything more, Quinn. This ring is beautiful. Thank you for thinking of it."

"You're welcome." He raised her hand to his lips, then sighed. "That still doesn't resolve the issue at hand though."

Footsteps, punctuated by the loud tap of a cane, echoed in the hall.

Julia tugged her hand back and rose. "Mrs. Middleton? Can I get you something?"

Dressed in her bathrobe and a frilly white nightcap, the elderly woman came toward them. "Couldn't sleep. Came down for some hot milk." She pointed a bony finger at Quinn. "It occurred to me as I lay awake up there that you two might need somewhere to spend your wedding night."

"We were just discussing that very topic." Quinn moved forward and put his arm around Julia. "I confess I forgot to book a room for the evening."

"No point in spending your money if you don't have to. I have a perfectly good wing not being used at present. You're more than welcome to stay here."

Julia reached out to lay a hand on the woman's arm. "Mrs. Middleton, will you be all right alone on your floor?"

"I'll be fine." She winked at Julia. "A bride must think of her husband at a time like this."

Julia's mouth fell open, her face heating. What was her employer thinking? She knew Julia's situation and the reason for accepting Quinn's marriage proposal. Why would she assume—?

"Thank you for your kind offer, ma'am," Quinn said. "If Julia is in agreement, we will gladly accept."

"Very well. It's settled. I'll have Allison make up one of the rooms." Mrs. Middleton squinted at Quinn. "Are you still planning on traveling to England in the near future?"

Quinn hesitated only a moment. "I am. I'll be leaving in a week's time."

"In that case, why don't you stay here until then? Then you'll at least have a few days together, and you can save money in the meantime." She pointed her cane at him. "As long as you don't mind your bride helping me during the day."

Julia blinked, her mouth opening and closing. A whole week with Quinn? The idea both thrilled her and sent shivers of terror down her spine.

"That's most generous of you, ma'am," he said, his lips twitching. "I believe I shall enjoy my stay with you."

Julia hung her wedding dress in the wardrobe of the room she and Quinn had chosen and closed the door. Quinn might be moving into the house, but she planned on returning to her regular room across from Mrs. Middleton tomorrow. One night sharing a room with Quinn would be unnerving enough. Besides, part of her job was to be close at hand, should Mrs. Middleton need her at any time, day or night. Staying on the opposite side of the house, in another wing entirely, was out of the question.

She took a seat on the tufted ottoman before the vanity table and picked up her brush. As she combed out her long hair, she gazed at herself in the mirror. This was not how she'd imagined looking on her wedding night. Brow furrowed. Eyes anxious. Pale. Pregnant.

She brushed her hair harder until all the tangles were out, then she purposely twisted it into a thick braid, as she did every night. No need to invite any thoughts of romance. Her simple cotton nightgown and plaid bath robe would also dissuade Quinn of any such notion. Not that he gave any indication of that.

She rose from the seat, pulling her lapels more tightly around her neck. Despite the fire in the hearth, a lingering chill made her shiver. This part of the house was shaded by large maple trees in the yard, and even in the warm weather, the air felt damp.

Julia eyed the large bed in the center of the room, and nerves jumped in her belly. Soon Quinn would return with his belongings, prepared to stay here for the duration. Even though they'd agreed to a marriage in name only, doubts swirled in Julia's head. What would he expect to happen tonight?

She walked to a door on the far side of the room and tried the handle. It opened into a connecting room. Perhaps this had been the suite Mrs. Middleton had shared with her husband years ago when they were first married. She peeked in and looked around. The space looked entirely more feminine and had probably once belonged to her mistress. It was fairly common, especially back then, for each spouse to have their own quarters.

It was obvious, however, that although the main bedroom had been hastily cleaned, made up with fresh linens, and a fire set to burning in the hearth, the connecting room had not. Thick layers of dust coated the furniture, and there was no fire to warm the space.

Julia sighed and closed the door. Somehow she would have to share this room with her new husband. Maybe she could make him a pallet on the floor. The area rug looked thick enough to provide some comfort. All she needed were some extra blankets.

Heavy footsteps sounded in the hallway, and seconds later, a knock sounded on the door.

Julia whirled around. Her hand flew to her throat. "Come in," she called.

The door creaked open, and Quinn stepped inside, carrying a brown carpetbag. "I see you've gotten comfortable." He smiled as he set the bag on the floor. Then he took off his hat and laid it on the dresser. "This looks very cozy. Quite an improvement from my cot at the Y."

Julia's stomach dipped. The poor man. How could she ask him to sleep on the floor after all he was doing for her? She glanced at the small divan near the window. She could fit on it without too much trouble. For one night, it would have to do.

"Is anything wrong?" Quinn had come over to stand in front of her.

"No. Nothing." She moved a step backward.

"Then why do you look like you want to jump out the window behind you?"

Julia's gaze darted from his face to the bedpost, and she forced a laugh. "Don't be daft. I'm a little . . . unsettled. That's all." She wrapped her arms in front of her. "Anyone would be in a similar situation."

"Do you mean newlyweds on their wedding night?"

Heat flared in her cheeks. Was he making fun of her?

"I'm only teasing, Julia. A poor attempt to lighten the mood."

He reached for her hand. "It's really not that bad, you know. We have a pleasant room with a lovely fire and a bed that looks very comfortable. I do believe I'll have a good night's sleep for the first time in ages."

Nervous tingles shot up her spine. She tried to disengage her hand, but he squeezed tighter.

"Maybe we should clear the air," he said, "and then you can relax."

"What do you mean?"

He led her to the divan. "Have a seat."

She perched on the edge of the green velvet settee. When he sat beside her, she folded her hands in her lap. It was silly to be nervous. Quinn was a reasonable man, kind and honorable. But she'd never had to spend the entire night with a man before.

"Julia, what can I do to make you feel more comfortable?" His gray eyes searched her face. "Shall I sleep on the floor?"

Guilt flashed through her. Had he read her mind? She met his gaze, noting for the first time the fatigue lining his features. After all he'd done for her, she couldn't ask that of him. She took a breath for courage. "That's not necessary." She glanced at the bed. "I'm sure there's plenty of room for both of us."

The lines eased. "Thank you."

He rose and walked to the wardrobe, where he removed his jacket. "Is there a lavatory nearby?"

"Yes. Down the hall on the right."

He smiled. "I'll be back in a few minutes. Feel free to claim whatever side of the bed you'd prefer."

By the time Quinn returned in his nightshirt, his clothes neatly folded over his arm, Julia was under the covers. The strain of the day had left her weary, and now with the warmth from the fire and the comfort of the soft mattress, Julia's muscles finally began to relax.

Quinn laid his clothes over a chair, then proceeded to climb into the bed.

It was so large, Julia could have stretched her arm out over the mattress and still not have touched Quinn.

He smiled at her. "Good night, Julia. I hope you have pleasant dreams."

"Good night, Quinn. And thank you. It was a lovely wedding."

"Yes, it was." He moved over to kiss her cheek. Then he turned onto his side, but peered back over one shoulder at her. "My brothers used to tell me I snore. If I do, you have my permission to hit me."

Chuckling, Julia slid deeper under the covers. Surrounded by warmth and an unexpected sense of peace, she surrendered to sleep.

CHAPTER 28

The days following the wedding passed in a blur. Each day, while Julia worked helping Mrs. Middleton, Quinn spent time with Harry, exploring the sights of Toronto and taking him shopping for new clothing suitable for an ocean crossing. The lad's amazing recovery continued to astound him. Mrs. Chamberlain insisted it was due to prayer and to the fact that Harry felt safe and loved.

Quinn could believe it, for Mrs. C. had gone above and beyond the call of Christian duty where Harry was concerned . . . to the point where Quinn worried how she would cope when the boy left her care.

Her devotion to Harry—and to Julia, for that matter—was why Quinn insisted they let Mrs. C. know about their marriage. Julia had reluctantly agreed, and on her next afternoon off, they sat down with Harry and Mrs. C. and told them about the wedding. Mrs. C. had sent Harry off on an errand to the kitchen so she could question Julia in more detail about the pregnancy. The dear woman had been nothing but sympathetic, reducing Quinn's bride to tears. Then the landlady had come right up to Quinn and wrapped him in a tight hug. When she pulled away, she'd wiped her eyes with her apron.

"You're a good man, Quinten Aspinall. Not many people I know would do something so noble."

Quinn had shaken his head in protest. Any man with principles would have done the same for someone he cared about. Besides, how could he have left Julia to fend for herself? She was literally alone in the world, with no family, few friends, and a baby on the way. Not to mention a predator out to gain control of her child. No, he never could have lived with himself if he hadn't done everything in his power to protect her. Having a husband would give Julia the respectability she deserved.

After the talk with Mrs. C., Julia appeared more settled and more at peace than she'd been since Quinn had first met her. And they had fallen into a comfortable routine.

Each afternoon, after spending time with Harry, Quinn returned home to eat dinner with Julia and Mrs. Middleton. After the meal, the three would spend a quiet evening by the fire, playing cards or listening to the radio while the women knitted. Every night around eight o'clock, Mrs. Middleton would grow weary, and Julia would help her upstairs to bed. Then Julia would return, and they would have an hour or so alone until Julia became tired herself and had to turn in.

After the initial wedding night, she'd tried to move back to her old room near the widow. However, Mrs. Middleton insisted that Julia spend the little time she had with her husband before he left. Rather reluctantly, Julia had conceded but had claimed the adjoining room to Quinn's, maintaining that her restlessness would disturb Quinn's sleep. Despite the fact that he'd agreed to a marriage in name only, he couldn't help but feel the sting of rejection. Truth be told, he'd enjoyed sharing the bed with Julia that one night, waking to find her beautiful face so peaceful in slumber, her hair loosened from its braid and spread out over the pillows. However, if she felt too uncomfortable to sleep next to him, he'd not force the issue.

And perhaps in the long run, it was wiser to avoid temptation. Because each day, Quinn's heart grew more firmly entwined with Julia. And it became harder and harder not to reach out and hold her, to try and kiss her again. From the few kisses they'd shared, he sensed she held some affection for him at least, and if Quinn was patient, he hoped she'd come to care for him as much as he did her. And that once the baby was born, she would choose to stay in the marriage.

Though he had every hope of eventually making their union a true one, he realized he needed to take his time and tread with caution. Julia had already had one bad experience with a man. He did not want to scare her off by tipping his hand.

Not yet anyway.

The days slipped by, and before Quinn knew it, it was time for the train ride to Halifax. When he'd first imagined taking this trip, he'd been eager to be on his way back to England. But now that he and Julia had wed, anticipation for the voyage had turned to dread. How could he bear to put an ocean between them? How would he say good-bye to the woman who had become so dear to his heart? It would be easier to wrench off a limb and leave it behind than to leave her.

But after all his efforts to find his siblings and get them to come home, he couldn't abandon his plan now. Not while his mother still needed him.

Quinn rested somewhat easier, however, having taken care of the most important thing to ensure his wife's safety while he was gone. Without telling Julia, he'd tracked down Richard Hawkins at his residence and paid him a visit, just long enough to flash the marriage certificate at him and announce that he and Julia had wed. He wanted to make certain that if Hawkins ever learned that Quinn had left the country, the cad knew he had no chance with Julia, that she was a married woman, and the child belonged to them.

The man's insults and vile curses, followed by the slamming of the door in Quinn's face, had given him little satisfaction. However, it was the best he could do under the circumstances without giving in and physically throttling the man. But he would never disgrace Julia that way. Having a husband in prison would be worse than no husband at all.

The day of departure arrived with little fanfare, other than a sick feeling in the pit of Quinn's stomach.

Julia, Mrs. Chamberlain, and even Rev. Burke insisted on accompanying Quinn and Harry to the train station to see them off. Becky had come to Toronto the day before and spent the night at the boardinghouse with Harry. She wanted them all to travel together, and Quinn was grateful to her for making things easier for him.

The only disappointment was Cecil. Since he hadn't called to leave any message, it seemed unlikely he would join them. But, as Quinn had finally started to accept, he couldn't control the actions of his siblings. They had their own ideas about how to live their lives, and all he could do was try to respect their wishes and let God's will for their lives play out as intended.

Still, Quinn scanned the crowd for Cecil in the slim hope that his brother had changed his mind. He could tell by Becky's furtive glances that she was doing the same thing. Disappointment crashed over her features when she caught Quinn's eye and he shook his head. Three out of four siblings would have to do.

Despite the early hour, heat shimmered around the platform in a haze, promising a scorcher of a day ahead. Quinn had already started to perspire and wished he hadn't worn his waistcoat. Harry looked much more comfortable in his white shirtsleeves, short pants, and suspenders.

Quinn stopped and set down his bag, his nerves vibrating like a live electric wire. He hadn't managed one single moment alone with Julia this morning. She'd been up before Quinn, tending to Mrs. Middleton the entire morning. Maybe his wife had purposely orchestrated their last hours together to ensure they wouldn't be alone.

The thought of having all these people on hand to witness his good-bye to Julia made him want to scream. She stood beside him now, looking so beautiful in her blue dress and matching hat, it made his heart hurt. How he would miss her expressive brown eyes, her infectious laugh, and the way her nose scrunched when she was thinking. These last few days together had been wonderful, but he feared that once he left Toronto, their relationship would never be the same.

If only he could send Becky and Harry on without him.

Quinn ground his jaw together, purposely setting aside all temptation to do just that. He pushed a hand into his pocket to touch the cold metal of the key his father had given him, reminding himself of the vow he'd made long before he knew Julia. He had to see this task through. Only then would he allow himself to face his future.

"I hear a whistle down the tracks." Harry's excited voice drifted over the noise.

Quinn's heart stalled in his chest like an automobile lacking sufficient fuel. Time was running out. He needed to make these last moments with Julia count. He looked over to find her watching him, unshed tears glimmering in her eyes. Did she feel as bereft as he at their impending separation? Or did she believe he was abandoning her?

Without a word, he turned and pulled her tight against his chest. "I will be back before the babe arrives," he whispered fiercely. "I promise you that."

"I know you'll do your best." She sounded so forlorn, so resigned.

He held her away from him so he could see her face. "I'll do better than that."

"But your mother—"

"No matter the circumstances, I will return. Nothing is more important than you and the baby." He looked deeply into her eyes. "Please believe that."

She stared back, a tear escaping. "I'll try."

The train whistle shrilled louder. Looming closer.

Without asking permission, he cupped her face in his hands and bent to kiss her. One last, perfect kiss that would have to sustain him until they met again. She clung to him, returning his embrace with unexpected passion, and in that moment, Quinn regretted not having more time with her, not having the chance to shower her with affection and show her how much he truly cared. Would it have made a difference? Would it have bound her heart more firmly to his?

He'd never know now.

The only thing he could do was entrust their future to the Lord and accept His will for them. Until that time, Quinn would remain patient and faithful, as long as she needed him.

Reluctantly, he stepped away and wiped a stray tear from her cheek. "Take good care of yourself, Julia."

"And you. I wish you safe travels."

He patted his breast pocket. "I have the letter for your uncle. You have the marriage certificate in a safe place?"

"I do."

"And if you have any trouble, promise you'll seek Reverend Burke's assistance?" He didn't have to name the person who could cause the trouble.

"I will." She shuddered.

A gust of wind swirled around the tracks, ruffling the women's skirts and lifting strands of Julia's fair hair across her cheek. She pushed them away with the back of her hand.

People on the platform scurried toward the arriving train. Smoke billowed into the air as the brakes squealed to halt the metal beast.

From the corner of his eye, Quinn saw Mrs. Chamberlain squeezing Harry in a tight hug.

Soon passengers began disembarking, mingling with those waiting to board. Apprehension built in his chest as their final moments together hurtled toward them. With supreme effort, he tore his gaze from her and reached for his bag.

"Quinn?" Anxiety swirled in her brown eyes.

"Yes?"

"I . . ." She closed her mouth, blinking hard.

He waited, not daring to breathe.

"I'll be praying for you. And your family." She dropped her gaze to the ground, hands clasped in front of her.

Quinn stared at the subtle curve of her cheek, the cast of her lashes, the trembling of the lips he'd just kissed. This was one of those crucial moments that might never be repeated. Nothing must be left unsaid between them. He reached a finger under her chin and tilted her face up. "I love you, Julia. You are the most important thing to me, and I will be back for you. Don't forget that."

A smile trembled on her mouth as more tears flowed. "I . . . I'll be waiting for you."

With a sigh, he pressed a last tender kiss to her lips, and tasting the salt of her tears, he blinked back moisture of his own.

"All aboard!" The conductor's cry echoed over the platform.

Quinn stepped away from her magnetic pull to bid Mrs. Chamberlain and Rev. Burke good-bye. He put an arm around Harry and went to join Becky, who stood farther down the platform. "Come on, lad. Let's find some good seats."

"I want to sit by the window." The boy's eagerness made Quinn smile. At least one of them was happy to be leaving.

Becky and Harry climbed the steps. Quinn followed. At the opening to the car, he turned to find Julia once more. She lifted a hand in a final wave. His heart pinched in his chest, but he nodded to her and disappeared into the train.

Once they found a seat and had stowed their luggage, Harry settled by the window, Becky beside him. Quinn sat opposite them, but his focus remained out the window until he found Julia's hat among the remaining people on the platform. As the train chugged slowly into motion, he gazed unblinking until the blue dot was no longer visible. Then he closed his eyes and prayed for the Lord's protection on his wife and unborn child.

Harriet wiped the dining room table, now empty after the evening meal. The boarders had all gone up to their rooms for the night, and she'd sent Mrs. Teeter away, needing solitude to do these mindless chores in order to keep occupied and not obsess over the glaring absence of one young boy in the house.

Never did she imagine she would get so attached to a child that quickly. She'd only felt this bereft a few times in her life. Once, after her parents' deaths, when forced onto the ship that would take her away from her homeland. The second time, when she'd learned of her sister's death, and the third, when she'd lost her beloved husband.

How could saying good-bye to a boy she'd known for only a few weeks cause her such devastation?

A loud knock sounded on the front door.

Harriet wiped the tears from her cheeks and huffed out a weary breath. "Who could that be?" she muttered as she made her way to the entrance.

Geoffrey stood on the porch, visible sympathy softening his features. "Good evening, Harriet. May I come in?"

Her stomach swooped. She knew he was coming to make sure she wasn't too upset after Harry's departure. But in truth she wanted to be alone and nurse her hurt in private. "Actually, I'm about to turn in for the evening, Geoffrey. Perhaps tomorrow—"

In a manner most unlike him, he pushed past her into the foyer. "Why don't you put your feet up by the fire and I'll make the tea?" he said as he swept off his hat.

Realizing there was no use trying to dissuade him, she heaved a great sigh. "Very well."

He offered her a brief smile before disappearing toward the kitchen.

Harriet finished tidying the dining room and went to sit in her chair beside the fireplace. Minutes later, Geoffrey bustled in with a tray. He set it on the table and handed her a china cup, her favorite one with yellow roses, and a plate of shortbread.

"Thank you." She took a sip, allowing the perfect blend of pekoe, milk, and sugar to seep into her soul while her tense shoulder muscles relaxed.

"Nothing like a good cuppa, I always say." Geoffrey took the seat opposite her and lifted his own beverage.

"I appreciate your efforts to cheer me up," she said after a few moments of silence. "But you really don't need to concern yourself. I'll be much more myself tomorrow."

One brow rose. "Doesn't mean I can't be here to help you tonight."

She smiled and set her cup on the table. "You really are such a dear friend."

His expression changed, just a flicker of displeasure, and then his usual easygoing demeanor returned. He reached for a piece of shortbread. "I know you'll certainly miss Harry, even though he stirred up a lot of unrest from your past."

"That I will. For the first time, I experienced what it would've been like to have my own child." Her throat tightened. "I have to admit, it felt really good." She'd made peace with being childless years ago, but every now and then, the longing for a family of her own tugged hard on her heart.

"I know that still bothers you at times." He gave her a pensive look. "My late wife struggled with the same grief."

Harriet pushed up from her chair and walked to the fireplace. "I'm thankful Harry might be able to reclaim part of his childhood by reuniting with his mother. That makes missing him almost bearable." She ran a finger over the framed photo of her sister. "I've come to the realization that you were right, Geoffrey. I never really got closure after Annie died." She turned to face her friend, a decision she'd been toying with suddenly solidifying in her mind. "In order to achieve that, I believe I might need to return to Hazelbrae."

"I always wondered why you've never been back," Geoffrey said quietly.

"I couldn't face going back into that house." Tremors raced through her. "I was too afraid to relive the trauma of Annie's death."

"Are you sure you can face it now?" He stood up and moved toward her.

She straightened her spine. "I hope so. But I fear that if I don't try, I may never fully heal."

Geoffrey took one of her hands in his, a determined look on his face. "Then I'm going with you. You won't have to do this alone."

Harriet's lips trembled. "I was hoping you'd say that. I'd feel much better with you by my side."

"I'm certain that facing your past will do you a world of good." He patted her hand and released it. "Now, I suppose I'd best be on my way."

She walked with him to the front door.

Geoffrey reached for his hat from the hall tree. "Just let me know when you plan to leave and give me a bit of time to clear my schedule."

She nodded but couldn't answer, her throat tight.

He bent to kiss her cheek. "I'll call you tomorrow. Sleep well, my dear."

As he strolled down the walkway, she watched his retreating back, not certain how she'd gotten so lucky to have such a wonderful man in her life.

CHAPTER 29

Three days after leaving Toronto, Quinn stared at Becky, Harry, and Cecil standing together at the rail of the ship in the Halifax harbor. Quinn still couldn't believe their brother had surprised them by turning up in Nova Scotia mere hours before they were set to sail. He credited the occurrence to God's doing, working on Cecil's heart to give him the courage to leave his post.

As the crew scurried around in preparation for their departure, the wind whipped Becky's skirt about her legs and threatened to pull the hat from her head. She had one arm wound through Cecil's, as though he might change his mind at any moment and run down the gangplank.

But Quinn doubted that would be the case, for as Cecil told Becky, he didn't plan on returning to Canada. Ever again.

Secretly, Quinn believed something rather significant must have transpired for Cecil to change his mind about coming back to England, but he chose not to question his brother. If Cecil wanted to tell them, he would do so in his own time.

Meanwhile, Quinn gave quiet thanks for the realization of his plan to bring all his siblings home. Now, if only Mum's health improved, they'd truly have their miracle.

A shout went up from the deck once the gangplank was pulled in. Excitement rippled through the passengers as the grand ship moved slowly away from the dock. Yet Quinn's chest compressed with a new grief, for this meant he was truly putting an ocean between himself and Julia.

Lord, keep her safe until I see her again.

Much later in the day, once Quinn had discovered his sea legs, he approached Becky, who was seated on a deck chair. It had occurred to him, after observing the rapport his three younger siblings shared, that he really didn't know his sister and brothers anymore. After all, he hadn't lived with them for nine years, ever since he'd left to find employment following their father's death. Perhaps it was time to remedy the situation. With Cecil and Harry napping in their cabin, he had time for a private chat with his sister.

Becky had given up on her hat and had tied a kerchief over her hair instead. She wore a heavy woolen shawl to ward off the cool sea air.

"How are you finding the voyage so far?" he asked, claiming the chair beside her.

She lifted her face. "It's quite pleasant. At least the weather is lovely, though I suspect the farther north we go, the colder it will get."

"That's true. When I came over in May, it was much brisker than this. I plan to enjoy the sunshine for as long as possible." He glanced at the papers in her hand. "A letter already?"

"From Ned. He must have slipped it in my bag when I wasn't looking." A smile trembled on her lips. "It's my first love letter."

Quinn realized how lucky his sister was to have found such a good man, yet his gratitude was tempered with more than a little shame at his initial reaction to Ned. "I'm happy for you, Becky. I'm sure he will make a fine husband."

"He will. I've never met a kinder person. I'm so fortunate to have him." She sighed. "Which made leaving all the harder. But Ned insisted I need to make peace with the past in order to start our future together with no regrets."

"A wise fellow."

"What about you?" She tilted her head. "Are you ready to tell me the story behind your sudden marriage to Julia?"

Quinn deliberated with himself for a second but quickly decided that his family needed to know the truth. "As you probably noticed, Julia is with child."

"I did notice." She stared at him. "Are you the father?"

He hesitated. It would be easy to claim the child was his, take the brunt of Becky's judgment upon his shoulders rather than reveal the true circumstances. But Quinn felt Julia would want Becky to know the truth.

"Unfortunately, no. An unscrupulous cad took advantage of Julia's trusting nature and left her in a compromised position. After several months, he found her again and started making trouble. I couldn't stand to see her at the mercy of such a man, so I offered to marry her and be a father to her child."

Becky's eyes went wide. "But that's a huge sacrifice, Quinn. Why would you do such a—" She stopped. "Oh. You're in love with her, aren't you?"

He met her frank stare and nodded. "I am, though I don't know if she returns my feelings." He frowned. "I hope you don't think badly of her. Julia is a kind and generous person, one who trusted too easily. She didn't deserve to have this happen to her."

Becky reached out to pat his arm. "Of course I don't think badly of her. From the little time I spent with her, I came to admire her very much."

They sat in silence for several minutes, watching the white wisps of clouds overhead.

Finally, Quinn dared broach the topic weighing on his mind. "Becky, would you tell me about your life with Mum after I left to work for the earl? The real story of how things were?"

The more he'd gone over the past and tried to fit the pieces of the puzzle together, he still couldn't fathom what had led his mother to such a desperate act as to surrender her children . . . unless circumstances were not as she'd made them seem.

Becky's features darkened. "It's not a time I care to relive."

"I take it things weren't as rosy as you made out when I came home for a visit?"

"No." Her shoulders sagged. "Mum made us put on a brave front for you, saying you worked hard to keep us clothed and fed, and we owed you a cheery disposition." Her forehead furrowed. "But it was far from happy. Most days we had barely enough food for one meal. The three of us would go out and beg in the streets while Mum cleaned houses and took in mending."

Guilt squeezed Quinn's chest. "Why wasn't there enough money? I thought my wages would have been sufficient."

She glanced over and shook her head.

He waited for her to explain further.

At last, she sighed. "There would have been plenty, if Mum hadn't taken to the drink."

"What?" He'd never once seen his mother touch an alcoholic beverage.

"Turns out she'd been taking a wee nip in secret ever since Dad died, but she managed to hide it. After you left, the nips became more and more frequent until soon she didn't go out to work anymore, wasting what precious money we had on liquor." The hardness in Becky's voice matched the set of her jaw. "One day, she said she was very sorry but she couldn't keep us any longer. She told us to pack our things. Then she took us to the orphanage and left us there."

"Sweet saints above." Quinn scrubbed a hand over his jaw.

"At first, it was a relief. No more begging. No more coping with Mum's drinking. And at least we had food every day. But then the director told us we were being sent to Canada, and they packed us all onto the ship."

How had he been so oblivious to what was happening? To the horrors they'd endured? "I'm so very sorry, Becky. I had no idea."

"How could you have known, when she hid her drinking from you?"

The slow burn of anger twisted Quinn's gut. He'd felt so sorry for his mother, when all along she'd brought most of this on herself. And here he'd been scrambling to rectify the situation, blaming himself for not being a better provider for his family.

Becky squeezed his fingers, her gloves warming him. "Don't be too hard on yourself. Or Mum. Sometimes adversity brings out the best in people, and sometimes it brings out the worst."

"To be honest, Becca, I'm grateful you agreed to come at all after what Mum put you through. No wonder you were reluctant to leave."

Becky's forehead crinkled. "Ned made me realize that I need to see her again, to tell her I forgive her, and to finally let go of the past. Before it's too late." She paused. "At first, I hated Mum for her drinking and what it led to, but then again, if she hadn't put us in the home, I'd never have come to Canada and met Ned." Her whole face softened at the mention of his name.

"To be fair," he said slowly, "Mum believed it was a temporary measure. She didn't know they had any intention of sending you abroad."

"I know. It was all part of God's plan, I suppose."

Scowling, Quinn scratched his chin. "Perhaps. Though hearing the whole story now, I'm having a hard time with forgiveness myself."

"Give it some time." Becky patted his arm. "I finally learned to accept that Mum just isn't as strong as we are."

Quinn looked at his sister with new appreciation. "You've turned into a fine young woman, Becky. I'm very proud of you."

"Thank you, Quinn." She tucked the folded letter into the pocket of her jacket. "Try not to have too many expectations when we see Mum again. That way you won't be disappointed if things don't turn out as you'd hoped."

"I'll keep that in mind."

Quinn didn't bother to tell Becky about his initial plan to find a home where they could all live together. He was thankful he'd let go of that idea after realizing he wouldn't get the earl's farm. If his mother was still chained by her need for alcohol, he couldn't in good conscience bring her into their home, especially with a young child like Harry. After what the lad had been through, he needed a stable, loving environment.

But it was too soon to speculate about all that now. Quinn would have to wait and evaluate his mother's condition when they arrived.

And then he'd let events play out for all of them as God intended.

Eight days later, after docking in Southampton and traveling by train to London, Quinn checked them into a modest-looking boardinghouse. The room consisted of two twin beds, a chair, and one dresser. He would let Cecil and Harry have one bed, Becky the other, and Quinn would make do on the floor. If he could, he'd have gladly paid for two rooms, but the advance on his wages had dwindled to practically nothing. In fact, he'd even dipped into the funds meant for Julia's return voyage, certain the earl wouldn't mind adding it to Quinn's mounting debt.

Tomorrow, Quinn would stop in at his employer's townhome to discover whether his lordship was residing there at present or was staying in Derbyshire. He hoped the earl might be in a position to offer Cecil a job in his household. Quinn thought the boy would do well as a groom at the Brentwood stables or even as a footman, if there was an opening.

After an uncomfortable night's sleep, the four of them met in the dining room for breakfast to discuss their next move. Thankfully, most of the boarders had left for work, so they had the room to themselves. Though the eggs were a tad cold, the savory bacon and sausages filled Quinn's empty belly.

As he sipped his first good cup of British tea, he leaned back against the rough wooden chair. "Where should we start today?"

"I suppose we should see Mum." Becky set down her fork. "But I'd like to go by the shops first. I have a few things I need to buy."

Cecil and Harry said they'd go with her.

Quinn supposed delaying their trip to the infirmary by a couple of hours wouldn't really matter. "Fine. That will leave me time to call on Lord Brentwood." He took out his pocket watch. "I'll meet you back here at ten o'clock."

Not wanting to waste a minute, Quinn left the boardinghouse on foot to walk to the townhome on St. James Square. As he breathed in the familiar scents of London, his chest expanded with a sense of well-being. Seeing the city through fresh eyes, he found the street vendors and traffic, local shops and uniformed bobbies brought forgotten feelings of nostalgia to the surface. Toronto was a vastly different city—cleaner and newer than London. Still, each had its own merit.

When he reached the townhome, Quinn walked around to the servants' entrance and knocked on the kitchen door. Nerves jumbled in his belly. Would Lord Brentwood be here? If so, how would he react to everything Quinn had to tell him?

One of the kitchen maids answered. "Mr. Aspinall," she exclaimed. "Whatever are you doing here? We weren't expecting you."

Quinn removed his cap and stepped inside. "I've just returned from Canada and was wondering if Lord Brentwood might be in residence?"

The girl beamed at him. "Yer in luck. His lordship's in town for the week. Business to attend to, or so we hear."

Relief overshadowed dread for the moment. "Excellent. I'll ask Mr. Davis if his lordship has time to see me."

Quinn made his way through the kitchen, which was unusually empty, and up the narrow servants' staircase to the main level.

Mr. Davis, the butler, met him in the hallway. "Mr. Aspinall. What are you doing here? I thought you were in Canada."

"I was, but I'm back now, and I need to speak to his lordship, if possible. It's important."

The butler inclined his head. "Very well. I'll let him know you're here."

A few minutes later, after being told the earl would see him, Quinn approached the library and knocked on the heavy wooden door. He clenched his damp palms into fists and prayed for a favorable outcome to this meeting.

"Come in." His employer's familiar voice rang out.

Quinn entered the study, strong memories of his first years of employment surging to the forefront. Nothing in this room had changed since that time when he'd been a lad of about Cecil's age. He'd been every bit as nervous that day as he was now.

"Mr. Aspinall." The earl looked up from his desk with a smile. "You've returned at last. Please, have a seat."

Quinn took one of the chairs, his mouth going dry in anticipation of the conversation to come. "We arrived yesterday, my lord. I wanted to see you as soon as possible. It is fortuitous that you are in residence."

The older man's face turned serious, pinning Quinn with an unnerving stare. "Did you find her?"

Quinn met the man's gaze. "I did."

"But she's not with you." A deep frown lined the man's forehead. "That does not bode well, I take it."

Quinn reached into his pocket and removed Julia's letter. His fingers trembled as he considered the news it contained, and he prayed the man would be reasonable upon learning all that had befallen his niece. "Julia asked me to deliver this to you."

The earl took the envelope. "Can you tell me how she's doing? Is she well?"

"She's fine, my lord. But she has explained everything in the letter."

Quinn's stomach churned as he waited for the man to open the envelope. How would he take the news of their marriage? Would he throw Quinn out on his ear? Or would he be grateful for the protection Quinn had provided her?

Slowly, the earl chose a letter opener from a drawer and slit the flap open. With a sigh, he opened the pages and began to read.

Quinn tried hard to remain still, to keep his foot from tapping. Discreetly, he rubbed his palms on his pant legs. The crackle of flames in the hearth and the ticking of a clock were the only sounds to break the silence. He glanced repeatedly at the earl's face as he read. When the color drained from Lord Brentwood's cheeks, Quinn knew he'd learned of Julia's condition and their subsequent marriage.

The earl tossed the pages down with such force they slid across the desktop. "You mean to tell me that you and my niece are married?" he thundered.

Quinn swallowed. "We are."

A few choice words passed the other man's lips as he surged to his feet. He crossed to the sideboard, where he poured a large splash of brandy. With one gulp, he swallowed the contents and banged the glass back down, seemingly oblivious to the early hour of the day.

Quinn forced himself to take even breaths. He needed to give the man a minute to come to grips with the situation.

Lord Brentwood raked a hand through his thick gray hair. Then, with another glare at Quinn, he resumed his seat, gathered the pages, and read the remainder of the letter. When he finished, he folded the papers and set them in front of him.

Quinn wished he knew exactly what Julia had written. What she'd told him about the baby's paternity. Maybe then he'd have an idea how to appease her uncle. He cleared his throat. "Let me assure you, sir, that I care for Julia very much, and I intend to do everything I can—"

His lordship held up a hand. "Nothing you say will make this situation any better. Every calamity I feared would befall my niece has come to pass. She is a ruined woman."

Quinn shot to his feet. "She is nothing of the sort. Julia is an amazing woman. Brave, strong, and selfless. I am proud to call her my wife."

The earl stared at him like he'd sprouted horns. "You might be proud, but I certainly am not." He swiped a hand over his mouth. "At least she had the good sense not to come back here and bring further shame to this family."

Quinn's gut clenched as though he'd received a physical blow. "Because she married someone from a different social class? Doesn't having a respectable husband count in your world?"

"You know the answer to that as well as I." Lord Brentwood glared at him. "I don't mean to be cruel, but you're a mere servant, while Julia comes from a noble lineage. No one in our class would deem her marriage respectable. Not to mention the baby."

Though Quinn had been prepared for a less than enthusiastic response to their union, he'd counted on the man's good opinion of him to temper his reaction. However, it had become obvious that his only value to the earl was as someone who could shine his shoes or pick out a suitable necktie for dinner. Quinn stiffened his spine. "I'm sorry you feel that way, my lord. I suppose it was foolish of me to think you'd be grateful that Julia is safe and that I've done everything I could to guarantee her well-being and protect her. If you'll excuse me, I am needed elsewhere." He turned and crossed the room but paused at the door. "Just to be clear, I am tendering my official resignation as your valet. I wish you and your family Godspeed." He gave a slight bow and left the room.

This time he did not return to the servants' entrance. Instead, he walked boldly through the entry hall, past the surprised butler, and exited through the main front door.

CHAPTER 30

After his disastrous meeting with the earl, Quinn thought the day could get no worse.

He was mistaken.

At the Camberwell Infirmary, the head nurse did not seem inclined to let the four of them see their mother. Quinn had to use his most persuasive skills to finally convince her.

"You should prepare yourself," the woman warned. "She's not long for this world."

"I'm sure once she sees her family," he countered, "she'll soon be on the road to recovery."

The woman only sniffed.

Quinn returned to the area where Becky, Cecil, and Harry were waiting. "We can go in. But be warned. The nurse said Mum is not doing well."

"All the more reason she needs to see us." Cecil rose and straightened his jacket.

"Exactly what I told her. Now let's go in. Quietly."

Becky kept a protective arm around Harry as they entered the dimly lit ward. Quinn nearly gagged at the dreadful odors of illness and unwashed bodies. Becky pulled out her handkerchief and held it over her nose.

Never had he wished more fervently that he could have afforded a private hospital for their mother.

The room contained twelve metal-framed beds, six on each side. Quinn headed to the far side of the room, near the rectangular windows, where Mum had been when he'd last seen her.

Sure enough, she lay on the last cot. Her face looked gaunt, the hollows in her cheeks more pronounced. Her graying hair splayed out over her pillow.

"Oh, Quinn." Becky's anguished whisper said it all.

Harry rushed to the bedside. "Wake up, Mum. It's me, Harry. We came all the way from Canada to see you." He put his hand on the bedrail. "Becky and Cecil are here too."

Quinn stood back and allowed the others access to their mother. After all, they were the ones she needed to see.

Her lids flickered, and slowly her eyes opened.

"My baby." Mum raised one of her hands toward Harry. "Is it really you?"

"Yes, Mum. But I'm not a baby anymore. I'm twelve now."

Her frail fingers touched Harry's cheek. A tear escaped, sliding onto the thin pillow.

"I'm here too, Mum." Cecil moved closer.

"Cecil. Look at you. All grown up. You look just like your father." She turned her head. "Rebecca, is that you? My goodness, you're a real lady now."

"Hello, Mum." Becky moved forward and grasped their mother's hand. "I'm here for a visit, but I'll be going back to Toronto soon to get married."

Their mother's pale eyes widened. "Married? But you're so young."

Quinn frowned. It seemed Mum had never received Becky's letter. Either that or she'd forgotten her news.

"I'm old enough to know a good man when I find one. A man as good as Daddy." Becky kept her tone soothing, and for that Quinn gave her great credit. She'd held back any ill feeling or resentment she bore her mother, as though sensing what the woman needed to hear.

Mum looked at each of her children. "I'm so sorry I couldn't take care of you. I thought you'd be better off in the home. I had no idea they'd send you across the sea." More tears brimmed in her eyes.

"We know, Mum." Becky smoothed the hair from her forehead. "It's not your fault."

Quinn blessed his sister for saying that and hoped that she had truly come to believe it herself. As he had.

At last, Mum's gaze landed on Quinn, and her lips trembled. "You kept your promise, son. You brought them all back to me."

He swallowed hard and nodded. "I told you I would."

She gave a wan smile, then turned to Harry. "I want to hear all about what you've been doing. But first I need to rest awhile."

A patient in another bed began to cough. Suddenly Quinn became aware of how much space the four of them were occupying. Now that Mum had seen everyone, they could take turns visiting with her so as not to tax her strength. Her eyes had already drifted shut.

"Come on, everyone. Let's give Mum a chance to rest. We can come back later, maybe one or two at a time."

They all assembled back in the waiting area, a windowless room with two rows of plain wooden chairs.

Becky dropped onto a seat with a sigh. "I'd like to talk to Mum alone when she wakes up, if nobody minds."

"I don't mind." Cecil slouched in a chair against the wall and pulled his cap over his eyes.

"Fine with me." Quinn chose a chair near the door. "Let's give her an hour or so to rest before you go back."

Harry sat beside Becky, his head on her shoulder. It wasn't long before he nodded off.

After half an hour of sitting, Quinn's muscles began to twitch, begging for movement. With nothing but torturous thoughts of the earl and Julia to scramble his brain, he needed some room to breathe before he went barking mad. He pushed to his feet and jammed on his hat. "I'm going for a walk. Tell Mum I'll be back later."

Without waiting for a response, he exited the building.

The first draw of fresh air, laden with the smell of salt and fish, filled him with new energy. Taking long strides, he headed back toward the boardinghouse. He had something he needed to do before he changed his mind.

At the front desk, he paid the proprietor for some notepaper, ink, and a pen, then headed to their room. Though still rankled by Lord Brentwood's harsh reaction, Quinn couldn't leave things as they stood. After all, he was still the man who had taken a chance on Quinn as a footman, and he was still Julia's uncle. In addition, Quinn owed the earl the money he had advanced him for the job he had just quit. Quinn wanted to make it clear he would repay him as soon as he found a new position. There were a few other things he wanted to say as well, and the best way to ensure he could say his piece without he or the earl losing their tempers was in a written note.

Half an hour later, Quinn blew on the last page to dry the ink. He'd laid his heart out on the paper, explaining how in Canada his marriage to Julia would not be viewed as a disgrace, and that Quinn would always ensure Julia and the babe were well provided for. He thanked the man for all the years of employment and even dared to mention that his brother Cecil would make an excellent groom at the Brentwood stables if the earl needed any extra hands. Quinn included a small portion of the funds he had left as a show of good faith for repaying the loan. Below his signature, he penned the address of the boardinghouse as well as the infirmary where he could be reached. Whether or not the man responded would be up to him, but at least Quinn had done what he could to make things right between them.

Quinn sealed the envelope, put it in his pocket, and left the inn. He passed by the earl's townhome, where he left the letter with Mr. Davis, and continued back to the infirmary. By the time he reached the waiting area, he felt much more settled.

He'd done the best he could by his employer. The rest was in God's hands.

"Are you ready for this?" Geoffrey's deep voice pulled Harriet from her surveillance of the road in front of her.

The hill didn't seem quite as daunting as it had the last time she'd been here. And the house itself could actually be called picturesque. Perhaps forty-five years had given her enough distance to view Hazelbrae with dispassion.

"I'm ready." She clutched her handbag tighter, looped her arm through Geoffrey's, and began the steep climb to the residence.

As they entered the intimidating front door, she did her best to quell the nerves rolling through her system. Unlike the last time she came here, she wasn't a little girl anymore. She was a survivor. A woman of substance who ran her own business. A person not to be trifled with.

And with Geoffrey beside her, a steadying presence in his dark suit and clerical collar, there was no reason to assume the worst.

"Good day, ma'am," Geoffrey said when they reached the reception desk and he'd doffed his fedora.

The stout woman looked at them. "May I help you?"

"I'm Reverend Geoffrey Burke. And this is Harriet Chamberlain. We'd like to speak to whomever is in charge here."

"Do you have an appointment?"

"No. But we have traveled quite a distance for this meeting."

"May I ask what your visit is concerning?"

Harriet stepped forward. "My sister and I came here many years ago as young girls. Unfortunately, my sister died here, and I have some questions I'd like answered."

The woman's mouth fell open for a moment. She quickly recovered and rose. "Please wait here. I'll find out if Mrs. Whitaker can see you."

"Thank you."

Several minutes later, the woman returned with a taller woman in her wake.

The statuesque brunette stepped forward, hand outstretched. "I'm Mrs. Whitaker, the directress here."

"Nice to meet you. I'm Reverend Burke, and this is Mrs. Chamberlain." Geoffrey smiled at the woman.

"What can I do for you?" She looked at them both warily.

"May we speak in private?"

"Of course. Follow me." Mrs. Whitaker glanced at the receptionist. "Hold my calls for the next half hour, please."

Harriett's stomach churned as they entered the directress's office. As she scanned the room, memories flooded her senses. Coming here as a terrified child, awaiting placement. Being summoned here when Annie died.

Once they had all taken seats, Harriett lifted her chin. "Mrs. Whitaker, I came here many years ago with my older sister as a Barnardo child. We were given different placements and subsequently separated."

The woman nodded.

"I won't bore you with the details of my life, but I will tell you my sister Annie suffered the pain and humiliation of an unwanted pregnancy at the hands of her employer, and with nowhere else to turn, she . . ." Harriet faltered, words failing her.

Geoffrey laid his hand on her arm, his gaze on the directress. "In a moment of despair, Annie took her own life. She was only fifteen years old."

"That's terrible. I'm so sorry." Mrs. Whitaker's brow furrowed.

"At the time of her death," Harriet continued, "I was overwrought, being only twelve years old myself. I never found the courage to return and find out where she'd been buried. I hoped you might be able to look up her records."

"I can try." The woman pursed her lips. "What was your sister's surname?"

"MacPherson. Annie MacPherson. She died in 1875."

"While I'm not totally familiar with the history of this establishment, I do know that most of the girls who passed away while living at Hazelbrae were buried on a plot of land behind this building."

"Is there any way to find out for certain?"

"I can check, but it might take some time."

"We don't mind waiting," Geoffrey said.

Mrs. Whitaker inclined her head. "Suit yourselves. But I will ask you to wait in the outer room."

"Certainly." Geoffrey rose and extended a hand to Harriet. "We'll take a walk about the property and meet you back here later."

As they exited the main entrance, Harriet took her first deep breath since their arrival. She inhaled the fresh air infused with the floral scents from the surrounding gardens, and the tightness in her chest eased.

"Shall we attempt to find the burial grounds?" Geoffrey asked. "Perhaps we might discover the grave ourselves."

Harriet doubted it, but she allowed him to take her by the arm.

They strolled across the lawn to a rear gate that opened to a less manicured area beyond. Wordlessly, they walked amid the taller grass mixed with wildflowers. When they came to the edge of a wooded space, Harriet spied rows of tiny white crosses. She froze for a split second before surging forward. How could there be so many girls buried here?

Her throat constricted as she spotted a larger carved cross. Slowly, she approached it until she could make out the words.

In memory of all the precious souls lost here. May they rest in peace. Amen.

Harriett's vision blurred, and she bowed her head. If only someone had cared enough about Annie to provide her with protection, perhaps her sister wouldn't have felt the need to take her own life. If only Harriet had been with her, maybe she could have made a difference.

Tears dripped down Harriet's cheeks. Somewhere in this field, her dear sister and unborn child were likely buried.

"Oh, Annie," she whispered, "I'm sorry I couldn't save you."

A warm arm came around Harriet's shoulder. She turned her face into Geoffrey's comforting embrace. As if sensing that words were unnecessary, he merely rubbed her arm, his silence providing the solace she required.

When she quieted, he passed her his handkerchief. She blew her nose and dabbed her damp cheeks.

"It doesn't look like there are any names inscribed on these markers," he said. "I can't imagine how they'll be able to locate Annie's remains."

"Maybe they have a map or some such reference in the office. They must have had to keep records. These can't all be anonymous souls with no one to remember them." Her voice trailed off at the thought.

"You're probably right. Shall we head back and see if Mrs. Whitaker is ready for us?"

"You go ahead. I'd like a few minutes alone if you don't mind."

"Take all the time you need."

When he'd gone, Harriet walked the length of the property, taking in every cross, searching for even one that might bear some type of marking. But all the crosses were identical. Plain white, no words. Harriet returned to what appeared to be the midway point and bowed her head. These poor girls deserved someone to remember them, to pray for them. And if no one else would do it, she would.

How long she stood there Harriet had no idea except that the heaviness in her lower legs told her it had been a while. When she raised her head at last, she saw Geoffrey and Mrs. Whitaker walking across the field toward her. The breeze blew the tall woman's hair around her face, and she clutched a piece of paper in her hand.

"Mrs. Whitaker," Harriet said, "I didn't mean to make you hike all this way."

"I don't mind." She held out the paper to Harriet. "I found a reference to your sister. It indicates she is buried in a grave marked number 32. Here's a map of all the site numbers."

Harriet scanned the pencil sketch of the property with the rows of crosses numbered in order.

"I believe each cross is marked on the back. If you find number 32, you'll have your sister's resting place."

Harriet looked up. "Thank you. It will be most comforting to know for certain which one belongs to Annie."

"Shall we look together?" Mrs. Whitaker's kind smile made Harriet's throat cinch.

She nodded, and the three of them began to search each cross for a number.

Very soon, Geoffrey called out, "I've found it. It's this one over here."

"I'll give you two some privacy," Mrs. Whitaker said. "When you're finished, come back to the house and I'll have some tea waiting."

"Thank you. Oh, and Mrs. Whitaker, do you know if anything would prohibit me from adding a marker to Annie's grave? Perhaps a small plaque with her name and dates?"

"I'm not sure of the policy, but I'll check the handbook and hopefully have an answer by the time you return."

Harriet nodded, then turned back to the plain cross.

The very least Annie deserved was to have her name visible so anyone visiting here would know she was so much more than just cross number 32.

CHAPTER 31

SEPTEMBER 1, 1919

Quinn stood at the bottom of the ship's gangplank, waiting as Becky said her good-byes to Cecil and Harry. A light mist hung in the air, threatening a harder rain to come. Quinn leaned his boot on a nearby crate and smiled at Harry's exuberant hugs. Today, Becky was leaving to return to Canada. Harry had tried to coax her to stay longer, but with her wedding tentatively scheduled for the end of the month, she felt she had stayed long enough.

It had been four weeks since they left Toronto, including twelve days of travel time and almost three weeks of visiting Mum each day at the infirmary. Quinn supposed Becky had stayed much longer than she'd originally intended, and he was grateful for the extra time because, just as Quinn had hoped, their mother's health had shown a marked improvement after seeing her children again. The doctor had called it nothing short of a miracle to see her rally the way she had. In fact, he said if she continued to improve, she might be released within the next week or two.

The only problem was, Quinn didn't know where he would take her.

With her weakened lungs and heart, the doctor advised she needed a clean, warm environment to live in, not the drafty, germ-infested workhouse. If Mum was stronger and able to make the ocean voyage, he'd have taken her back to Canada with him. But the trip would only set her health back, if she even made it there alive.

Which left Quinn trying to come up with a viable alternative here in England. He'd already started making inquiries in the area about possible work and had taken on a few odds jobs here and there to pay for their room and board.

He'd yet to hear back from the earl, which meant he likely wouldn't respond to Quinn's message. He'd hoped Cecil might find employment with him. Then at least one of them would have a decent income.

Quinn calculated the time he had left before Julia's baby was due, which was sometime before Christmas. That meant he had less than three months to find a more permanent job and a suitable place for his family to live before he returned to be with Julia in time for the birth.

But would a new employer even allow him the time off to make such a long trip? His gut screamed with the frustration of needing to be in two places at once.

The only other option rested with Cecil and Harry. If Cecil could secure a decent job, and Harry start doing some deliveries like Quinn used to do, then perhaps they could afford to rent a small cottage while Quinn was away in Canada.

"Do you ever stop worrying, big brother?" Becky's teasing voice drew him out of his thoughts. "You're going to have permanent ridges etched into that hard head of yours if you're not careful." She laughed out loud, a pretty, carefree sound that drifted in the wind.

His lips twitched in response. Becky looked so young and happy today, obviously eager to get back to her fiancé. He tried hard not to envy her the freedom to do so. "I wish I could go with you," he said. "You're certain you'll be all right traveling alone?"

Quinn had half-expected Cecil to return to Canada with her. But when he questioned his brother, Cecil admitted that he'd burned his bridges with Mr. Sherman. When he'd asked the farmer for some time off to visit his ailing mother, the man had coldly refused, and for the next week, Sherman had found continual ways to punish Cecil, reminding him that he was nothing but cheap labor. Finally, Cecil made the decision to leave for good, not taking time to contact Quinn but simply heading straight for Halifax. The fact that Cecil had breached his contract, risking potential punishment and forfeiting any money owing him, showed Quinn how intolerable his circumstances had become.

"I'll be fine," Becky said. "I'll find a nice group of women and stay close to them." She reached up to kiss his cheek. "And I'll be sure to deliver your letter to Julia in person once I've had a chance to settle in."

"I appreciate it." Quinn swallowed hard. "I want you to know how grateful I am to you for making this trip. I realize it cost you a lot to do so, but as you can see, it was worth it for Mum."

Her face softened. "She is much improved. I never thought that would be the case when we first got here."

He nodded. "I prayed it would. That knowing her children were all safe and alive, she would find a renewed will to live."

"What are you going to do now, Quinn?" Becky kept her voice low.

He set his jaw. "Whatever I have to do to ensure my family stays together."

"And Julia?" Her brow furrowed.

"I'll go back in time for the baby's arrival. I promised her that."

"But what then? I might be wrong, but I didn't get the impression Julia intended to return to England."

Tension snapped up Quinn's spine. He didn't even know if Julia would want to stay married to him once the baby was born. "I'll face that problem when the time comes." He reached out to squeeze Becky's hand. "I only wish I could be there to attend your wedding. I can't imagine you not having your family with you on your special day."

Moisture welled in her eyes. "It would have been nice. But as long as I have Ned, that's all that matters."

The ship's horn blared, causing a flurry of activity on the dock.

"I'd better get on board." Becky threw her arms around Quinn in a tight hug. "Take good care of everyone, and I'll see you when you get back to Toronto."

"Be happy, Becca. You deserve it."

"I will." With one more hug for Harry and Cecil, Becky grabbed her bag and rushed up the gangplank. At the rail, she found a spot between the passengers and waved down at them.

Cecil and Harry waved back, but Quinn just stood and stared, wishing with every fiber of his being that he was going back with her.

"Mr. Aspinall? There's a message for you."

Quinn halted on his way through the boardinghouse lobby and headed over to the desk.

A clerk handed him a slip of paper.

Quinn unfolded it and read the few words jotted there. Instantly, his heart started to race.

Come to the house tomorrow at ten o'clock. We have unfinished business. Lord Brentwood.

"What is it?" Harry hovered at Quinn's elbow.

"The earl wants to see me tomorrow." Quinn glanced at Cecil. "I suppose we'll find out then what he has to say." He tapped the paper against his palm. "I will pray very hard tonight that he sees fit to grant you a post at Brentwood. That would be good news indeed." His brother knew Quinn had asked about a possible position for him there.

"I won't hold my breath," Cecil huffed.

Harry's eyes widened. "Maybe I could work for the earl too."

"I don't know, lad." Quinn ruffled Harry's hair. "Let's wait and see what tomorrow brings."

The next morning, Quinn accompanied his brothers to the infirmary and left them visiting with their mother while he went to meet the earl. He prayed the whole way over, asking for the Lord's help to accept whatever the man had to say.

After the previous night's rain, today had dawned cool and sunny. When Quinn arrived at the townhouse, Mr. Davis informed him the earl was out in the back garden. Quinn thanked him and walked around the outside, through a side gate to the rear of the house.

The earl was seated on the terrace, reading the morning paper.

Quinn stood at attention beside the table until the earl looked up. Then he gave a slight bow. Even though he was no longer in the earl's employ, old habits died hard.

"Mr. Aspinall. Thank you for coming. Please, join me."

Hiding his surprise, Quinn pulled out a chair and sat down.

"Would you care for some tea or a crumpet?"

"No, thank you, my lord. I just ate."

The earl motioned to a maid hovering behind him. She quickly came forward to refill his cup. He added milk and sugar, leaving Quinn waiting for him to get to the reason for the visit.

"Thank you for the letter you wrote," his lordship said at last. "It showed great dignity in the face of my adverse reaction to your news."

"I didn't want to leave matters on a sour note. Not after everything you did for me when I desperately needed work." Quinn tried to relax on the hard chair. "Also, Julia cares about you a great deal and worries about your opinion of her." He tilted his chin. "I told her that if you truly cared about her, her welfare should be all that mattered."

"You're right." The earl's gaze slid away. "I'm ashamed to say my first thought was how her circumstances would affect my family's social status. Once I read your letter and had time to consider the situation from all angles, I came to the same conclusion. Julia's happiness and well-being are what's most important."

Quinn clenched his fingers together. Was this a dismal attempt at an apology?

The earl patted a linen napkin to his lips, then set it back on his lap. "I also appreciate the noble gesture you made on behalf of my niece by marrying her. You went beyond the call of duty, and as a gesture of thanks, I'm prepared to honor the offer I initially made you."

Quinn stiffened. "Do you mean the tenant farm?"

"Precisely."

"But I didn't fulfill your requirements."

"Not to the letter, but you did find my niece, and you did ensure her safety. And you have facilitated the start of a reconciliation between us, if Julia's letter is any indication. I have written back to her, offering my apologies for our estrangement and assuring her that it is my wish that we find a way to move forward." The earl drummed his fingers on the tabletop. "As long as we don't advertise the fact that she married beneath her station, no one will really be the wiser."

Irritation snapped along Quinn's nerves. "You plan to hide your niece away like you're ashamed of her?"

The earl sighed. "That's not what I meant." He rose and crossed the terrace, hands in his pockets. "My daughter, Amelia, is about to make a very advantageous match with the son of a duke. Their betrothal will be announced very soon."

Quinn waited for him to continue, willing his system to settle.

"By the time Julia's child is born and you're ready to bring them back—likely next spring, I would assume—Amelia should be wed. I can't take the chance that any perceived stain on Julia's reputation might cause the duke to change his mind about uniting our families." He turned to give Quinn a hard stare. "Will you agree not to interfere with this marriage?"

Quinn gritted his teeth, picturing Julia's hurt at not being welcome at her cousin's wedding. "I will explain the situation to her and make sure we stay away until after the ceremony. Though if Amelia's fiancé truly cares about her, it shouldn't matter who her cousin has married."

"A lovely notion, but I fear reality is not quite so forgiving." He resumed his pacing. "Now, back to my offer of the farm."

Quinn's mind whirled with possibilities. His initial reaction was to refuse the offer outright. But in truth, he owed Julia the chance to voice her own opinion on the matter. "Thank you for your generosity, sir, but I will need to discuss this with my wife first."

The earl returned to the table and resumed his seat. "A prudent response. I hope Julia will realize the merit of my offer. Where else could you obtain your own property with a working farm and a home to live in?"

Indeed, wasn't that the dream Quinn had entertained the whole time he was in Canada? It would be perfect for his mother and brothers as well. "Unfortunately, it will be some time before a letter reaches Julia and she sends her reply."

The man studied him. "In the meantime, let's address the other request you made in your letter."

"My brother."

"Correct. You said he'd been working on a farm in Canada for several years?"

"That's right. He's a hard worker. And he's good with horses."

"What about your youngest brother? Didn't he also work on a farm?"

"He did, but it was . . . far from a pleasant experience." Quinn sucked in a deep breath and slowly exhaled. Why did he want to know about Harry?

The earl frowned. "I'm sorry to hear it. Still, I imagine the boy learned a fair bit over the years."

"He did."

His lordship stroked his chin in a thoughtful manner. "Then what I propose is that you move your family onto the farm now. Between the three of you, you should be able to manage the work. And when you leave for Canada, the boys should be able to keep things running smoothly until your return, perhaps with a little help from some of my other tenant farmers."

Quinn's pulse leaped in his veins. His dream of having his family back together shimmered before him once again. He rose to pace the terrace alongside the earl. "Why would you take such a risk? Surely there are a lot of contenders for the farm."

"True. But none of them is married to my niece." The earl gave him a frank stare. "And they haven't proven their loyalty to me." He turned toward Quinn. "Consider this a gesture of goodwill, proof of my sincerity to reconcile with Julia."

"What if she wants to stay in Canada?" A muscle twitched in Quinn's jaw.

The earl shrugged. "We can adjust the plan if Julia is against the idea."

Quinn quickly tried to process the situation, a flare of hope igniting in his chest. If he accepted, he and his brothers could move onto the farm immediately and get the house ready for his mother. With the three of them working hard through the fall, they could have the property well in hand before Quinn had to leave for Canada around the beginning of December. "Has anyone been tending the land recently?"

"I had a temporary man overseeing the property. Everything is in decent shape. Except for the house, which will need a good overhaul."

Quinn approached the man and stretched out his hand. "Then I accept your offer, sir."

His lordship stood and clasped Quinn's hand. "Excellent. I'll be leaving for Derbyshire tomorrow. Shall I plan for you and your brothers to arrive within the week?"

"That should be fine." If Mum wasn't ready to leave by then, he'd make arrangements until she could join them.

"I look forward to a prosperous relationship. I only hope my niece agrees."

A niggle of unease crept into Quinn's gut. This arrangement hinged on Julia, and unfortunately, she was the unknown factor in all of this.

Quinn nodded. "As long as it's God's will for our lives, then I believe she will."

As he headed back to the infirmary to tell his brothers the good news, he prayed Julia would be as pleased with the outcome as he.

CHAPTER 32

Harriet stepped out the door of the Dr. Barnardo's Home with Geoffrey right behind her. They had met with the administrators of the facility and had presented their plan for having clergy members take turns visiting the farms to ensure the proper treatment of their young wards. Happily, Geoffrey had recruited a dozen clergy from different Christian faiths in the area, all eager to help in their campaign. The only task remaining now was to create a schedule and begin implementing it.

"The meeting went well, don't you think?" Geoffrey positioned his fedora on his head and glanced over as they walked.

"Better than I expected," she said.

"How about I buy you lunch to celebrate?"

Harriet released a slow breath. "I'd like that. Thank you." With a firm lift of her chin, she did her best to put her melancholy behind her. She was slowly getting used to life without Harry, as well as other changes in the boardinghouse. Emma and Jonathan had left to return to England, and though Julia lived nearby, she was busy with her position as companion to Mrs. Middleton. Harriet reminded herself every day that her role as proprietress was an ever-changing one. She knew better than to get too attached to any one tenant, for they always left her at some point or another.

Yet lately, a pervasive loneliness had seeped into her very bones.

Geoffrey opened a door for her, and she stepped into a dimly lit restaurant. As her eyes adjusted, she looked around and frowned. This was not some everyday eatery. This was a fancy restaurant with white linen tablecloths and candles for ambience. She turned and almost smacked into Geoffrey's chest. He grasped her elbow to steady her.

"This is too posh, Geoffrey. Couldn't we just get a sandwich in a diner?"

"I want to treat you to a nice meal. How long has it been since you've been to an elegant restaurant?"

She blinked. In all honesty, she couldn't remember. She was always too busy with her boarders, making sure their meals were appealing and the residence was clean and inviting.

"Your inability to answer says it all." Geoffrey smiled. "Please allow me to spoil you a bit."

A hostess appeared. "A table for two?" she asked brightly.

"Yes, please," Geoffrey answered before Harriet could protest any further.

She huffed out a breath and followed the woman across the room. Geoffrey was quick to pull out a chair for her. She sat down, her handbag on her lap.

The hostess set two menus on the table. "Your waiter will be right with you."

"Relax, Harriet. I want you to enjoy this." Geoffrey set his hat on the empty chair and took a seat beside her. He picked up a menu and began to read. "I believe I'm in the mood for a thick steak."

"Then I hope you have a thick stack of bills to pay for it," she muttered as she scanned the entrées.

Geoffrey chuckled. "It's not like I eat steak every day." He lowered the menu. "Anything strike your fancy?"

She looked up. "I think I'll try the Waldorf salad."

"A salad is all you're going to have?"

"Yes. Why?"

He stared at her. "You're right. You can choose whatever you wish. But please don't worry about the cost."

She focused back on the menu. "If spending money makes you

happy, I'll be sure to leave room for an extravagant dessert." She struggled to hide a smile, her mood definitely lifting. Keeping this man off guard proved very satisfying.

After they had ordered, Harriet did her best to soak in the lovely atmosphere and appreciate Geoffrey's gift. "This is very nice. I'm sorry I wasn't as enthusiastic as you probably hoped."

"Not to worry. As long as I manage to distract you from your troubles for a while, I'll be glad."

She frowned. "Have I seemed that unhappy lately?"

"To be honest, yes. I've missed my best friend's sunny nature." He reached over to cover her hand with his. His warm eyes radiated concern. "I'm hoping she'll come back to me soon."

Harriet's throat tightened. Why were tears so near the surface at every turn lately? She looked down at his hand, relishing the strength paired with gentleness. Where would she be without Geoffrey in her life? Without him to steady her, to lift her spirits, to go out of his way to ensure she was taken care of?

Like a true partner would. . . .

"Harriet." The strange timbre of his voice made her lift her head.

Her breath caught at the intensity in his expression, and her heart began to beat an unnatural rhythm. "What is it?" She hardly dared voice the question.

"You and I have been friends for more years than I care to count," he began. "All the way back to when I was a relatively new rector and you and Miles helped me start up the Newcomers Program."

She wanted to look away but found she couldn't. What if he was about to tell her he'd been assigned to a parish in a different city? What would she do without him around the corner?

"Recently I've been growing restless, and I find myself wanting to make a change. Before it's too late."

Her free hand fluttered to her throat. She was right. He was leaving her. And he'd chosen a fancy restaurant to impart the bad news. Her mouth went completely dry. How was she ever going to wish him well when part of her would be dying inside?

"So I've decided to be brave and ask for what I want." He caressed her fingers with his thumb, his eyes on her face. "Harriet, will you do me a great honor and marry me?"

Her mouth fell open. Every thought flew from her head. "You're not moving away?"

"Moving? Why would you think that?"

"You . . . you said something about being restless and wanting a change."

He gave a hearty laugh. "Moving is not the type of change I'm interested in. I want someone to come home to at night. Someone to share all aspects of my life. And I want that someone to be you." He leaned closer and kissed her softly, with just enough heat to make her heart gallop in her chest. Then he pulled back to look at her. "I can see I've stunned you with my proposal. Maybe you'd like some time to consider it before giving me an answer?"

"That would be . . . reasonable."

"Oh, I almost forgot." He reached into his pocket and took out a small box. "I probably should have led with this, but it's been forty years since I've proposed to a woman." He opened the box to reveal a square-cut emerald ring with two small diamonds on either side. "I've had this since last Christmas, waiting for the right time to ask. I finally realized I was wasting precious days we could be together, and that no matter the answer, I needed to know."

Tears blurred her vision. He'd even remembered she didn't like ostentatious diamond rings. That emeralds were her favorite stone. "Oh, Geoffrey." Her voice broke.

His smile faded as he closed the lid. "It's all right, Harriet. No one said you had to return my feelings. If friendship is all you can manage, then I'll have to live with it." Sorrow shadowed his features, dimming the light in his eyes.

Her heart squeezed. "You didn't let me finish." She swiped at her damp cheeks. "I don't need time to think it over, because . . ." She inhaled and let out a breath. "I would be honored to be your wife."

His brows shot upward. "Really?"

"Really." She managed a wobbly smile.

His face broke into a wide grin. Then he leaned in and kissed her once more. This time, she reached over to cup his cheek and kissed him back.

When he moved away, his eyes were shiny with tears. "I love you very much, Harriet Chamberlain. But I never dared to hope you could ever consider me as more than a friend."

She lifted one shoulder. "Lately when you've been over in the evenings and leave for home, I've been wishing you didn't have to go." Heat rushed into her cheeks.

"I feel the same way. It's hard going back to an empty rectory. I almost bought a dog for company."

Harriet gave a shaky laugh. "A dog might be nice. I haven't had a pet in years."

"Then maybe we'll get one together." He laughed too, the sound freeing all the tension within her. "Should we see if the ring fits?"

"Please do." She held out her left hand, but then stopped. She still wore her former wedding band all these years after Miles's death, as she felt it gave her more respectability as a boardinghouse owner. With a steadying breath, she wriggled the gold band off, kissed it, and deposited the ring into her handbag. Then she held out her hand again.

"You're sure?" Geoffrey asked.

"Positive."

He took the emerald from the box and slipped it onto her finger.

"It's perfect," she said. "And so are you."

"I'm far from perfect, Harriet, but I'll do my best to be a good husband to you."

"I already know you will be. You are the most thoughtful, caring man I've ever met. And I'm blessed to have you in my life."

Joy beamed from his face. "I must warn you. I don't want a long engagement. So as soon as I can find a minister to marry us—"

She held up a finger. "A short engagement is fine, but I will need some time to put my affairs in order."

"What affairs?"

"Well, for one thing, I'll have to see about selling the boardinghouse. As a minister's wife, I'll have my work cut out for me. I don't need to be worrying about boarders too."

"I hadn't really thought about that." He laid a hand on her arm. "Are you certain you're willing to give up the business? After all, it's your last tie to Miles."

"To tell you the truth, I think the time has come to let someone younger take on the responsibility. Besides, if I make a commitment to you, I intend to give it all my energy and devotion."

He shook his head. "I didn't think it possible to love you even more, Harriet Chamberlain, but right now, I do."

Quinn guided the horse and buggy along the dirt lane that led past Brentwood Manor to the tenant farms beyond, being careful not to jostle the wagon too much. To his extreme gratitude, the rain had stopped yesterday, and a cool wind had dried out the mud. A nervous energy buzzed through his system. He couldn't quite believe that today would see the fulfilment of his dream, and he would at last bring his mother to her new home. A place where she could feel safe with her family around her. A place where she could heal and never have to fear living in squalor again.

Another benefit of Mum's time in the infirmary was that her need for liquor appeared to have faded. As long as they could keep her from starting again, the doctor had told him, she should be fine.

Quinn glanced sideways at her. She sat tall on the bench seat, staring straight ahead. In the bright light of day, the toll the years had taken on her were evident in the sallow skin and the deep grooves around her eyes and mouth.

"The farms are over the next hill, Mum. Ours is the second one we'll see."

From the firm press of her lips, Quinn could tell she was working hard to contain her emotions. "I can't believe how lovely the countryside is here," she said. "After living my whole life in the city,

I never dared imagine what it could be like." She inhaled deeply. "The air is so fresh and clean. I feel healthier already."

Quinn grinned at her. "That's the best news I've heard all day."

"I still can't believe you managed this." She pulled her new blue shawl, one Quinn had bought for her travels, more closely around her shoulders.

"The earl is a generous man, and he appreciates loyalty among his staff. Apparently, I impressed him with my service."

"And the fact you married his niece has nothing to do with it?" Mum's lips twitched.

Quinn shrugged. "At first, our marriage was a detriment to the situation, since his lordship believed Julia had married beneath her. Only by the grace of God did he have a change of heart and offer me the farm in gratitude for keeping Julia safe."

"The grace of God indeed," she murmured.

They passed the first tenant farm, and not long after came upon their land. Quinn's chest swelled with pride at the progress he, Cecil, and Harry had made over the past several weeks. With Mum strong enough that they could leave her in the nurses' care, he and the boys had spent most of the time at the farm. Cecil's knowledge of crop rotation and plowing had proved more than beneficial. Even young Harry's experience with farmwork served as a great bonus in their efforts.

"Those are our fields, Mum. We'll grow several different crops once we get the ground ready. And Cecil hopes to raise pigs as well." He pointed. "There's the house over to the right."

Her face brightened. "It looks big. I'd pictured a one-room cabin."

"You'll be amazed. There are two separate sleeping quarters, with a common living area. And a loft where Cecil and Harry sleep. There's even a rough indoor privy."

He guided the animals toward the farmhouse, knowing his mother would need to rest soon. There'd be ample time to show her the rest of the property later.

"This is wonderful, Quinten," Mum said as he helped her to the ground.

Luckily, the house came with the basic furnishings provided, which would save them a good amount of money. Over time, Quinn planned to build more furniture to add to what was there. And he hoped his mother would make use of her sewing skills to fashion some new curtains, linens, and bedcovers. The rugged stone walls with wooden trim might be rustic compared to the earl's home, but to his mother it would seem like a palace.

He opened the door and ushered her inside the main room. To the left was the kitchen area with wooden cupboards, a cast-iron stove, and a good-sized table and chairs. To the right, two large easy chairs flanked the hearth around a cotton rug.

"It's lovely." Tears appeared in Mum's eyes. "I haven't had a house to call my own since your father died." She reached out a hand to him. "Thank you, son. For not giving up on me when you had every reason to."

He grabbed her hand and squeezed, his eyes burning. "Never."

She smiled and moved farther into the room. "It could use a woman's touch, but overall you've done a wonderful job with the place."

"All we really did was clean. I knew you'd want to fix it up the way you'd like."

She nodded, her throat working. "I can't wait to get started."

Quinn pointed to the small hallway. "Let me show you to your room. I think you must be ready for a rest after our long trip."

"That sounds heavenly. My own room and my three sons right here. What more could a mother ask?" She turned to him, her eyes glowing with emotion. "You have done a great job, Quinn, getting our family back together. Your father would be so proud of you."

Quinn swallowed hard, then ducked his head so she wouldn't see the tears forming. He'd waited nine long years to hear those words. Nine years since the day he'd made the promise to his father. Nine hard years where he'd almost given up hope of ever fulfilling it.

The soft click of his mother's bedroom door told him he was alone. He wiped a hand across his eyes, attempting to sift through his jumbled emotions. Pulling the iron key from his pocket, he rolled it between his fingers. Then he crossed to the front door to the nail protruding from the jamb. There he hung the key as an ever-present reminder of the vow he'd made and had now fulfilled.

"I hope Mum's right," he whispered. "I hope you're proud of me, Dad. Of all of us."

Quinn glanced around the interior of the house, letting the full realization of his accomplishment sink in. He'd achieved his dream, completed his mission. Yet as he stood alone in the kitchen, waiting for the expected feelings of elation to rise up and envelop him, his stomach dropped. Even though his mother's praise had warmed him through and through, a trace of unrest persisted.

Because one crucial element was missing.

Without Julia by his side to share in this moment, his victory seemed hollow.

He blew out a long breath. Had he sacrificed one dream for another?

He walked to the window to stare out at the fields where his brothers were working. The date for Julia to give birth was drawing closer by the day. It was time for him to focus on one more very important promise he had to keep.

And God willing, he intended to do so.

CHAPTER 33

NOVEMBER 15, 1919

Julia looked at the staircase and attempted to gather the energy to go up to her quarters. Now that she was so far advanced in her pregnancy, Mrs. Middleton insisted she rest each afternoon. Yet the effort to climb the stairs was too daunting.

Perhaps she'd just put her feet up in the parlor and rest near the warmth of the fire.

She walked over to the sofa and pulled a knitted afghan across her lap. Then, with a long sigh, she took Quinn's letters from her pocket and opened them. In truth, she'd long since memorized every word he'd written, but it still brought a measure of comfort to reread them. Running her fingers over the very ink he had penned somehow made him seem closer.

Becky had brought the first letter to her in person two months ago upon her return from England, and they'd had a nice visit. Becky told her all about the voyage, the cramped room in the boardinghouse they'd stayed in, and her mother's amazing, albeit slow, recovery. In his next letter, Quinn had written that he would soon get his mother out of the infirmary and spoke of his pride in now having a home to take her to. Julia had actually wept tears of happiness when she read of his anticipation for his mother to see it for the first time.

Yet the fact that this home was one of her uncle's tenant farms troubled Julia. Quinn had made it clear that the final decision as to whether or not they accepted her uncle's gesture rested with her. But it appeared that Quinn had already assumed she would want to continue their marriage and that she would agree to return to England. Which only added to the guilt she wrestled with at the possibility of having to destroy Quinn's dream if she chose not to go back.

To refuse, however, would now have additional consequences. In a letter, her uncle had offered his sincerest regrets at their estrangement and had made it clear that his offer of the farm was given in thanks for Quinn's loyalty and as an olive branch in the hope that she would return to Derbyshire after the baby was born. So if she declined Uncle Howard's generous offer, she would not only break Quinn's heart, she would further alienate her uncle.

Julia folded the pages with a sigh. In truth, she missed Quinn desperately. Missed his calming presence, his quick wit, and his charming smile. The way he always made her feel safe and cared for. And she couldn't help feeling a little jealous of the cheery tone of his letters. What if he became so consumed with his new life on the farm that he didn't come back to Canada?

Back to her like he promised.

It didn't help that she was nearing her due date, and he'd made no real mention of when he might return. Perhaps he never would and simply couldn't bring himself to tell her. What would she do then?

That depressing idea had taken root and wouldn't shake loose, forcing her to admit the very real possibility that she would face her future alone. To combat her anxiety, Julia spent much time in prayer, reminding herself that God was on her side and everything would be fine. No matter what Quinn ended up doing, she was strong and capable and would do whatever it took to keep her child safe.

Julia leaned back on the sofa and closed her eyes, calling to mind the last time she saw Quinn at the train station. Once again, her heart had lagged behind her head. Over the course of their days together, he'd become increasingly essential to her well-being, and it wasn't until the day of his departure that she'd acknowledged the truth. She *did* love Quinn—quite desperately, in fact. And she couldn't imagine her life without him. But when she should have told him her true feelings, she couldn't make her tongue release those few precious words.

Would it have changed anything if she'd told him sooner?

A throat cleared, causing Julia's eyes to open.

Mrs. Banbury stood in the doorway, gazing down her nose at Julia. As Julia's pregnancy had become more and more apparent, so had the woman's disapproving air. She held out an envelope. "This came for you."

Julia struggled to her feet to accept the paper. "Thank you, Mrs. Banbury."

Despite the woman's thinly cloaked hostility, Julia always tried to be polite, hoping if she treated the woman with kindness that perhaps one day she would realize not all English citizens were horrid creatures.

The woman left without another word, and Julia resumed her seat. She looked at the envelope and a shiver ran down her spine. The return address was from a Toronto solicitor. Surely this could not be good news.

She ripped open the flap and took out the single sheet of official letterhead.

> *You are required to appear before the magistrate at the Toronto courthouse on Thursday, November 27, 1919, at two o'clock to defend charges by Dr. Richard E. Hawkins regarding the paternity of your unborn child.*

As the words sank into her brain, she gasped and covered her mouth.

Dr. Hawkins was demanding she go before a judge to discuss her pregnancy. What on earth would she do now? All it would take was one question from the judge and the truth of her baby's paternity would be revealed.

Panic raced through her, causing her breath to grow shallow. Breathing was already hard enough with the babe pressing against her lungs. She rose and stretched her diaphragm, intentionally slowing her intake of air. It wouldn't do for her to pass out.

She laid a palm on her belly, comforted to feel the flutter of life inside her. Slowly, her system settled as her breathing evened out. She would not allow anyone or anything to separate her from her child. Especially not its unscrupulous father.

Even though her husband wasn't here, she still had their marriage certificate. As Quinn had told her, the child was his by law. But what if the judge asked her under oath to identify the true father? What would she do then?

She retrieved the paper from where it had fallen on the floor, Quinn's words coming to mind. *"If you have any trouble, promise you'll seek Reverend Burke's assistance."*

As much as she hated to inconvenience anyone, she would have to once again ask for help. Alone, she stood no chance of keeping her child. But with a clergyman beside her to give her some semblance of credibility, just maybe she'd have a fighting chance.

She would also enlist Mrs. Middleton's assistance. Find out if the woman had a solicitor of her own whom Julia could hire to represent her. One thing Julia knew for certain, she couldn't take on Dr. Hawkins in court without a professional on her side. Someone who knew the law and what rights Julia had as the baby's mother.

She took in a steadying breath, feeling the rightness of her decisions. If it took six months of wages to pay her employer back, it would be worth it to be rid of Dr. Hawkins once and for all. And to know her baby was safe.

Thursday the twenty-seventh dawned cold and snowy, with a thick layer of white covering the ground. In one way, Julia welcomed the weather since it afforded her the opportunity to wear a heavy woolen cape. The bulk of the cloak hid the advanced stages of her pregnancy, and only a boor would ask her outright about the child's imminent due date.

She hoped.

Upon learning of Julia's dilemma, Mrs. Middleton had insisted on hiring a solicitor for her. She'd also wanted to accompany her to court, but Julia refused to hear of it, remembering from her wedding day the long corridors and steep flight of stairs in the building. The dear woman wouldn't be able to manage those. In addition, there was no guarantee how long the process would take, and Julia didn't want to tax Mrs. Middleton's strength.

But Julia wouldn't be alone. Mrs. Chamberlain had insisted on coming with her and Rev. Burke today.

"Quinten warned us that fellow could cause trouble," she'd said. "I won't hear of you facing that man alone."

Julia had not been able to suppress her tears of gratitude. "Thank you, Mrs. C. I don't know what I'd do without you."

And now, as the pair arrived to pick Julia up in the minister's automobile, Mrs. Middleton saw her off at the front door with a hug. "Don't worry, child. My solicitor will handle everything. You just stay strong."

If only it were that easy. Especially with her queasy stomach threatening to rebel and the dull ache across her lower back that had plagued her since early morning.

"I'll do my best." Julia managed a smile. "Please pray for me, Mrs. Middleton. I need all the divine intervention I can get."

They arrived at the courthouse and found a parking spot just down the road. The short walk to the imposing stone building did nothing to quell Julia's nerves at the thought of facing Dr. Hawkins again. She paused at the foot of the stairs below the arched stone entranceway and recalled the words of her favorite Bible verse, one that always provided her with comfort.

The Lord is my strength and my shield; my heart trusted in him, and I am helped.

Julia held those words close as she followed Mrs. C. and Rev. Burke into the building, where the weight of justice seemed to echo within its very walls. How strange to be back here again. The last time, she'd been a nervous bride who never could have imagined returning under these circumstances. Would the law be her undoing, or would the judge uphold Quinn's legal position as the rightful father of her child?

Before her, a large split staircase led to the second story. Having no idea which way to go, she made her way over to a receptionist to ask directions. The woman pointed down the main corridor to another hallway, at the end of which she would find the courtrooms.

On the way there, Julia began to feel unwell, her body slick with perspiration. When they came to a women's lavatory, she excused herself to splash cold water on her face, hoping it would alleviate the nausea. But as she exited into the corridor, the tightness in her chest spread over her whole torso.

"My dear, come and sit down. We have a few minutes yet." Mrs. C. ushered her over to a bench outside the courtroom.

A large clock on the wall ticked away the minutes, increasing her trepidation. She tapped one foot against the tiled floor, every nerve in her body jumping.

Rev. Burke came to sit down beside her and held out his hand to her. "Why don't we take this time to ask for the Lord's help before we go in?"

"That's a good idea." She gave a shaky smile. Prayer might be just what she needed. She placed her chilled fingers in his warm ones and took Mrs. C.'s hand with the other. When he bowed his head, she closed her eyes, drawing strength from the devout man's steadying presence.

"Lord, we ask for your help today. Be with Julia as she faces the man who betrayed her. Protect her and her child, Lord, and give the judge the wisdom to make the right decision for all involved. In Jesus's name we pray. Amen."

Julia's throat thickened. "Thank you. For the prayers and for coming with me today." She gulped in a breath. "I only wish Quinn could be here."

The minister squeezed her hand. "I consider it a privilege to stand with you in his stead."

"We both do." Mrs. C. gave her a quick hug.

The courtroom doors opened, and several people exited, followed by two solicitors.

Rev. Burke rose immediately and assisted Julia to her feet.

A man approached from her right. "Good day, Mrs. Aspinall."

"Mr. Nelson. It's good to see you." She'd already met the solicitor once at Mrs. Middleton's house, where she'd explained the situation, and he'd assured her he'd do his best to protect her child. "These are my friends, Reverend Burke and Mrs. Chamberlain."

"Nice to meet you." Mr. Nelson gave a tight-lipped smile. "If you're ready, shall we go in?"

She drew in a fortifying breath and nodded.

They entered the interior of the courtroom. Only a few people sat in the rows of seats behind a wooden railing separating the spectators from the lawyer's area. A somber-looking man in black robes and a gray wig sat high on the judge's bench.

Once he spied them, he banged a gavel on the desk. "Next case on the docket, Dr. Richard Hawkins versus Mrs. Julia Aspinall."

Mr. Nelson escorted her to the front of the room. "Here we are, Your Honor. Mr. Eugene Nelson representing Mrs. Aspinall." He motioned for Julia to sit at one of the tables in front of the bench.

Julia glanced over her shoulder to see Mrs. C. and Rev. Burke taking their seats behind her.

The judge turned his attention to the other side of the room. "Mr. Kendall, I assume you are representing Dr. Hawkins."

"Yes, Your Honor."

"Very well. You may proceed."

Julia stiffened on the hard chair, resisting the urge to glance at Dr. Hawkins.

Mr. Nelson leaned over and whispered in Julia's ear. "Remember, it's vital that you do not react to whatever he says. We will have our time for rebuttal afterward."

She nodded, staring straight ahead at the judge. Her stomach cramped, and she prayed she wouldn't retch. This whole ordeal was humiliating enough without that.

Mr. Kendall spoke for several minutes, relaying the history of Dr. Hawkins's relationship with Julia.

The judge appeared to listen intently, and when the lawyer finished, he said, "So, to sum up, Dr. Hawkins claims that Mrs. Aspinall, while unmarried, entered into a physical relationship with him, which he believes resulted in her pregnancy."

"Correct, sir."

"And subsequently, after having no contact with Dr. Hawkins for several months, she married another man." The judge peered down at a paper on his desk. "A Mr. Quinten Aspinall, who has now returned to his homeland of England, effectively abandoning her and the unborn child."

A sharp cry escaped Julia. "That is not true!"

"Mrs. Aspinall. Please restrain yourself." Mr. Nelson's sharp whisper hissed in her ear.

She clamped her lips together and bowed her head. Her heart pumped loudly in her chest, and she couldn't seem to draw in enough air.

"Please continue, Mr. Kendall."

"Dr. Hawkins contends that Mrs. Aspinall is lying about the paternity of her child and that she married another man in order to deprive him of his only progeny. Thus, he believed his only course of action was to bring the matter before the court and have the woman swear to the identity of the true father under oath."

The judge frowned. "Why is Dr. Hawkins so certain the child is not Mr. Aspinall's?"

"The marriage took place when Mrs. Aspinall was already advanced in her pregnancy. Unless she had relations with *two* men out of wedlock, which of course given the circumstances could well be within the realm of possibility, the child is more likely to belong to Dr. Hawkins. He believes that in order to cover the shame of her condition, she coerced some unsuspecting fool into marrying her."

Julia bit her lip so hard she tasted blood. Tears of shame and anger pooled in her eyes, and she blinked hard to keep them from falling. At this moment, she was thankful that Quinn wasn't on hand to witness this degradation. He certainly would have created an unpleasant scene and perhaps gotten himself arrested in the process.

"I suppose the only manner to ascertain the truth of the situation is to have Mrs. Aspinall come forward." He stared at her. "Ma'am, if you will approach the witness stand, the bailiff will swear you in."

Dear Lord, help me. . . .

Mr. Nelson stood and put a hand under her elbow to help her rise. She paused for a moment to steady herself. There was no way to avoid it. She would have to admit Dr. Hawkins was the father of her child and throw herself on the judge's mercy. What would he do? Would her marriage certificate save her, or would he disregard it as a mere ruse?

Despite her unsteady legs, she made it up to the platform and sank onto the chair.

Glancing out over the room, her gaze fell on Mrs. Chamberlain, who smiled and nodded her encouragement.

Then the bailiff approached carrying a black Bible with gold lettering. He held it out to her. "Place your left hand on the Bible and raise your right hand. Do you swear the testimony you are about to give is the truth, the whole truth and nothing but the truth, so help you God?" His voice boomed over the silent room.

The Lord is my strength and my shield.

Julia ran her tongue over her lips, then stiffened her spine. "I do."

Mr. Kendall came forward, a smug look on his florid face. "For the record, state your name, please."

"Mrs. Julia Holloway Aspinall."

"Mrs. Aspinall, is it true you were married in July of this year?"

"Yes."

"And you are soon to give birth?"

She swallowed. "Around Christmas, yes."

Mr. Kendall leaned on the railing in front of her, his small eyes staring hard. "Mrs. Aspinall, is Dr. Richard Hawkins the father of your child?"

She clutched her handbag until her fingers ached. Under the weight of Richard's stare, as well as the disapproving whispers of several other spectators, a deep resentment began to well up within her. Why was she being made out to be the villain here? Mr. Kendall had done nothing but attack her reputation. Made her out to be a woman of loose morals. But he hadn't given the court a true account of her situation. Shouldn't the judge have all the facts before making his decision?

She turned her head. "Your Honor, may I say something before I answer the question?"

The robed man studied her for a moment. "I suppose I can allow that. Go ahead."

She swallowed and did her best to ignore the lawyer's glare.

"Mr. Kendall made it sound like I had a long-standing relationship with Dr. Hawkins, and that I participated willingly in . . . having relations with him. But that is not the case." Despite the excruciating agony of discussing such personal details, she lifted her chin. "It happened only once, at a time when I was heavily medicated, as per Dr. Hawkins's orders. I didn't . . ." She paused and, steeling herself, turned her gaze on Richard. Some type of intense emotion burned in his eyes. Was it hatred or fear?

"You didn't what, Mrs. Aspinall?" The judge frowned at her.

She clenched her fingers together and gathered her courage. "I did not consent to having relations with him."

Commotion erupted from across the room.

"That's ridiculous. . . ."

"She's lying. . . ."

"My client is a respected physician . . . he would never . . ."

Bits and pieces of their words drifted by her. Images darted across her line of vision. The red face of the other attorney. Richard's stunned expression. Her own solicitor shouting, trying to be heard above the din.

Three sharp raps of the gavel finally stilled the chaos. Julia realized she'd been holding her breath. The growing discomfort in her lower back that had plagued her all morning now intensified, radiating through her whole body.

"Are you accusing Dr. Hawkins of a crime, Mrs. Aspinall?" the judge asked. "Think carefully before you answer, because what you are insinuating is a very serious charge."

He was scolding her like a wayward schoolgirl. Of course he would side with a respected physician and assume she was lying. How could she make him believe her?

She twisted on her seat in an attempt to catch Rev. Burke's eye. Could he step in to support her or say something in her defense? He merely shook his head, the sympathy on his face bringing hot tears to her eyes.

"Mrs. Aspinall. I asked you a question." The judge's sharp voice sliced through her. "Are you saying Dr. Hawkins forced—"

"Ah!" A razor-sharp pain ripped across Julia's abdomen. She bent over her knees, breathing hard.

"Mrs. Aspinall, are you all right?" The judge's voice echoed from a distance.

She couldn't answer him, too intent on drawing oxygen into her lungs.

"Mr. Nelson, if your client is unable to proceed, we can take a brief recess for her to compose herself."

"Yes, Your Honor."

"You are excused for the moment, Mrs. Aspinall. You may step down."

Perspiration beaded on Julia's forehead. She gripped the railing and attempted to rise, but the pain intensified. She bit her lip to keep from crying out again.

"Let me help you." Mr. Nelson's kind voice barely registered.

Julia released her grip on the rail and grasped his hand. Just as she went to take a step down, another spasm knifed through her. She screamed and pitched forward, crumpling to the ground as everything around her went black.

CHAPTER 34

Quinn unfolded himself from the taxicab, paid the driver, and stood looking at the house before him. It felt like forever since he and Julia had shared their few precious days together here as husband and wife. Forever since he'd kissed her good-bye.

A slow smile spread across his face. Would his wife be happy to see him? Would she throw herself into his arms and shower him with affection? He had certainly imagined such a scene the whole way here. He'd purposely refrained from sending a telegram to announce his arrival, wanting to see the surprise and pleasure on Julia's face when he arrived on her doorstep. How would she look now in the advanced stages of her pregnancy? Glowing with health and happiness? Or wan and pale, worn down by the weight of the child?

He prayed she was well and that they would have several more weeks together before the baby made its arrival. Selfishly, he wanted this time alone with her, to reconnect with his wife and show her how much she meant to him. He also wanted to ascertain how Julia felt about him. What if she resented him for his long absence, for choosing his mother's welfare over hers?

He drew himself up tall. If that was the case, he'd do everything in his power to make it up to her and let it be known that from now on, she and the child were his main priority.

With renewed determination, he ran lightly up the stairs to the front door and knocked. A few seconds later, Mrs. Banbury opened the door.

"Hello, Mrs. Banbury. It's good to see you again." He gave the dour woman his best smile.

"Mr. Aspinall. We were not expecting you."

"Indeed. I wanted to surprise my wife. May I come in?"

The woman pursed her lips but stood aside for him to enter. "You may. However, I must inform you that Mrs. Aspinall is not here."

Something in the flat way she made the statement caused the hairs on Quinn's neck to rise. It didn't sound as if Julia had gone out to the market or to visit a friend. "Oh? Will she be back soon?" His heart thumped, belying his attempt to remain nonchalant.

"Not likely. She's in the hospital."

Alarm raced through his system. "Is she ill? How is the baby?"

The clip-clop of footsteps accompanied by a cane echoed on the tiles. "Mrs. Banbury, is this any way to treat a guest?" Mrs. Middleton's scowling countenance had the woman retreating.

Quinn moved forward. "Mrs. Middleton, what happened to Julia? Why is she in the hospital?"

"Come in and I will explain." She limped toward the parlor.

With little choice, Quinn followed her, his thoughts racing. All he wanted to do was rush to Julia's side, but apparently Mrs. Middleton had other ideas. What if she was trying to find a kind way to relay some terrible news? What if Julia had come down with a serious illness? What if something had happened to the baby? Julia would be beyond devastated.

"It's good to see you again, Mr. Aspinall. May I offer you some refreshments?" Mrs. Middleton asked as she settled in her armchair.

"No, thank you, ma'am. I just need to know about my wife. Is she all right?" *Of course she isn't all right if she's in the hospital.* He perched on the edge of the sofa, elbows leaning on his thighs.

"She's out of danger for the time being." Mrs. Middleton set her cane beside the chair.

"What happened?"

"Several weeks ago, Julia received a summons to court from Dr. Hawkins."

Quinn's blood pressure shot upward. He'd had a bad feeling the man would not relent, even given proof of Julia's marriage.

"I had my solicitor, Mr. Nelson, take her case, but unfortunately it seems the stress of appearing in court and being forced to testify took its toll on her. She collapsed in the courtroom and went into early labor."

Quinn leapt from his seat. "Labor? Does that mean . . . ?"

Please, Lord, let it not be so. He'd promised Julia to be back in time for the baby's birth. Instead she'd had to handle going to court and premature labor all alone. How would he ever face her again?

"It was touch and go for a while, but the doctors managed to stop the labor. However, given her elevated blood pressure, they feared for both her life and the child's and have therefore kept her in the hospital on bed rest."

"I have to see her. Which hospital is she in?"

Mrs. Middleton tilted her head. "Before I tell you, I must insist you compose yourself. Julia is in a delicate state. Remaining calm is of utmost importance to her health. When you see her, you must not upset her in any way. No discussions of Dr. Hawkins or the court appearance—or any other subject that might cause her undue distress." She stared at him. "Do I make myself clear?"

He had the sensation she was scolding him for something. "I'd appreciate you speaking plainly, Mrs. Middleton. What other subject are you referring to?"

"It's no secret that your lengthy absence, as well as uncertainty about your relationship, has been weighing heavily on Julia these last weeks. I hope you'd have the good sense to avoid any such discussion right now, especially if it might upset her."

"I understand." He swallowed hard, refusing to let fear grab ahold of him. "I'll do my best to ensure she stays calm, ma'am." He lifted his chin. "But as long as Julia wants me there, I will stay by her side."

She gave him a measuring look. "Fair enough, Mr. Aspinall. Just don't give her too much of a shock."

Quinn had never been so thankful to be able to wield the title of husband. Using it gave him immediate access to Julia as well as privileged information about her condition from the head nurse.

"She's doing much better, Mr. Aspinall," the stout woman told him. "Staying in bed has been the key to keeping her blood pressure at acceptable levels."

"And the baby?"

The nurse smiled. "So far, so good. It was a blessing the doctors were able to stop labor when they did. Each day in the womb is a better chance at your baby's survival."

Quinn's neck heated, not used to discussing such issues. "May I see my wife now?"

"Of course. Room 323. Down the hall on your right."

"Thank you."

As Quinn approached the room, his hands tightened around the bouquet of carnations he'd bought at the gift store. He didn't want to arrive empty-handed and hoped the floral offering would help soften his unexpected arrival after such a long absence.

Once he entered the ward, he quickly spotted Julia in the bed next to the window. She lay asleep, unmoving on the pillows, the blankets pulled high over her expansive middle. He moved toward her, his heart beating hard in his chest.

He'd forgotten how beautiful she was. Her fair hair framed her face, accentuating her appealing features—the long lashes, delicate brows, and pert nose. The pregnancy had added a plumpness to her face and fullness to her lips. How he'd missed her. He longed to hold her hand, to kiss her cheek, but he didn't wish to disturb her rest.

Thank you, Lord, for letting me get back in time.

When she didn't stir, Quinn took a seat beside the bed, content to simply gaze at her. However, the effects of traveling for more than a week soon caught up with him, and he'd almost dozed off when he sensed her rousing.

She yawned and stretched. Then her eyes widened as she noticed him.

"Hello, Julia." He kept his voice to a whisper, not wanting to alarm her. "How are you feeling?"

She blinked, pulling herself to a sitting position. "Quinn? Is it really you?"

"It is. I'm finally back." He smiled, though perspiration gathered under his collar. Would she be glad to see him? Or furious he'd stayed away so long?

She reached out a hand toward him, tears welling in those beautiful brown eyes.

He leaned forward and grasped her fingers, warmth flooding through him.

"I'm so happy you're here," she said. "You have no idea how hard it's been—"

"I'm under strict orders not to discuss any distressing topics." He handed her the bouquet. "These are for you."

She smiled and brought the flowers to her nose. "They're lovely. Thank you. If you leave them on the windowsill, the nurse will take care of them when she returns."

He did as she asked, placing them beside two other arrangements, one from Mrs. Middleton, the other from Mrs. Chamberlain.

"When did you get here?" she asked when he returned to his chair.

"Late last night. Too late to bother you, so I checked in at the YMCA." He winked. "Just like old times."

She gave a light laugh, and the knot of tension in his chest loosened. So far, she seemed pleased to see him.

"When I came to the house this morning, Mrs. Middleton told me you were here."

Her brow furrowed. "Did she tell you about the courthouse?"

"She did. But again, it's a topic I was warned not to mention."

When she started to argue, he held up a hand.

"There'll be plenty of time to discuss all that. Right now, I just want to sit with you and thank the good Lord for keeping you and the baby safe until I got here."

Julia's lips quivered. "I'm grateful for that too. I've been dreading having to go through this birth alone."

He squeezed her hand, wishing he could impart his strength to her. "I'll be here from now on. You have my word."

"I knew I could depend on you." She gave a sleepy smile, her eyelids drifting shut again.

A sliver of alarm went through him. She'd just awakened. How could she be tired again?

As he settled back in the chair to wait, he vowed to devote all his energy to helping her regain her full strength in order to bring a healthy child into the world.

"You don't need to worry anymore," he said softly. "I'm here now. I'll take care of everything and make sure no one bothers you again."

Julia gradually came out of sleep, conscious of a new feeling of peace. For the first time in a week, she'd slept well, not fearing Richard Hawkins would suddenly appear and try to claim her child.

She blinked and glanced at the chair beside the bed. Quinn's large frame filled the space. His eyes were closed, his head resting against the wall. How long had he been sitting there like her own personal guard? No wonder she'd slept so well.

She took a moment to study him, the cleft in his chin, the fall of hair across his brow, the long lashes against his cheek. Her recollection of his good looks paled in comparison to the reality before her. When he opened his eyes and caught her staring, heat rushed into her cheeks.

A slow grin crept over his face. "Do I pass inspection?"

She looked down and busied herself fixing the covers. She wanted to tell him he looked more handsome than she remembered, but the words would not shake loose. And then as her fingers grazed her sizable middle, she realized how different she must appear to him. Would he find her repulsive now?

"What is that grimace for?" he asked.

She glanced over at him. "You might pass inspection . . . but do I?"

He held her gaze. "You're as lovely as ever. Even more so, as an expectant mother should be."

"I wish I could believe you. I feel as enormous as an elephant." She gave a nervous laugh.

"A temporary state until your beautiful baby arrives."

"Our."

"Pardon?"

"*Our* beautiful baby." She frowned and laid a protective hand on her stomach. "You do still want to be a father to my child, don't you?" She held her breath, waiting for his answer. Perhaps he'd had time to reconsider the ramifications of parenting another man's child, and now, faced with the trouble Richard was causing, wanted no part of the drama.

Quinn reached for her hand. "Of course I want to be the babe's father. I'm sure once I meet this little person, I will fall madly in love with him or her."

Julia pressed her lips together. Did that mean he still cared for her? Or was she just another obligation he had to fulfill? "You've had a lot of time to reevaluate this whole situation. I wouldn't blame you if you had changed your mind." Her throat tightened. It was only fair to give him the opportunity to back out of their arrangement. After all, he now had everything he'd worked so hard to achieve. He'd found his siblings, his mother's health was restored, and he'd secured a home for them all.

"Julia, I would never go back on my promise to you." His eyes glistened. "If you can forgive me for staying away so long, I'll spend every moment from now on making it up to you."

Her lips quivered, relief spilling through her. "Of course I forgive you. I'm just happy you're here."

He leaned forward and kissed her—a gentle kiss filled with

promise. The promise of a life shared together, where she wouldn't have to face every hurdle alone.

"Rest now," he said. "We can worry about the future later."

Quinn was right. She would do herself and the baby no good fretting about events she couldn't control, like whether or not Richard would continue to harass her or if she would have to go back before the court. Quinn was here, and that was all that mattered for now.

She leaned back against the pillows with a sigh and smiled at her husband. "Now, tell me all about your farm."

CHAPTER 35

The next morning, Quinn left Mrs. Middleton's, whistling off-key. The elderly woman had insisted he move back into the room he had occupied after the wedding, and Quinn had gratefully accepted.

On the way to the hospital, he stopped to buy some chocolates he knew Julia liked. The clerk tied the package with a bright red ribbon. He smiled, imagining how she would enjoy the sweets. He also had a book in his pocket that Mrs. Middleton had lent him, saying Julia would love the story. Reading it together would help pass the time; it felt so long just sitting and waiting.

When he arrived on the third floor, a nurse waylaid him before he reached Julia's room.

"Mr. Aspinall. Thank goodness you're here. Your wife has gone into labor and has been asking for you."

"What? When?"

"About an hour ago."

"Why didn't anyone call? I would have been here sooner."

"I did, sir. I left a message with the housekeeper, who assured me she would pass it on."

Quinn frowned. He hadn't seen Mrs. Banbury this morning since he'd skipped breakfast, intent on getting to the hospital as soon as he could.

"Where is Julia?" he barked, immediately regretting his curt tone.

"I'm sorry, sir, but fathers are not allowed in the delivery room."

"I promised my wife she wouldn't be alone. Now, you can either show me, or I'll search every room until I find her myself."

The young nurse bit her lip. "Very well. Follow me."

She led him down one corridor after another until he was lost in the maze of the hospital. Finally, they passed through a set of double doors marked Labor and Delivery.

The woman came to a stop in front of a nurse's station and pointed to a door. "Your wife is in there. Let me go in and make sure the doctor is not examining her. I'll come back and get you."

"Fine, but if you don't return soon, I'm coming in."

The nurse quickly disappeared through the door.

Before it shut completely, Quinn strained to see inside, but other than some equipment and a steel table, he could see nothing.

Frustration coursed through his veins. He realized he was clutching the now-battered box of chocolates, so he set it on the nurses' desk. He could always buy more tomorrow. If Julia made it safely through the delivery, he'd buy her a dozen boxes.

The door opened, and the nurse emerged. "You may go in for a moment, but then you must stay in the waiting area." She gave him a smile. "Everything is going to be fine."

"Thank you." Quinn paused to gather his wits, then entered the room. The smell of antiseptic and other mysterious medical odors hung heavy in the air. He ignored everything except for the woman in the bed. "Julia. I'm here, love."

Her hair was plastered against her head, soaked either with perspiration or from someone wiping her brow. Her forehead was wreathed in lines of worry, but they relaxed the moment she saw him.

"Quinn. Thank heavens. I was afraid you wouldn't be able to find me."

He reached out to take one of her hands in his. "Nothing could keep me from you. Now that I'm here, you can relax and—"

She grunted and squeezed her eyes shut.

"Breathe, Mrs. Aspinall." An older nurse stood by the bedside. "Slow and steady. That's it."

"Where is the doctor?" Quinn demanded. Surely with his wife's tentative condition, the physician should be here.

"Oh, he pops in and out. But he's not needed till the end. We have hours to go yet."

"Hours?"

Julia gripped his fingers so hard his bones ached.

"How will she endure the pain for so long?"

The nurse raised a brow, and her lips twitched. "Your first child, I take it?"

He nodded, his gaze fused to Julia's face.

"Every baby is different, but most firstborns take a long time to appear."

The pain must have subsided, for Julia relaxed her grip on his hand and the tension in her face lessened.

"Kiss your wife good-bye. The next time you see her, she'll be holding your son or daughter."

Quinn scowled. Every nerve in his body twitched. How could he leave, knowing she was in such distress?

"Trust me," the nurse said as she moved toward him. "She's in good hands. I promise."

"If there's any way I can be of help, I'll be right outside."

"Help?" The nurse chuckled. "Expectant fathers aren't much help at a time like this. It's the woman who does all the work."

"I wish I could do it for her." Quinn turned to Julia and squeezed her hand. "I know you'll get through this, love. I'll be in the waiting room, praying for you both." He felt the sting of tears behind his eyes as he leaned down. "Remember, you're not alone."

She opened her mouth as if to say something, but instead her face contorted with pain, and she grasped his hand in another bone-crushing grip.

Once the contraction ended, the nurse smiled. "You did well, Mrs. Aspinall. Rest until the next one." Then she turned to Quinn. "All right. Off you go and let us do our work."

He only had a moment to kiss Julia's cheek before the nurse literally pushed him out of the room.

When the door shut in his face, he stood staring blankly at the gray windowless slab. Never in his life had he felt so helpless.

A hand touched his arm. It was the younger nurse from before. "Let me show you to the waiting area," she said gently.

With no other recourse, he allowed her to lead him away.

Fourteen long hours later, a man in a blue hospital gown appeared in the doorway of the waiting area.

The other expectant fathers in the room looked up.

"Mr. Aspinall?"

Quinn rose, his knees and back stiff from sitting so long. He'd been praying harder and harder as time wore on, loath to move from his seat lest he miss the doctor. "Yes?"

He struggled to gauge the man's demeanor to determine if he came bearing bad news or good.

The man's face broke into a wide smile. "Congratulations, sir. You have a fine baby girl."

Quinn allowed himself to breathe, his chest swelling with relief. *We have a daughter. A little girl to spoil.* He stumbled a few steps closer. "And my wife? How is she?"

The man's smile dimmed. "She had a hard time of it and lost a lot of blood, so naturally she's quite weak."

Quinn fisted his hands at his side. "Will she be all right?"

"Barring any unforeseen complications, I'm confident she will make a full recovery."

Quinn released a breath. *Thank you, Lord.* "Can I see her?"

"The nurses are just finishing up. Give them about fifteen more minutes, and you can go in and meet your daughter."

"Thank you, doctor." Quinn shook the man's hand. "I appreciate it very much."

The men in the waiting room congratulated Quinn. He thanked them, all the while watching the clock for the moment he could see Julia. He would not relax fully until he saw her with his own eyes.

Julia leaned back against the pillows, grateful for the nurse's ministrations. The woman had washed Julia's face and neck with a clean washcloth and re-braided her hair.

"We must look our best when that handsome husband of yours comes in." The nurse winked at Julia. "Where is your shawl? Oh, here it is." She draped the cloth around Julia's shoulders. "Now, let's get that little angel."

From the bassinet in the corner, she picked up a swaddled bundle. Then she came over and held her out to Julia, lowering the head into the crook of Julia's arm.

Tears sprang to her eyes as she gazed down at her daughter. The tiny rosebud lips, the button of a nose, the impossibly small lashes against porcelain skin.

My daughter.

Julia's chest swelled with a rush of the fiercest love she'd ever known. At the same time, a deeply protective instinct rose inside her, and she knew she would die to protect this tiny life. "She's perfect."

"Yes, she is." The nurse smiled down at her. "I'll let your husband know he can come in now."

The door opened, and almost immediately the woman returned. "He was waiting right outside. I'll give you two a little time alone. If you need anything, just call."

Julia looked over to see Quinn hovering in the doorway, a look of concern darkening his features. Waiting for such a long time, not knowing what was happening, must have been terribly hard on him. She held out her hand. "Come and meet our daughter."

Quinn took a hesitant step forward, his gaze never leaving her face. "How are you? The doctor said you had a difficult time."

"I'm tired and a little weak. But I've never been happier." She smiled at him and moved the blanket away from the tiny face in her arms. "This little one made all the pain worthwhile."

Quinn walked over and leaned in to take his first look. His brow furrowed, then all at once, the tension in his face eased. "She's so small."

"Actually, she's a good size, the doctor said. Seven pounds, three ounces." Julia ran a finger over the baby's velvety cheek. "Do you want to hold her?"

Quinn's eyes grew wide. "I don't know if that's a good idea."

"Of course it is." Julia set her jaw. It was important that he bond with the baby as soon as possible. To feel the same incredible connection she did. "Bring a chair over."

He hesitated, then did as she asked, taking a cautious seat. "Now what?"

"Hold out your arms and make sure to support her head."

Julia placed the baby in his arms, adjusting the blanket around her face. The little girl scrunched her perfect little nose, then settled in with a soft sigh.

Julia could tell the exact moment Quinn's heart expanded with love, exactly as hers had. His entire face softened, and tears shone in his eyes.

"She's beautiful." He raised his head. "Just like her mother."

Their gazes held until the baby squirmed in his arms, claiming his attention.

"So, Mrs. Aspinall," he said, "what do you intend to call her?"

Julia wrapped her fingers around the end of her braid. "If you have no objection, I was thinking of Evelyn. After my mother."

"Evelyn Aspinall." He smiled. "That has a regal sound to it."

"Do you have a suggestion for a middle name?" Julia glanced at his profile as he stared down at the baby, mesmerized.

"You want me to choose a second name?"

"Yes." She reached over to lay a hand on his arm. "I want you to feel that she's your daughter too. Because she is—in every way that matters."

Quinn's Adam's apple bobbed, and he cleared his throat. "My mother's name is Mary. If it suits you, I know Mum would be honored."

"Evelyn Mary Aspinall. That's perfect." Julia smiled at him, her heart filled to the bursting point.

Doubts about the future still plagued her, but in this moment, Julia chose to focus on her blessings, to give thanks to God for the safe birth of her beautiful baby and for bringing Quinn back to her. Whatever else God had in store for her, she would discover as time went on.

For now, she'd simply bask in the joy of this most special day in her life.

CHAPTER 36

The day after Evelyn's birth, Julia leaned back in her hospital bed with the baby in her arms. She'd just finished feeding her, and now as Julia gazed down at Evelyn's perfect features, she relished the peace and contentment on her newborn's face.

Thank you, Lord, for this precious gift. May I always be a good mother to her and do whatever I can to keep her safe.

With the warm weight in her arms, Julia's eyelids grew heavy, but worried that she might lose her grip on the baby, she fought to stay alert until the nurse came to take Evelyn back to the nursery.

Footsteps brought Julia's eyes open. But instead of a nurse, Richard Hawkins stood inside the door.

Julia tightened her hold on Evelyn, clutching the tiny bundle closer to her chest as a protective wave surged through her. What was he doing here? If he thought she would let him have any access to her daughter . . .

"I heard you'd had the baby." Richard removed his hat, his eyes straying to the swaddled bundle, then back to her. "I wanted to come by and see how you're doing."

"I'm fine, thank you." Julia kept her gaze steady. She'd known she wouldn't be able to keep the news from him. As a physician with privileges at several hospitals in the city, he would have access to any information he wanted. And though she'd tried to mentally prepare herself for this moment, her heart still thumped unevenly in her chest.

"You had a girl." He came farther into the room, standing awkwardly by the foot of the bed. Once again, his gaze darted to the baby, whose tiny face was just visible from inside the blanket. A look of pure agony flashed over his features.

Something about his demeanor stirred Julia's sympathy. She'd expected him to come in uttering threats, but this unassuming attitude had her baffled. "Would you . . . like to see her?" she asked hesitantly.

He nodded and moved to the side of the bed.

Julia shifted the cloth away from the infant's face so he could see his daughter more clearly.

"She's beautiful." He stared at Evelyn for several moments, his throat muscles working, then he raised his head. "I want you to know that what you said in the courtroom had a profound effect on me." His gaze faltered, shifting to the baby again. "I owe you a deep apology for my actions. In my arrogance, I made a lot of erroneous assumptions about our relationship, which caused me to take liberties that were very wrong."

Julia shifted the baby's weight, unsure how to respond to this seemingly remorseful man in front of her. Was it a ruse to get her to allow him access to the child, or did he sincerely regret his actions?

He paused and ran his hand over the back of his neck. "I got caught up in grief and in my own selfish desires and didn't stop to consider that you might not feel the same about me. I hope you can find it within you to forgive me."

She studied him for a moment, searching for some evidence of an ulterior motive for his apology. "If you are truly sorry," she said quietly, "then you'll leave us alone. My daughter will have a good home and a good father. Let us live our lives in peace."

His attention flickered back to the baby, who had begun to squirm in Julia's arms, her tiny face scrunching up as though preparing to cry. He straightened. "If you'd given birth to my son, this would have been a much harder decision. I would never willingly abandon my heir, a son to carry on the Hawkins name." He exhaled slowly. "But I will abide by your wishes . . . if we can both agree to let the unfortunate matter between us rest and not invite further legal action."

Julia blinked, barely able to believe she'd heard him right. If her silence was all he wanted, then she could certainly agree to his terms. In truth, she had no wish to go through an arduous court proceeding, subjecting herself and Quinn to harsh judgment. Richard's apology had helped somewhat to ease her wounds. And now she had her precious baby, whom Julia wouldn't trade for the world. She nodded. "Very well. I can accept that."

The lines of tension in his face softened, and he took a step backward. "Despite everything, I wish you well, Julia." He gave a slight bow and turned toward the door.

"Richard, may I offer you some advice?"

Her words halted his departure, and he turned, his brows lifted in question.

She leaned forward in the bed. "Make an effort to repair your relationship with your wife. Surely there is something between you worth salvaging."

A wry smile twisted his lips. "Ah, a romantic until the end, eh, Julia?"

"Perhaps. But I believe that a marriage should be preserved, if at all possible."

"Well said, young lady." Rev. Burke entered the room, coming to stand beside Richard. "Ending a marriage should never be undertaken lightly. Not until every solution has been explored."

Richard's features became shuttered. "I'll keep that in mind. Good day to you both."

Julia released a long breath, the tension draining from her muscles as he exited the room. Could the threat from Richard really be over? She bent to kiss Evelyn's forehead, thankful that Quinn hadn't arrived to find him here. Heaven only knew what he would have done.

"Dr. Hawkins didn't threaten you again, did he?" Rev. Burke pulled up a chair beside the bed.

"No. Believe it or not, he apologized." She shook her head. "And he's agreed to leave us in peace."

"It seems our prayers have been answered."

"Indeed, it does."

But a niggle of unease wound through her. What would this mean for her and Quinn going forward? Would he feel his duty fulfilled now that the baby had arrived and the danger from Richard had been resolved?

The minister leaned forward. "Tell me, Julia, have you been able to forgive Dr. Hawkins for what he did to you?"

Julia gazed down at her sleeping child, for the first time without the fear of losing her, and her heart swelled with gratitude. "I think I will be able to in time. I already feel a tremendous weight lifted off of me."

"I'm glad." He paused. "I hope this means you've forgiven yourself too."

Julia frowned.

"Before you married Quinten, you confessed you felt some degree of culpability for Sam's death and for not rebuffing Dr. Hawkins. Have you come to see things a little clearer now?"

She pursed her lips, considering. "I believe so." She stroked a finger down Evelyn's soft cheek. "I still wish I'd handled things differently, that I could have done more for Sam, but I . . . I know I did the best I could under the circumstances. With Sam and with Dr. Hawkins."

Rev. Burke patted her arm. "With the past behind you, hopefully you'll be able to focus all your attention on this beautiful child and the wonderful future in store for you."

Julia lowered her gaze once again so he wouldn't detect the uncertainty that plagued her. Perhaps the only course of action was to wait and see how God's plan for her life would unfold over the coming weeks.

Because right now her marriage "in name only" was beginning to chafe like a pair of ill-fitting shoes. She only hoped that once she and Quinn had the chance to talk, they would both be of like mind about what their future would hold.

CHAPTER 37

February 10, 1920

The snow had not stopped for the past five days, leaving the city blanketed in a thick, fluffy quilt that appeared as soft as cotton. But after shoveling Mrs. Middleton's property continuously for days, Quinn knew the truth. The snow packed a significant weight. The strain in his shoulders, arms, and back attested to that reality.

Not that he was complaining. In fact, he welcomed the physical work. Welcomed the proof that he had accomplished something worthwhile. Even though he'd have to repeat the process again in a few hours if the snow continued to fall.

Quinn straightened and stretched his back, then leaned on the handle of the shovel to survey his handiwork. Once more, the walkway was clear all the way to the road, flanked with waist-high banks of snow. In truth, the landscape around him was beautiful—pristine and pure. The air crisp and invigorating. But it still didn't help to shake the restlessness that had plagued him of late, nor the guilt for even acknowledging such feelings.

How could he be so ungrateful after all the gifts God had bestowed on him? He should be filled with joy, yet deep in his spirit, he felt . . . empty, unfulfilled. Mrs. Middleton had been more than generous, allowing him, Julia, and the baby to stay with her these past two and a half months, especially since Julia had only recently resumed her duties as the widow's assistant.

Yet with little to occupy his time, Quinn couldn't help but feel like a kept man. Ridiculous, he knew. Still, his thoughts continually drifted to England and the farm that awaited him there. Spring would soon be nearing, and his brothers would be planning to till the soil in preparation for the crops. Quinn should be there to help them. Not spending his days idle, doing nothing but odd jobs for Mrs. Middleton or some of Rev. Burke's parishioners who required his aid.

Of course, he helped Julia with wee Evelyn. Watching that sweet baby grow was a source of constant joy. But also one that reminded him of the other unfulfilled longing in his life.

His relationship with Julia.

Quinn set the shovel against the house, then clomped up onto the porch, knocking the snow from his boots. Instead of going inside, however, he leaned against one of the porch columns and looked out over the snow-covered street.

Ever since Julia and the baby had come home from the hospital, she'd taken up residence in the room adjoining his, keeping the door closed at night. To avoid disturbing him with the baby's cries, she'd said. Yet night after night of staring at that closed door felt like a silent form of rejection.

The proverbial and literal wall between them.

Did Julia ever lie awake in her bed next door and think of him with the same longing he felt for her? Or was she perfectly content to continue with their marriage in name only?

When Quinn had offered Julia the protection of his name, he'd thought he could accept such an outcome. However, the more they bonded as a family, the stronger his feelings for Julia had grown, and every night that he slept alone in the huge four-poster bed, the lonelier he became. But the shame of his selfishness would not allow him to broach the subject with Julia. Instead, he plied the heavens with earnest prayers for the Lord to work on Julia's heart and, if it be His will, allow her feelings to grow to match Quinn's. Maybe if he had some sliver of hope of that ever happening, he could live with the frustration awhile longer.

Behind him, the front door opened, and someone stepped onto the porch.

"What are you doing standing out here in the cold?" Julia's scolding tone was mixed with teasing. "You'll soon have icicles forming on your brows."

He tried to manage a smile but failed. "Just admiring the scenery."

"And brooding, it looks like." She came up beside him and laid a hand on his arm. "Is something bothering you, Quinn?" she asked softly. "You've not been yourself lately."

So, she had sensed his discontent too. He exhaled, his breath hanging in the frigid air like a wispy cloud. Perhaps it was time to confess some of his angst. "I'll admit I've been feeling restless. Living here with no real purpose. Not able to work to provide for my family. It goes against everything I've been raised to believe."

She frowned, her mouth turned down, and he silently berated himself. He should never have burdened her with this. She had enough to contend with, being a new mother and all.

"I had no idea you felt this way," she said. "Why didn't you say anything?"

He shook his head. "I didn't want to bother you. I thought it would pass, but that doesn't seem to be the case."

She shivered, pulling her cloak closer around her.

"You should go inside," he said. "You don't want to catch cold."

"Not unless you come with me. Let's continue this conversation indoors where it's warm."

"I'd rather forget it altogether." Now that he'd voiced his grievance, it sounded petty and selfish.

"No, Quinn. I won't forget it. It's time we had a serious talk about the future."

He blew out another breath. "You're right. But it will have to wait until later. I promised Mrs. C. I'd help her with some repair work today."

"Fair enough," she said with a pointed look. "I'll see you at dinner and we can discuss it then." She turned toward the door. "Give Mrs. C. my love."

Quinn's heart sank as Julia disappeared into the house. She seemed disappointed in him. What if she'd come to the conclusion that their marriage had been a mistake after all? Could he face leaving her and the baby behind, this time for good?

Later that afternoon at the boardinghouse, Quinn banged the last nail into the bannister, then shook the rail to make sure he'd secured it tight enough. Satisfied it would pass Mrs. C.'s inspection, he picked up the container of nails and headed down to the hallway below.

"If a whole barrel of monkeys were swinging on that rail, I doubt it would move." Mrs. C.'s voice came from behind him.

He turned to face her. "It should be a lot safer now." He placed the hammer in the landlady's toolbox, a feeling of accomplishment spreading through his torso. He hadn't felt this useful in a long time. "Any more repairs needed today?"

"Not right now. Though I'm sure I'll have more projects to do before the property goes up for sale."

He wiped his hands on a rag. "I'm still surprised you're selling this place, Mrs. C. You seem like part of the woodwork here."

A wistful expression crossed her face. "It was time. Besides, I'm starting a whole new life as a pastor's wife. I'll have no time to be a landlady."

He managed a true smile. "I'm sure you'll be very happy in your new role."

A knock sounded on the front door.

"Oh good." Mrs. C. headed to answer it. "You'll get to see Grace and that adorable nephew of hers."

She opened the door and Grace entered, carrying a small boy. The cold air and a flurry of snow snuck in with her. Grace hugged Mrs. C., who promptly scooped the child from her arms. He was snugly wrapped in a thick yellow blanket, with only his eyes and two red cheeks peeking out.

"Look how big this young man is getting." Mrs. C. pulled more of the blanket away from his face. "He must be walking by now."

"Running is more like it." Grace laughed, then looked past Mrs. C. as she shrugged out of her overcoat. "Quinn? What are you doing here?" She rushed over to give him a hug.

"Grace. It's good to see you." He'd often thought about his friends from the voyage over, still amazed at how quickly they had all bonded. Emma and Jonathan, who had recently announced their engagement, were now living back in England. But he had no excuse not to see Grace. She and her new husband lived here in the city. "I'm helping Mrs. C. with a couple of repair jobs. How are you?"

Grace took a step back and smoothed a hand over her dark hair, her brown eyes sparkling. "I feel wonderful."

"Marriage certainly seems to agree with you." He couldn't help the tiny twinge of envy as he thought of his own uncertain relationship.

"It does indeed. In more ways than one." Her exuberant laugh filled the hall.

"No!" said Mrs. C., her eyes wide.

"Yes!"

"Oh, my dear, that's wonderful."

Quinn looked at the giddy women and scratched his head. "I'm missing something. What are we talking about?"

Color spread into Grace's cheeks, but nothing dimmed her smile. "Andrew and I are expecting a baby."

Mrs. C. hugged her, squeezing the little boy between them. "Your husband must be over the moon."

"He is. We're both thrilled Christian will have a sibling to share his childhood."

Quinn studied the boy who looked so much like Grace and marveled how she hadn't hesitated to raise her late sister's child. Originally, he hadn't quite understood her determination, but now with baby Evelyn in his life, Quinn could appreciate the depth of Grace's commitment. "Congratulations, Grace. You deserve this happiness after all you've been through."

"Thank you, Quinn. And so do you."

"Come into the parlor and sit down," Mrs. C. said. "No need

to stand in the hall all day." She carried the boy into the room and sat him on her knee while she began to remove the blanket from around him.

Quinn hovered in the doorway for a moment, not sure how to bow out of what would surely be woman talk. But he hadn't seen Grace in ages, and it would be rude not to visit for a few minutes at least.

"Tell me, how is that precious baby girl of yours?" Grace asked as he took a seat on the sofa. "Mrs. C. told me all about her, but I want to hear it from you."

A smile came easily to his lips. "She's growing every day. And finally sleeping through the night."

"That's always helpful. Especially for her parents." Grace winked at him.

His neck heated at her implication, his gaze sliding to the patterned carpet. With Grace's marriage so blissful, she wouldn't begin to understand his complicated situation.

When he glanced up, he saw that Grace was busy removing little Christian's sweater and hat and thankfully appeared oblivious to his discomfort.

"How is Andrew?" Mrs. C. asked. "Still busy with his father's hotel?"

"Always. Though it will be better once the Valentine's Day Gala is over."

Mrs. C. bounced the boy on her knee. "I hope he manages to make time for you, dear. After all, you're still newlyweds. And it's important to keep the romance alive."

"Andrew always makes time for us." Grace smiled. "Last night he cooked dinner for me and had his mother mind the baby. It was wonderful." She sighed, a dreamy look coming over her face.

"He cooks for you?" Quinn's brows rose. He'd love to see such an expression on Julia's face, but by the time he ever learned to cook, Evelyn would be starting school.

"Andrew is always doing things to make me feel special. And of course, I'm happy to reward his efforts."

The two women laughed out loud.

Quinn rubbed his hands on his thighs, his thoughts suddenly swirling. Since he'd been back, there'd been no romance at all between him and Julia, mainly because of the baby. But maybe that was the problem. He'd been focused on helping Julia with Evelyn whenever he could and keeping the firewood stocked. Practical things to prove his devotion. But maybe a romantic gesture was needed to show Julia how he truly felt about her. "What sort of things does Andrew do?" he asked cautiously.

Grace pursed her lips. "Well, he often brings me flowers from the greenhouse. Or takes Christian for the afternoon to give me time to myself. Or arranges a night out for the two of us. He's quite creative actually."

"You're a lucky woman," Mrs. C. said. "Some men never learn how to keep the spark alive in a marriage. I was fortunate that my Miles was romantic as well."

Quinn's thoughts flew back to the intimate meal he'd shared with Julia at the inn in Peterborough. The prelude to their first kiss. Perhaps he could re-create that evening and remind Julia of the spark that once existed between them.

Or perhaps even ignite a new spark. His pulse sprinted to life. He would woo his wife as if they weren't already married, and hopefully it would help them determine the direction their future would take.

It was certainly worth a try.

The clock in the hall began to chime the hour.

Quinn blinked. If he was going to plan something special, he'd better get moving. He stood up. "I really should be going. Julia will start to worry." He bent to kiss Grace's cheek. "It was lovely to see you again, Grace." He looked over at Mrs. C. "Don't forget, I'm available for any other jobs you need doing. Just not tonight."

"Good-bye, Quinn." Grace laughed. "And give Julia our best."

CHAPTER 38

Julia checked on Evelyn in her cradle, sleeping contentedly with her thumb in her mouth. As she ran a finger over the baby's satiny cheek, Julia's heart expanded with love. She still couldn't get over the miracle of this beautiful child. That she'd grown in Julia's womb and was now a living, breathing human being.

Did all new mothers feel this way? Amazingly powerful, like they could do anything, achieve anything, now that they'd given birth? Becoming a mother had changed Julia in subtle ways—made her stronger, more courageous. This new little being depended on her for everything, and Julia knew she could take on the world for her daughter's sake.

Fortunately, she no longer had to worry about Richard Hawkins, a fact she gave thanks for every day.

She straightened, her thoughts spiraling back to Quinn and the unsettling conversation they'd had this morning. She'd hoped these past few weeks would have solidified their union, not made matters worse. Though Quinn had been nothing but thoughtful since Evelyn's birth, he'd treated Julia more like a sister than a wife, keeping a polite distance between them, and had given no indication that he wished for their marriage to change.

But lately, Julia had sensed a shift in her husband's mood. Watching him this morning brooding on the porch, hearing him voice his discontent aloud, had snapped her out of the bubble she'd been living in. She'd been too focused on the baby, she realized, and hadn't considered how Quinn must be feeling.

"Living here with no real purpose. Not able to work to provide for my family. It goes against everything I've been raised to believe."

Of course it did. For the better part of his life, Quinn had been responsible for his family, working hard to earn every shilling he could. These last two months must have been extremely difficult for him—living on what he would view as the charity of a widow. It must chafe at his pride and his sense of integrity not to earn his keep. No wonder he kept trying to find odd jobs to do.

And he'd borne it all without complaint for her sake.

Julia moved to the bed and folded a blanket she'd tossed there. She could no longer ignore her husband's growing unhappiness. If it meant releasing him from his commitment, then she would do so, even if it broke her heart to let him go. After all he'd done for her, granting him his freedom was the least she could do.

If they were to have a future together, she wanted it to be because he loved her, not because his ingrained sense of duty chained him to her.

Be bold, Julia. No more waiting for Quinn to declare his feelings. No more fear of the unknown.

Tonight she would take charge of her life again and trust that God would work all things out for their mutual good.

A soft knock sounded on the adjoining door. Her heart sparked like a backfiring auto.

Lord, please be with us during this conversation, and help us to follow your will for our lives. No matter what the outcome.

On a quick inhale, she moved to open the door.

Quinn stood on the other side, a tentative smile on his face.

Her mouth fell open, and her pulse began to race. He was wearing his good suit, the one he'd worn at their wedding, and looked incredibly handsome, his hair freshly combed and a striped tie at his neck.

"Why are you dressed like that?" she blurted out.

His lips twitched. "I'm here to request the pleasure of your company at a dinner for two this evening." He gave an exaggerated bow.

Her hand fluttered to her throat, her fingers brushing the worn neckline of her old blouse. She'd stopped wearing her better outfits since Evelyn seemed determined to stain every one. "That's thoughtful of you, but I can't"—she waved a hand toward the cradle behind her—"leave Evelyn."

"You don't have to. We'll dine right here in my room by the fire." He gave her a slow smile that made her pulse skitter. "Why don't you meet me in fifteen minutes? The food should be here by then." He winked at her and closed the connecting door.

Julia gulped in a nervous breath, her plans for the evening suddenly forgotten.

Mrs. Middleton had been more than pleased by Quinn's request for a private meal in their quarters, eager to help him pull off his romantic surprise.

"About time," she'd said and shook her head as though he was a slightly daft child.

Then the dear woman had instructed her cook to comply with Quinn's instructions, and the two had planned some of Julia's favorite dishes for the menu. Mrs. Neville also supplied him with a tablecloth, napkins, and candles to decorate the small table in his room. Flowers would have been perfect too, if he'd had time to visit a florist.

Now as Quinn surveyed the scene, satisfaction curled in his chest. The room looked as romantic as he could get it. He only hoped Julia would appreciate the effort.

He paused to say a heartfelt prayer, asking the Lord to give him the right words to let his wife know exactly what she meant to him.

And if you're so inclined, Lord, could you bring her around to my way of thinking about England? If not, then help me to accept that too.

A polite knock sounded precisely fifteen minutes later.

Quinn attempted to calm his rioting nerves as he opened the door.

Julia stood there in a gauzy blue dress, hands clasped in front of her. She'd taken her hair down and wore it loose.

He swallowed hard. "You look lovely. Please, come in."

"Thank you." Her nervous gaze slid past him to survey the room. She took a few steps forward, leaving the connecting door ajar, then stopped. "Oh, Quinn. This is wonderful." She ran a finger over the tablecloth and the china plates. "How did you manage all this?"

"With a little help from Mrs. Middleton and her cook." Knowing he needed to take his time, he resisted pulling her into his arms. "Why don't we enjoy our meal, and we can talk afterward?"

He held out a chair for her. The silky ends of her hair grazed his fingers.

Quinn took the other seat and laid a napkin on his lap.

A fire blazed in the hearth, and two taper candles graced the table, casting a subtle glow over Julia's beautiful face.

He lifted the cloth covering her dish and smiled. "I hope you're hungry. Mrs. Neville went out of her way to make this for us in a short amount of time."

"Fried chicken and mashed potatoes? My favorite."

"Good. I was hoping I'd remembered correctly. We might even have chocolate cake for dessert." He gave her a deliberate wink.

Color bloomed in her cheeks. "You're re-creating our night in Peterborough," she said quietly.

"I'm trying." He studied her as she stared at her plate, wishing he could read her mind. "I wanted to give you a special evening. I hope I haven't overstepped."

"No, of course not. This is very . . . thoughtful." She picked up her fork and began to eat.

Quinn did the same, and for several minutes, they ate in silence, with only the crackle of the flames to break the stillness. He glanced at Julia's plate and his stomach dropped. Far from enjoying the meal, she was toying with the food on her plate.

Suddenly she set down her fork. "I have something I need to get off my chest or I won't be able to eat a bite."

One glimpse of her troubled face and Quinn's spirits fell. This romantic evening was not going the way he'd hoped. Where had things gone wrong?

Julia glanced up at her husband, dismayed by the wretched expression on his face. She still couldn't understand why he'd arranged this dinner. If he hadn't been so miserable earlier in the day, she might have been thrilled by his efforts. But something didn't seem right. Was he trying to make up for his admission earlier, to prove that he wasn't as unhappy as he appeared?

"I've been thinking about what you said this morning. I'm sorry you've been so discontented lately, Quinn. I never wanted to be a burden to you."

His head snapped up, eyes blazing. "You're no burden, Julia. Never think that."

"But you're not happy. That much is obvious."

His gaze slid away. "I've been feeling a little restless. That's all."

She fingered the napkin on her lap. "Be honest with me. Do you feel trapped here with me and the baby?" Though it pained her to ask, it was beyond time for them to be truthful with each other.

"Not trapped. Just . . . in limbo." He released a long breath. "I'm used to working from sunup to sundown, and these months of inactivity, along with the blasted snow, have me climbing the walls."

That made sense. While she had much to occupy her time caring for Mrs. Middleton and the baby, Quinn must have felt at loose ends.

"I didn't realize how hard this must be for you," she said carefully. From his frown, she knew there was more he was holding back. She reined in her impatience and waited for him to continue.

The candles flickered, casting shadows over the tablecloth.

"The truth is," he said, "that I can't help thinking about the farm. I want to be there to help my brothers with it." He stared miserably at his plate.

Of course he'd want to go home. On the farm, his hard work would be valued. He'd have a purpose to his days.

"That brings me to what I need to say." She took in a breath and rose. "Could we move to the settee?"

His mouth pressed in a grim line, and he nodded.

They crossed the room to the small sofa, and he sat down beside her, looking as uncomfortable as she felt.

"I know we agreed to a marriage in name only," she began, "with the stipulation that once the baby was born, we would reevaluate our situation." Dread pooled in her stomach, but she squared her shoulders. "You've sacrificed a great deal to protect me and the baby, and I will forever be grateful for everything you've done for me."

"Julia, I—"

"No, please, let me finish before I lose my nerve." She wet her lips. "It's time that I put your needs first. And so I am officially releasing you from your debt to me. I want you to be free to live your life as you planned before I derailed it. And if you need to go back to England, I understand." Her voice broke, and she blinked hard to hold back tears.

When he met her gaze, a host of emotion swirled in his eyes. "Is that what you want, Julia? For us to go our separate ways?" He sounded weary.

Her heart thudded unevenly in her chest. If she told him the truth, he might feel even more obliged to stay. Yet, didn't he deserve the truth at last?

Be bold, Julia.

"No, it's not." She swallowed, shoring up her courage. "What I really want is for our marriage to be real. To be true partners and raise our daughter in a loving home. But not at the expense of your happiness." She held her breath. Her whole future would hinge on his next words.

He looked into her eyes with such intensity that the air leaked from her lungs. "You want our marriage to be real?"

"I do," she said softly.

An incredulous smile spread across his face. "I want that too. That's why I arranged this dinner. To show you how much you mean to me." He took her hands in his. "I love you, Julia. More than the day we married. I want to share everything with you and love you as a husband should."

Heat burned up her neck to her cheeks, and her heart threatened to fly from her chest.

"I love you too," she breathed. "I realized it right before you left, but somehow I couldn't say the words."

His smile widened. "You have no idea how I've longed to hear that. But I didn't want to pressure you."

"And I didn't know how to bring it up."

Staring into her eyes, he tugged her to her feet. Her free hand landed on his solid chest. The smell of Ivory soap and his spicy cologne wrapped around her like a hug.

"If you don't mind," he said, his voice husky, "I'd like to kiss my wife now."

She laughed, joy bubbling up through her, feeling suddenly light enough to float across the room. "I'd like that too."

He wound his fingers through the hair at the back of her neck, sending a host of shivers down her spine. Slowly he leaned forward and brushed his lips against hers with just a whisper of contact. Then he fused his mouth more firmly against hers.

She returned his embrace with an eagerness that shocked her. How she'd longed for this closeness again. The feel of his strong arms around her. The taste of his lips on hers. This was where she belonged. With Quinn, she'd found her place in the world at last.

When he moved away, her heart still beat a quick tempo in her chest. He rested his forehead against hers, and she waited until her breathing evened out to look at him. "As much as I want to keep kissing you, there's another important issue we need to discuss."

His expression sobered. "England."

"Yes."

The flames crackled in the hearth. Her glance shifted to the remains of the meal still on the table, one more reminder of everything he was willing to do to please her. From helping change Evelyn's nappies, to chopping firewood, to always treating her with respect and honor. If he could give up everything for her, she could do no less. She laid her palm against his cheek. "If your happiness means moving back to England, then Evelyn and I will go with you."

"Really?" His eyes grew round. "You're willing to come home? To face your uncle and all that would entail?"

"I am." She smiled up at him. "Because with you by my side, I know I can face anything."

He stared at her for a moment, then cupped her face with his hands and kissed her again. When they finally parted, he took her hand. "Julia, would you do me the honor of marrying me again—this time in a church? I want to pledge my life and my love to you before God."

Tears pressed against her lids. The first time they wed, she'd made sure it was more like a business arrangement than anything else. But this time, she was ready to say her vows and share her heart in a sacred place. She nodded. "I would love to."

He smiled, and the love that glowed in his eyes warmed her from the inside out. "Then I'll speak to Reverend Burke tomorrow."

"We are gathered here today to witness Quinten and Julia restate their marriage vows before God." Rev. Burke's voice boomed out over the sanctuary of Holy Trinity Church.

The minister had been more than pleased when asked to perform a church ceremony for them and had offered to christen baby Evelyn immediately afterward.

What more perfect way to start their lives together?

Though Quinn tried hard to focus on the man's words, his mind kept wandering to every detail of his glowing bride before him. The profusion of pink and white flowers she held in front of her, the long lashes that swept her cheek when she looked down, and the fullness of her lips that trembled ever so slightly as she smiled. She'd never looked more beautiful than she did right now.

"Quinten, wilt thou have this woman to be thy wedded wife? To live together after God's ordinance in the Holy Estate of matrimony? Wilt thou love her, comfort her, honor and keep her, in sickness and in health, and forsaking all others keep thee only unto her as long as you both shall live?"

Quinn fought back the lump in his throat as he looked into Julia's brown eyes. Every trial they had endured had led to this moment, culminating in this pledge of love. "I will."

"And Julia, wilt thou have this man to be thy wedded husband? To live together after God's ordinance in the Holy Estate of matrimony? Wilt thou love him, comfort him, honor and keep him, in sickness and in health, and forsaking all others keep thee only unto him as long as you both shall live?"

Julia smiled and nodded. "I will."

They gazed at each other, their promises vibrating in the air between them, so much more meaningful than before.

Rev. Burke cleared his throat. "Do you have the ring?"

Quinn took out the plain silver band from their first ceremony. He'd wanted to buy her something fancier, but Julia wouldn't hear of it. *"I love my ring,"* she'd said firmly. *"We can have it consecrated, but I don't want another."*

He handed the band to the minister.

Rev. Burke quickly blessed it. "Place the ring on Julia's finger and repeat after me: 'With this ring, I thee wed and with all my worldly goods I thee endow: In the name of the Father, and of the Son, and of the Holy Ghost. Amen.'"

Quinn slid the ring onto Julia's finger, and in the hush of the sanctuary, repeated the solemn words, his promise now weighted by a new sacredness.

Rev. Burke raised his head from the book. "With the saying of holy vows and the giving of a ring, I pronounce that Quinten and

Julia are indeed husband and wife, both legally and in the eyes of God." He paused to look out over the congregation. "Those whom God have joined together let no man put asunder."

Quinn's chest filled with so much emotion he feared it would burst. He beamed down at Julia, who smiled through a veil of tears.

The minster leaned forward and winked. "If you'd care to kiss your bride, I won't object."

In keeping with the holiness of the moment, Quinn leaned in and gave her a firm but chaste kiss. He hesitated for a moment, his lips hovering near hers, then unable to resist, he pulled her in for a more substantial embrace that hinted at the passion simmering beneath the surface.

A titter of amusement rippled among the guests. Julia's cheeks were as rosy as her flowers when they parted, though she didn't look at all scandalized.

"If everyone would stay seated for another minute," Rev. Burke announced, "we will now baptize the Aspinalls' infant daughter."

Mrs. Chamberlain, who had been holding the baby during the ceremony, came forward to hand Julia their daughter. Dressed in a white knitted gown and bonnet, Evelyn slept peacefully, not stirring until the minister poured the water over her forehead.

The simple beauty of the ceremony, dedicating their child to God, brought another rise of emotion to Quinn's throat.

Lord, thank you for entrusting this precious child to me. Help me to be the best father I can. And the best husband to Julia. May I never take them for granted.

After the baptism, Rev. Burke invited everyone down to the basement for a reception that the church ladies had kindly provided.

Quinn stood with Julia in the narthex, greeting each guest and thanking them for coming. At last, Rev. Burke brought up the rear, Mrs. Chamberlain by his side.

Quinn shook his hand. "Thank you for doing this, Reverend. It meant a lot to have our marriage sanctioned by God."

"You're most welcome, lad. I'm delighted that you and Julia have made this a permanent arrangement."

"You and me both, sir. An answer to my prayers to be sure." Quinn bent and kissed Julia's lips. Evelyn gurgled her approval.

Then he lifted the baby from Julia's arms, took his wife by the hand, and walked forward into their future.

A future that looked brighter than any dream he could have imagined.

EPILOGUE

MARCH 30, 1920

Seven weeks after Julia and Quinn's wedding, everyone gathered in Holy Trinity Church once again for another happy union—the marriage of Reverend Geoffrey Burke and Harriet Chamberlain.

The audience—a far larger one than had attended Quinn and Julia's ceremony—applauded as Rev. and Mrs. Burke headed down the main aisle of the church. Dressed in a cream-colored suit with a matching netted hat, Mrs. C. beamed at her new husband as they passed their guests.

Quinn put his arm around Julia and gave her a light squeeze. She looked up from the baby in her arms to bestow him with a brilliant smile, and he couldn't resist kissing her. His heart thudded with joy as it did every time they embraced.

Little Evelyn waved her plump fists. Coming up on four months old, her bright eyes taking in everything, she was the second greatest joy in his life, next only to her mother.

Seated beside them in the pew, Jonathan and Emmaline wore matching grins. They had traveled all the way from England to attend the ceremony, a fact that had touched Mrs. Chamberlain deeply.

"Mrs. C. looks so beautiful in that outfit," Emma whispered. "And so incredibly happy."

Jonathan raised a brow at his fiancée. "Reverend Burke took long enough to declare his intentions. But better late than never, I always say."

Emma laughed. "That seems to be your motto in life, Jon. One I'm determined to change, by the way. I don't plan on waiting much longer for our own wedding ceremony."

"I have to agree with you there, Miss Moore." He dropped a quick kiss on her lips as they rose to exit the aisle.

Quinn chuckled, scarcely able to contain the happiness that swelled in his chest. In a matter of days, he, Julia, and the baby would be sailing back to England, in the company of Jonathan and Emma. Of the group of friends that had met nearly a year ago on the ship, only Grace had chosen to remain in Toronto. Quinn glanced across the aisle at Grace and her husband. Andrew held Christian on his lap, trying to thwart the lad's attempt to escape. Grace glowed with good health, her belly now round with the baby they expected in another few months.

Looking back, Quinn had to admire how far they had all come in a relatively short space of time. He, Grace, and Emma had come to Canada, each with their own hopes and dreams for the future. And after enduring hardship and loss, they had all found their path.

Surely the hand of God had been on their lives every step of the way.

Even Mrs. Chamberlain and the good reverend had found joy of their own. Quinn marveled once again how God had used him and his siblings not only to heal Mrs. C.'s childhood wounds but to bring about a positive change to Dr. Barnardo's organization. She and Rev. Burke now had a team of clergy in place to supervise the children more closely and ensure they would no longer fall victim to abuse.

To Quinn's surprise and delight, Julia had told him she wanted to do something similar to help the Barnardo children back in England and had asked Quinn to work with her on this new mission.

Upon hearing this, his heart had swelled with admiration for his bride. Julia's dedication to helping others was one of the reasons he'd fallen in love with her in the first place, and he'd been only too happy to agree to help her with this cause, one near and dear to his family. He suspected his mother would be eager to join in her crusade as well.

Now, as Quinn and Julia followed the congregation outside to greet the newly married couple, he stopped to pull his wife and daughter into a warm embrace. "Are you happy, Julia?"

She smiled up at him. "I've never been happier. I can't wait to start our new life in England."

He still couldn't get over the fact that she was willing to come with him. "You realize the farmhouse is a far cry from the luxury you were used to at Brentwood. It will take time to fix it up the way you'd like."

"We have the rest of our lives to work on it." She paused to give him a mischievous look. "Though you may want to get started on that extra room for the children."

"Why? Evelyn won't need her own room for . . ." He paused as her words registered. "Did you say *children*?"

"I did." Her lips tipped up in a secret smile. "If my suspicions are correct, we'll be adding to our family much sooner than we anticipated."

Quinn's throat grew tight. Tears stung the back of his eyes. Too moved for words, he simply kissed her. "I love you, Julia. You have made me the happiest man in the world."

She reached one hand up to caress his cheek. "Let's keep this news to ourselves for now. After all, it's Mrs. C.'s day to shine."

"Right you are. Though it's Mrs. Burke now." He paused, scratching his chin thoughtfully. "I don't think I'll ever get used to calling her that."

Julia laughed and shifted Evelyn onto her other hip. Quinn put his arm around his wife. "Let's go and celebrate with our friends."

As they walked toward the stairs, Quinn whispered a prayer

of gratitude for the abundance of blessings they had received. He knew with absolute certainty that by keeping God at the forefront of their lives, all things were truly possible.

And no matter what the future might hold for his family, they would weather it together, with love.

A NOTE FROM THE AUTHOR

Dear Readers,

When the subject of the British Home Children in Canada was suggested to me as a possible topic for a book, I confess I'd never heard of them. Not in all the time growing up in Ontario—where a large majority of these children were sent—and never in any of the educational studies I'd undertaken. So to find out about these children and the role they played in our country's history was indeed surprising.

I learned that from the late 1860s up until about 1948, over one hundred thousand children of all ages were sent from the United Kingdom to Canada to be used as indentured laborers, mostly on Canadian farms. There were many organizations involved in the migration of children out of England, but I chose to focus on the homes run by Dr. Thomas Barnardo.

Of the one hundred thousand children sent to Canada, twenty thousand (some reports say thirty thousand) came from the Dr. Barnardo's Homes. Although Dr. Barnardo's organization was not the only one involved in this endeavor, he became the most influential figure in child migration of the last half of the nineteenth century.

Though these children were believed to be orphans, only a small percentage actually fell into that category. The majority of children placed in homes such as Dr. Barnardo's came from families that, through sickness or the death of one of the parents, had fallen on hard times. In many instances, this was thought to be a temporary measure until the family's circumstances improved. Countless parents did not realize that their sons and daughters would be shipped off to another country.

Once in Canada, the children were sent to various receiving homes across the country to be distributed to the farmers who were looking for help. Though the intentions of the people in charge were good, and they believed they would be providing these children with the opportunity for a better life, the reality did not measure up to the ideal. The majority of children were treated miserably by their employers and made to feel subhuman, as though they didn't matter.

Not surprisingly, as they grew into adulthood, most of these children never spoke about the topic because they were either too traumatized or too ashamed to relive it. In fact, often their own families had no idea of the difficult circumstances that had initially brought their loved ones to this country or the hardships they had endured.

In Ontario, a lady named Lori Oschefski spearheaded a movement to unearth this chapter in both England and Canada's past and shed light on these brave souls. Her own mother was one of these children and had kept it a secret until well into her eighties. Ms. Oschefski is the founder of the British Home Children Advocacy and Research Association. This organization has quickly moved to the forefront of the British Home Child awareness movement, not only in Canada but across the world. Ms. Oschefski is very active in communities across Ontario, bringing the story of the British Home Children to the public by giving many presentations on the subject.

I did consult several times with Ms. Oschefski via her Facebook group, and I thank her and the other members who offered me suggestions and stories of their own relatives.

I must confess that while I tried my best to be as factual as possible, I have taken some artistic license with a few of the situations that occur in the book. Although I used the actual name of the superintendent of the Barnardo receiving home at the time, a Mr. Hobday, I made up all interactions with this character, and he is strictly a fictional representation of the real Mr. Hobday. I also made up the cemetery and the rows of white crosses at the Hazelbrae receiving home in Peterborough. I believe the Hazelbrae girls were actually buried in a local cemetery; however, I thought it would be more dramatic to have a private burial ground on the property itself. I did try to find out the name of the person in charge of the home at the time of my story but was unable to come up with the information, so I created Mrs. Whitaker. Again, she is a purely fictional representation, who in no way reflects on any real directress who worked there. The actual Hazelbrae residence, renamed the Margaret Cox Home for Girls in 1912, closed in 1922 or 1923, and was completely torn down by 1939. Today, a black granite heritage plaque stands near the site with the names of the over nine thousand children who came through Hazelbrae and the dates they arrived.

Any mistakes in my portrayal of the Aspinall children's experience with the Dr. Barnardo organization are purely my own and do not in any way reflect on the research I've done in writing this book. I only hope that my story helps shed a little light on such a daunting subject.

Interestingly enough, another wonderful Christian author named Carrie Turansky was writing about this topic at the same time I was. Her novel, entitled *No Ocean Too Wide*, came out in June 2019. It's a wonderful book, and I recommend reading it to see how her fictional account handles the same subject matter.

If you care to learn more about these children and their stories, please check out the British Home Children Facebook page for lots of great information: www.facebook.com/groups/Britishhomechildren/. I also recommend https://upsanddownsofhomechildren.wordpress.com/about/ and https://canadianbritishhomechildren.weebly.com/.

I hope you enjoyed Quinn's quest to find his siblings and the romance he finds along the way.

Blessings until the next time,

Susan

ACKNOWLEDGMENTS

This story was an important one to tell, and because of the weight of the subject matter, I did the most research I've ever done on a book to date. Thank you to Lori Oschefski, founder of the British Home Children Advocacy and Research Association, for all her efforts in bringing this issue to light and making the information available to the public.

Many others helped bring this story to print:

I'd like to thank my agent, Natasha Kern, for her support, her wisdom, and her kindness.

Thank you to David Long and Jen Veilleux, my editors at Bethany House. Jen, your attention to detail amazes me! I know you do everything in your power to make my story the best it can be. And my thanks to the entire team at Bethany House, who work so hard to make our books shine.

My heartfelt gratitude goes to my two amazing critique partners, Sally Bayless and Julie Jarnagin, who give such great advice.

And, as always, thank you to my family for their love and encouragement.

Thank you to my wonderful readers and influencers. I appreciate you all so much, especially those who take the time to let me know how my words have impacted them.

Susan Anne Mason describes her writing style as "romance sprinkled with faith." She loves incorporating inspirational messages of God's unconditional love and forgiveness into her stories. *Irish Meadows*, her first historical romance, won the Fiction from the Heartland contest sponsored by the Mid-American Romance Authors chapter of RWA. Susan lives outside Toronto, Ontario, with her husband and two adult children. She loves red wine and chocolate, and is not partial to snow even though she's Canadian. Learn more about Susan and her books at www.susanannemason.net.

Sign Up for Susan's Newsletter!

Keep up to date with Susan's news on book releases and events by signing up for her email list at susanannemason.net.

More from Susan Anne Mason

In this fascinating glimpse into high society of Toronto after WWI, three individuals embark on an unpredictable journey from England in search of a loved one and unexpectedly find more than they could have ever imagined.

CANADIAN CROSSINGS: *The Best of Intentions, The Highest of Hopes, The Brightest of Dreams*

You May Also Like . . .

As Chicago's Great Fire steals away their bookshop, Meg and Sylvie Townsend make a harrowing escape from the flames with the help of reporter Nate Pierce. But trouble doesn't end when their father is committed to an asylum after being accused of murder. They must prove their father's innocence before the asylum truly drives him mad.

Veiled in Smoke by Jocelyn Green
The Windy City Saga #1
jocelyngreen.com

All of England thinks Phillip Camden a monster for the deaths of his squadron. But as Nurse Arabelle Denler watches him every day, she sees something far different: a hurting man desperate for mercy. But when an old acquaintance shows up and seems set on using him in a plot that has the codebreakers of Room 40 in a frenzy, new affections are put to the test.

On Wings of Devotion by Roseanna M. White
The Codebreakers #2
roseannamwhite.com

Gray Delacroix has dedicated his life to building a successful global spice empire, but it has come at a cost. Tasked with gaining access to the private Delacroix plant collection, Smithsonian botanist Annabelle Larkin unwittingly steps into a web of dangerous political intrigue and will be forced to choose between her heart and her loyalty to her country.

The Spice King by Elizabeth Camden
Hope and Glory #1
elizabethcamden.com